MR.

JENNIFER MILLER
& JASON FEIFER

NICE GUY

GUY

 ST. MARTIN'S GRIFFIN ≋ NEW YORK

MR. NICE GUY. Copyright © 2018 by Jennifer Miller and Jason Feifer.
All rights reserved. Printed in the United States of America. For information,
address St. Martin's Press, 175 Fifth Avenue, New York, N.Y. 10010.

www.stmartins.com

Designed by Anna Gorovoy

The Library of Congress Cataloging-in-Publication Data
is available upon request.

ISBN 978-1-250-18988-2 (trade paperback)
ISBN 978-1-250-18989-9 (ebook)

Our books may be purchased in bulk for promotional, educational,
or business use. Please contact your local bookseller or the Macmillan Corporate
and Premium Sales Department at 1-800-221-7945, extension 5442, or
by email at MacmillanSpecialMarkets@macmillan.com.

First Edition: October 2018

10 9 8 7 6 5 4 3 2 1

ADVANCE PRAISE FOR *MR. NICE GUY*

"In *Mr. Nice Guy*, one brave couple does what most of us would never dare: give brutally honest feedback about last night's sex. The result is an incredibly funny, fiendishly smart, deliciously NSFW romp you won't be able to put down."

—Sascha de Gersdorff, executive editor, *Cosmopolitan*

"In their addictive comedy, Miller and Feifer have captured not just the heady mix of young ambition and uncertainty that many readers will recognize, but also New York City in a precise moment of transition, when one generation is fading but the next isn't quite ready (or willing) to take its place. We can all find a bit of ourselves in *Mr. Nice Guy*. For better or worse."

—Neil Janowitz, editorial director, Vulture.com

"This pitch-perfect take on modern romance is far more than a guilty pleasure. It's also a timely battle of the sexes, taking aim at deep-seated assumptions about who wields the power—in the corner office, and in the bedroom."

—Stacy London, host of *What Not to Wear* and *Love, Lust or Run*

"A juicy insider's tryst through the ever-shifting world of the glossy magazines." —Jo Piazza, author of *The Knockoff*

"Witty, sexy, sweet, and utterly engrossing, *Mr. Nice Guy* stakes out fresh battleground in the war of the sexes. With its twisty plot and fizzy cast of characters, this is a joy ride you can't predict nor put down until the surprising end."

—Amy Scheibe, author of *A Fireproof Home for the Bride*

"An addictively entertaining and deliciously sexy debut."

—Julie Garwood, *New York Times* bestselling author

To the many, many dating sites we tried before finding each other:
Thank you for (eventually) working.

And to all the editors who have taken us seriously: You're to thank
(and to blame) for what follows.

PART ONE

CHAPTER 1

Just shy of 9:00 A.M., his underarms already brackish, Lucas emerged from the Chambers Street subway and joined the throng of pedestrians converging on One World Trade. For a month now, he'd been making this trip alongside the tourists and suits, the Truthers and Staten Island émigrés. He loved the commute, August heat be damned. In fact, he couldn't believe his luck. To be here, finally, in New York, working inside that gleaming scepter of polished glass. The building's spire pierced the impossible blue, seemed to stab straight through the sun. It reminded Lucas of a batter at the plate, pointing to the outfield.

A cynical person would have been embarrassed by such grandiose thoughts. But Lucas couldn't help himself. Though only a fact-checker—an invertebrate on the media food chain— he thrilled to enter One World Trade's echoing lobby each morning. He loved how the tap of his ID commanded the security bar to swing down and simultaneously summon the elevator. He rarely shared the car with anyone else. Everyone in this elevator bank worked in magazines, which meant they didn't arrive until at least 10:00 A.M. But Lucas hadn't yet adjusted to these so-called media hours. By 10, it felt as though half the day had already shriveled in the heat. And Lucas couldn't afford any missteps. Too many people back home believed it was only a matter of time before he skulked back below the Mason-Dixon. They eagerly awaited his contrite return to the old life, the one he'd lived so well until he ruined everything and went to New York: that "polluted, sweaty cesspool of liberalism." These were his grandmother's exact words.

"People sweat in Charlotte," Lucas had argued. "But they don't smell!" his grandmother retorted. "Unless you're rich, New York is like a slum. It's like India."

Lucas's grandmother had never been to New York or India. But that was beside the point. In dropping out of law school after a year and breaking up with his (wealthy, pedigreed) fiancée six months shy of their wedding, he'd dashed the hopes and expectations of his family. Never mind that Mel had dumped him. Everyone, including Mel herself, believed that Lucas should have done more to salvage the situation. Instead, like a coward, he'd run away—and to Yankeedom of all places!— turning his back on the people, the very culture, that had raised him.

With the exception of his older brother, Sam, Lucas hadn't spoken to his family once since arriving in Manhattan a month ago. But so what? This was the place he'd longed to be, and he was working at *Empire Magazine,* the place he'd always wanted to work. So what if he inhabited a poorly ventilated box and only made thirty-three thousand pre-tax dollars a year?

The elevator doors slid open at the twenty-ninth floor and Lucas stepped out.

EMPIRE

Painted opposite the elevator bank in massive black letters, the word was the visual equivalent of a bullhorn or a punch in the face. And why shouldn't the empire—as everyone called their floor—intimidate? The magazine was a fifty-year-old New York City institution headquartered in Manhattan's newest bastion of hopefulness and pride.

Heading toward his desk, Lucas walked past the glass-walled offices of the magazine's editors—its ruling class—their large windows overlooking Lower Manhattan and the East River. He passed the cubicle banks, dense as Iron Block buildings, where the proletariat—the staff writers, designers, marketers, and other assorted minions—produced the bimonthly publication. He was well into the suburbs of the empire by now, approaching the outpost of interns. And then, finally, the cluster of fact-checkers. How absurd that the fact-checkers should have less desirable real estate than the interns, but so it went. These were the exurbs, backed against a windowless wall, unwarmed by the sun. Lucas knew he shouldn't complain. He'd only been at *Empire* for a month. His career, he reminded himself, would take persistence and time. And yet his initial leap of faith had catapulted him so far, so fast. Should he not continue to bound with the same speed?

Lucas sat down at his tidy desk. His colleagues' workspaces were cluttered with papers, on which they'd scribbled and typed the minutiae—the facts—of the upcoming issue. But Lucas let nothing pile up, literally or figuratively. He'd come to New York to unburden himself. And yet in so doing, he now had a year's worth of law-school debt to worry about. To make matters worse, his work frequently reminded him of his penury. Just now, for example, he was fact-checking a story about a celebrity chef whose restaurant featured a "gold menu." For a few thousand dollars, you could have a gold-flecked Kobe burger or a margarita with a gold-dusted salt rim. It was amazing to think how less than a decade ago the same people who paid bank for gold-baked branzino had been crying on the floor of the stock exchange.

Lucas tried to work, but before long he was checking his ex's Facebook page. Just two months after their breakup and Mel was already "in a relationship." The new suitor's page was private, so Lucas had limited material: height and build (tall, sturdy), clothing (khakis, popped collar, baseball hat), and name (Cal Braden). In short, a lacrosse-playing frat bro. If New York had its Masters of the Universe, then Dixie had its Kings of Douchery. It was obvious from these photographs that Cal Braden couldn't wait to give a pretty southern girl a big rock, and a big house, and a big brood of children styled head to toe in Vineyard Vines. Lucas didn't want any of that. And yet some deeply embedded muscle strained with the discovery that Mel had exchanged him for this newer, preppier model. Oh, and she'd untagged herself from all of Lucas's photos. They'd been together for six years—four at college and two afterward—and it was like he never existed.

"Jesus, Luke. It's been a month already. You've got to quit sucking up to the boss. You're making the rest of us look bad."

Lucas quickly minimized Facebook and swiveled around. Franklin, short and snub-nosed, his hair spiked like porcupine quills, stood there drinking a Venti iced coffee, the plastic still sweating from the heat.

"What time is it?"

"Ten thirty." Franklin pulled his Jack Spade messenger bag over his head.

Had he really been looking at pictures of Mel for an hour?

"How many times do I have to tell you, Luke: Nobody knows we're back here."

If nobody knows we're back here, Lucas thought, *then I'm not making you look bad.* Still, Lucas was convinced that his colleagues would eventually come to respect his work ethic. *That Luke,* they'd say. *He hustles.* At some point, the brass would take notice. Otherwise, Lucas would succumb to the same fate as Franklin, who was still checking facts three whole years after arriving at *Empire.* How could someone languish like that? If Lucas had been smart enough to flee Charlotte immediately after college, he'd surely be an editor by now.

Then again, he'd just wasted an hour on Facebook. His self-loathing felt like a cement block. Somebody might as well push him into the East River.

"What're you working on?" Franklin leaned over the cubicle wall.

"The Best Restaurants package."

Franklin frowned. "*Empire* must be in trouble or we wouldn't be covering this shit. Every single issue of *Washingtonian* is the Best Restaurants issue. And every issue of *Boston* magazine is 'Best of Boston,' which is funny, because everything in Boston is the worst."

Lucas disagreed. There was still plenty of actual culture in *Empire*—political analysis and at least three meaty features each month. The magazine held the same world of promise that had captivated him back in college when he happened to pick up a copy at Barnes & Noble. He'd started subscribing, to the confusion of his dorm mates and later to Mel, who never understood why he cared about some recent scandal involving the mayor's daughter, or the city's gentrification battles, or the rise of sketchy Chinatown bathhouses. Nobody back home understood how the glossy pages transported Lucas into a world equally full of glamour and grit, of modernity and history, of culture from the subterranean to the heavenly. Everything you wanted to talk about, and see and experience, was captured within *Empire*.

"How long before they had you checking big features?" Lucas asked now.

"So precocious, this kid!" Franklin snickered. "It's adorable."

Franklin could make all the fun he wanted. A year from now, he'd still be stuck in the exurbs, checking the veracity of other people's stories. *But not me,* Lucas thought. *I'll be writing them.* He closed Facebook and got to work on his thousand-dollar hamburgers.

CHAPTER 2

At precisely 11:13 A.M., Lucas received an email from the Editor-in-Chief's secretary. He was being summoned.

Many months later, when Lucas picked through the rubble of his career, attempting to unearth the bomb that had led to its implosion, he decided it had all started here, with this missive. At the moment, however, he could hardly guess what the Editor wanted with him. Jay Jacobson was one of the city's most formidable media moguls. Inside *Empire,* he was a benevolent despot: feared, revered, discreetly criticized for his capricious nature, but, above all, obeyed. Among themselves, the staff called him Jays, a play on his alliterative name. It was a small, inert act of rebellion, secretly sanctioned by the despot to give the proletariat an illusion of control.

Lucas read and reread the email—"4pm, Mr. Jacobson's office"—trying to determine whether this request was good or very bad. He only realized that he was exhaling heavily, and repeatedly, when Franklin's head popped up, whack-a-mole style, from the divider. "Dude, what's with the asthma attack?"

"Jays wants to see me."

Franklin frowned. "Well, when you greet him, make sure you bow deeply, from the waist."

"Ha-ha," Lucas said, though later that afternoon when Lucas went to prep in the bathroom he tried out an experimental bow in front of the mirror. He felt—and looked—ridiculous. Lucas righted himself. Then he straightened his tie. He was the only person in the office who wore one to work every single day and, like his commitment to an early arrival, the decision had raised more than a few eyebrows. And yet look how smart he'd been! Making your mark was about preparation, about being ready for anything at a moment's notice. "You were born to work here," he whispered as he gave himself one final once-over and smiled to make sure there wasn't anything stuck in his teeth. "You're going to impress the shit out of this guy."

But first he had to get himself past the Editor's assistants, Florence and Phyllis. These were Jays' loyal sentries: hefty women of indeterminate middle age who had worked at *Empire* as long as anyone could remember. Despite their doughy appendages and double chins, they projected a stone-like severity. At times, it seemed they were asleep with their eyes open. People called them the Sphinxes.

"Pst! Lucas!" Alexis was beckoning him. She was Jays' third assistant, the one who did most of his busywork. Petite to the point of fragile, she looked as though she might shatter, should she accidentally bump into something. Her breasts, however, were enormous. Lucas had heard a senior editor refer to them as "French," and since then he'd had a difficult time keeping his eyes on Alexis's face. At least he made a concerted effort to do so; plenty of others, both male and female colleagues, did not.

"You can go right in," Alexis said, and then, with an air of conspiracy, whispered, "Just don't look those women in the eye or you'll turn to stone. And when you leave, make sure you back away. Slowly."

"Right, thanks," Lucas said, because his nerves were too ratcheted up for a witty response. And also, maybe it was good advice? He could feel the Sphinxes' eyes on him as he walked, following him in a reptilian sort of way. He knocked and was told to enter.

The afternoon light in Jays' office was blinding. It was like walking into a prism: dizzying and dazzling, everything fractured. "Hello?" Lucas blinked repeatedly, frantically. Was he really blowing this already?

"Good to meet you!" Jays stood up from his desk and suddenly the room snapped into focus, as though physically altered by the man's impeccably clothed, strapping physique. Lucas had known plenty of alpha men at UNC, but this guy could have been a movie star. He was in his mid-forties but somehow looked ageless. His chin and nose were perfect, sculpture worthy. His eyes were a deep cerulean blue, and his teeth gleamed. He met Lucas in the middle of the room and presented his hand. Jays' sleeves were rolled up, his forearms strong and hairless.

Does he wax his arms? Lucas hesitated before gathering himself. "Great to meet you, too," he said, and shook, remembering to keep his fingers firm.

"Please." Jays motioned to a sitting area where a beautiful distressed-leather couch, an armchair, and a coffee table polished to the point of invisibility were arranged on a white shag rug. Jays relaxed into the chair. "How're you settling in at *Empire*, Luke?" he asked.

"I'm great," Lucas said, trying to unobtrusively size up the Editor. Jays wore a crisp linen oxford with two open buttons and—Lucas noticed—no undershirt. Light gray slacks and black Gucci horsebit loafers. No socks. The only thing missing from this picture was a tumbler of scotch. Some of the editors' desks were veritable bar carts, but Jays' didn't have a single bottle of alcohol on display. What he did have was an entire wall of shelves lined with identical notebooks. It was one of the Editor's well-known eccentricities that he preferred writing by hand (with a Lamy 2000 extra-fine-nib pen, which Alexis ordered on Amazon for the affordable price of $134.99) inside a bespoke leather-bound ledger. Every few months, a box of them arrived from Milan. Each notebook was rumored to cost hundreds of dollars.

"I'm thrilled to be working here," Lucas said.

Jays smiled serenely. "I'm very happy to hear it. You know, Luke, we generally don't hire people who come to us so totally green."

Lucas started to sweat.

"Housman said you were a go-getter."

Dan Housman was number two on the masthead. Both he and Lucas had been Sigma Chi at UNC, albeit many years apart. It was the only reason Lucas's application had made it out of the HR slush pile.

". . . which makes sense," Jays continued, "because I gather that Sigma Chi isn't usually available to someone whose father, well, sells cars?"

It was true; Lucas's fraternity brothers were the sons of bankers and corporate executives. They all paid full tuition. But they'd welcomed Lucas in, seeming to delight in the novelty of him: this salt-of-the-earth representative. Never mind that Lucas's backyard straddled one of Charlotte's most affluent suburbs or that his parents belonged to the city's third most desirable country club. At parties his fraternity brothers could say, . . . *and this is Lucas, whose dad actually sells cars!* Lucas didn't mind. It was, after all, a mutually beneficial arrangement.

But hearing "sells cars" out of Jays' mouth made Lucas cringe. "Actually," he said as gently as possible, "my dad owns the dealership."

"To be the son of a car salesman," Jays continued, "and to have the audacity to walk right into a fraternity where you didn't belong—"

Was he being insulted? He couldn't tell.

"—is the kind of initiative that I admire."

Hold on. Jay Jacobson *admired* him?

"I have to say, Luke, that I was impressed by your application. It's been a long time since I've seen someone with so much passion for this magazine. Such a familiarity with what we do. And to be the son of a car salesman from North Carolina!"

Out of Jays' mouth, "North Carolina" might as well have been Madagascar. And yet it hardly mattered. The Editor admired him. The Editor was impressed by him!

"But here's a secret I'll share with you, Luke."

Jays leaned forward in the chair. Up close, Lucas saw that the Editor had a small shaving nick on his jaw. It was also true about his eyes: They were a little too close. Lucas relaxed a little.

"By dint of fate, or God, or what have you, I also had the misfortune to be born in a less than advantageous location. Beloit, Kansas, if you can believe that. Sometimes I wonder: When there's New York, can there also be Kansas? Do you understand what I'm saying?"

Lucas wasn't sure, but he nodded. He was suddenly hyperaware of the motion of his head rocking back and forth on his neck.

"Sometimes, we must forge our own way in the world,"

Jays continued. "We must rewrite our origin stories. It's what you are doing, and I respect it tremendously. That line in your cover letter, about wanting to remake yourself 'in the image of New Amsterdam.' An editor could call that overwrought, Luke."

Lucas felt a 103-degree fever triangulating between his cheeks and forehead. He'd debated that New Amsterdam line for days before finally deciding that a little poeticism might help distinguish him from the other applicants. How could he have been so stupid?

"But it shows your hunger. Your ambition. And in the end, even the best writers need good editors. A guiding hand."

Lucas nodded. He *was* hungry. And Jays saw it. Franklin was wrong; Jays *had* been watching.

"I can see that you're a fiercely dedicated young man. A person who has the potential to do great things here."

"Thank you," Lucas said. He felt like adding a "sir" but feared it would sound ridiculous.

Jays stood. "I want you to feel comfortable coming to me if you have any questions or problems, Luke. My door is open."

"I appreciate that," Lucas said, again stifling a "sir."

"Now, do you have any questions for me, Luke?"

Lucas had not been prepared for this. "I guess I'd love to know if you have any specific advice for me?" Lucas could have slammed his head against the wall. How uninventive could you be? Yet for some reason, Jays seemed to find the question amusing.

"You wrote it yourself," he said, chuckling. "Remake yourself in the image of *Empire*. You were born a North Carolina boy. Go become a New Yorker."

"Yessir," Lucas said, letting his head go full nod. Who would have expected Jay Jacobson to be so welcoming? This was not the remote and fickle autocrat he'd been warned about. This was a person who appreciated Lucas for the man he really was—or at least the man he wanted to be.

"And Luke?" Jays said. "Quick question. Whose tie are you wearing?"

Lucas had no idea. His grandmother had purchased it from Macy's, and as little as he knew about fashion, he knew "Macy's" was the wrong answer. "Brooks Brothers," Lucas said, thinking it sounded safe.

"Huh." Jays nodded. "Mine are Gucci. They might look good on you."

"Thank you!" Lucas exclaimed, though that wasn't exactly a compliment. He backed up a few paces, then turned and shut the Editor's door behind him.

Lucas floated past the Sphinxes, his smile bright as the streaming Manhattan sun. He felt positively baptismal, like he'd emerged a sparkling new version of himself. The naysayers—his parents, his grandmother, Mel, Cal fucking Braden—could all go screw themselves. Lucas had been blessed by Jay Jacobson, ruler of the empire.

"Well?" Alexis asked as Lucas walked by her desk. "Do you still have a job?"

Lucas didn't want to cheapen his conversation with Jays by discussing it. He wanted to go somewhere private and think it over, sentence by sentence, word by word. But Alexis was waiting. "He had some pretty harsh things to say about my cover letter."

Alexis frowned. "That's rough."

"He also said I might look good in Gucci."

Alexis grimaced.

"What's wrong?"

"OK, listen carefully. As soon as you leave tonight, you need to go and buy yourself some ties. Nice ties. Only not too nice—not Gucci nice. But stylish. Michael Kors maybe?"

"What's wrong with—?"

Alexis cut him off. "If you get the right ties, I don't think he'll let you go."

"Let me go! Over a tie? Are you kidding?"

Alexis shook her head. "No offense, Luke, but you don't know where you are yet. Jays will be paying attention to your ties now."

Lucas nodded. He didn't know what to make of Alexis's assessment, but it was clear that Jays had given him a test, one that he must pass. There was only one problem. "I can't afford to buy new clothes."

"Stock up on those dollar bagels from the street-corner carts in the morning," Alexis said. "That's what I did my first full year here. You can make your paycheck go a long way on those bagels."

For the rest of the day, people were unusually nice to Lucas. According to Franklin, Lucas's firing was all but guaranteed. Why else would Jays have bothered to call him in and criticize his cover letter? "It's such a shame," Franklin said disingenuously. "You've only been here a month."

That night, he and Alexis invited Lucas for drinks. A "just in case" good-bye party, they called it. Of course, Lucas wasn't going anywhere, but he couldn't exactly say, *Jays said he admired me.* He'd make enemies of them both. "I'll meet you at the bar," he said as the day wound down. "I've got an errand to run."

By the time Lucas arrived, Franklin was so drunk he was sweating large circles under his arms. "What'dya buy?" he asked, pointing at Lucas's Bloomingdale's shopping bag.

"Nothing," he said, though in this case "nothing" cost about half of his paycheck. He pulled the bag toward him, but

Franklin managed to grab it. In went his hand and out came a fistful of tissue paper and silk ties.

"Well, well!" Franklin exclaimed. "Who knew that Luke was such a devotee of Beau Brummell?"

"Who?" Lucas asked, snatching the ties back.

"The original dandy. He polished his boots with champagne. Before him, the only proper necktie color was *blanc d'innocence virginale*. But clearly," Franklin scoffed, "that's not you."

Lucas felt his face turn a color that was decidedly not *blanc d'innocence*. Meanwhile, Alexis was laughing so hard that her delicate body looked ready to shatter. Hiccupping, she told Franklin that she'd played a little joke on Lucas: told him to wear designer ties or he'd definitely be shit-canned. Franklin nearly spit out his beer, and Lucas lunged to protect his ties.

"You made all that stuff up?" He forced a smile. First thing tomorrow, he would return the ties before his checking account was the wiser.

"Let's raise a glass to Luke," Alexis said, "and toast his relatively decent chance of retaining employment."

The three of them clinked. Lucas was feeling better. They'd never embrace his hustle if they didn't like him. But they seemed to. "So Jays isn't really as crazy as you guys've been saying?" Lucas asked. "I mean, that's why I believed you, Alexis."

"Oh no, he's crazy," Franklin said. "Or he makes everyone crazy, at least. Every decision in this office is made because someone's guessing what Jays wants but is too afraid to ask him. He'll still kill a story you've been fact-checking for weeks, months even."

Alexis wiped the last tears from her eyes. "He falls out of love with something that he's assigned and then blames the editor or the writer—or both—for wasting his time."

"Good thing I'm just a fact-checker then," Lucas said, and the others laughed.

The evening continued with more talk of Jays' antics. Rumor had it that during a brief tryst with a high-end interior designer the Editor had spent an ungodly amount of company money outfitting his dining room with an ornate crystal chandelier. "We're talking Versailles-style," Alexis said. "I heard it cost ten grand."

"I heard it cost *twenty*," Franklin said.

"Who's doing the expenses?" Lucas asked. "Somebody must be keeping track."

"Why not wait until you've been here awhile and then let us know what you think?" Franklin said, finishing off his drink. Lucas remembered what Alexis had said earlier that day: *You don't know where you are yet.* But she'd been joking, having fun at his expense. This talk of Jays' expense reports was obviously more of the same.

CHAPTER 3

It was 12:30 A.M., and the evening was in full blossom. About now, the tattooed girl with brown bangs agreed to a second drink. About now, you sped along Central Park West, your taxi windows down, the dazzle of gilded doorways rushing by. About now, as you rollicked toward the next bar with a group of people you'd only just met, you mustered the courage to take a pretty stranger's arm.

These were Lucas's fantasies of New York. They weren't climactic moments—when you gained entry to the penthouse party in the West 80s or actually took the pretty girl into your bed. Events realized were too easily ruined. The real excitement lay on the glorious cusp.

And yet, for Lucas, the cusp was a lonely place to be. He stood at the corner of Bleecker and Cornelia Streets, clutching his bag of expensive ties. His colleagues, having dispersed to their significant others (Alexis) and their Tinder prospects (Franklin), had deserted him. Meanwhile, the West Village buzzed with activity. Bars were packed. Long-legged women strode arm in arm down the sidewalks. Herds of Jerseyites wandered past, the men with meringue-stiff hair, the women squeezed into sausage casings that passed for dresses. Lucas had no group, no pack, to call his own. Yet he was desperate to feel a part of these streets. And that meant he was going to have to choose a bar. It meant he'd have to talk to a woman he didn't know.

At Christopher Park he paused. To his left was the former Lion's Head bar, where Pete Hamill said a "glorious mixture of newspapermen, painters, musicians, seamen, ex-communists, priests and nuns, athletes, stockbrokers, politicians and folksingers" had all "bound together in the leveling democracy of drink." Lucas knew this, for the same reason he knew about anything in New York: *Empire* had written about it. But no longer would he have to rely on the secondhand telling. He could now experience these places in the flesh, absorb their spirit through osmosis. It was only a shame that the Lion's Head technically ceased to exist. Now it was an NYU dive called Kettle of Fish.

Inside, college students drank cheap beer and played Connect Four. Thirtysomethings and neighborhood locals clustered around the bar. Lucas stood helpless, gripped by indecision. Maybe he should just go home. He thought about his cramped apartment with its fluorescent lighting and grimy floors. *Fuck it.* He pulled up a stool. He hung the shopping bag on a hook, carefully, as though the silken bounty were a nest of sleeping snakes.

He eyed the Macallan 12 but thought about his wallet and settled for a Jack Daniel's on the rocks. Nearby, a trio of women complained about their law firm. One of them was petite, with a jaunty blond ponytail and perky breasts. Lucas should offer to buy her a drink. But then what about her friends? And even if he could afford to buy them all drinks, wouldn't the gesture come off as creepy—like he was hitting on all of them at once? What did a man do in this situation? Silently cursing his inexperience, Lucas caught the eye of one of the women. It wasn't the pretty one. Lucas smiled anyway, but she'd already averted her gaze. This was a disaster.

He pulled out his notebook and a pen. If he looked artistic enough, or mysterious enough, maybe a woman would come talk to *him*. But Lucas couldn't shake the feeling that everyone was watching him, judging the fact that he was twenty-four and had no idea what to do with himself at a bar, alone. Or that he was at a bar alone to begin with. He needed to order another drink—that, at least, he knew how to do—so he downed the rest of his whiskey in a gulp, then signaled for the bartender.

And that's when he saw her.

Her dark brown hair, which fell in a thick sweep over one tanned shoulder; the critical arch of her eyebrows; the sexy bump in her otherwise delicate nose; her long fingers turning a glass of red wine; and, most of all, her sternum. It was the result of her dress—black with a V-shaped plunge that revealed a wide expanse of lightly freckled skin. The cut, he realized, was the exact shape as Christopher Park. Only instead of facing east, the tip of this triangle pointed south, downward toward regions unseen.

Lucas had never given any thought to a woman's sternum. Why would you when there were breasts in the vicinity? (He momentarily thought of Mel, whose large breasts he had loved, despite her complaints that they created unflattering side-boob.) This woman's breasts were modest at best. But in the moment, nothing seemed more appealing than the flatness in between: bare and exposed. Almost proud. It was like the sternum was issuing a challenge: *Come on over, Lucas; see how close you can get.*

Mel had always expressed hostility toward lone women in bars. Clearly, she'd say, they were either desperate or slutty. Otherwise, why submit yourself to the kind of men who went to bars to meet women? Lucas never argued, but he disagreed. Why was aloneness an automatic sign of depravity? It was like he knew this day—this specific day, in which he sat alone at a bar—would come. And yet Lucas swore he could read that sternum like a crystal ball. In his future: immediate rejection. Only how else was he going to remake himself in the image of Manhattan? Not by sitting here, ruminating. Not by *not* trying. If only he had some pretext for talking to her. What a loser he was, afraid to strike up a simple conversation.

He needed to grow a pair. He gave the woman another cautious glance. She was scribbling on a bar napkin. Hadn't he basically been doing the same thing? Maybe it was a sign. Awkwardly, he maneuvered through the throng until there she was, mere inches away. She was even more stunning up close. She'd done some dark makeup thing to her eyes, a technique, Lucas realized, that Mel had spent years attempting unsuccessfully. His heart throbbed in his ears. "Excuse me?" he said.

The woman looked up and gave Lucas the briefest of onceovers, a glance that said, simply: *He'll do.*

Lucas needed to say something else, but what? He felt a sudden sympathy for every man who had ever attempted to use a line on a woman. Those men weren't sleazebags! They were terrified! And rightly so, because the woman was starting to look impatient. Lucas was sinking. If only he could be honest: *Cut me some slack. I've never done this before.*

But then, remarkably, she saved him. "I'm Carmen." She held out her hand.

"Lucas," he said, and slipped his fingers into hers. They were soft and warm. He felt his body flush. "Nice to meet you."

"So what brings you over to this side of the bar, Lucas?"

This was it. He was going to either start swimming or die a cold, watery death. "I was—well, I was wondering if you needed a piece of paper."

"Paper?" She sounded intrigued.

"Well, that napkin you're working on looks about tapped. I thought maybe you'd like some actual paper."

"And you have some?" The woman smiled, but just at the corner of her mouth. "Do you travel the bars of New York dispensing office supplies to women in need?"

"On occasion," Lucas said. In fact, Mel had often berated him for taking his reporter's notebook along when they went out. She accused him of being distracted and, worse, weird. But ever since Lucas had read a profile in *Vanity Fair* about Jay Jacobson's obsession with writing in notebooks, he'd started carrying one with him. Of course, his wasn't expensive Italian leather, but a cheap pad from Staples. He pulled it from his back pocket and ripped out a few pages. "And don't worry," he said coyly. "There's more where this came from."

Carmen frowned.

You moron! "I just mean I've got plenty," he corrected himself. "In case inspiration strikes."

"Ah. Let me guess: NYU MFA program. Aspiring novelist."

"Journalist," he said, relieved. He was pretty sure that "writing program grad student" was a deal breaker. He thought about mentioning *Empire*, which might even impress her. But if she discovered that he was only a fact-checker, he'd find his ass tossed back onto Christopher Street. "You're a writer, too?" he asked, nodding at the napkin.

"Of a kind," Carmen said. But she didn't seem eager to elaborate. "So you're what—twenty-two, twenty-three?"

"Do I look that young?" It occurred to him that he might have gotten in way over his head. It wasn't just that Carmen was obviously a thousand times sexier and more sophisticated than

Mel. She was also older. Early thirties older. Though weren't more older women picking up younger men these days? *Empire* had recently run a story on just this topic. Carmen smiled and flipped her hair over her shoulder. The scent of some large-petaled flower blossomed in the beery air.

"Would you like another glass of wine?" he asked.

"Sure, Lucas," she said. "You can buy me a drink."

Luckily, he was able to get the bartender's attention without much trouble and order Carmen's drink.

"Another Jack, bub?" the bartender asked.

"Macallan Twelve," Lucas said sharply, and gave Carmen a look that said: *What self-respecting person drinks Jack?*

The drinks arrived. "Your *Macallan,* sir," the bartender said, rolling his eyes. "And a Pinot—on the house." He nodded at Carmen as though the two of them were sharing a private joke. Lucas bristled. But never mind. He and Carmen clinked their glasses. This was actually happening.

"So, Lucas," Carmen said. "How's your night going? What brings you out here alone?"

He wasn't sure if she was flirting or deciding what caliber of loser he was. "My friends got tired," he said.

"But not you." She eyed him steadily.

"Not me," Lucas said, and nearly choked on his Macallan. He waited for her to say something. It seemed like her turn, but he feared another awkward silence. "I came in here because it used to be a big writers' spot, in the sixties and seventies. I wanted to check it out."

"You sure you're not in grad school?" Carmen laughed.

Lucas's face burned and he took a large sip to cool his nerves. "Have you been in New York a long time?" he asked.

"Born and raised on the Upper West Side. I'd never live anywhere else."

"I know what you mean," he said. "I've been trying to get here my whole life."

"All twenty years of it."

"Really," he protested. "I'm not that young."

She nodded skeptically.

"But I've only been here a month."

"What took you so long?"

"My ex. She wouldn't even consider moving."

Carmen nodded solemnly. "Well, we New Yorkers certainly don't want anyone like *that* around. But you on the other hand—New York is happy to have you."

At that moment, someone behind Lucas jostled him and he bumped rather hard into Carmen. Some of his drink splashed onto her lap.

"Sorry," he said, panicking. "I'm really sorry. Let me get you something—a napkin?" He reached for the one on the bar, but it was covered with her writing. He cursed, frantically signaling to the bartender.

"It's fine, Luke," Carmen said. "Relax."

He needed to stop acting like a spaz. Glancing down to regroup, his eyes fell onto Carmen's dress. It was tied with a knot, just a few inches above her hip. Oh, how he wanted to give that knot a tug.

"Are you OK, Luke? You're sweating."

"It's hot in here," he said. And then, because the alcohol was finally doing its job, he said, "Maybe we could talk someplace with a little more breathing room?"

Carmen finished off her wine in one large gulp. "I know a place." She slid off the stool. In her heels, she was taller than him. Mel had barely come up to his shoulder. But forget Mel. This night was not about her. This woman was most certainly not her.

"Are you ready?" Carmen asked.

You have no idea, Lucas thought. Only then he remembered the ties. Luckily, half his paycheck hadn't vanished in the hands of some drunken stranger. "OK," he said, holding the bag and meeting her at the door. "After you." Carmen looked back at him and stumbled a little. He realized that she was quite drunk. He took her arm, grateful for the chance to steady her. "Where to?" he asked.

"Thisaway," she said, slurring just a little. Then she led him into the street.

CHAPTER 4

It had been six years since Lucas woke up beside a woman who was not Mel. In fact, it had been exactly that long since he'd been in a bed with another woman at all. He was, a friend had told him recently, a "fucking virgin." Not as in *that guy's a fuckin' virgin!* But more like, *that guy has had sex, sure, but he hasn't fucked. He is a virgin at fucking.* This analysis made Lucas anxious. Both he and Mel were virgins when they met during freshman year of college and both were equally relieved to dispense with the title. But while Lucas had sex with one person—and then, well, sex, and then sex, and then, as long-term relationships tend to go, less and less of that sex—his friends had moved on to sex with acquaintances and strangers, which was an entirely different skill. Which meant Lucas had a whole new virginity to lose.

Miraculously, Carmen didn't seem to notice his inexperience, and everything worked more or less the way it was supposed to. There were a few hiccups, but nothing disastrous. And now he was lying beside a gorgeous woman, on a sunlit Saturday morning, in the West Village, after his very first one-night stand.

Lucas stretched, feeling his heels glide along the luxurious bedding. He'd always assumed that sheets were just sheets, the phrase "thread count" just a marketing ploy, and so he opted for the cheapest. It turned out that sheets could be magic. And a bed could be as expansive, downy, and white as a puff of cloud. He had to pee, but he didn't want to move from this spot. Ever.

But what if there's more sex? If so, he couldn't do that on a full bladder. So, reluctantly, he climbed out of bed. The bedroom was impeccably clean, with furniture that had neither been salvaged from the street nor purchased at Ikea. If he ever wanted to bring a woman back to his own bedroom, he'd have to part with the other half of this month's paycheck and then some.

Lucas tiptoed into the bathroom. A wicker basket beside the toilet was a schizophrenia of magazines: *Elle*, the *Economist*, last week's *Times'* Sunday magazine, and *Us Weekly*. No *Empire*. He wondered what kind of writing Carmen did. It seemed strange that they'd had sex and yet he knew nothing about her. But wasn't total detachment the point of being single in New York? He could pick up another woman tonight and nobody would question him. Nobody even had to know! Never in his life had Lucas enjoyed such anonymity. Back home in Charlotte, privacy was a foreign concept.

Lucas washed his hands, wondering what came next. Was he supposed to wait until Carmen woke up and then excuse himself? Make coffee? And where should he be—dressed and waiting somewhere, or should he just climb back in bed? Suddenly, the idea of morning sex seemed presumptuous. What would Jays do? Lucas thought about it. Jays, he decided, would get dressed and leave, and then he'd text later that day to thank

his lady friend for a great evening. And that would be the end
of it. Gracious and confident. But Lucas did not have Carmen's
number. As he debated, he looked himself over in the mirror.
When he and Mel had first started dating, she admitted that
her friends found him cute. They liked his dark blond hair and
big brown eyes, and of course his cheekbones—prep-school
cheekbones, Mel called them. And if her friends had also considered his head to be just a little too small for his body, they
kept this detail to themselves. Lucas was fairly self-conscious
about that particular deficiency and often assessed the head-
to-neck-to-torso ratio of the men he encountered. Clearly, Carmen hadn't minded this flaw. Or she'd been too drunk to
notice. It was dark in that bar, after all.

Lucas dressed quickly. He considered leaving his phone
number, but that seemed like a very un-Jays thing to do. Lucas
would have been perfectly happy to see Carmen again, but he
didn't want her to think that he *expected* a call. And who knew?
Perhaps they'd meet again, at a party or on the street, like in a
Woody Allen movie. That would be *so* New York. Lucas took a
final look at Carmen in her cloud bed and then shut the apartment door behind him.

Once outside, Lucas entered a small café, where he purchased a *New York Times* and a black coffee and settled in to
read. He couldn't focus. In his mind's eye, he was pressing his
cheek against Carmen's sternum. They'd wasted no time upon
entering the apartment. She hadn't even bothered to turn on the
lights. He'd kissed her on the mouth, then on the neck, then
on both of her breasts over the fabric of her dress and, finally,
as though this were the true prize, the bare space between them.
Then he'd reached out his arm and tugged at the knot of her
dress. The fabric had not dissolved in his fingers, as imagined.
He'd struggled a little to get it undone, but eventually the tie
loosened and slipped. The dress fell open. Lucas gasped. She

stood in her heels. Her bra was see-through, right to the nipples, and her thong was a triangle of so little surface area, it might have been sewn from a shadow. Lucas had briefly flashed back to the porn he'd watched alone in his old apartment, surreptitiously, when Mel was out. There was always some innocent-looking girl, in glasses and maybe a ponytail, going about her innocent day. And this innocent girl would become shocked or incredulous or aghast that somebody made a pass at her. But then her shirt or dress would come off, and she'd have on nothing underneath. Or a slutty tattoo. Or a landing strip. And it always ruined the moment, this lack of narrative consistency. And now here was Carmen, bringing what seemed like a major writing flaw to life. When she got dressed that morning, she'd actually prepared to be undressed.

So there she stood, beautiful and bare, and Lucas was still fully clothed. He wondered if Carmen didn't look a little annoyed—*am I going to stand here half-naked all night?*—but it was dark and Lucas wasn't worrying anymore. He followed Carmen into her bedroom, where she began to remove his shirt, her practiced fingers navigating the buttons one by one. She loosened his tie, slid her hands down to his belt. He could feel something happening inside of him, something almost religious in its power. Like his afternoon baptism in Jays' office, this, too, was a kind of conversion. He had met a beautiful woman at a literary bar and she had taken him home to her apartment. By the end of the night he would no longer be a fucking virgin. By the end of the night he would be remade—reborn in the morning sunlight as a New Yorker.

Lucas returned to the undressing. Carmen had loosened his tie, slid her hands down to his belt . . . loosened his tie, slid her hands down . . . loosened his tie . . .

"Oh shit!"

In the coffee shop, people looked up from their newspapers.

Lucas buried his face in his hands. He was a fuckup, the greatest fuckup in the history of fuckups. Because right now sitting on the floor in Carmen's apartment was a hefty portion of his paycheck. Amidst all the indecision of how to make a masterly exit, Lucas had left behind his bag of designer ties.

CHAPTER 5

A week later, at a house party in South Slope, Lucas made out with an elementary-school teacher. She was chubbier than the women he usually liked. Being on the lanky side himself, he sometimes felt dwarfed by athletic types or women whose hips were double the width of his own. But he liked her plastic-framed glasses and full, pouty lips. They'd talked easily; he'd made her laugh. People were dancing in the living room, so they retreated to the bedroom, where they ended up on the bed, tumbling uncomfortably on a heaping pile of purses. This was so easy, he'd thought to himself. And he knew it was because of Carmen. Carmen was older, more attractive and much more sophisticated than the elementary-school teacher. A schoolteacher, to be clear, whom he could fuck! As a college student, he'd lost his virginity to another college student. That was the expected, singular option. But this was a part of adulthood he'd never considered—the buffet of professions, of real people with important functions in the world, who are also feral, sexual creatures. That lawyer he saw on the subway that morning? She fucks! The receptionist at his dentist's office? She fucks! If Carmen had wanted him, then why not these other women? The idea left him inspired.

"So, want to . . . ," he started to ask the schoolteacher, though swiftly he realized he wasn't sure what should come next. He paused and regrouped. "Um, come back to my place?"

"You're sweet," she said, touching his cheek. "But I don't think so."

Sweet? Lucas flushed. "I don't understand," he said. "Did I do something wrong?" Was it the way he kissed? Something about his tone?

"No . . . ," the teacher said tentatively, climbing off the bed. "I'm just not interested." She seemed annoyed, almost affronted. Did she think he was trying to pressure her? That wasn't it at all. He just wanted some feedback.

"Wait," he said, but the teacher scowled and quickly left the room.

Lucas sat for a moment amidst the purses. Purses of professional women who might not fuck him after all. He imagined dumping the contents onto the covers, scouring the objects for answers. Because a new, troubling thought was sinking in: What if Carmen was a blip? An accident? A trick perpetrated by the universe to make him think that he was reasonably attractive and passably suave? What if he was ugly and awkward? An ugly, awkward, (still mostly) fucking virgin.

Weeks passed and Lucas discovered that picking up one woman did not necessarily lead to picking up another. For nights on end, he found himself with no plans, no place to go. Nor had he heard from Jays. Their one-on-one had felt so promising, and then . . . nothing. Every day at work felt like an at-bat for the Charlotte Knights, the Triple-A baseball team he loved from home. *Maybe today. Maybe today.* But none of the scouts was calling.

Lucas gave himself a pep talk: Wasn't the challenge of the city what made it so amazing? Wasn't there dignity—and even romance—in the striving? Wasn't that why he moved here?

Because back home, his parents cared only for the winning team and the top league. It was why, when Lucas was little, they'd moved into a neighborhood that they could barely afford; why they constantly worried about money, even while his mother insisted on only doing volunteer work; why they were so eager for Lucas to get a law degree from UNC, marry into the Woodward clan, and then go work for Mel's father's firm. Essentially, move from the minor leagues of status and wealth into the Big Show.

And then, one day in late September, the scouts finally picked up the phone. "Jays can't make it and wants you to fill in for him and show support," read an email from the Sphinxes.

Beneath that, they had forwarded an invitation, the entirety of which was: "Jays!!!!!!! Been too long, my friend! Release party for the Casa Madera Black! VIP room at Wilde's! Would mean the world to see you there! XO, Lori."

Lucas stared at the computer screen. Jays could have asked anyone to take his place, but he'd gone right to Lucas. It was tremendously exciting. And terrifying. How could Lucas possibly represent Jays at an exclusive event? Or show the proper amount of support to the Casa Madera Black, whatever that was? Or socialize with the other VIPs, whoever they were? In an excited panic, he forwarded the invite to Alexis. At the top, he wrote: "!!!!!!!" It seemed the lingua franca of these exchanges.

Within seconds, Alexis responded: "Welcome to the publicity event gravy train!" She went on to explain that TV studios, billion-dollar-valuation tech start-ups, liquor conglomerates, and hell, even high-end pen manufacturers all knew that the one surefire way to get a bunch of editors in a room was to rent a swanky event space and distribute free alcohol and hors d'oeuvres. These events happened every night and editors who were lucky enough to receive invites could go for days at a time without having to cook dinner or otherwise pay for groceries, so long as they were willing to make meals out of Kobe beef sliders, tuna tartar crostini, and grilled cheeses stuffed with prosciutto—which, of course, they were. Salt-rimmed glasses of mescal or whiskey would precede and follow.

"Even after the recession this stuff is happening?" Lucas typed back.

"I know, right? Can you imagine what it was like before?"

"But what do these companies expect in return?"

"In theory, coverage. But they almost never ask. We live in a land of excess. Have you been in the products closet? I haven't paid for my own body wash since I started here."

Lucas had not been in the products closet. Lucas was currently paying for his own body wash. The world was opening up.

"Honestly, Franklin and I are too low on the totem pole to get these invites, so please write this publicist back immediately and tell her you want 'a plus-two.'"

And so Lucas walked back to his desk and emailed Lori the publicist. Five minutes later, she responded: "Lucas!!! So great to meet you. You're confirmed with a plus-two. Can't wait to see you at Wilde's!!"

How was anything this easy?

The next afternoon, a $125 bottle of Casa Madera Black arrived for Lucas via messenger. By that evening, Lori had sent

Lucas two more invites, one to a vodka party the following week and the other to a new wine bar in Tribeca called September Issue. It was the pet project of some chef Lucas had never heard of, and the small plates were supposed to be inspired by high-end fashion photographers.

"I'm just a fact-checker," Lucas told Alexis. "Won't all these companies be upset if they figure out I have zero editorial control?"

"You assume they have any idea how magazines work," Alexis replied.

"Isn't that their job?"

Alexis shrugged. "You've got to stop worrying so much."

But Lucas could not stop worrying. In advance of the Wilde's party, he'd spent hours scouring *Empire*'s recent fashion coverage, trying to assemble some combination from his own closet that passably resembled one of the shoots. He honestly wasn't sure whether Jays now expected him to wear fashionable ties or not, so he'd gone out and reluctantly spent the other half of his first paycheck on replacements. He prayed that one stylish accessory might compensate for the unremarkable quality of his shirt, pants, and shoes.

After work, Lucas, Alexis, and Franklin took the subway to Grand Central. Crossing Park Avenue, Lucas squinted down the manicured median. The farther you went, the more money per square foot. In his mind's eye, he imagined single-home town houses with their creamy façades and wrought-iron railings, luxury boutiques, and expensive restaurants.

Franklin must have noticed Lucas's wistful expression, because he snorted. "The Upper East Side is disgusting. It's all stuck-up rich people, entitled tweens snorting cocaine, and dogs that look like rats. Anyway, we're here."

Across the street was a red awning stamped with the Wilde's logo: a silhouetted dandy wearing a flamboyant cravat. The bar was housed inside a boutique hotel: six stories of pristine red brick. The doors were manned by a pair of high-heeled, air-brushed women, who smiled over their clipboards. One of these girls had hair so dark and liquid, Lucas expected her to be standing in a black puddle. The other had a blond camel-like hump of hair pinned over her forehead.

Lucas gave his name. "Ah, you're VIP," said the dark-haired publicist. "Present this at the door to The Study at eight thirty." She handed Lucas a bronze coin engraved with the Wilde's logo.

"Don't we need medallions, too?" Franklin complained.

"Oh, come on!" Alexis groaned, and pulled Franklin into the party. Red-faced, Lucas followed.

Inside, the décor was a mix of dark wood and hardcover books. Fireplaces glowed with fires that transmitted neither smoke nor smell. The bartenders fabricated elaborate cocktails, their hands flourishing bottles like skilled magicians. Waiters passed miniature fried-fish sandwiches on brioche buns, small triangles of Welsh rarebit, and gourmet "chips" doused in truffle oil. The trio drank a round of cocktails upstairs and then wandered down to the basement. This was the actual Wilde's bar, cozy and dim, with paintings of fox hunts and aristocratic women wearing dresses that Franklin immediately identified as belonging not to the Victorian Era, during which Oscar Wilde lived, but the Edwardian period, which officially started after the playwright's death.

"So fastidious, you fact-checkers," Alexis said as she sipped her old fashioned.

Franklin rolled his eyes. "Luke, it's almost eight thirty," he said testily. "Don't you have somewhere to be?"

———

Lucas had been nervous about The Study, because he expected Jays' sort of people: editors and socialites and artists who knew one another from their many exclusive galas and Hamptons time-shares. But Lucas couldn't imagine Jays among these people in ordinary work clothes, standing alone, their faces bathed in digital light. How many were only pretending to be engaged with emails and texts, fearful of looking uncomfortable and unmoored? Lucas was about to join the crowd in its collective cowardice when his eye fell upon a young man, about his own age. He was distinctive, because he did not have a phone at the ready—and because he was comically overdressed, clad in a tuxedo and accessorized with a walking stick. He was also phenomenally awkward looking—ugly, to be frank—with large eyes beneath a sloping forehead; bullish nostrils; and a couple of distracting Sharpie-black moles on his cheek.

This unfortunate character stood uncomfortably close to a young woman, who regularly shifted her eyes between her phone and the doorway. They engaged in a strange kind of dance, in which the woman kept taking tiny steps backward and the man would scoot forward to make up the distance. In this way, Lucas watched them move halfway down the bar. He'd seen assholes invade a woman's personal space before, but this individual didn't exactly appear to be hitting on his unwilling interlocutor. Mostly, he seemed clueless about some basic social cues.

"Lucas!" His name burst from the mouth of yet another stilettoed publicist. "Lori, from Hot Biz PR! Terrific to meet you! I see you've noticed Nicholas Spragg! I got a note that you two should connect!" She buoyed him across the room on a wave of verbal enthusiasms. Meanwhile, Spragg's victim, sensing that she'd finally been freed, turned her grateful eyes on Lucas and vanished.

"Lucas Callahan!" Lori exclaimed. "Nicholas Spragg! Nicholas Spragg! Lucas Callahan! I'm thrilled to introduce you!

You're both new to the city! I'm sure you'll have plenty to talk about!" Then Lori was retreating on treacherous heels.

Nicholas took the opening. He leaned in, causing Lucas to step back a bit, causing Nicholas to step forward a bit, the dance resuming uninterrupted with a new partner. And as it happened, Nicholas launched into a personal synopsis. He'd recently moved to New York from Europe. Where in Europe? Lucas asked. "Oh, here and there. Paris and London. Berlin." But he wasn't actually European? Well, "Continental" was his preferred term.

"Oh," Lucas said, and noted that Nicholas looked disappointed by this lack of enthusiasm. But then he was telling Lucas about his long Germanic history and how his great-grandfather was a Bavarian count. "Our family still owns castles, which are literally packed to the gills with centuries-old works of art."

"Huh," Lucas said, a bit flummoxed, by both the strangeness of these claims and the uncomfortable proximity of Nicholas's face to his own. Nicholas then launched into a monologue about his task of managing the collection, making sure that everything was properly restored and appropriately loaned. Though he'd just come from "the Continent," he might soon have to return. There was trouble with a particular portrait that was meant to go to the Uffizi but ended up at the Louvre. "A horrible mess," he said.

"So you're an art dealer?" Lucas asked. He was eager to slot Nicholas into a recognizable role in the world. At the core of all this man's bluster, he must *do* something, right? But Nicholas gave Lucas a cryptic look and replied that he "dealt" with "all sorts of things."

Lucas searched for the right response. He came up with: "I love your cane."

"Oh, thank you!" Nicholas exclaimed. "This belonged to my great-grandfather the count. This is ivory from an elephant tusk." He paused to see how this explanation was going over. In response to Lucas's polite smile, he frowned, then added, "And would you know that my great-grandfather shot the elephant himself?"

"No kidding," Lucas said, beaten into submission. "That's extraordinary."

Now Nicholas beamed. "It is, isn't it? He wanted to teach me how to shoot, but he died when I was six. He was a force. Even at ninety, he would carry me on his shoulders and call me 'the little king.'"

"He sounds like a fascinating man," Lucas said.

At that moment, Nicholas's phone buzzed. "I've got to run!" he announced, and shook Lucas's hand heartily. "This has been quite a capital evening. I hope we stay in touch." He produced a cardholder—were the letters *NS* encrusted with actual diamonds?—and extracted a thick piece of paper with "Nicholas Spragg" written in the center. There was no contact information. There was, in fact, no other information at all. *Well,* Lucas thought as the enigmatic young man retreated, *so much for that.*

Twenty minutes later, the tasting was over and The Study began clearing out. Lucas couldn't imagine why Jays needed anyone to stand in for him tonight, but he hoped he'd adequately fulfilled his role. He returned to the main rooms, now tightly packed, and almost immediately stumbled upon a familiar sound. It was the unmistakable booming baritone of his roommate, Tyler. Lucas craned his neck, but no luck. He'd have to follow the voice.

It didn't take long. Tyler detonated a laugh and Lucas felt its force like a gust of wind. It was amazing that someone so short, barely notching five-six, could produce such a sound. Then again, Tyler was the very embodiment of compact power; he had the dense body of an old-timey wrestler, only minus the waxed mustache and unitard. The two of them made a visually ridiculous pair: Lucas slim and gangly, Tyler stocky and short. But they were rarely together, because Tyler was perpetually out.

They'd met via craigslist when Tyler's previous roommate moved out. "I know people at *Empire*," Tyler said when Lucas visited the apartment. "If you want to move in, that's cool." Lucas had expected a more thorough vetting and wondered if he should be suspicious. But he desperately needed a cheap room. And as Tyler said, "poor journalists need to stick together."

Tyler had been in New York a year longer than Lucas. Before that, he'd worked in Boston for a free weekly paper given out in the subway. Part of his job was to follow the elite of Boston to their galas and benefits and then produce columns about the personal muddying of their political lives (and vice versa). He managed to do this successfully for three years, an especially impressive feat in Boston, an insular town with a small core of power brokers. But that was Tyler, as Lucas was learning: Nothing stuck to the guy. He was too charming, too friendly, and too loud, really, but in a way that was more endearing than annoying. No matter what he wrote or whom he pissed off, everybody felt like his best friend. It's why he'd been poached by Noser.com, a New York–based website that produced investigative snark, largely about the media. It was sophisticated gossip, one step above Page Six and designed for people too embarrassed to be seen reading a tabloid.

Lucas wondered if Tyler was a little embarrassed by his new employer, because he now interviewed and wrote under the pseudonym J. P. Maddox. Lucas considered pseudonyms dishonest; Tyler argued that human beings had multiple personas. Tyler was Lucas's roommate. J. P. Maddox was a media reporter. They lived different lives, served different functions in the world.

Now Tyler caught Lucas's eye and waved him over to his

small group. "This is Lucas," he announced. "My new roommate."

"I'm Sofia. Pleased to meet you." The young woman beside Tyler extended her hand, and Lucas shook it, feeling a little breathless. She was gorgeous: tall and lithe, with long brown hair. She wore a crisp men's button-down, dangerously unbuttoned. But what struck Lucas most were her eyebrows: dark and thick. "Courageous," oddly, was the word that came to mind.

Lucas struggled for something witty to say, but before he could think of anything, the other member of their group slid his arm around Sofia's waist. Of course she'd be spoken for. And yet by *this* guy? The boyfriend wore a flannel shirt and a lumberjack beard but also metallic gold Nikes, a pair of red Beats around his neck, and a Supreme baseball cap. He seemed to be awkwardly suspended between stereotypes.

Then the boyfriend—who still hadn't introduced himself—wandered off in search of another drink.

"As you can see," Tyler said, "Sofia's dating a hopster."

"I'm sorry," Lucas said. "A what?"

"Hopster. Hip-hop hipster. It's helpful, really: Every month, when Sofia finds a new man, I get to learn about a new subculture I wished didn't exist. Last month was an abcaster."

"Which is?" Lucas asked.

"An abstract podcaster. There's one episode that's just Sofia breathing for an hour."

Sofia frowned, but she seemed more amused than annoyed. "You're giving my new friend here a very bad impression of me." She winked at Lucas and his heart fluttered. Her voice brought to mind terraced gardens and olive trees. "What's the point of living here if you're not going to take advantage of all the—"

"Bizarre sexual proclivities?"

"*Diversity*, Tyler."

"Sure, whatever. Actually, Lucas, seeing as you're new to the city, I think you can take a lot of inspiration from Sofia. She's an urban explorer in the grandest of senses. I've never met someone more willing to try anything."

Sofia smiled. "Well, I didn't move here to sit in my apartment."

"I thought urban explorers climbed bridges and snuck onto subway tracks," Lucas said.

Sofia turned to Lucas. "Well, there are many kinds of explorers. But I *have* always been curious about the abandoned railroad beneath the West Side Highway. We should go sometime."

"I'd love that," Lucas said. "I could even pitch it to the magazine."

"That's fantastic!" Sofia said, and Lucas felt his heart soar. Until the hopster reappeared.

"Well, we should be getting on to Ames's book party. Luke, we could probably, almost certainly get you in," Sophia said.

Andrew Ames, Lucas knew, was a *New York Times* book critic known for his prickly attitude toward self-important, navel-gazing memoirists. He'd also just released his own memoir.

"I'd love to," Lucas said. "But I'm here with some friends."

Sofia leaned toward Lucas. She smelled of cut grass. "Until next time, then."

"Hold up, folks." Tyler looked up from his phone, eyes gleaming. "Before we jet, I must read the latest from your esteemed publication, Lucas. The Internet is ablaze over Carmen Kelly."

Carmen Kelly wrote "The Sophisticated Sensualist," *Empire's* dating and sex column. It was the only part of the magazine in which Mel had shown any interest, which Lucas found strange. What use did people in a long-term committed relationship have for tips on dating and one-night stands?

Sofia bent over Tyler giraffe-like, as though the top of his head were a low-lying shrub. "I hate that woman. Truly. Listen to this," she said. "'We reached my place. I could see Guy's panic. Something was supposed to happen, but he didn't know when, where, and in what order. If I gave him a written-out schedule, he'd have thanked me and studied it.'"

"What's there to hate?" Tyler protested. "Nobody sleeps with Carmen Kelly without knowing that he'll eventually end up ground into dust. Have you met her around the office, Lucas? She's the one human being capable of frightening those horrible Sphinxes."

"I don't think she comes into the office," Lucas said. "But how do you know Jays' secretaries?"

Before Tyler could answer, Sofia said, "You're assuming the men who fall into Carmen's clutches know who she is."

"It's all anonymous, so who cares?" Tyler said.

Sofia snorted, but it was a cute, delicate kind of snort. "If she was writing about *you*, I don't think you'd be so sanguine, Tyler. Maybe she *is* writing about you."

"Do you take me for that much of a sexual naïf? Listen to this: 'I experienced what I can only describe as his inexperience. He was trying so hard, poor Guy. He must have thought that he was highly sophisticated—quite sexually fluent, if you will. Instead, I was reminded of what the estimable Walter Kirn said about Aaron Sorkin: His "dialogue is how stupid people imagine smart people sound."'"

"That almost makes sense," Sofia said.

"But it's still impressively mean," said Tyler.

"Can we go now?" the hopster asked, speaking for the first time.

As Lucas listened to them bicker, he began to experience an uncomfortable sensation. He could swear that the room was filling with water and that he was sinking, quickly losing oxygen. Because by the Walter Kirn reference he knew—and he was certain that, somehow, at any moment, Tyler, Sofia, and even the hopster would know it, too: Carmen from the West Village was actually Carmen Kelly. And she was writing about him.

The Sophisticated Sensualist
By Carmen Kelly

I intimidate men. As a dating columnist, it's the cost of doing business. And it means that the guys I date are the ones bold enough to hit on me—which is to say those with big offices, even bigger egos, and positively massive bank accounts. Ladies, I know what you're thinking: They're all compensating for *something*. But so what? Sex is never a given, even if you have flown me out to Vegas for front row seats at the Octagon. (Though I have learned a thing or two about how to break an arm at the elbow; this generation of high rollers wouldn't know a *Pretty Woman* move if Julia Roberts personally bit them in the ass.)

Lately, though, the fancy meals and trips have started to feel staid. So I recently decided to try something new—i.e., a nice guy. Just a regular dude who can't afford a meal at Gramercy Tavern or 11 Madison Park (let alone a private jet to Vegas) and who would probably be grateful to have a woman like me take him home.

A few weeks ago, I entered a little spot in the Village, not at all classy, where a decent glass of Pinot only costs eight bucks. It was about midnight and I was sitting at the bar, waiting to see who or what would swim by. Dear reader, with you always in mind, I was taking some notes on a napkin when, to my surprise, a kid materialized. He looked to be twenty-two, twenty-three tops. He had terrific cheekbones (youth!) but an unfortunate haircut (youth!). He looked like he'd just wandered off the set of *Oklahoma!*

"Excuse me," he said, looking absolutely terrified. And then . . . nothing! He just stared at me, frozen in time. Eventually, he said he'd come to offer me some paper, because I was running out of room on my napkin—and then, wouldn't you know it, he actually produced paper. Working with what you've got! I applaud that, and, in my head, gave him a name: Mr. Nice Guy. In the name of research, I then took Mr. Nice Guy home.

Banker boys will do one of two things on the way from a bar to a bed: They'll either start the heavy petting right there in the cab because they think they're in an Axe body spray commercial, or they'll drop not-very-subtle hints about how experienced and excellent they are, hoping that, when they fail to get it up or finish too fast, it'll seem like a fluke. Mr. Nice Guy did neither. We decided to stroll—ah, late summer!—but he kept his distance, roughly the width of three city trash cans, the whole way. As we went, he asked me questions, first-date style: How do I like the city? What's my favorite band? My favorite color? So curious, this boy! It was refreshing. Until we reached my place.

Upon his entering my apartment, Mr. Nice Guy's panic was palpable. Something was supposed to happen, but he didn't know when, where, and in what order. If I gave him a written schedule, he'd have thanked me and studied it. Finally we shed our clothes—he tried helping me out of mine, but I'll do that myself, thankyouverymuch—and then I experienced what I can only describe as his inexperience. He was trying so hard, poor guy. He must have thought that he was highly sophisticated—quite sexually fluent, if you will. Instead, I was reminded of what the estimable Walter Kirn said about Aaron Sorkin: His "dialogue is how stupid people imagine smart people sound."

Mr. Nice Guy was doing what he thought other people do, not what his body told him felt right.

To wit: Sex with Mr. Nice Guy was like reading the overwrought prose of a first-year MFA student or—ugh—an undergraduate poetry major. Yes, the banker boys can be too distant, too disconnected, just parking their faces between my breasts like they're storing a bottle of whiskey on the rack. But Mr. Nice Guy was unleashing something. Me on top, me on bottom, it didn't matter—he tried to gaze longingly into my eyes, so much so that I had to close them to keep from cracking up.

His technique? It was fine. Every one-night stand is a little awkward and I was impressed by his stamina. But his behavior afterward was too novice to let stand. Depending on the chemistry—which is to say, depending on whether it's clear there should be more sex the next morning—a man is allowed to stay the night, but only to deliver the goods come sunshine. Mr. Nice Guy stayed, a real bummer because he snored and stole the covers. And then, when I woke up the next morning, he was gone. Vanished! There was no coffee waiting for me, no note thanking me for a nice night (even if it wasn't). And, to add insult to injury, he left the toilet seat up.

When I settle down—if I settle down—it won't be with a banker boy. (Sorry, gents! But keep calling for now.) But my little experiment taught me something about nice guys off Wall Street: They're excited, they're eager, but they need to get laid a thousand more times before they're real men. Maybe some of you ladies will be kind enough to help them—and please teach them some manners when you do. Thank-you notes may be passé in this digital age, but common courtesy is timeless.

CHAPTER 6

The Internet was like one massive highway pileup, and Lucas couldn't look away. By 9:00 A.M. the next day, Carmen's column was undergoing a thorough analysis throughout the Web. "Carmen Kelly Wins the Internet," one site declared. A conservative news site ran a photo of her in a skimpy dress and wrote: "American family values are under assault, and this Manhattan seductress is leading the charge." A frat-boy site ran a list called "15 Ways Carmen Kelly Will Criticize You in the Morning." (Number 7: "You only gave me four orgasms.") *Be-Damed,* an affiliate of *Noser,* laid out an argument straight out of Feminist Theory 101. "Women are assumed to be inherently empathetic," the writer explained. "So when a female like Carmen Kelly behaves in a non-empathetic manner or employs even a drop of condescension, it upends everybody's notions of female as nurturer, caretaker, compassionate mother-figure, etc. That's why men hate Kelly today. She makes them sad and lonely, with no-body to kiss their boo-boos."

And, of course, there were the tweets: an army of anony-mous men calling Carmen a slut, and worse; a campaign of women calling on Twitter to shut down those anonymous men's accounts; and the reporters in New York one-upping one another with jokes. "Welcome to sex with unimpressive writ- ers. Here in Brooklyn, we call that 'Tuesday,'" wrote someone from *Noser.*

As the target of Carmen's "drop" of condescension, Lucas felt strangely disconnected from it all. He wanted to hate her, but that meant siding with the chorus of sexist men, which he found appalling. And her defenders, like *Be-Damned,* seemed all too eager to lump him in with that crowd anyway.

"Hey, look at this!" Franklin said from inside his cubicle and to nobody in particular. "J. P. Maddox at *Noser* has written an open letter to Mr. Nice Guy. They want him to write a rebuttal."

In half a second flat, Lucas was standing over Franklin's computer screen. "No shit," he said. "You think he should—I mean, *will*?"

"Whoa there!" Franklin sputtered. "Look who's suddenly a gossipmonger."

Lucas slunk back to his cube. He was terrified of being iden-tified and publicly humiliated. But he was also indignant. His performance wasn't so bad . . . was it? Because what if he'd read the night all wrong? What if everything she said about him was true?

No. He should trust himself, to be more like Jays. He would write that goddamned rebuttal! He grabbed his laptop and headed outside. Sitting on a bench, he typed furiously for twenty minutes—invective after invective, witty phrase followed by sharp, wounding metaphor. And as his fury spilled onto the screen, he felt a pure, invigorating rush. Most of the time, he was a slow and careful writer. He made outlines with bullet points and sub bullet points. And yet Carmen said that sex with him was "like reading the overwrought prose of a first-year MFA student." It was all Lucas could do not to throw his computer against the sidewalk. He was *in magazines,* which made him a laborer, not an artist. You could hunt through his work for days before stumbling across a mixed metaphor or, god forbid, an adverb. Also, he thought most poetry was stupid. So there.

But everything he'd written so far was foreplay. Now that he was reaching the climax of his argument, he could barely contain himself. His fingers flew across the keys as the letter's most pointed, devastating, and forceful thought began to co-alesce. It built, as though pressurized, until he couldn't contain it any longer. And all at once, in a burst of consonants and vowels, the sentence shot from his fingers onto the screen. Lucas sighed and sat back, breathing hard. His hands fell from the keys. He was spent. He could have passed out right there on the park bench.

Now to get this sucker printed. He wasted a good twenty minutes trying to think up a decent, anonymous email address to create and finally settled on IAmNiceGuyNYC@gmail.com. Because he was, after all, a nice guy. A decent person, unlike Carmen Kelly. He was willing to own at least that part of her description.

He typed J. P. Maddox's email address into the computer, then paused. Sure, *Noser* had asked for the rebuttal, but it would be so much more devastating to have his response printed in *Empire* itself! Tyler would be pissed, but he'd deal. Lucas replaced Maddox's email address with Dan Housman's.

"Dear Mr. Housman," Lucas wrote. "I am the person who had the unfortunate experience of spending the evening with your columnist Carmen Kelly last month. I have written a rebuttal for your consideration—one that corrects the 'facts' presented by Ms. Kelly. You have my permission to run it. Thank you for your consideration. Sincerely, Nice Guy."

He pressed "send." Then he hurried back to the office. He wanted to be there when the email landed.

But by 4:00 P.M., he'd heard nothing. Unable to stand it any longer, Lucas took a stroll past Housman's office. He knocked, but when Housman called him in he found Jays, wearing perfectly tailored gray pants and complaining about his hamstrings.

"They're so *tight!*" Jays groaned, and reached his arms toward his feet.

"Sorry," Lucas said immediately.

"About my hamstrings?" Jays asked, his face still bent toward his knees. "Unless you're a five-foot-five gay man named Rocco with a BMI of eighteen-point-five then my hamstrings aren't your fault. Or your problem."

Housman gave Lucas a look, but Lucas couldn't tell if the expression said *come in* or *get out*.

With another groan, Jays righted himself. "So, Luke." Jays swung his head abruptly toward the door. "Maybe you can advise us. Carmen's recent victim has made contact. 'Mr. Nice Guy' is how he signed the email. I mean, really?"

"It *is* what Carmen called him," Housman said.

"It's not bad—the rebuttal," Jays went on. "The guy's intelligent. A few great lines actually."

Lucas tried to swallow his smile.

"You OK, Luke?" Housman asked. "You look a little . . ."

"Constipated," Jays said. Which did the trick of erasing Lucas's grin altogether.

"Of course it needs a serious edit, starting with the name. I'm nixing the 'Mr.' It sounds like those ridiculous Roger Hargreaves characters—Mr. Jelly and Mr. Tickle. Anyway, when Carmen called him a grad student she wasn't kidding."

Lucas swallowed the insult. "Are you going to run it?" he blurted.

"That's why I like our new hire, Housman. Young Luke has a fire in him. But we definitely don't want *Noser* taking control of this thing. The publisher is already on my ass about our Web traffic." Jays glanced at Housman. "It's a stroke of luck that Nice Guy decided to send the letter to us instead of those muckraking pre-schoolers. I mean is anybody at *Noser* older than twenty-five?" Jays seemed not to remember that Lucas was only twenty-four. "So here's where we're at: The writer of this rebuttal could be any huckster. How do we know it's really him?"

"Wouldn't Carmen be able to verify the guy's identity?" Lucas offered.

"I think it's better if we leave Carmen out of this for now," Jays said. "In fact, Luke, I'd prefer that you keep this conversation between the three of us."

"Of course," Lucas said, puffing up a little. He'd just received his first state secret and straight from the emperor's mouth. "What about asking the writer a question about Carmen that he'd only know from . . . uh, experience?"

Jays nodded, though he looked skeptical. Lucas decided to pivot and dismiss his own idea. It would demonstrate that he could self-critique. "Although I'm sure there's no shortage of men with those kinds of details," he said.

Jays stopped nodding. Housman grimaced.

"I didn't mean it like that. I, uh . . . that was really insensitive." Lucas stared at the floor.

"No, you're right," Jays said. "She has had many gentleman callers, which means that we can't necessarily trust what any one man has to tell us."

"Um," Lucas said. "What if we—"

"Housman and I will think of something, Luke. Thank you for your input."

"Oh," Lucas said. "OK." He had to redeem himself. But how?

"Talk to you later," Housman said, not quite looking Lucas in the eye.

Lucas slunk back to his desk, ruminating over his mental impotence.

"What's going on with you?" Franklin said when Lucas collapsed into his chair. "Two hours ago you bounded in here like you'd won a gold medal and now you look like you've been fired." Franklin leaned eagerly around the cubicle divider. "Have you been fired?"

"No," Lucas said. "Sorry to disappoint you."

CHAPTER 7

L ater that night, Lucas received an email. Technically, Nice-GuyNYC received the email, but Lucas was having messages to the fake account forwarded to his personal one.

Dear Nice Guy,

We appreciate your considered response to the column written by Carmen Kelly, which appeared in this week's issue of *Empire*. Though we have never published a full-length response to one of her columns before, we are entertaining the idea of publishing yours. However, your column must be fact-checked in order to verify that you are indeed the person about whom Ms. Kelly wrote last week. The easiest route is for you to come forward and reveal your identity, so that Carmen can confirm it.

If you are not willing to do that, then I will need you to confirm a few details about the night in question.

1. The name of the bar at which you and Carmen met, as well as verification from someone else at the bar that you were there with her.

2. The address of Carmen's apartment, as well as verification from the doorman that you went home with her.

3. A specific detail about sex with Carmen that nobody else would know.

Sincerely,
Jay Jacobson
Editor, *Empire*

As Lucas read, a series of thoughts sped into his mind, stopped short, and crashed: He could never reveal his identity; he had no proof they'd met at Kettle of Fish; Carmen's building had no doorman. And then Lucas began traveling to the logical conclusion of the letter: If Jays wanted an explicit sexual detail about Carmen in bed, it meant that either Carmen was now part of the discussion or . . .

No. Jays clearly wanted to keep her out of the discussion.

Which meant someone else would have to verify.

And only Jays and Housman knew about this.

And Housman, who got married like a month ago, was definitely not sleeping with Carmen.

Which meant that Jays was (is!?) sleeping with Carmen.

Which meant that Lucas had slept with the same woman as Jay Jacobson.

Which meant Lucas was in the same league as Jay Jacobson! Which meant that in alluding to Carmen's many sexual partners Lucas had also deeply insulted the woman Jay Jacobson was (is!?!?) sleeping with.

Which meant that Lucas just told his boss, the most powerful man in New York media, that he's just another dick in a lineup of dicks.

Lucas was screwed. And yet he'd never felt more elated. It was like he'd just cracked the modern version of *The Da Vinci Code*. But now it was time to focus. He needed to get Jays proof—and quickly. It was after midnight, but Lucas grabbed a pen from his desk, tiptoed past Tyler's door, and booked it to the West Village.

It was a Tuesday night and Kettle of Fish wasn't crowded. Lucas sat down at the bar and ordered a beer. To his relief, he recognized the bartender. "Do you remember me?" Lucas asked.

"No," the bartender said without even looking up.

"I was in here a few weeks ago? I was talking to a woman over there in the corner. Her name is Carmen Kelly."

"Ms. Kelly."

"Yes!" Lucas said. "You know her."

The bartender nodded. "That magazine she works for isn't really to my taste. But she doesn't act like a big shot. Never has."

Carmen, humble? Please. But Lucas nodded. "So, um, here's the thing. My friends and I are huge fans. But, see, they don't believe that I actually met her. They've been busting my balls for two weeks now." Lucas had never used the phrase "busting my balls" before, but it seemed like appropriate language for a brusque neighborhood bartender. "They're calling her my imaginary girlfriend."

The bartender frowned. "What do you want from me?"

"Well, I was hoping that you could kind of provide some testimony for me. You know, like a quick video saying that I'm not a lying piece of shit."

The frown deepened. "Forget it."

"OK, yeah, I know it's a lot to ask," Lucas said, nodding as earnestly as possible. "You wouldn't have to say anything about her, though. Just the fact that I met her."

"What's your name?" the bartender asked skeptically.

"Guy."

"No way, Guy. I don't remember you. And even if I did, I wouldn't get involved in your dumb game."

"There's got to be some way to verify—"

"I said no. Do you need to hear it again?"

"No, sir," Lucas mumbled. He slapped down some money and slunk morosely out of Kettle of Fish.

Having failed his first test, he wasn't sure that attempting to pass the others mattered, but he headed for Carmen's apartment anyway. Indeed, there was no doorman. Was that just a trick question? He wrote down the address and then scanned the mailboxes for her apartment number. It felt odd to be fact-checking his own one-night stand. If only he could confirm the "why" of it all. Why had Carmen taken him home? Was he just an easy victim? Hadn't there been anything about him that she'd found charming or likeable?

It seemed so pointless and, honestly, a little gross to make your living looking for other people's flaws. But worse, her column had destroyed his memory of that night, tarnished the pride he felt waking up beside her. She didn't even realize she'd done it. Or maybe she did and simply didn't care.

Lucas looked up at Carmen's building. He couldn't remember if her apartment looked out over the street or not. Part of him wanted her to peer out and see him standing there. He hadn't failed. Not entirely. He was trading the excitement of one new experience for that of another: having his first published piece of writing in a notable magazine. Even if he wasn't going to be paid for it. And even if nobody knew that it was his.

Lucas pulled out his phone right there on the street and signed into the Nice Guy email account. He sent the address and apartment number, noting the lack of a doorman. He told Jays the name of the bar and hoped that would suffice. Now all he needed was a sexual detail. "Carmen kept asking me to pull her hair," Lucas wrote. "It was frustrating, because no matter how hard I pulled, it never seemed to be hard enough." He sent the email, hoping the facts checked out to Jays' satisfaction.

The UnSophisticated Sensualist
By "Mr. Nice Guy"

Carmen,

I'm sorry I was attracted to you. I'm sorry I was excited that you took an interest in me—or appeared to. You have my deepest apologies for the way I didn't treat you like a piece of meat during the walk to your place. You have my humble regrets for kissing you too passionately. I atone for touching you too gently. It is with a heavy heart that I admit I looked into your eyes as you—should we get real?—rode my cock, your tits bouncing, your breathing heavy. "Fuck me fuck me fuck me fuck me fuck me," you said.

That is what you said. In your column last week, you somehow left that part out.

To the nice men of this city you insulted, insinuating that they're all worthless because I didn't measure up to your expectations: I am sorry about that. Most of you are probably better lovers than me. I didn't represent you well. I appreciate your pity, if that's what you have to offer. But I'd rather take your righteous indignation. Because what the hell is wrong with being excited and showing it? What's so bad about feeling lucky and appreciative? That's what we're being judged for, of all things? Women like

Carmen, throwing $100 bills out the window and laughing at the people desperately trying to grab one because, to them, $100 is a lot of money?

I was only trying to be genuine—inexperience and all. But women like Carmen don't want honesty. And if you don't satisfy their every whim and desire, they'll punish you for being yourself.

I'm trying not to be petty.

Yeah, maybe I kissed Carmen too much like I kissed my ex. Muscle memory. But I was with her for years. So yet again, I'm sorry. Most of us at least give long-term partnership a shot.

Back up. Not trying to be petty . . .

Nope, let's be a little petty. Carmen, the woman who prides herself on her sex life—you know what she's like in bed? Stiff, at first. It was like she was waiting for me to warm her up. But two minutes later she's yelling. Yelling! "Fuck me fuck me, fuck me, fuck me!" There wasn't passion in it. More like instructions. Like she was a drill sergeant. She didn't say that in her column either. Here's something else: She said she avoided my eyes. No. I kept looking into her eyes—"gazing," as she described—because she wouldn't break the eye contact. I liked it, sure. Eye contact is sexy. But she liked it, too.

Carmen, I don't know what the hell you're looking for, but I think it was more than a simple screw.

I do stand by one thing you said about me: I am a nice guy. Most of us are. And we're not going to bars like it's *American Gladiators*—all antagonistic and bringing our A Game. We're just trying to have fun, and hope that the women we meet want the same. But you never wanted that. You don't seem to like the banker guys you always talk about, but you don't like guys like me either. That's my problem? No. It's yours. If you found what you were looking for, I guess you'd have nothing left to write about.

CHAPTER 8

Jays, that ass, had printed a rebuttal to her column. A *rebuttal*! Readers could say whatever they wanted in the online comments. They could skewer her on social media. But the rabble hordes—which Lucas obviously was part of—did not have the right to besiege her in the pages of *her* magazine. And yet Carmen knew it was pointless to argue with Jays. The issue with Mr. Nice Guy's rebuttal had sold more physical copies than any week over the previous twelve months: more than *Empire*'s coverage of the hurricane that turned Lower Manhattan into a temporary Atlantis; more than the interview with the school shooter who'd terrorized that elementary school upstate; more than the cover story about the transgendered Republican congressman.

What was wrong with New York? Where was its respect for privacy—for dignity? She herself had grown up in a small Hamilton Heights apartment, her bedroom an alcove separated from the living room by a shoji screen. Her father, an MTA administrator of Irish stock, and her mother, a high-school Spanish teacher from Colombia, had encouraged her to make it her own. "Always preserve your own space," her mother had said. "Your own space is sacred." And so Carmen had gotten creative with paints and floating shelves and paper lanterns purchased in Chinatown.

When she started publishing "The Sophisticated Sensualist," her parents weren't thrilled. But they came to understand that Carmen's column wasn't Page Six. Nor was it *Noser*, which churned out public epistles of snark and narcissistic oversharing. Like her childhood alcove, the column was Carmen's own space, and through it she provided a voice to women throughout the city. It wasn't exactly bra burning in the streets. But it did expose and lambast the city's most sexist and misogynistic denizens. People thought everything was great for women these days. All this talk about "the end of men," a great calamitous finale for the power-hungry gender. But that was far from true.

Case in point: Carmen had not come to *Empire* to be its sex columnist. Years ago, she'd been hired to write on a variety of issues and, likely because she was an attractive woman in a mostly male newsroom, been shunted into the role of sex whisperer. The gig was steady, at least, but felt like a closet reminiscent of her childhood bedroom. Now, as then, she was doing whatever she could to make the space her own, while also preserving her dignity. The requirements of her job didn't make it easy. Maybe it was inevitable that Jays would turn on her. But it hurt to see how enthusiastically her beloved city—and its women! her peers!—reveled in her misfortune.

And then, just as she was on her way to *Empire* to give that narcissistic shit Jays a piece of her mind, he had called—personally—and asked her to lunch. Hearing his voice, so cordial and smug, made her want to throw the phone at a nearby store window. But he was the source of her monthly paycheck, which was high enough that she could almost forgive the lack of benefits. So now, instead of yelling at him in his office, Carmen sat at a table for two at The Standard Grill, waiting for Jays to roll in. She hated being first.

Like a desperate lover, she had primped for this lunch, hoping both to punish (show him what he was missing) and to pander (woo him back). As much as a feminist as she was in the pages of the magazine, she'd been less than exacting in her own love life—her *real* love life. She hated herself for this. Still, she'd gotten her hair blown out and donned some killer stilettos.

Jays was a sucker for Louboutin. "Tough on the outside," he'd once whispered into her ear, "but raw and red underneath." He liked her to wear them and nothing else. He bought her a pair that never left his bedroom. Instead, he liked to watch her run her tongue up and down the silky leather. He'd wanted to stick the heel in her ass, and she'd let him get as far as the outer rim. She had agreed to stand over him as he lay on the ground and hover one heel just above his crotch. *Closer, Carmen. Closer.* It was terrifying. (What if she tripped?) But it was also empowering. (What if she did trip?) Sex with Jays was unlike any she'd ever had. And she never wrote about any of it. It was too difficult to explain, these acts that sounded like crass fetishism or erotica schlock but, in fact, represented a rare mutual vulnerability.

"Hey, Car." Jays strode up and kissed her on the cheek. Their on-again-off-again affair of two years had only been officially over for just three months, though Jays looked predictably unflappable. Carmen hoped he would not try to make small talk or force her through the painful process of looking over the menu. Food added indignity to difficult conversations.

The waiter arrived. He knew Carmen, and he wasn't making eye contact. Which meant he'd read Nice Guy's attack. *Well, screw him.*

"Listen," Jays said as soon as the waiter walked away with their drink orders. "I'm a shit for printing that column. I'm well aware."

"Owning up doesn't make you a better person," Carmen said. But it was the smart play. Jays knew the one thing that politicians never learned: Denial increases the appearance of guilt. The truth—or some semblance thereof—killed all desire for gossip.

"Look, Car. It's not personal."

She snorted.

"I'm not trying to bullshit you. If you were running the magazine, and that guy's rebuttal popped up in your inbox, wouldn't you publish it, too? That column was publicity gold. It was going to get attention. And frankly, I hate to say it, but your column has been getting a lot less attention lately. It's repetitive, besides which, I think we both know you're aging out of the single-woman-on-the-prowl shtick."

As he made his case, Carmen began issuing her own silent refutations. The column was going just fine, thank you. Certainly none of the men she'd been writing about seemed to think that she was "aging out" of anything. In fact, she had every reason to believe that she was growing more desirable as she approached her sexual prime. Surely Jays knew that women hit maximum orgasm capacity in their early thirties. If anyone needed an age check, it was him! Forty-two and still treating the city like a frat house. She realized that she was clenching her fists under the table.

"Anyway, what happened this week was new and exciting. So that's what I wanted to discuss. How do we capitalize on it?"

She just looked at him. She wanted to hate him, but she felt both his physical proximity and his emotional distance like an ache. She wanted to take his beloved Louboutins and stomp on his heart. She wanted nothing except for him to say, *Carmen, I love you.* But he wasn't going to do that, and the reason, she knew, was simple. People called Jays inscrutable, but his actions followed a consistent logic: Jays did what was good for Jays. It wasn't personal. He was never spiteful. When Jays treated you well, it was because you were good for Jays. When Jays treated you poorly, it was because your suffering was good for Jays. Now Carmen burned with embarrassment, because she'd stupidly believed—or deluded herself into believing—that these rules didn't apply to her. Somehow she'd convinced herself that she was the one genuine, non-transactional thing in Jays' life.

Or maybe part of her had known the truth all along. Maybe she kept coming back because she liked being good for Jays. Because it made *her* feel good.

"How do you mean—*capitalize?*" she asked.

"That's what I'm asking you. We learned something this week about what our readers want, and I want to give them more of it. But it's your column. What do you think?"

Carmen couldn't remember the last time Jays asked her advice about anything. She thought about it for a moment, as Jays looked at her expectantly. "What if I do a series in which I only date nice guys for a month?"

Jays pursed his lips. "No, no. I don't think that's what got people fired up."

Over the next few minutes, Carmen tossed out every idea she could think of. Pick one nice guy, and try to turn him into a jaded asshole? Or better yet, hold a nice guy contest to see if any of them could turn *her* into a wide-eyed ingénue? She was even willing to set up a janky cardboard booth in Central Park, like Lucy's psychiatry booth in *Peanuts*, that said "Will Date

Nice Guys," and then write about what happened next. But Jays just kept shaking his head, repeating, "We need to fire people up."

Carmen was growing frustrated. "What do you want—a series in which every ex of mine trashes me in a nasty column?"

"Of course not," Jays said. "We're not hanging you out to dry. This is still your space. Your voice."

Your space, your voice. Never had she heard him talk like this before and it caused her to flush with excitement. "There's so much I could write about, Jay. I could get into the nitty-gritty sexual politics of all kinds of relationships. I could cover ageism, the LGBTQ community, go inside the world of fetishes, investigate polyamory and open marriages. Instead of writing about myself, I could actually start reporting. Real journalism."

"Interesting," Jays said, "but I don't think it would be provacative."

"But it would be! I'd be looking deep into the how and why of how people think and love and fuck. That would definitely change things up."

Jays just shook his head. "We can't replace a first-person sex and relationships column with a detached intellectual foray into sexual politics. Readers want titillation. They want *you.* And, besides, I already have plenty of reporters to do that other stuff."

And if I don't have reporting experience, she thought, *it's because you haven't given me any.* Now Carmen was angry. Her column was a box whose boundaries could be stretched, but never broken. What a coward Jays was. He claimed to be innovative and cutting edge, but he was afraid to take any significant risk. Just like 99.9 percent of magazine editors everywhere. "You want provocative?" She searched for something so patently absurd that Jays would finally realize how narrow-minded he was being—and that it was time to start taking her seriously. "OK, here's provocative. Why not set up a sexual cage match between me and that guy who slammed me? Every week we can fuck and then fight about it."

Jays' face lit up. "That's great! Tell me more."

"Wait, what? I was joking."

"Jokes are where some of the best ideas come from. Seriously, Carmen, I think you've stumbled onto something brilliant."

"I mean . . ." She felt like she was walking into a trap. Had Jays already thought of this? Had he merely been waiting for her to think of it, too? In any case, he was off and running.

"We could do it as a weekly series. A kind of back-and-forth between you and Nice Guy. And—oh! We could call it 'Screw the Critics.' A nice double-entendre."

Jays wasn't a wordsmith. It probably took him hours to come up with that. When did he think of it? Carmen wondered. Yesterday? This morning?

"I don't know, Jay. It's like putting sex with me on Rotten Tomatoes: 'Last night's sex was twenty percent fresh and eighty percent totally twisted'? It feels wrong."

"Look, unless you're totally repulsed by this guy, then why not try it out? At least you'll have the chance to fight back. As it stands, Nice Guy's got the last word."

Jays knew exactly where to aim. She was not totally repulsed by Nice Guy, despite his inexperience. And yet this arragement felt . . . not like prostitution, exactly, but perhaps like being mated at a zoo. But what choice did she have? She considered the question. Jays understood her circumstances here, and the position he was putting her in. She could say no, and risk whatever happened next. Based on how the conversation had started, Jays would likely cancel her column. She could walk away entirely, but that left her with no job and no platform, and it would look like she'd been defeated by Nice Guy's rebuttal. No. Neither option sounded good. She hadn't wanted to be a sex columnist in the first place, but that's what she was. At the very least, she couldn't let it end like this, bested by Nice Guy and Jays—a pair of little boys.

"You can take some time to think it over," Jays said, breaking the silence.

Carmen looked up and met his eyes. If she was going ahead with this, it would be on her terms. She was already thinking ahead, to her next meeting with Nice Guy and how she was going to call the shots. But first, she had to deal with the man sitting across from her. "I want a full-time position with benefits," she said.

Jays looked startled. He had clearly not expected her to negotiate, a sign of how truly cocky he'd become. He should have known better; she wasn't just going to roll over. And he'd clearly forgotten how well she knew *him*. He wanted it to happen. He already felt invested. She could see it in his face. That's what gave her leverage—not a lot of leverage, really, but enough.

"I want a full-time salaried position. No more contract. And I want to have a title. Call me editor-at-large, and put it on the masthead."

Jays opened his mouth to respond, but Carmen cut him off.

"And I want an office. For the one day a month that I feel like coming in. I don't care who you have to kick out."

Jays sucked in a breath. "All right," he said.

"And," she interjected before he could steal her momentum, "I'm setting the terms of this thing. I'm not just going to jump back into bed with Nice Guy. We're going to take it slow, build up to the climax, as it were. If you give the readers what they want right away, they'll get bored."

"Always an eye for narrative." Jays nodded approvingly. "But you and Nice Guy have to file successful reviews for at least two months. Otherwise the deal's off."

"What do you mean 'successful'?"

"I want four hundred thousand online readers per column."

"Online readers?"

"It's a digital world, Carmen. I'm watching Web traffic now," he said. "So if we're good here, I'll set it up with Nice Guy and then send you his email. You can file your first review by the regular deadline and we'll take it from there."

"You put all of this in writing for my lawyer," she said. "Then we'll move forward." She stood up and collected her bag. She felt tall and powerful, towering above Jays in her Louboutins. And, yet, the rush of total victory eluded her. Negotiating the terms of a contractually bound fuck buddy was not what Sheryl Sandberg had in mind when she instructed women to Lean In.

Still, Carmen felt competent. She hadn't been *totally* steam-rolled—a small and perhaps pathetic kind of success, but also the only one available to her. Working with what she had, she'd harnessed that same resourcefulness from her childhood bedroom. She wasn't much different from Jays, in this way. She was taking care of herself, first and foremost, as always.

CHAPTER 9

It was Sunday night, just a few days after Jays had presented his proposition to Nice Guy: a regular sexual exchange between him and Carmen to be followed by columns penned by each, reviewing the other's performance. Lucas was elated. Jay Jacobson had given Nice Guy and his skills (*all* his skills) a strong vote of confidence. Because if the Editor didn't think Nice Guy could spar with Carmen—on the page and in bed—he wouldn't have offered up such prime real estate in the magazine.

Of course, all this happened by email. And Jays had no idea that Lucas was Nice Guy. And so long as Nice Guy remained anonymous, Jays had written, there would be no money. Clearly, the Editor was trying to incentivize Nice Guy to come forward. But that was out of the question, both for the sake of Lucas's job at *Empire* and for his reputation. (Imagine if his family and Mel discovered what he was up to?) Still, if the columns became wildly successful, Lucas reasoned, he'd have enough leverage to make Jays revisit the financial question. In the meantime, he was going to be published every two weeks in *Empire! Life* was good.

But for now, he'd have to keep his identity—and therefore his elation—under wraps. He arrived at a Chelsea restaurant to join Tyler and Sofia for dinner. The restaurant was narrow and dark, with oil-stained carafes of Chianti on display. It was owned by Sofia's cousin, who plied them with free antipasti and wine. Sofia said the place was once the headquarters of a small-time Mafioso who gifted the restaurant to Sofia's great-uncle to repay a debt.

"It's a cute story," Tyler said. "And obviously apocryphal. Seeing as you're in the facts business, Luke, could you help me prove the lady wrong?"

"Leave him alone," Sofia said. "It's Sunday night."

"Lucas is always working," Tyler said. "He's a regular Tracy Flick."

Lucas met Tyler's eyes and quickly looked away. *Noser* had already mounted a campaign to uncover Nice Guy's identity, helmed by Tyler himself.

"Tyler is threatened by anyone who appears to be working harder than him," Sofia said.

"I'm absolutely working harder," Lucas said. He'd learned that a head-on approach always worked best with Tyler. Sure enough, Tyler nodded approvingly.

"Anyway, there's no reason for the two of you to compete. You're barely in the same field. *Empire's* the equivalent of the literary beach read and *Noser's* basically a tabloid."

"I thought we were both in journalism," Tyler said.

"Is that what they're calling *Noser* these days?" Lucas said. Sofia laughed.

"You work at *Noser,* too!" Tyler protested.

"I'm a contract photographer." Sofia waved her hand dismissively. "I might as well be working for the Sears catalog. It doesn't matter. My work isn't who I *am*."

Both Lucas and Tyler stared, as though she'd just spoken heresy.

"You have to be invested in your work," Sofia said. "Of course you do. But the idea that my passions should—or even could—be contained within my daily endeavor to pay the bills is absurd. The pictures I take in exchange for a paycheck aren't exactly art—"

"Ask Sofia to show you some of her extra-curricular work," Tyler said. "It's fairly risqué."

"I'm intrigued," Lucas said, hoping for specifics.

But Sofia wasn't finished with her argument "When all of your passion goes into your work, what's left for, I don't know, *passion?* Most people I know—most women especially—aren't really living. They're singularly focused on the end game: the best job, the best man, and so on. They spend all their days slamming doors shut instead of throwing them open. I'm sorry if I sound like a bitch, but that's sad."

"If you couldn't already tell, Sofia doesn't have a lot of female friends," Tyler said.

"God forbid you ever meet my ex," Lucas said, and the others laughed. "But seriously. You're genuine. You obviously don't let anybody punish you for being yourself. I wish I could have learned that lesson about six years ago."

Sofia looked up quickly, then back at her wineglass.

A moment passed.

"So, Lucas," Tyler said, breaking the silence, "tell Sofia about that party you went to last week at Hamish McGregor's penthouse."

Sofia looked impressed. "He's the city's hottest art dealer."

"All the furniture looked like spaceships," Lucas said. "And some of the people there might have been walking sculptures. It was superweird."

"McGregor has sold a ton of work to Jays," Tyler said. "It's on display in his various interests. Honestly, Luke, your editor has a finger in pretty much everything, not to mention half of the women in—"

"Ugh, stop." Sofia scowled.

Tyler grinned. "Anyway, he's an investor in three or four hot restaurants, a couple of cushy bars, a club downtown. I've heard he's angling his way into development—high-end condos and a hotel."

"Sounds like you've been *nosing* around," Lucas said.

"Congratulations, you're the first person to think of that pun!" Tyler said.

Lucas, slightly less confident than he was a second ago, sipped his wine.

"So," Tyler continued, "why did Jays send you to Hamish McGregor's ugly penthouse?"

"I think I'm becoming a kind of protégé?"

"You mean upscale errand boy?" Tyler asked.

Lucas made a face.

"Anyway, I ran into this guy I met a while back named Nicholas Spragg. Sofia, maybe you can help me figure him out. He says he manages his family's art collection, from all the family castles. But the first time we met, his great-grandfather was a Bavarian count. The next time he was a Hungarian duke."

"That doesn't seem so crazy," Sofia said. "Maybe on one side it was a count from Germany and on the other side a duke from Hungary?"

"Sure, except that I Googled him, and it seems his father owns Kingswood Hotels."

Tyler nodded. "So they're loaded."

"Nicholas said he was born in London, but he's actually from a town called Apex, in Idaho, where Kingswood is headquartered."

"If I was from Idaho, I might say I was born in London, too," Sofia said.

"Oh," Lucas added, "and he's *phenomenally* awkward. People only put up with him if they happen to know the size of his bank account. In which case, they're obsequious as hell. Otherwise, they can't get away fast enough. But Nicholas doesn't seem aware of the difference. He's got this strange . . ."—Lucas searched for the right word and only one seemed to fit— "innocence."

At that moment, Lucas's phone rang. The number was just a string of zeros. "Look at this." He held the phone up for the others to see.

"Well, go on. Answer it!" Tyler instructed.

Lucas did. "This is Britta Packham, attaché for Mr. Nicholas Spragg," said a woman with a sharp British accent. Lucas's eyes widened at the table, causing Tyler's and Sophia's to widen even more. "Nicholas requests your company tomorrow evening for dinner and entertainment. Can you attend?"

"Yes?" Lucas said, giving his compatriots a perplexed look.

"The car will pick you up from your apartment at eight P.M. sharp. Please dress for dinner." Britta Packham, attaché for Mr. Nicholas Spragg, hung up.

"That was Nicholas Spragg's 'attache,'" Lucas said. "Is that a thing?"

"Is he a major general?" Tyler asked.

"If he is, I haven't heard that story yet. But the attaché—well, Nicholas—invited me out to dinner and 'entertainment' tomorrow night. What does that mean?"

"This sounds fascinating," Sofia said, leaning forward, her chin propped on the back of her palm.

"He's sending a car to pick me up," Lucas said, almost in protest. "How does he know where I live?"

"Well, whatever happens, I'm sure it'll make a terrific story," Tyler said. "And tomorrow's a Monday. How much trouble can you really get into?"

CHAPTER 10

The "car" turned out to be a limousine, and it sat double-parked outside Lucas's building. "We've got a reservation!" Nicholas called out testily as Lucas rushed out of his building. "Ticktock."

Lucas climbed in. The limo's seats were leather and tufted, and the car had a waxy smell, as though recently cleaned. Nicholas was sitting alone holding a tumbler of scotch. Next to him a bottle of champagne relaxed in a bucket of ice. Lucas stared at it, unsure of what it signaled.

"For the ladies," explained Spragg.

Lucas looked around the empty limo. Were these ladies hiding in the trunk?

"We're meeting them at dinner," Nicholas continued. "I offered to pick them up, but they had some prior engagement. They're socialites. You know how it is."

Lucas did not know how it is, but he gave a commiserating nod. "How do you know them?" he asked.

Spragg cleared his throat. "Oh, they're friends of a friend—a guy I knew from my junior year in Paris who recently moved to Hong Kong. He's been making all kinds of introductions from abroad. Honestly, without him I'd be sunk. Turns out," Nicholas said, and eyed Lucas, "we can't *all* land on our feet with instant invitations to the best parties."

It was a hard comment to parse. Was Nicholas accusing Lucas of social climbing? Or was he identifying a fellow climber in arms? Either way, Lucas thought it best to distance himself from . . . well, whatever Nicholas was. "Honestly," he said, "I only go anywhere special when Jays—er, you know, Jay Jacobson— can't make it."

"Yes, Jay!" Nicholas exclaimed. "I think we might see him later on. I texted him about our after-dinner plans. He's a stand-up guy."

"Oh!" Lucas said. "If you're texting with Jay, then I'd say you've got the keys to the kingdom."

"Yes, I suppose that's true," Nicholas said, his voice tinged with sadness. "Have you texted with Jay today?"

Today, he said—as if texting with Jays were a daily multivitamin. No, Lucas admitted: He didn't even have Jays' number.

This news seemed to brighten Nicholas's spirits considerably. He sat silently for a moment, bathing in some untold joy. And then the limo began to slow, stopping outside an unassuming restaurant in Tribeca. This, Spragg explained, was Luca, New York's newest adventure in molecular gastronomy. Lucas had read about the culinary trend in *Empire,* albeit a few years back. The food was part science experiment, part modern art, and Lucas had wondered why anyone would spend a fortune eating a hybrid between a Kandinsky and a Petri dish.

Lucas and Nicholas found the socialites at the bar, sipping

cocktails from what looked like test tubes. The women looked like publicists but with more expensive haircuts. The blond one waved when Nicholas walked in. "Just as Henri described you," she said—pronouncing the name "On-ree"—and gave him a kiss on each cheek. Her name was Corinne and she wore a very tight, very short black dress with long sleeves and boots molded so tightly to her calves, they looked painted on. She was beautiful in an anorexic, crystalline kind of way—not unlike the drink in her hand. The brunette was equally attractive but more like a red wineglass: buxom with cascading brown hair and a wide, welcoming smile. "I'm Katherine, but call me Katie," she said, which seemed unnecessary: Didn't Katies just call themselves Katie? Even as she shook Nicholas's hand, she was looking at Lucas, intimately, almost conspiratorially, as though the two of them already shared a host of tantalizing secrets.

The maître d' led them to a corner table. "Cheers!" Nicholas announced, and they were seated. "Here's to a capital evening."

The women kept the conversation running smoothly, peppering the men with questions. Predictably, Nicholas steered the conversation toward his ever-growing roster of questionable relatives. Lucas was far more interested in the women themselves, but he felt unsure of the etiquette. Were socialites like hipsters, who refused to call themselves what they obviously were? Was it rude to ask what they did for a living, given that the whole point of being a socialite was that you didn't actually *do* anything? And if that question was off-limits, then what could you ask?

In the end, the questions were moot, because once the food began to arrive they were all too nonplussed to concentrate on anything else. Mushroom-scented foam floated like sea scum upon a tan-colored broth, and an accompanying plate of diminutive petals and leaves seemed to have been arranged with tweezers. This was followed by a single oyster bathed in a bright yellow liquid, dotted with black caviar and surrounded by three tea-green crackers dolloped with a pungent-smelling black cream. And then the challenges began: a round of sweetbreads, then foie gras, and then the marrow of some animal's neck. Nicholas and the socialites dug eagerly into each, but these were not foods Lucas wanted in his mouth, let alone his stomach. As each course was swept away by the white-gloved waitstaff, Lucas hovered in horrified anticipation of the forthcoming plate of hearts or livers or other heinous body parts. Finally, what arrived was a cloud of kale-flavored cotton candy atop a slice of rare tuna. Relief.

A number of glasses of wine into the meal—there was a new one for nearly every course—Lucas found himself speaking exclusively with Katie. He wasn't quite sure when or how this split had happened, but he felt grateful to be paired with her instead of Corinne, whom he'd come to think of as the crystal queen. Katie was full of questions, almost reporter-like in her directness. They discussed their favorite books and magazines. She loved the *New Yorker* and made a point of reading every issue in full—a feat, Lucas suddenly realized, that only socialites would have the time to accomplish. She wanted to know from start to finish how an article was fact-checked and appeared to see his position as not simply important but heroic. "The truth," she said, pointing to a spate of recent media scandals and embarrassments, "lies in your hands."

Out of anyone else's mouth, Lucas would have found this statement overblown. But Katie looked at him earnestly when she said it, leaning in flirtatiously, her long hair brushing his shoulder. She was either genuinely impressed with him or very good at flattering men. He decided he didn't care which was the truth. He was also sliding quickly from tipsy toward drunk.

"You and Corinne don't seem at all alike," he whispered to her.

"You two don't seem so much alike either," Katie said, nodding toward Nicholas.

"I can't really afford dinners like this," he admitted. "I'm just here—well, I'm here because he invited me."

Katie smiled. "Well, I'm here because Corinne invited me, so I guess that makes us a pair." She reached down and squeezed his hand. The touch point of her fingers sent a shiver up Lucas's arm.

Dinner concluded after 11:00 P.M. Back in the limo, now fulfilling their destiny, the women opened the champagne. Nicholas poured a glass of scotch and handed it to Lucas. "I'm all right," he said, waving the glass away. "I've got to be up at six thirty if I want to get a run in before work."

"Don't be ridiculous," Nicholas said. "The night is young."

Of course, Lucas thought, he was the only one of them who actually had work in the morning. "If I come in hungover, Jay will have my head."

"Jay will live," Nicholas said, forcing the drink into Lucas's hand. "And so will we!" He knocked twice on the partition and the limo took off, speeding up the West Side Highway. Nicholas cozied up to Corinne and, in seconds, the two of them were kissing. It was a strange and shocking moment—not only the proximity of these two people unabashedly making out but also the sight of this model-esque woman pressing her red lips against Nicholas's homely mouth, his acne scars, his moles. Lucas looked at Katie, who smiled at him. She leaned over and kissed his neck, then his cheek, then his mouth. Lucas shut his eyes, actively trying to block out the adjacent lip smacking. This proved easy enough when Katie slid onto his lap and pushed him back against the seat.

The car stopped at Eleventh Avenue and 53rd outside a

high-rise apartment building. They filed past a formidable-looking bouncer into the lobby. The walls were inset with bubbling fish tanks, full of brightly colored schools. The floor was glass, and an entire ocean seemed to flow beneath their feet. When a massive stingray slid by, Lucas flinched. The women smiled serenely. Maybe that's what made you a successful socialite: the ability to treat the most ostentatious things as ordinary.

Presently, a kimono-clad woman appeared and bowed deeply before them. "Welcome, Mr. Spragg," she said, and extended her hand toward an open elevator. "Have a pleasant evening."

"This is Manhattan's first love hotel," Nicholas explained as the elevator flew them toward the sky. "A place where couples are afforded a few hours of privacy and where businessmen can take a midafternoon nap. Don't look so scandalized, Lucas!" Nicholas slapped him on the back. "They're common in Japan. I'm surprised that *Empire* hasn't already written about this place, but maybe you should keep it to yourself. We wouldn't want it getting too popular."

The "we" in this sentence seemed to refer to Corinne and Katie, with whom Nicholas exchanged a sly smile. For just a moment, Lucas felt that something about all of this—the dinner, the women, the very mutual understanding among the group—was eluding him. But the feeling quickly passed. Katie was stroking the back of his hand with her thumb. He looked at her and she tilted her head toward his shoulder, so he put his arm around her and drew her in close.

Stepping out of the elevator, they entered a passageway lined by paper screens and smelling strongly of tatami mats; the love hotel was taking its Japanese theme seriously. Another kimonoed woman instructed them to remove their shoes and then led them to a small dimly lit room where the air pulsated with entrancing Asian-infused electronica. Two hookahs smoldered beside a low table and plush cushions.

"I didn't think those were Japanese," Lucas mumbled, mostly to himself. He was feeling sleepy, lulled by the music and dim lighting.

"I asked for them specially," Nicholas replied. He looked a little hurt. "You don't like them?"

"Oh yes, they're very nice," Lucas said. But he was distracted by Katie's nails trailing up and down his back.

For the next hour, they cuddled in their respective pairs, chatting and drinking and blowing smoke rings. When Lucas glanced at his watch, he saw that it was after 1:00 A.M. But he didn't want to go home anymore. He wanted to stay here, in this strange, smoky place, with this beautiful woman who was massaging his neck and who genuinely seemed to like him— unlike a certain sex columnist. And why not enjoy Nicholas's generosity? This was an experience the likes of which he never could have imagined back in Charlotte, let alone yesterday. It was just as Sofia had said: Doors were meant to be opened. Now that he was here in New York City, Lucas intended to walk through as many as possible. He need only let the experience lead him.

And now the experience was leading him toward the joint that Nicholas had lifted from an ebony box sitting in the center of the table. And it was leading him toward those lines of white powder, which Nicholas had tapped out and cut along the tabletop. Lucas had never done cocaine before. It seemed dangerous. But after the other three snorted through a rolled hundred, Lucas knew that he would do it, too, because why not try everything at least once? Because he wanted keys to the next room and the next. The night drifted on. There was dancing, and kissing, and drinking, and smoking, and more kissing. At one point, Lucas found himself between both women, his ass pressed against Corinne's dress, his groin thrust toward Katie. The women were kissing him, swaying with him. Hands were untucking his shirt, though he couldn't tell whose hands. He felt like he was melting to the floor, dripping through the women's hands and lips like water. And then Nicholas appeared, looking angry and hissing something into Corinne's ear. He took her hand, and they left the room. Lucas started to ask Katie what that was about, but Katie only smiled as she guided Lucas to the floor and began to trail her lips down his shirt toward his pants. At that point, all questions flew out of his head.

Lucas woke, naked, on a mattress spread on the floor. He was massively hungover, his skull throbbing rhythmically, as though to the tick of a second hand. He was in one of the rice paper rooms—a different one from before—and alone. His clothes were folded neatly on the floor beside the mattress. There was no sign of Katie. No condom wrapper, no errant earring. Not even a lingering whiff of perfume. How had he ended up in here? Had he spent the night alone? It seemed doubtful seeing as he was butt naked. He'd never once woken up in the morning with so many blank hours behind him. The last thing he remembered: the uncomfortable sensation of sucking more drugs up his nose.

Lucas managed to get dressed, but then he couldn't find the door. He pushed at one rice-paper panel, then another, but the screens didn't budge. "Hello?" he called out. "I want to leave. Hello?" How deep within the love hotel could he be? He considered leaving by force: Surely he could punch his way through these paper walls? But then one of the panels slid back and a kimonoed woman appeared. She looked a little frightened at the sight of Lucas, so frantic and disheveled. He stormed past her and ran to the elevator. In the lobby, the security guard did not look up as Lucas hurried over the stingrays and out onto the street. When he reached the office, Franklin was just settling in. "It's ten-oh-one," he said, and wagged his finger. "You're late."

CHAPTER 11

Six days later, Lucas skulked through the West Village, his eyes darting to and fro like the caricature of a Cold War spy. He was going to meet Carmen for their first professional rendezvous. In the surrounding apartments, people washed down their takeout pad thai with cheap beer. They were staving off the despondency of a Sunday evening, while Lucas was meeting a beautiful woman for a risqué magazine column. He couldn't have asked for more. Well, he could have asked Carmen to be less of a jerk. She'd taken days to confirm their first official meeting. Was she playing hard to get? Or was she just a sore loser? Lucas—aka Nice Guy—had tapped into a well of popular sympathy and she just couldn't handle it. No matter. Lucas was going to be magnanimous. He'd be the bigger man. And before he knew it, he'd be enveloped in her beautiful cloud bed.

"Hi," Carmen said, upon opening the door. She didn't bother to invite him in but retreated immediately to the couch. Lucas stepped into the apartment and closed the door behind him. He'd showered, shaved, and dabbed on cologne, whereas Carmen looked like she'd just woken up from a nap. She still managed to look sexy in a loose-fitting T-shirt and messy pony-tail. But the message was clear: She didn't give a crap.

They sat across from each other in the living room. Lucas tried to keep his eyes off Carmen's shoulder, exposed *Flashdance*-style by her scooped shirt. He considered apologizing, but as several hundred readers had pointed out in their comments, he had nothing to be sorry for. And yet he wanted to start this . . . project? experiment? liaison? Whatever it was, he wanted to start it on the right foot. "So, listen," he began. But Carmen spoke over him.

"Here's the thing," she said.

Was she about to apologize? Maybe this was already going better than expected. Lucas began ticking off all the things he'd need to do during their sex tonight. Be more assertive. More confident. More—oh, crap, he'd stopped actually listening to her.

". . . and that's why I'm not going to sleep with you," she concluded.

"Wait, what?" So much for Carmen's concession speech.

"We're going to write the columns, Lucas. But we're not basing them on sex. At least not any sex that we're having with each other. I'll make out with you. We can fool around a little bit to get some color. But you and I will not be having inter-course."

"So then why did you agree to—"

She interrupted. "You know, it's not quite fair, is it? Keeping your identity secret."

"I just . . . can't." His mind flashed uncomfortably to the look on his grandmother's face at opening a copy of *Empire* and reading about his sexual exploits and humiliations. "I'm not a grad student by the way." He gave Carmen a searing look. "I actually work at *Empire*."

"Oh, come on."

He nodded. "I've been a fact-checker there since July."

"That fucker," she said to herself. Then to him: "OK, so besides Jays, who at the magazine knows about this?"

"Nobody knows. Jays doesn't know."

Carmen looked startled, then impressed. He could sense that she was making some kind of mental recalculation. "Well, aren't you full of surprises," she said.

Lucas didn't respond. He just watched her. For a good thirty seconds, they only looked at each other in silence. "And," he finally said to break the silence, "I'd appreciate if you didn't tell Jays."

Carmen didn't acknowledge the comment. "We might as well get this show on the road," she said, then stood up and walked to him, skirting the coffee table. She knelt in front of him and fixed her dark eyes on his own. For the first time, Lucas understood what people meant when they talked about drinking in a person's gaze. He imagined kissing Carmen's eyes. He thought about suctioning his lips against her eyelids and lightly pulling. How bizarre was that? He had never been attracted to anybody's eyelids before.

Then Carmen was kissing him deeply. His body flooded with warmth. His fingers tingled. He kissed her back, leaning into her, circumnavigating the tip of her tongue with his own. She murmured, so he ran his tongue around hers again.

Abruptly, she pulled away. She reached for a notebook on

the coffee table, flipped it open, and began writing. Lucas watched, dumbfounded.

"What are you doing?"

"Taking notes, Lucas," she said. "Shouldn't you be doing the same?"

"Right now? In the middle of—"

"What did you think this was going to be?" Carmen asked, impatient.

"I th-thought . . . ," he stammered. "You don't have to be so transactional."

"This is work, Lucas. We are colleagues and this project is about mechanics. Now, do you need a piece of paper and a pen?"

"I can type on my phone."

"Fine. Let's take a few minutes to jot down our initial impressions and then we can give it another try." She scooted away from him on the couch so that he couldn't see what she was writing. Every so often, she reread her work and chuckled to herself. Clutching his iPhone, Lucas closed his eyes and searched for the warm, tingling sensation of a few minutes ago. But there was nothing. Only the inert object in his hand.

Nice Guy and Carmen Kelly: The Reunion

Valued Readers,

Welcome to "Screw the Critics," the first-of-its-kind experiment. We're answering a question none of us has the stomach to investigate ourselves: Can unvarnished, honest feedback make someone a better lover? New York was atwitter these last few weeks as our sex columnist, Carmen Kelly, excoriated a young man after a one-night stand—and then the man, who we're calling Nice Guy, shot back in the same pages. But rather than nurse their wounds alone, they're reuniting in the sheets—this issue and every issue—to review each other in *Empire,* take each other's words to heart, and become intimate once again. What will happen? You'll only find out here.

Yours,
Jay Jacobson, Editor, *Empire*

Nice Guy,

When the Texan arrived at my place, as he did every week for quite some time, I took off my shirt before he'd taken off his shoes. Whenever I invited the Chef over, he let himself through the front door; I'd lie naked in bed and wait. These were men who deserved the welcoming, with their charm and skill and confidence. Then you waltzed into my apartment last Sunday, cologne slicked to your neck, and expected the same treatment. You expected sex. Fuck-buddy status isn't some raffle you win, Nice Guy. It's a job you earn—a job with expectations, a results-oriented task—and you haven't earned it yet. Yet here we are, all the rules mashed into nonsense: You wrote into a magazine and, much too much like a raffle, literally did win a job. And that job is to be my fuck buddy.

Lucky you, I suppose. But not lucky me.

If this is our burden, then my role is clear: I must teach you how to be like the Texan, like the Chef, or at least the closest to those men that you can muster—if not for your sake, then at least for my own sanity. But we will not get there quickly. The thing they had, and the thing you lack, is instinctiveness: They knew how to touch another body, how to move with it, how to lead it. When you touch me, you're like a teenager holding a baby for the first time—all searching for guidance, as if the baby is going to tell you how it wants to be held. The baby will not tell you. But I will, here, in these pages. When we're in person, you'll just have to figure it out.

And that's why we started on Sunday like we were at eighth-grade prom: We made out for a little, and, aware as I was of your erection, I wasn't going to help you with it.

You're a so-so kisser. A little reactionary, always one beat behind, waiting to see what I'll do first. Kissing is like a jazz tune: There's a riff that the band repeats—be-bap-be-bap—and then the musicians solo, return to the riff, solo again, and so on. The riff is the simple kiss, and you're good there. Your lips are soft, and you move them well. The solo could use some work, though. You don't go on very long; I think you get lost in it, unsure how fast to move your tongue and how long to open your mouth, and so you return to the riff, until soon enough the song is mostly just be-bap-be-bap on repeat. Work on that. If you can get there, I might let you touch my breasts.

Carmen,

Do you know what teenage boys do when they're home alone? Two things, mostly. One, they masturbate. And two, they try figuring out why the girl they're infatuated with is so intimidating. Why is she so confident? Why is she making things so difficult? Then the teenage boy grows a few years older, and discovers that the girl wasn't actually any different from him. No girl was. Everyone at that age was nervous and fumbling! Nobody knew what the hell they were doing. It's a life-changing revelation.

But you, Carmen. You are every teenage boy's nightmare come true, because you are highly skilled at playing the intimidator. You are trying to make me question myself—maybe even my self-worth. But I'm not falling for your games. For starters, I'm going to tell readers exactly what happened on Sunday.

I showed up at your apartment expecting to start this grand experiment of ours, but from the get-go you decided you weren't going to play fair. You'd decided that we wouldn't be having sex that day—as if, you know, we hadn't already done it once before. We'd just be kissing, you said. It was like you were trying to trick me or throw me off guard. But fine. We kiss. And then you break away and write down some notes, and snicker to yourself. Then we repeat the whole process four times. What the hell, Carmen? What were you trying to prove anyway?

So, what can I report to our readers? Uh, I can confirm that you have a nice couch. It's a comfortable place to sit while being humiliated. Maybe next time, I can sit there while you read old sexts of mine, on speaker, to my mother. And the kissing? I wish I could insult you, but you're good. You kissed me the way someone kisses when they want to be remembered. I kissed you back with equal passion all four times. Though I doubt you're woman enough to admit it. But I know what I know, Carmen. You're not intimidating me and you're not playing me. Game on.

CHAPTER 12

Carmen had convinced Jays that the columns should move slowly. This was a striptease, not porno, and the game was to keep readers wanting more. The slow build would raise tensions. The cliff-hangers would get people talking. She had not, however, told Jays that she never planned to sleep with Lucas again—that doing so would cross a line she had drawn for herself.

For his part, Lucas wasn't sure he saw the difference between having sex and doing many of the other things that (he assumed) were still on the table. He often found foreplay more intimate than sex; there was more touching, more exploring, more mouth. But he wasn't going to give Carmen a reason to declare anything else off-limits. No sex for a while? Fine. This was his chance to master everything else—what Mel was afraid of, or uncomfortable with, or that, truth be told, he and she had skipped once sex became routine. Once, a few years ago, Lucas felt a sudden desire to kiss Mel's butt cheek, and so he flipped her over and did it. And then he moved a little closer to her crack. And closer. And it felt naughty and exciting, even though he wasn't quite sure what to do when he landed in between—and then Mel turned to him, concerned, and said, "What if I fart?" And that was that.

Carmen, for all her faults, would not worry about things like farting. Carmen was a pro. She could probably hold a fart for hours.

But this also meant that Carmen would never take pity on him. So if he was going to stick his nose into some part of her body, he better damn well know what to do when it got there. It wasn't easy to dish out criticism when he was so outmatched. Carmen was the better lover. She was also a precisely honed argumentarian. He'd had a burst of momentum—and, let's face it, a lot of luck—with his initial column. But there he'd criticized the situation as a whole, not the play-by-play. And so, on the subject of kissing, she trounced him with turns of phrase and baited him into saying things that hadn't seemed sexist at the time. (He now realized that "saying things that hadn't seemed sexist at the time" is its own genre of "saying things that are sexist.") It was embarrassing.

"Maybe we threw this kid in too fast," Jays told Housman, who then reported this to Lucas. "If he can't win some of the rounds, we might have to call the match."

Tyler had his own take, of course. After "Screw the Critics" debuted, he posted on *Noser,* writing under his pen name J. P. Maddox, to declare open war. "The first time Carmen Kelly scorched Nice Guy in the pages of *Empire,* I made the poor sap an offer: 'Don't allow Carmen to feast on your tender Nice Guy flesh,' I said. 'Rebut! Refute! I will give you a platform to do so, and help restore your good (albeit anonymous) name!' But instead, as we learned with a jolt this morning, Nice Guy took my idea straight to the Evil Empire. So now, I am declaring *Noser* the resistance." Maddox then debuted a column called "Screw Off!," a forum for readers to insult Carmen and Nice Guy.

Within an hour, "Screw Off!" had 142 comments. "Once after a hookup," the first read, "this guy literally farted as he walked out my door, and I thought that was the worst. But no. Nice Guy's column is the worst. Miss you, fart guy."

Now it was the evening, and Tyler was sitting on the couch in his and Lucas's living room still reading reader responses. "Look at this!" Tyler exclaimed. "Now we've got a commenter called Rogue Empire, who claims to be an *Empire* employee. We've got a mole!"

Lucas rolled his eyes.

"Here's what they say," Tyler continued. "'Rampant speculation among the staff about Nice Guy's identity. Many believe it's click-bait fiction. What won't Jay Jacobson do for page views?'"

"I'm sure Jays wouldn't make this up," Lucas said, trying to sound unsure.

Tyler wrinkled his nose. "Either way, I wish I could write these Nice Guy columns."

"But that would defeat the whole purpose," Lucas said. "The reason it's entertaining is because people know it's real."

"No, it's entertaining because people like to read about sex," Tyler said. "But Nice Guy's problem is that he's a slow driver in the left lane. The guy has to keep up or move over. Readers may love a very public airing of sexual grievances, but even more than that, they want a fight. And right now it's a beatdown."

"So if you were advising Nice Guy, what would you tell him?" Lucas asked.

"OK, I see what's happening. You're going to pass off all my good advice as your own in order to get promoted at work. Advising the competition is professional treason."

Competition? Lucas didn't think so. *Empire* made news. All

Noser did was talk. But Lucas shook it off: Tyler was joking. And anyway, Tyler knew which way this relationship flowed. "You're going to tell me," Lucas said, "because you're hoping I'll learn who Nice Guy is. And then maybe I'll tell you."

"Nah, you're too trustworthy. But roommate to roommate: Didn't Carmen write an article a while back about her favorite literary sex scenes? I'd tell Nice Guy to do a little reporting. Use her own desires against her."

Lucas found Carmen's old column, only to discover that readers had largely ignored it. There were only a handful of comments, a rare act of collective disinterest in Carmen's writing. The reason, it seemed, was the column's sincerity. It was heartfelt: a rare clear peek into Carmen's mind, which Lucas could now use to his advantage. He jotted down the titles she'd recommended—*A Sport and a Pastime,* set in France in the 1960s; *The Lover,* set in French colonial Vietnam; and a couple of works by Anaïs Nin, who, wouldn't you know it, was French. Then he went to the library and checked them out. He read them diligently but was disappointed by how languid and abstract they were. He supposed he'd been expecting something more like *Fifty Shades of Grey*—something obvious, with a flashing neon arrow pointing toward Carmen's clitoris. A manual, maybe, like the *Kama Sutra.* But all he had here was: France. Was she turned on by croissants?

There was one volume missing, though. *Romance of the Bones* wasn't at the New York Public Library. After many hours calling booksellers, he finally tracked down a copy at a rare bookshop deep in the canyons of Midtown. On the first crisp Saturday of fall, he ventured out in search of it.

He found the shop in a run-down building huddled in the Garment District and took the creaking elevator to the second floor. The place was musty and packed with books. Lucas dinged the bell beside the register, but no clerk materialized, so he wandered around the store, pausing before a shelf of nineteenth-century social manuals. He pulled one out—*The Gentleman's Guide to American Manners*—and was just flipping it open when, from the corner of his eye, he noticed a familiar form slipping among the shelves. For a moment, he just stood there, blinking, like she was a spectre, a gathering of dust motes and light.

Lucas's colleagues had warned him that the longer he lived in New York, the more it would seem to collapse around him, like a trash compactor; everyone he knew would be thrust at him. You had to be careful sharing gossip while out to dinner, they said, because inevitably you'd turn around to find the subject in question eating pork cheek not three feet away. (This exact thing had once happened to Franklin, precipitating not one but two breakups.)

Lucas hadn't believed his colleagues. In a metropolis as vast and complex as New York, what were the chances that two people who knew each other would ever wind up in the same place at the same time? But here was Sofia, very much flesh and blood, her boots creaking over the uneven floors.

"Hi," Lucas said.

Sofia turned around. "Well, hi," she said with surprise. "I thought nobody knew about this place."

Lucas nodded sheepishly, as though he'd stumbled into her private boudoir. In response, Sofia seized the book from him and flipped it open. "'Published 1893,'" she read. "You know this advice is dated?"

"I just picked it up," he said. "It seemed fun." *Better she catch me with this,* he thought, *than a novel called* Romance of the Bones.

Sofia flipped the pages. "Ah, this should be enlightening.

'In the Presence of a Lady,'" she read, and cleared her throat. "'When entering a crowded streetcar, a lady should leave the door open. It is quite permissible for her to appropriate the seat of the man who gets up to close it.'" She looked up at Lucas. "I like that rule. It's wily."

"Seems a tad obnoxious to me," Lucas said.

Sofia rolled her eyes. "Let's see what other gems we've got." She flipped further. "Now this is interesting," she said. "'If you meet a lady of your acquaintance in the street, it is her part to notice you first, unless, indeed, you are very intimate.'" Sofia nodded, looking gravely at Lucas.

He was supposed to say something clever here. "Indeed," he managed.

"So what this means," she said, "is that either you and I are very intimate or you are very rude."

"So I was just supposed to ignore you? Or stand here looking at you until you noticed me? That doesn't seem right."

"So we're not very intimate then?"

Lucas's face reddened. She was flirting! And yet the logistics of simultaneous intimacy with two women seemed overwhelming, especially since he had to keep one of them a secret. *The Gentleman's Guide to American Manners* would call his situation problematic, to say the least.

"You haven't answered the question, Luke!" Sofia smiled invitingly. "But before you do, I should explain *why* this wise rule of intimacy was established." She read: "'The reason is, if you bow to a lady first, she may choose to acknowledge you, and there is no remedy; but if she bows to you—you as a gentleman cannot cut her.'" Sofia considered this for a moment, still looking at the book. "That doesn't work out very well for the woman."

"Why not?" Lucas asked.

"Well, by this reasoning, a lady's got to put all her cards on the table. She's got to say up front, 'I like you.' And then our *gentleman"*—Sofia spoke this word with obvious disdain—"so as not to be a total asshole, has to return the gesture. Even if he's not interested. So the lady could easily walk away believing that he's interested in her when, in fact, the opposite is true."

"Except in this scenario, the woman would *know* the customs of the time. She'd know better than to assume anything. I'd say she's got the upper hand. If you'd ignored me, I'd have no remedy!"

"But I didn't ignore you." She stepped toward him until their bodies were almost touching.

In that moment, all of Lucas's concern about Carmen—not to mention the fact that he had not yet laid hands on the book he'd come here to collect—flew straight out of his mind.

CHAPTER 13

The afternoon, past its apex, was now tumbling toward dusk. They'd walked for a long time in Central Park and had drinks at a small café on Madison Avenue. Then, after an interminably long subway ride to Brooklyn, entered Sofia's spacious one-bedroom overlooking the Brooklyn Bridge. Lucas sipped a gin and tonic in silence, admiring the view, and when he glanced back Sofia was standing in the bedroom doorway, leaning against the frame. Silently, he stood up and walked toward her. In a rush, their shirts had come off and they tumbled onto the bed. It was a sleek, utilitarian object—vaguely Japanese—and low-set. Even as their limbs tangled, Lucas's thoughts turned to Carmen's cloud bed, a place into which a person could sink and cocoon. Sofia's bed was hard, the sheets pulled taut, an intentional buffer against comfort.

But forget Carmen and her apartment! He reached for the clasp of Sofia's bra and she let him remove it. But when he slid his hands toward her waist, she pulled them back up. Lucas was a little perplexed; Sofia did not seem like the kind of person to take things slow. Soon she rolled away and stretched out on the bed.

"Time for a break," she said. Lucas looked at her quizzically, but her smile was so warm that he immediately felt at ease. Maybe he was getting her *too* excited. Maybe that's why she wanted to slow down.

"This is an amazing apartment," he said, turning his head toward the bedroom window, nearly the length and width of the wall. The bridge looked especially emblematic, with its American flag silhouetted against the sky. Like a postcard. Beyond it stretched the East River and the jigsaw puzzle of Lower Manhattan.

Sofia yawned. "I've been here for almost ten years. It's a good thing I bought it when I did."

"You own this? Jesus. I can barely afford the cubbyhole that Tyler and I are renting. He calls it the body fridge. Though we only have one air-conditioning unit, so it's actually just the opposite."

Sofia pointed to vents near the ceiling. "Central air," she said apologetically.

"Wow," Lucas breathed. "What I wouldn't give . . ."

"Well, it's my parents' money. It's got to be good for something."

"My mother would have a heart attack if she heard you talk about money—or your *parents*—that way."

Sofia shrugged. "Well, they're dead."

"Oh God, Sofia." Lucas sat up quickly. "I'm so sorry I said that."

She shook her head dismissively. "You didn't know. And since you're wondering, it was a small-jet crash when I was three."

"I don't know what to say."

"Don't say anything then." Sofia sat up. As she did so, the sheet covering her breasts slipped away. He was turned on but also discomfited by his arousal—given the conversation.

"Stop looking at me like that, Lucas. I'm not a charity case." She flicked his arm.

"How would you like me to look? You're naked, and we're talking about your parents' plane crash."

"Well, definitely not like I'm some pauper-orphan. Because clearly"—she motioned to the bedroom—"I'm not a pauper."

"Sorry," Lucas said. "From now on I'll only look at you like you're an orphan."

Sofia stared at him, her mouth open. Then she grabbed a pillow and smacked him. "You just made a joke about my dead parents!" She smacked him again, this time laughing.

Lucas shielded his face, unable to suppress his grin. "I know. That's fucked up, right? But I knew you'd find it funny."

"Oh, you *get* me." She chuckled. "How cute."

Now it was Lucas's turn to take up arms. He threw the pillow at her chest and then they were playfully batting each other. Soon they were stripping off the rest of their clothes and tumbling together, naked, exposed to the Manhattan skyline.

Later, they lay side by side, watching the city wink at them through the darkness.

"That was fun," Lucas said. He turned on his side and ran his finger down Sofia's long neck and across the edge of her shoulder. Sex with her had been very different from sex with Carmen. Now that he had a fresh point of comparison, he understood that what he'd taken for the columnist's experience was actually an obsession with control. She'd directed the action, precisely so that it suited her notions of what should happen—when and how. Of course she hadn't liked his eagerness and passion. That would have required her to relax. But she was an uptight, Type A lover.

Lucas sat up abruptly and started fumbling in his pant pocket for his phone. That was a good observation, the "Type A lover" thing. Just the kind of theme that should go into his column.

"What's going on?" Sofia asked.

"Work thing," he mumbled, his thumbs flashing.

"Uh-huh." Sofa sat up and folded her legs beneath her. She observed him coolly, and when he didn't look up she said, "I'm fairly certain that *The Gentleman's Guide to American Manners* would frown upon a young man, sitting naked beside one lover, taking notes about another one."

Lucas's thumbs froze. Maybe he could pretend she hadn't said anything.

"What was that thing you told me at my cousin's restaurant? 'Always be genuine. Don't let anyone punish you for being yourself.'" Lucas glanced up to find Sofia observing him with wry amusement. "You've got to be more careful, my friend." She tsked her finger. "It's risky, quoting from your own column in casual conversation. You're lucky Tyler didn't notice. I'm actually pretty surprised he didn't."

Lucas tried to put the pieces together. *Be genuine. Don't let anyone punish you for being yourself.* Did that sound like him? Did he say that? *Oh. Oh yes.* He'd written almost those exact words in his initial rebuttal as Mr. Nice Guy, and then, like a cocksure dumbass in love with his own words, he blurted it out and—

Should he play dumb? Call it a coincidence? Say he'd read the column so many times that it got stuck in his head? No way she'd believe that. Because here she was, watching him squirm, grinning slightly and, of course, naked. It was all too much. She'd caught *Noser*'s big scoop. She was going to out him.

"I am so screwed." Lucas pushed his fingers into his eyes. He felt like throwing up—a careening, stomach-twisting sensation of helplessness that was all too familiar. It dredged up memories of Mel, asking again and again why, after four years, then five, he wasn't 100 percent certain about their future together. There'd been so many of these unbearable nights, with him saying he loved her and her, crying, telling him that "love" wasn't the same as "in love." It had gotten to the point that the very sound of a woman blowing her nose triggered a Pavlovian response in Lucas: the desire to run. To get as far as he could from their relationship and, most of all, from his own emotional impotence.

"Sofia, please don't tell anyone. If Jays realizes who I am . . . my job, my career . . ." He was starting to feel short of breath. How could he have been so careless?

"OK," she said, like it was nothing.

"No, Sofia, I mean it."

"So do I, Lucas. Why would I want to hurt you?"

Lucas nodded, doubtful. "So you're not mad?"

"Why would I be mad?"

"Because I lied to you."

Sofia lay back, her legs folded Indian-style. Lucas's eyes traveled from her pubic bone up her stomach and across her breasts, which now lay flat against her chest. He could see the dark points of her nipples, her long, graceful neck. She arched her back, stretching. As he watched her, his mouth hung open just a little. Good God, even now, in the depths of panic, he wanted to press himself on top of her.

She finished her stretch and sat up, her hair a mess around

her face. "I'm not your girlfriend." She smiled. "You don't owe me anything."

"Mel would have gone apeshit."

"Your ex?"

He nodded.

"Well, I am most certainly not her. But I am curious. Were you writing about me? Can I see?"

The notes he'd made described everything that was wrong with Carmen's style of lovemaking in contrast to all that was right about Sofia's. He handed her the phone. "What do you think?" he asked after a minute. It occurred to him that almost immediately his fears of career ruination had morphed into a desire for professional validation.

"It's sweet of you to praise me like that."

"OK. . . ." He waited for her to say more. Surely she was taken with the deftness of his argument—about how Carmen couldn't derive pleasure without dictating his every move, whereas Sofia had no physical blueprint. She'd organically allowed their bodies to fall into sync, so much so that they'd even come together.

"Are you hungry?" she asked. "I can order something."

"Wait—that's all you have to say?"

She gave him a devastating look, like he was a puppy, happy and oblivious, trotting across a dangerous intersection.

"What, Sofia? Spit it out."

"I like you a lot, Luke. I think you're handsome and funny. You have a lovely body."

"But—"

"There was nothing organic about our sex just now."

"I don't understand. You were faking it?"

"The orgasm? No, that was real."

"OK, so what's the problem?"

"Well, the thing is, I gave myself the orgasm."

Lucas slid back from her on the bed, as though the distance of a few inches would lessen the coming blow.

"Look," she said, "men generally don't know what they're doing. It's not their fault—it's hard to know a woman's body, especially the first time. But if I wasn't able to make sex pleasurable on my own, I'd be having a lot of disappointing sex."

"So you're saying that I'm bad."

"Not bad exactly, but . . . after we started making out, I actually wasn't sure that I wanted to sleep with you. Because the kissing was—it was like we were dancing and you kept stepping on my toes." She gave him a look: *I'm sorry, but it's true.*

"And?" he said.

"But we were having so much fun, so I thought, 'Why not?' Only it was just kind of . . . so-so. I'm sorry, Luke. I'm no fan of Carmen's, but she wasn't entirely wrong."

Lucas stood up. "Excuse me," he said coldly, and went into the bathroom. He sat down on the toilet and buried his head in his hands. Then he got up and stood in front of the mirror. Could he really be that bad? Could anyone actually be *that bad at sex?* All his life, he'd figured sex was like pizza: At its worst, it's still pretty good. At least, Mel had never complained about his performance. If anything, *he'd* been the disappointed one. She treated oral sex like a necessary, mildly unpleasant task, like washing the dishes or vacuuming. And she always wanted to have sex the same way, lying on her stomach. The lack of variation frustrated him. Not that he'd ever said anything about it. He'd worried about offending or angering her. And anyway, hey, it was sex. At least he was having it.

Sofia knocked on the door. "I'm sorry. I thought you'd want the truth."

Mel never complained to Lucas about sex, so for six years he'd taken her silence as a sign of satisfaction. It never occurred to him that her silence might be the same as his own. Which meant that he and Mel had likely been underwhelming and disappointing each other for years. At best they were prudish and at worst cowards. Prudish cowards. Maybe if they'd been more honest with each other, things would have ended differently, or not at all. Lucas looked out the bathroom window at the flickering city. How many couples were breaking up right now? How many people were untangling their limbs and turning away from each other, frustrated? How much heartache could be avoided if people would only say what they were really thinking?

Lucas opened the bathroom door. Sofia had wrapped herself in a silky, Asiany kind of robe. "I had no business saying those—" she started to apologize. But Lucas cut her off.

"Will you help me?"

She looked at him quizzically.

"The other day, Tyler said this thing to me—about how Nice Guy could use help. He was joking, but . . ."

A slow smile spread across Sofia's face. "You want me to be your sex coach?"

"I mean, that's kind of an embarrassing way to put it." He nodded at the bed. "It's a weird thing to ask. I'll totally understand if you—"

"I love this idea!" she exclaimed, and threw her arms around his neck. "This is going to be so much fun!"

"You're sure?"

With her arms still draped over him, she pulled away slightly. "I can help you," she said. "I totally can." And then more to herself, "Carmen won't know what hit her. Oh, this is going to be so good." She kissed him deeply, and the warmth of her mouth seemed to suffuse the whole of his face. She detached her mouth, turned from him, and began to pace, as though searching for the solution to a complicated problem. "We could say we're 'dating.' I'd be the perfect cover; people would never suspect you."

Lucas hadn't expected Sofia to be so accommodating, and for a moment he wondered if there wasn't something a little odd about her enthusiasm. But she'd said that she was passionate about sex. And she clearly liked him. Maybe she wanted an excuse to spend time with him. And was that so incredible? Why shouldn't a witty, beautiful, cultured woman want to be with him—or even just "with" him?

"OK, coach," he said. "When do we start?"

CHAPTER 14

A week later, Lucas and Carmen had their second on-the-record meeting. When Lucas arrived at the budget hotel that Jays had booked for them, Carmen was already there, sitting upright on the bed, notebook in hand. "Your column was very immature," she said. "Now lie down."

There was a suspicious stain on the comforter, but Lucas obeyed. And just like last time, Carmen set the rules, which were so rigid that Lucas wondered if she'd been charting their sexual acts on a spreadsheet. Worse, every few minutes Carmen would stop abruptly to write something in her notebook, leaving Lucas wet lipped, heart pounding, his body maddeningly abuzz.

Still, he felt more confident. He'd seen Sofia three times that week, for a grand total of seven "training sessions." One night, they had sex at 8:30 P.M., then again at midnight, an unexpected blow job at 4:00 A.M. followed by sex again before work.

He didn't know his body was physically capable of all that stimulation. Even with Mel, he tended to withhold a little bit of himself during sex, because to focus on pleasure was to risk triggering an early orgasm. But now his body could barely recover. He didn't have to worry about being overwhelmed with pleasure; it was nearly impossible, like being able to drink without fear of getting drunk. And this gave him a new kind of confidence that transcended Sofia's bed. He'd had enough of Carmen calling all the shots.

"You can't keep stopping," he said, finally. "It doesn't feel natural."

Carmen laughed. "Nothing about this situation is natural."

"I get that. But if we're going to take this column on, shouldn't we at least try to make the, uh, the *activities* feel as authentic as possible? I've been thinking a lot about it and I guess I've come to the conclusion that, well, maybe we could . . ." His newfound confidence was slipping.

"Spit it out, Lucas."

Lucas swallowed. "Don't you want people to take something away from what we write? You know, for their own relationships?"

Carmen tipped her chin back and laughed. She had a lovely throat. Significantly nicer than what came out of it. "Don't pretend you have some lofty goal. You're here because you want to fuck me and because you're hoping to advance your career."

"OK, sure. I want to write for the magazine. But that's not the *only* reason I'm doing this. I've been in relationships"—he prayed that his use of the plural sounded plausible—"where you can live with a person for months, even years, and never really know what they want." He flushed. "Sexually."

"This is my point, Lucas. We're not doing *activities*. We're kissing, touching, fondling, groping, rubbing, sucking, and licking. But you're so squeamish that you can't even talk about sex in its most basic terms." Carmen climbed off of his legs.

"That's not true!" Lucas protested. "I'm just trying to take this partnership seriously, elevate it, turn it into something worthwhile."

"Jesus! We're not sexual altruists working for the greater good. This is about making people buy magazines. And do you know how?"

"Apparently not."

"We're creating a titillating, tidy little circle of judgment. I'm going to judge you. You're going to judge me. And the good people of New York are going to judge both of us."

Lucas opened his mouth to refute this but didn't know where to begin.

"My column isn't about giving advice. It's about getting people off and turning them on. And that's accomplished by providing an open invitation for them to judge you. Judgment is the world's greatest aphrodisiac."

This was not where he'd expected the conversation to go. "But why would you want to be involved in that?" he asked, flummoxed.

Carmen slipped off the bed and stood in the middle of the hotel room. "Well, let's see. Because I'm strong enough not to care. I don't just take; I dish. And dishing on a public stage is power. I'm not crying into my Pinot with a bunch of girlfriends. I'm talking to the entire city. People may not agree with me, but they do listen. And the more that I put myself out there, the more power I attain. I stand so far above everyone; their judgments can't touch me."

"My judgment got to you. My first column."

"Like hell it did."

Now Lucas was angry. They *were* partners in this, despite

what she'd said. She should take him seriously. "There's a good chance people aren't judging you because of what you write. They're judging the fact that a woman your age is writing a column meant for a twenty-three-year-old. I mean you're what, thirty-five? Thirty-six?"

"I'm thirty-one," Carmen said, her voice hard.

"Exactly," Lucas muttered, and hopped off the bed, to face her on his feet.

"All right, fine. You want me to communicate with you, Lucas? Well, here's what's on my mind. I'm doubtful that you can do anything even halfway proficient or pleasurable with my breasts. But here they are, so please, by all means . . ."

Carmen pulled her shirt over her head and tossed it hard against the wall. Then she removed her bra and sent it flying. Lucas looked at her breasts. They were, he decided, *excellent*. It was what he'd have written down if he had a notebook in hand. And yet Lucas, for the second time in one conversation, opened his mouth and found no words to release.

"Do something to them," she stated. "You want to level up with me? You want to have more control? Get used to being judged, pal." She cupped her breasts hard with both hands, pushed them up, and held them there. She locked eyes with him and raised her eyebrows expectantly. Then she took her hands away; her breasts fell back down with a little bounce. "Last chance," she said. "Do something to my tits. Make it good."

Lucas paused. Then he stepped forward and went in face first.

CHAPTER 15

Dear Nice Guy,

Have you seen that movie *Turner & Hooch,* where a slobbering dog bathes Tom Hanks in saliva? I just saw the sequel—and it was you giving me the complete canine experience this week. It was called *Turner & Cooch.* (Or was Hooch the dog, not Turner? Don't ruin this joke for me, people.)

To eager men everywhere, here's a little advice on tit sucking: Don't go straight for the nipple. You're not a two-month-old and my breasts aren't there to pump you up with protein. This is sex, not nursing. For god sakes. I told Nice Guy to impress me, and he led with his lips like some laser-guided mouth missile. There is an entire boob that could use some

attention first. I want you to Make. Me. Feel. You. Kiss
the sides. Kiss the undersides. Cup them, caress them,
squeeze them. Squeeze them harder. I should have
woken up the next day a little sore. But Nice Guy was
the Niagara Falls of drool. Yuck. He'll probably write
that I stepped away after a few minutes. Well, yeah,
because I worried about drowning.

Here's what you could have done, Nice Guy: You
could have locked eyes with me; you could have
shown me that, yeah, you know my boobs are there,
but you're a man who's seen plenty of boobs before,
who knows exactly what to do with them and will do
it in due time. You could have stepped toward me,
strongly and confidently, eyes still on mine. Then
hands on my tits, coming upward like you're scooping
them up, like you're holding my whole body. Play.
Feel. Kiss me. Then go down. Press yourself into me.
Kiss. Inhale. Suck. You should know the order. Build
me up. And had you done all this, and done it right,
I'd have let you grab me around the waist and throw
me faceup on the bed, and then waited for you to
take your pants off, and then let you straddle me and
fuck my tits. Because that's how you do it, Nice Guy.
Or that's how you're supposed to.

See you next week. If I must.

Carmen finished writing next week's column on her iPhone.
She was standing in the middle of this dump of a hotel room,
her wet hair turbaned in a towel. She'd fumed all through her
shower, scrubbing her body red with anger. She felt only mildly
calmer now.

Carmen loved luxury hotels. She especially loved the novelty of spending the night in a hotel in her own city. For her birthday, she sometimes booked a ridiculously expensive room, savoring the sense of escape. A hotel room was like a blank canvas. For twelve hours, you could be anyone: artist, rock star, or high-powered executive. You could even be a writer in the old mold—stylishly accommodated, boozed, and fed while on assignment. And so, when she'd negotiated her contract with Jays, she said that she would not be made to feel as though she were renting a room by the hour. She wasn't asking for the Pierre. Just a decent-sized bathroom (preferably with a soaking tub), room service, and a firm bed whose linens had an acceptable thread count. This way, she could take back something for herself; at the end of each session with Lucas, she would relax for the night on *Empire's* dime. But Jays had not held up his end of the bargain. He'd put them in this two-star dump. It was infuriating, especially since she knew that the Editor himself would never stay anywhere that cost less than six hundred dollars a night. (She'd seen his expense report; not so long ago, some of those "work-related" itemizations had been itemized on her.)

And after tonight's encounter with Lucas, Carmen felt an almost desperate need to climb into a large porcelain tub. She had not felt this grimy in a long while. Possibly not since the gallery owner had tongue-raped her in the back of a taxi. He'd leaned in unexpectedly and shoved the hot, wormy muscle into her mouth. Carmen had been too startled—and the kiss was too short—to do anything. It was already over. The guy was getting out. He thought he'd been a gentleman, not asking her to come upstairs. Back home, she had literally considered washing her mouth out with soap. She vowed never to let anything like that happen again.

And yet that was the moment she returned to, in thinking about the last hour with Lucas. When she'd ripped off her shirt and bra, she'd done it as a challenge—a power move. He'd been blindsided by her breasts, by a body of which he was clearly in awe. If that wasn't power, what was? But if that *was* power, then why did she now feel sullied, outside and in?

She got dressed, left the hotel, and stood on the sidewalk, unsure where to go. In the past, she would have happily seated herself at some bar and waited for a man to pick her up. Now she cringed at the thought. Her closest friends, Martin and Dale, lived in Chelsea, not far away. But she knew how *that* would go: Too much white wine and then she'd be spilling everything. Martin couldn't keep a secret. Dale could, except from Martin. She couldn't help but think about Jays and what— or who—he was doing. The rake. She should have insisted they treat the columns like creative writing assignments. (And when Jays grew tired of foreplay and demanded that she and Lucas start fucking, that's exactly what Carmen would insist they do.) But she had succumbed to pride. Jays had issued her a challenge, and (unlike certain moments in the past) she was determined to face it honestly. Which meant she was trapped in this tussle with Lucas every other goddamned week. And *still* Jays claimed victory. Because nothing would change the fact that he'd broken her heart.

Carmen hailed a taxi and asked for the Museum of Modern Art. The museum had been closed for hours, but Carmen knew Charles, the night security guard. She'd been introduced to him years ago by her grandmother, a onetime Broadway actress, at a party hosted by a group of producers. Charles had regaled Carmen with tales of the museum's intrigues, and before leaving she'd delivered him a plate of fancy desserts and a playbill signed by her grandmother. Since then, he'd been happy to do Carmen the occasional favor.

"You've had a night?" Charles asked, letting Carmen into the spacious, silent lobby. It was his typical question. Carmen only called on Charles in her worst moments: those rare occasions when her confidence faltered, when she felt like a fraud, a hack, an outsider in her own city. She came to remind herself why she'd made such a difficult, capricious, and expensive place her home.

"I won't be long," she said. There was only one painting that Carmen wanted to see.

After she graduated from New York University with an English degree and with no idea what she wanted to do with her life, Carmen spent a summer backpacking across Europe. She visited the Louvre, Uffizi, and Tate. In Amsterdam, she went to the Van Gogh Museum, where she saw *Bedroom in Arles, Sunflowers,* and *Almond Blossoms.* But when she went looking for *The Starry Night,* she couldn't find it. She doubled back through the entire museum before finally flagging a docent.

"You are from America?" the docent asked, and smiled mischievously. "I am afraid *Starry Night* is at the Museum of Modern Art in New York."

Carmen had traveled thousands of miles, hoping to see a painting that was back at home. The moment clinched something for her. She still had no idea what she wanted to do with her life, but she was certain that whatever awaited her, it waited in Manhattan.

And so she visited this gallery on the fifth floor of MOMA when she needed to remember who she was and why she'd chosen this life. *The Starry Night,* the cliché of a million dorm rooms, always started Carmen's heart pounding. Not just because it was remarkable and absorbing—which of course it was—but also because, against all odds, it lived here. And because it was here, and not over there, it could belong to her—just as it belonged to every other person who, by their perseverance and their moxie, had struggled to carve out a piece of this city for themselves.

Carmen stood before the painting for half an hour, casting her troubles into van Gogh's turbulent sky. When she'd vanquished all thoughts of flight, all doubts and second guesses, she headed back downstairs, thanked Charles again, and hailed the evening's final taxi.

From the time that she could talk, Carmen had called her paternal grandmother Mira. "Miranda" was too difficult, but variations of "Grandmother"—"Granny," "Grandma," "Nana," what have you—were deemed unacceptable. Mira had spent her life bucking categories. As the daughter of Irish immigrants, she was expected to marry young and raise a brood of children. Instead, she frequently reminded Carmen that she'd been a divorcée at age twenty-five, in the 1950s, with a *child*. She'd made her living as a waitress, an artist's model, a girls' school gym teacher, and, in her last act, a celebrated actress. She'd been proposed to six times and managed to fend off five of these suitors. Then in her "succulent late sixties," she'd fallen madly in love with a white-bearded, Birkenstocked folk singer—"can you imagine, Carmen!" They lived out of wedlock for many years, until fourteen months ago, when a heart attack felled him. Now Mira lived alone in his creaky ground-floor apartment on Perry Street. It was rent-controlled to the tune of six hundred dollars a month, which was fortunate, seeing as she had almost no savings.

Carmen arrived there just past 11:00 P.M. and let herself in. Mira, always a night hawk, lounged on the patchy Baroque Louis XVI settee in one of her many "evening-in" getups. This one was a silky aubergine-colored robe and matching slippers procured from the depths of Chinatown. She was drinking hot chocolate and simultaneously working through a game of Solitaire, a biography of Czeslaw Milosz, and an episode of *House Hunters* on her iPad.

"Multitasking, are we?" Carmen slipped off her heels and walked across the uneven floorboards toward the lamplit living room. She kissed Mira on the cheek, breathing in her powdery scent and the fragrance of her lipstick, which given how much the woman had applied over eighty-six years was more or less permanent.

"Is everything all right?" Mira asked.

Carmen visited her grandmother multiple times a week, accompanying her on various outings and shopping expeditions. But evenings, Mira knew, were for Carmen's work.

"Don't mind me," Carmen said, and scanned the apartment's impressive built-in bookshelves. A rolling ladder, which provided access to the upper reaches, had long been Carmen's favorite detail of this little home. "I'll just find something to read."

"Oh please," Mira said. "There's chocolate on the stove. Or—I'm guessing you'd prefer whiskey?"

The galley kitchen was submarine-like, windowless and pulsating with greenish light. Most people would have found the apartment's 450 square feet claustrophobic. But Mira contended that they were enough: manageable enough, affordable enough. "I have a home," she'd say. "I have the Village for a backyard. What else do I need?"

Carmen could think of a few things, including natural light and a bathroom where your knees didn't hit the door when you sat on the toilet. But she knew how lucky Mira was. Now Carmen fixed her grandmother a new mug of cocoa and poured herself a drink. Back in the living room, she said, "I'm involved with something that's either very smart or very stupid."

"Something or someone?" Mira asked.

"Both."

Carmen could see that Mira was now revved up, as much as a woman pushing eighty-seven could be. There was nothing she'd loved more than puzzling through a problem. So Carmen explained everything—about the column, the deal she'd made with Jays, and the exchange with Lucas earlier than night.

"Are you comfortable with the physical arrangement with this young man?"

"At the moment. More or less," she said.

"And this corner you've backed into?"

"Corner?"

"Well, you did good for yourself, negotiating a new contract. But, Carmen, as soon as this column achieves its goal—gets the numbers up or whatever—what's to stop Jay Jacobson from firing you?"

Mira had met Jays exactly once. And from that encounter, she'd pronounced him the "Sultan of Smarm." From then on, she insisted on referring to him by his full name, like he was an evil spirit that must be properly labeled in order to be exorcized.

Carmen had assumed that "Screw the Critics" would grant her greater cachet in the mediasphere, more assigned pieces at higher word rates. But Mira was right. Jays could dispose of her when he got what he needed.

"You've got to think about the long game," Mira continued. "Professionally speaking, what do you really *want*?"

Suddenly feeling shy, Carmen traced her toe along the rug. Instead of the dusty threadbare object she was used to, her foot sank into plush fiber. "Wait, is this new?" she asked. "Mira, this looks expensive."

"It was—and don't give me that look, Carmen. Harry always treated this place like a short-term rental, even though he'd lived here for thirty years. He never fixed things, never invested in anything new. And, well, as I said, this is my home. At least until I step onto that Broadway stage in the sky."

"Very funny," Carmen said. But she suddenly understood what her grandmother was trying to communicate. Carmen needed to take responsibility for her career. She needed to own it. "I want a cultural position in this city that's equal to my intellect," she said. "And I want to be paid for it."

Miranda nodded. "Then go get it."

Carmen just shook her head. "A sex and relationships columnist becoming a public intellectual? Please."

"If I could elbow my way onto Broadway, then you can certainly expand your repertoire. After all, you're already on the inside."

"I'm stuck inside the sex-columnist ghetto, Mira. Whenever I pitch anything else I get, 'Nice writing, but this topic is outside your comfort zone.' And Jays isn't the only one dishing out that kind of condescending bullshit."

"You deserve to be liberated. The question is how?"

Carmen had been asking herself this question for years. She'd had big ambitions. After returning from her post-collegiate jaunt across Europe, she'd enrolled at Columbia Journalism School. The following summer, she'd actually secured an internship at the *New York Times*. But it was unpaid and she had a whopping amount of school debt from college and grad school. Meanwhile, her parents had retired, sold their Hamilton Heights apartment, and moved to Tucson, so she no longer had a place to crash. Reluctantly, she turned down the internship. But she refused to leave New York City—the pulse of the media world—to cover community board meetings in Bumblefuck, Pennsylvania, or even Nowheresville, New Jersey. She found her way into corporate copywriting, describing dresses for catalogs, and landed the occasional essay in women's magazines, which paid a glorious two dollars a word but often required her to amp up the ogle factor and play down the facts. When a friend told her that *Empire* was hiring Web writers on contract, Carmen jumped at the chance.

From the get-go, she understood that Jays had taken both a professional and nonprofessional interest in her. She also understood that if she took advantage of the latter she'd have a better shot at attaining her ultimate goal: her own column in the magazine. And so she figured out when to be confident with him and when to be coy. After just a year, to Carmen's delight, Jays delivered the prize. And maybe the gig didn't come with health insurance, but Jays had talked about cutbacks from the publisher, and how could Carmen argue with that?

Carmen had also come to like Jays: his passion, his ambition, and, despite his massive success, the vulnerability he harbored over his common upbringing. To the world, he used his humble roots as a humble brag, but behind closed doors, he was convinced that everyone considered him a hick. It was possible that, deep down, he still saw himself that way. But he guarded these feelings like precious gems. Carmen was the only one he let in, and this convinced her that she was different. Special.

Three years after she'd first come to *Empire,* they began dating in secret. When it came to Carmen's job or Jays' public love life, they had an unspoken understanding: Anything was game as long as it wasn't serious. This went on for years with the occasional blowup and breakup—inevitable given how stubborn, strong-willed, and jealous they could be. But they always returned. Most of the time, Carmen was happy.

Then she was no longer in her twenties and something shifted. It was such a cliché: Turn thirty and you start to worry about the future, about being alone. Yet Jays, nearing forty, seemed to feel the same. A new intensity had entered their romantic interactions, as though they were running out of time.

But why should that be? They were changing. Why couldn't their relationship change, too?

It was time, Carmen decided, to see whether they could thrive under the bright and exacting light of day, so she'd broached the idea of finding work elsewhere. Then they could go public.

At this suggestion, Jays cowered like a vampire caught at daybreak. He would not return her phone calls or emails. The Sphinxes repeatedly said his calendar was full. It felt worse, even, than if he'd fallen in love with someone else. Instead, this silence—her sudden banishment—revealed that she wasn't special at all. Like everyone else, she was a pawn.

Carmen waited to be fired, but the call never came. Maybe Jays feared she'd run to the press. Or maybe he was just a coward. Or maybe he was just waiting for something else to push her out—and then along came Nice Guy. There was no return to the way things were, she realized now. When "Screw the Critics" was over, she was over.

"I'm totally dispensable to Jays," Carmen said.

Mira swept up her Solitaire game and started to deal out cards for Gin. "Then you must make yourself indispensable."

"How many gimmicks can I really cook up? What'll I do—go on tour, teach people how to screw onstage? I'll have cameras follow me around. It'll be a total sensation."

Mira organized her hand, her lips pursed in thought. "That's not a bad idea."

"Mira!"

"Not the public sex, Carmen. The tour. Why not make a bigger name for yourself? *Brand* yourself, as they say. You'd be terrific on camera."

"And I'd talk about . . . ?"

"Well, the column you're writing for starters. The experience of reviewing and being reviewed. Juicy tidbits about mystery Nice Guy. Don't you think people would be curious? Don't you think they might—and should—learn something from you?"

Lucas had said exactly this, but Carmen kept that point to herself. "I'm trying to get out of the sex-writer ghetto, remember?"

"I'm merely suggesting a strategy, Carmen. You start with what you know—and what you're known for—and then you use that platform as your launching pad. You move from sex and relationships to sexual *politics:* reproductive rights, women in politics, cultural sexism. You respond to the news cycle, make yourself the go-to commentator. From there, you can talk about anything you want and people will listen. In short order *Vanity Fair* will run a profile titled 'The Reinvention of Carmen Kelly.'"

"Jays would never go for that. He's got a vise grip on the media spotlight. All the TV, radio, print—it's all him. His face is the *only* face of *Empire.*"

"Why do you need his approval?"

"Because he'd fire me."

Miranda laid down her cards. There was no need for her to say "gin"; a perfect hand stared back up at Carmen. "It seems to me that for the next few months at least you have an enviable degree of job security."

Carmen looked up. *Oh, wise, wise Mira.* "Because he can't fire me while the column is going well."

"And if his plan is to let you go anyway, you have nothing to lose. Though I suspect if you play your cards right he'll feel compelled to have you stay."

"And I might have other magazine opportunities by then."

"And a book deal or, better yet, a movie deal."

"Right, and the film will be called *Screw the Critics.*" Carmen rolled her eyes, but she was starting to feel genuinely rejuvenated. Lucas was just a child. How could she have allowed herself to be defeated by his nonsense? Moreover, and this especially delighted her, Jays was going to be pissed. He was going to be so pissed that the farthest reaches of the empire would feel his ire. Well, let it.

"I'll need to start with a late-night show," Carmen said. "I think that's the right audience. But I've got to do something absurd enough to go viral; otherwise nobody will pay attention. Like, I dunno, teaching some gawky PA how to kiss on air."

"That's brilliant."

"I was kidding!"

"I'm not."

Carmen pondered this. "I recently met a writer from *Late Night with Kyle Carter*. I guess it's worth a try."

"Oh, I adore that Kyle Carter! He is handsome and terribly funny. Tomorrow we'll go shopping for your camera-ready outfit."

"Let's not get ahead of ourselves, Mira."

Mira gathered up her silken robes and tucked her legs beneath her on the couch like an excitable teenager. "Yes, Carmen, let's!"

CHAPTER 16

Lucas lay awake, ruminating over that evening's encounter with Carmen. She'd issued a challenge—*Do something to my tits. Make it good*—and he'd diligently applied himself. He believed he'd done a good job; by that point, he'd had a week of coaching with Sofia. But he suspected his technique was irrelevant. Carmen didn't want a fair and honest critique. She wanted to embarrass him. And so, when she took off her shirt, she'd set a trap. He could accept her challenge and be portrayed as a failure, or he could reject it and get the same result; the game was rigged.

Lucas thought about this for a moment. He needed to hit her with a no-win choice of his own—throw her off-balance, regardless of whether she said yes or no. He sat up in bed; it was 3:00 A.M., but there was no chance of sleep now. He grabbed his laptop.

Dear Carmen,

I didn't realize it was possible for a woman to detach herself from her boobs, until you presented yours to me. (Readers, you should know: This week was dedicated to Second Base, and it happened standing up: Carmen took her shirt off and insisted I get in there, so I took her up on the invitation.) I want to be descriptive here, but most words for breasts are cliché. Are they voluptuous? Not really. Ample? Depends on who's measuring. Perky? Well . . . sort of, though they're just too large to completely escape gravity. Oh, hell, let's just be plain about it, because I mean to be complimentary: Your boobs are just really nice. They're more than a handful—just large enough that when I put my face in between them I can press them up against my closed eyelids. That's a little embarrassing to write, but I guess it's the point of these columns, so . . . the boobs-on-eyes thing has always been a turn-on for me. I don't know why. Maybe it's the intimacy of it—that I have to be really up against a woman, really involved with her body, to have her boobs against my eyes.

But though I had your boobs, I most certainly didn't have you.

You're really big on taking notes during our sessions, so I tried taking a mental ticktock of how you responded to a man's face in your boobs. For the first minute, you stood with your arms to your sides, like nothing was happening. Your boobs were there in front of me, though the rest of you seemed to have wandered off in search of a cocktail. But oh! Then you breathed deeply, twice. And finally, finally, you tentatively ran your fingers through my hair— not in a particularly erotic or encouraging way, and only once, downward to my neck. What was that? I'd like to think that I'd given you at least a twinge of pleasure in that moment. Then you stepped backward. You'd had enough, which is just as well. Carmen, you had driven me to a state I wasn't sure I was capable of: I was getting bored with boobs. And I love boobs. I love your boobs, in theory at least. Yet I now realize that there's a big difference between boobs in isolation and boobs on a living woman's body.

I'm trying now to think of what it was I did in the seconds before you touched me. Was it sucking your nipple just a little too hard? The flicking of my tongue? Circling of my tongue? Is that something you're into? It's so hard to tell with you. You give no feedback. And that, dare I say, is the sign of a lousy lover. You certainly seem confident of your sexual abilities, but I think your confidence is misplaced. You think you know what's right and wrong, which gives you the right to sit back and judge what's delivered to you. But a good lover is confident enough to say, "I like this; do more of it." A good lover is confident enough to reveal themselves. So, Carmen, here's what I think: You're hiding something from me. There's something about me that you like—something about me that you think is worthy—and you don't want to show it.

So I'm going to issue a challenge, here in these
pages, and readers can see next week if you'll take
me up on it: Let's get drunk. Let's get sloppy
enough that we can't hide things from each other.
Sloppy enough that handwritten notes would be
illegible in the morning anyway. I'm taking three
shots of Jameson before you and I meet next time,
and I challenge you to do the same. I'll bring a
bottle, so we can throw back some more. Let's see
what you're like when you're not thinking so hard
about what we're doing.

Lucas clicked "save," smiled, and settled back down into
bed. Finally, he had a plan.

The next morning, far too early, Lucas's alarm buzzed. He
dragged himself out of bed, showered, and headed out. He
was off to meet Nicholas Spragg, who'd resurfaced a few days
before with a brunch invitation. Lucas still felt a little weird
about the love hotel, but he was too curious about Nicholas to
say no.

They were meeting at Ice, a trendy glass box of a restaurant
in Greenwich Village west—or was it Meatpacking south?—in
which the décor was entirely transparent. Clear glass tables,
walls, even cutlery. Nicholas was already there, sipping a cappuccino at the see-through bar. Lucas quickly noted the tailored
khaki suit with its precisely folded maroon pocket square, the
checkered white and maroon shirt, and the maroon leather
belt. A third maroon object dangled from Nicholas's fist. It was
a leash, Lucas realized. And it was attached to the maroon
leather collar of a black dachshund.

"This is Saint Regis," Nicholas said. He smiled proudly, as

though he alone were responsible for the dog's existence. "Isn't he delightful?"

"Hiya, pup!" Lucas squatted and rubbed the dog's head affectionately.

When the hostess arrived to take them to the table, the dog would not budge. He was visibly shaking. After a minute of failed coaxing and cajoling, Nicholas finally lifted the puppy into his arms.

"Is he OK?" Lucas asked.

Nicholas frowned. "I hope so. A breeder dropped him off first thing this morning," Nicholas said, as though there were nothing particularly unusual about door-to-door pet delivery. "But we may not be a good fit."

Lucas could only imagine Nicholas abandoning the dog on some street corner and he dearly hoped the breeder accepted returns. "Why'd you name him Saint Regis?" he asked.

"It's the hotel where I've been living."

Lucas did a double take. Did he just say "living"?

"Did you know the Bloody Mary was invented at the Saint Regis?" Nicholas went on. "And John Jacob Astor, who built it, died aboard the *Titanic*. Anyway, as you can imagine, my father is absolutely aghast that I refused to decamp at a Kingswood property. But your average Kingswood is utterly devoid of elegance or charm. Do you know what I'm saying?"

Lucas did not, but he nodded anyway.

Nicholas leaned forward, his face flushing. "Back in the day, much of New York society lived in hotels. They'd 'take rooms,' stay on for months, and have all of their meals together. Everyone ate luncheon—so much nicer than 'lunch,' which sounds like a sneeze. And they dressed for dinner. They were cultured."

He said all of this wistfully, almost nostalgically. *Forget New York*, Lucas thought. *Nicholas should move to Charlotte and take up with Grandmother Callahan;* he'd have all the luncheons he could stomach.

"But, to be totally honest with you," Nicholas continued, "the Saint Regis isn't quite what I'd been hoping for. People don't really stay for more than a week and the crowd is, well, old."

Even Lucas, who knew next to nothing about fancy hotels, could have told Nicholas that. "Wouldn't you find a younger crowd at The Standard? Or The Bowery Hotel? Or one of those new places in Williamsburg?"

"Do you think those are places where you could congregate? I mean sit with your friends and drink cocktails and talk about city life? You must do that all the time at the magazine."

"Drink cocktails and talk about city life?" Lucas repeated with a smirk.

"I would love to be a fly on the wall during one of your editors' lunches. All of you discussing your fascinating stories. And in the evenings, taking off to these fashionable events, where you meet the city's most cultured and fascinating people. It must be a brilliant life."

Not long ago, this had been Lucas's own image of *Empire.* But the work was more ordinary than he'd imagined—just another office, really, where people did office things. Except for Jays and his deputies, everybody ate lunch at their desks, usually salad from the shop downstairs, coated in a dressing that left your mouth feeling what Alexis called squeaky. Meanwhile, the weekly publicist parties were not particularly exclusive. Even Kobe sliders got old after a while. And although the sporadic last-minute invites from Jays were truly a world apart, Lucas was so obviously the outsider at them, nothing more than a spectacularly mismatched body double. It seemed absurd for Nicholas to see him as part of some inner circle, especially since Spragg was the heir to a hotel fortune, partied with gorgeous socialites, and had (at least purported to have) Jays' cell phone number!

And yet Lucas recognized the longing in Nicholas's eyes, empathized with his unfulfilled desires. He supposed that everyone—even the most wealthy—desired things they could not have.

But what they could have was two hundred dollars' worth of brunch. Nicholas ordered a round of mimosas, a pile of fresh pastries, a stack of ricotta pancakes, and truffle-oil omelets. When the drinks arrived, he raised his glass. "Thank you," he said.

"For what?" Lucas asked.

"For your friendship," Nicholas said.

"Oh," Lucas said, a little confused. "Well, thank you."

No longer terrified, Saint Regis jumped up from Nicholas's lap and caught a croissant in his mouth.

Lucas walked home through the Village, enjoying the neighborhood that was so much quieter and cleaner than his own. But just as he turned the corner onto Perry Street, he nearly barreled into a woman laden with grocery-packed tote bags. "Oh," she said. "I'm sorry." She backed up half a step. And then, "Oh. Hi."

Lucas froze. It was Carmen, of all people. And yet this was her neighborhood, so what did he expect? She was not alone either. An old woman, wrinkled and gaunt with large, heavily lidded eyes, stood beside her.

"I'm Mira Kelly," the woman said, and stretched out a frail arm, encircled in flashing beads. "Carmen," the old woman mumbled, "your manners."

Carmen shifted the grocery bags. "Grandma, this is Lucas," she said curtly. "We're colleagues."

Seeing Carmen loaded down like that, Lucas felt a pang of guilt about the previous night. Attacking her age was a low blow. He'd now been in the media scene long enough to know that Carmen was absolutely too old for her column. She was playing a twentysomething's game. And it was a shame, because she was a really good writer—he had to admit that much. For all of his frustration with Carmen, it was still a point of pride that he was able to go head-to-head with her on the page.

"Let me help you with those," he said now.

"We're fine." Carmen shook her head.

"These are my groceries," Mira said, "so it's my right to insist that Lucas carry them the rest of the way."

Reluctantly, Carmen let Lucas slip the bags off her shoulders and onto his arms. Lucas and Mira began to walk side by side, with Carmen trailing behind.

"I'm sure you know of Mira Kelly, the Broadway actress?" Lucas asked now.

"You've heard of me?"

"Wait—it's you?" Lucas stopped, bewildered. How could this legend be Carmen's grandmother? "Three years ago *Empire* ran a fantastic profile of you. I'll admit, I didn't know you then, but after that story—wow! I'd kill to see you onstage. Are you in anything?"

Carmen looked a little stunned.

"That's quite a good memory," Mira said, clearly impressed. "I'm retired now. But you work at *Empire* with my granddaughter?"

"He's a fact-checker," Carmen said flatly. "He makes sure the names are spelled correctly."

Mira furrowed her brow at Carmen's rudeness. "Well, everyone starts somewhere," she said.

"This is us," Carmen said abruptly, stopping outside a building at the end of the block. It was only a few doors down from the café that Lucas had visited after his first night with Carmen, in his post-coital ignorance, before he knew better.

"Thank you so much for your help," Mira said. "And good luck at the magazine. I hope you'll forgive my granddaughter her crankiness. She and I were up far too late last night plotting world domination."

"Sounds like fun," Lucas said, handing Carmen the groceries. "See you at work," he said brightly, and thought of his column—his *challenge*—that was about to hit newsstands. She had no idea it was coming, and he liked finally feeling in control of something.

"Sure," Carmen replied, visibly relieved to be free of him. "At work."

CHAPTER 17

Lucas had never been a fan of late-night talk shows. The hosts were poor interviewers; their only real talent was the agile shuffling of oversized index cards. And the whole thing felt like a vestige of older times, when the most sophisticated thing on television was a guy on a stage talking to an audience. Today's viewers deserved better, Lucas thought. But still, he made an exception for Kyle Carter. The man was late night's newest star, but he'd started as a humble Internet creator, making YouTube videos out of his home. They were funny and weird and experimental. He once finagled a meeting with the marketing department at Froot Loops and berated them for ten minutes about their misspelling of the word "Fruit." In another video, he recruited five guys named Kyle and five guys named Carter and had them mud wrestle. (Team Carter won.) A late-night show seemed like an unnatural fit, but the network was clearly aching to reach a younger audience, and Carter wasn't about to turn down the paycheck. His show was decent, but not nearly as daring as his online stuff. There was sadness at the edges of his 1000-watt smile, a sense of loss. Lucas appreciated that.

And so, at 11:47 one night, as Lucas was sitting on the couch, he had Kyle Carter running in the background as he intermittently read the *New York Times* on his phone. It had been a few days since the new issue of *Empire* hit stands and Lucas had heard nothing from Carmen. She'd been obnoxious with the *Turner & Hooch* stuff, but Lucas had to admit that her advice had been good. Even he felt turned-on reading her preferred version of events. Still, he was enjoying a reprieve from her.

And then Carter said something that abruptly drew Lucas's attention to the show: ". . . please welcome the editor-at-large of *Empire Magazine* and the creator of the magazine's new blockbuster column, 'Screw the Critics'—Carmen Kelly!"

Lucas dropped his phone. On television, Carmen strode across the stage in glossy heels and a black dress, looking sexy as hell but also as erect and proud as the CEO of a Fortune 500 corporation. She leveled her eyes at the cameras as though America were her boardroom and in so doing wilted the egos (if not the dicks) of Carter's male audience.

Lucas's mouth dropped open.

"So this column of yours," Carter was saying, "is quite the *rousing* read." The house drummer budump-chinged.

"Tyler!" Lucas shouted. "Get in here."

Carter continued. "Some people have called you the country's first sex critic. Others say you're just the hardest woman to please in America. A lot of people are scandalized—and not just Republicans! In just a few weeks, your 'Screw the Critics' column has spawned a million conversations and some very hostile critics who are saying, well, screw you! Can I read from one of them?"

"Please," Carmen said.

"OK, so this is from the *New York Review of Books,* which I didn't know was allowed to print the word 'sex.' But here we go. '"Screw the Critics" promises unvarnished honesty, but its premise is a lie. It treats sex as a science, with Carmen Kelly holding all the equations. But in truth the only science here is that Carmen and Nice Guy have no chemistry. Sex is subjective. It is art. It makes no sense when held up to the microscope. And the only thing we really learn from "Screw the Critics" is that we should all be so fortunate to never sleep with either of these two.'"

Carter turned to Carmen. "Care to respond?"

"Well, first of all, I know that writer and he would be *very* fortunate to sleep with me," she said. Carter chuckled. "But I also disagree with the premise. Yes, sex is art. Hell, art is probably derivative of sex: It's our shoddy attempt to replicate the same passion and excitement that we feel with another person. But it is also science, because as any woman will tell you, there is absolutely a right and wrong approach. You can turn me on or turn me off, and that's biology at work. Nice Guy, for all his flaws, could one day turn me on—I really do believe that. But it won't happen until he learns a few things. Because bad sex is real, Kyle. I think we're all more or less familiar with the truth of that."

"I hope you're not accusing me of anything," Carter said, hamming up his mock despondency. "But hey, being good at sex is one thing. You say you're an *expert* at it. What makes you an expert?"

"Well, that *New York Review* critic claims to be an expert commentator."

"So you're saying an expert is just someone who declares themselves an expert."

"No, no, it's more than that," Carmen says. "They have to have a proven, trustworthy opinion. They have to be able to really show that they know what they're talking about."

"And how do we know your opinion is trustworthy?"

"Well," Carmen said, "how about a demonstration?"

Back in the apartment, Lucas was now on his feet. "Tyler!" he shouted. "Where are you? Get in here right now!"

Carter was loving this. "Surely you're not going to demonstrate the, um, art of sex on this stage?" he said. "This isn't HBO, remember."

"Oh, don't worry, this'll get steamy, but it won't get you in trouble with the FCC," Carmen said. "I believe you have a production assistant on this show named Adam?"

"We do," Carter said. "He's a talented young man. We promised you some airtime, Adam—this is your moment!"

The camera cut to the side of the stage, where celebrities usually made their entrance. Out sidled Adam, a gangly, unkempt young man dressed in ill-fitting jeans, a size-too-large T-shirt, and running sneakers. His eyes were magnified behind a pair of large glasses.

"Come on, Adam," Carter said, waving him over. "Don't be shy. Carmen won't bite . . . and if she does, we have a good workers compensation program here."

Adam shuffled slightly faster to where Carmen was standing. She opened her arms for a hug, her smile big and wide. And as soon as he leaned toward her, she threw herself into him like a reunited lover, kissing him deeply. His arms flailed for a few seconds, as though he'd been electrocuted. Then he settled in and wrapped his arms around her and kissed her back. If this was to be Adam's moment in the spotlight, he was seizing it. The audience went wild.

"Holy fuck!" Lucas shouted at the television.

Carmen and Adam finally disengaged. The poor kid looked disoriented.

"He volunteered for this," Carter told his audience, "but I don't think he really knew what he was in for. Did you, Adam?"

Adam shook his head.

"So how was that?" Carter asked.

Carmen nodded, impressed. "Pretty good."

Adam beamed.

"But the thing is, we don't want pretty good. Right? I mean, Adam doesn't just want to be 'pretty good.'"

She glanced at Adam. Clearly, he had considered the last thirty seconds a lot better than pretty good, but he wasn't about to argue about it on national television.

"We want spectacular," she continued. "And luckily, spectacular isn't as elusive as we may think. Adam, for example, could improve a little bit on his tongue technique. Now don't get me wrong. It was—"

"*Pretty good*," Carter said, exaggerating for effect.

"Right. But if Adam were to put his hands just about here on my shoulder blades, and hold me tight so I feel like he's confident and in control, and then move his tongue just a little less this way" (Carmen made a flicking motion) "and a little more *this* way" (she twirled the tip of her tongue counterclockwise) "I think he'd knock it out of the park."

"What do you think, Adam? You up for another try?"

Adam's face colored. He nodded, trying to look casual. Really, Lucas thought, he looked like he was about to pee himself.

"OK, let's give it a shot," Carmen said, flashing her peppiest smile. She beckoned him with her index finger and the audience began to cheer and holler. Then Carmen and Adam were locked together again, Adam's hands immediately on her back, just as she'd instructed. He squeezed her shoulder blades and then ran his palms down her back, landing them on her hips. He seemed confident and in control. When they finally pulled apart, Carmen was the one who looked flushed. "Wow!" she breathed. "Now that's what I call spectacular." The audience went ballistic. Adam the PA smiled like he'd won the Powerball jackpot, like that kiss had changed his life forever.

"Now, OK, before we let you go," Carter said, "I have to ask you: In this week's column, your anonymous partner, Mr. Nice Guy, issued a challenge. He wants you to get good and liquored up before meeting him next time, and writes: 'Let's see what you're like when you're not thinking so hard about what we're doing.' So, what's your plan?"

Carmen laughed the kind of practiced laugh that presidential candidates use when dismissing an opponent during a debate. "Let's put aside the fact that Nice Guy's suggestion smacks of insensitivity, given the important conversations we're having right now about alcohol and consent on college campuses. In a way, his desire to get drunk is reflective of many young men his age: When they feel intimidated, they look for a crutch to take the pressure off. We women don't really need that—do we, Adam? We're at the top of our game when we put our brains to work."

Adam nodded. "You're a great thinker, Carmen."

The audience laughed. Adam beamed.

"Now this is the kind of man we all deserve," Carmen said, and leaned over to kiss him one more time. As the two made out like high schoolers in the back of a movie theater, Carter wrapped it up: "Editor-at-large of *Empire Magazine* and the creator of 'Screw the Critics.' Carmen Kelly, everyone!" he practically yelled, and as the audience cheered, Carmen didn't even break lips with Adam. Her eyes remained closed. She just raised her hand and waved, and that image—Carmen in full control, her hand conducting an audience while her mouth conducted a man—was the last viewers saw before a commercial break.

And that's when Tyler ran into the room. "You won't believe what Carmen Kelly just did," he said to Lucas, oblivious of the many times he'd been summoned to watch. "Twitter is going insane about it."

Lucas turned off the television. He was no longer feeling so relaxed.

CHAPTER 18

The next day at work, Carmen was the sole topic of conversation. Lucas couldn't bring himself to participate in the gossip fest, but he had nowhere to hide. The Internet was alight with pictures of Carmen kissing Adam. In a moment of weakness, Lucas went to *Noser* to see what people were saying on that "Screw Off!" column Tyler had launched. It was a mix of Carmen defenders and condescenders—arguments over whether she was exploiting herself or being exploited, if she was a woman in control or just desperate for attention. "Not all heroes wear capes. Some just make out on television," a person named BklynBabe wrote. Meanwhile, whoever was behind the Rogue Empire account reported that Jays was in his office stewing over the whole ordeal. Apparently, her TV appearance was as much a surprise to the Editor as it was to everyone else. "It's like the Army just obliterated ISIS," Rogue Empire wrote, "and the president only found out about it via Twitter while taking a shit in the Oval Office en suite."

Lucas had to admit: Carmen had pulled it off. By making the column about her—not them, not the magazine, just *her*—she'd turned Nice Guy into a punching bag. He now existed simply to be knocked down, like the team that always loses to the Harlem Globetrotters. He'd become a stand-in, if only because Carmen couldn't have angry sex with herself.

His one consolation was a date with Sofia, planned for that evening. And yet as he got off the train in Brooklyn, he couldn't stop constantly refreshing Twitter on his phone, where, surprise, there was nothing but Carmen, Carmen, Carmen. He entered the restaurant and found Sofia waiting for him with two dozen oysters and a pair of martinis. She seemed to have memorized the best oyster happy hours in the city—one of those small New York particulars with which Lucas had immediately fallen in love.

"Hey," he said despondently. "Can you believe the shit show?" He picked up a jiggling crustacean from the platter of crushed ice and slid it into his mouth.

"That display on TV last night was a bald-faced publicity grab, a pathetic attempt to inject some excitement and purpose into her otherwise sad little life."

Sofia's fervor took Lucas aback. Sure, she didn't like Carmen. But where had this sudden loathing come from? Was it possible that Sofia was jealous? Certainly not of Carmen's looks. But of the spotlight and attention? Sofia couldn't possibly lust after something so crude.

"What you need," Sofia continued, "is some perspective. A reminder that your life is much larger and more complex than hers. Hold on to that, my friend, and it will buffer you against disappointments large and small."

Sofia obviously had something specific in mind, but she remained tight-lipped through dinner. Afterward, a taxi whisked them to Red Hook, an industrial neighborhood on the edge of the East River. Lucas knew that hip restaurants and new condos were popping up there. But their destination was a deserted stretch of warehouses, graffitied walls, and uneven, trash-strewn cobblestones.

"I should tell you that I'm doing this because of you, Lucas. Which already makes you about a million times more interesting than Carmen."

"I d-don't understand," he stammered, shivering. It was freezing, perhaps colder given their proximity to the water. "Doing what?"

"You're the muse for my next project!" She grabbed his hand and pulled him along. There were no streetlights and Lucas stumbled after her, as unsure of his footing as he was of her intentions. And yet: *muse*. The word was romantic. Thrilling. To be named such by Sofia was almost enough to dampen his increasing anxiety. Because she was now pulling him farther into the darkness, down a narrow alley.

"I think this is it." Her phone light illuminated a door. "A street artist I know told me about this place. It should be open."

Who knew what was behind that door! Squatters, homeless people, drug dealers. Lucas scolded himself for thinking like his mother. "But how am I your muse?" he asked, stalling.

"Don't you remember? When we first met, you said you wanted to go urban exploring. That turned me on to my new series." She held up her camera bag. "It's about the contrast between factory and flesh. We're going to bring abandoned spaces to life."

"We."

"Of course," she said. "I'll give you the honor of going first." She nudged him forward.

Lucas swallowed. He did not feel comfortable about this. Not one bit. When he'd offered to join her on such an adventure, he'd been three cocktails deep into a cushy media event. He never thought he'd actually end up trespassing. But he wasn't about to give Sofia a reason to doubt him, so he pushed the door open and led them into a room that was as cold and dark as it was vast. By their phone lights, Lucas could make out long production tables and rusted machines of indeterminate purpose that hulked ominously in the corners. The air smelled strongly of wood dust. Lucas moved his light slowly around the perimeter. And then, suddenly, he cried out. Because there, propped against a wall, were rows and rows of caskets.

"You found them," Sofia said blithely. "Excellent."

Lucas's heart pounded, his body buzzing with adrenaline. "You could have told me we were breaking into a coffin factory!" he snapped. Sofia had been setting up some battery-powered lights, but she went to him and pulled him close. Her warm body and earth-like smell calmed him. "I'm sorry," he apologized. "That came out wrong."

"No one said being a muse is easy." She kissed him deeply and it was like an infusion. His heart slowed; his body relaxed. Then she handed him the camera. "Point and click," she said. "Just wait until I'm totally undressed." She scampered over to the coffins. The next thing Lucas knew, Sofia had shucked off her coat and sweater. Off went her bra, followed by her shoes and pants. "Factory versus Flesh!" she called out as her panties landed beside her.

Lucas raised the camera to his eye. There she stood, bared to the dark, beautiful before those coffins. She'd chosen *him*, of all people, as her witness and recorder. Taken *him* to the threshold of an unknown door and urged him to open it. Appointed *him* her muse. Snapping away, watching Sofia laugh at the bitter cold, Lucas saw that she'd been right earlier. He'd needed a whole new perspective on things, and now he had it.

CHAPTER 19

Lucas came into work the following day feeling as though he'd been shot up with a confidence-boosting drug. He felt invincible against anything Jays—or Carmen—might throw at him. In fact, the day unfolded as though Carmen's media stunt hadn't happened. And then, in the midafternoon, something completely unexpected happened. An email arrived, directly from the Editor. It read: "Tonight, Wild Boar. 8 P.M. Much to discuss." It was the most coveted invitation he could have received—and not to a party in the Editor's stead but to dinner with the man himself.

The Wild Boar was a restaurant on one of the most beautiful blocks in the West Village. According to Franklin, it had been Jays' first major investment a few years back and was now a kind of vassal state to *Empire*'s capital at One World Trade. It's where Jays held court; his private dining room was an after-hours office. "Nobody from the office can eat there without an invitation," Alexis had once told Lucas. "I mean, it's not illegal. It's a free country. But if Jays found out, or if you ran *into* him . . ."

"Then what?" Lucas had asked at the time.

Nobody had an answer for this, because nobody had attempted to eat at the Wild Boar without an invitation.

But when Lucas arrived, safely invited, he was not directed to the private dining room. Instead, the hostess escorted him to The Gallery, a wide balcony overlooking the restaurant's sweeping floor. From here, Lucas could look down upon the walls bedecked with Basquiats and Mondrians and Warhols—could they possibly be real? He'd been expecting taxidermy, for some reason. There was none, not discounting the stiff hair confections and shellacked faces of the wealthy patrons.

And then there was Jays, just sitting at a table. It reminded Lucas of running into his grade-school teachers after school—when they were just out in the world, shopping or eating or doing other normal-person things, no longer on the clock in the role he defined them by. The Editor was just here. Eating. It was remarkable as it was unremarkable.

"Lucas," Jays said, waving him over. "It's good of you to join us."

Lucas had been so focused on Jays that he hadn't realized there was, in fact, an *us* at the table. Jays' dining companion looked somewhat familiar; the man had thinning hair and a fake tan and extended his hand to greet him. "Jason," the man said by way of introduction, and shook Lucas's hand firmly. A thick gold band flashed on his pinky.

"Jason's an old friend," Jays said, motioning for Lucas to sit. Lucas did, and a server promptly appeared. "You drink scotch, Luke?"

Lucas nodded. Jays then nodded to the waiter. The waiter nodded back and hurried away.

"So what do you think about the Boar?" Jays asked. Lucas considered which thing to compliment in order to impress Jays the most. But in truth, he had no insight into anything.

"I love the art," Lucas ventured. Neither man reacted.

"So Jay and I were just talking about the so-called 'mole' in your office," Jason said. "You know, Rogue Empire, who keeps posting on that *Noser* message board? I was suggesting to your Dear Leader here that a crackdown may be in order."

A recent Rogue Empire post had compared Jays to the North Korean dictator. It struck Lucas as highly unfair, but Jays didn't seem to mind.

"Letting people vent is an effective way to handle employee frustration," he said. "And, anyway, I doubt Rogue Empire is actually one of our employees. It's probably J. P. Maddox himself, trying to drum up page views. Pathetic."

"But if it *is* someone on the inside," Jason said, "I'm sure your loyal friends would keep their ears to the ground?" He nodded at Lucas.

If Rogue Empire was a mole, Lucas didn't have the faintest idea who it might be. Now his heart rate spiked. How could he possibly investigate his own colleagues?

"I would never ask Lucas to snitch," Jays said, looking mortified. "Luke, I hope you know that."

"Of course." Lucas swelled with relief. Yet again, the Editor had proved his critics wrong; he was a fair and decent person.

"So, Lucas." Jason twisted his pinky ring with agitation, clearly frustrated that Jays had shot him down. "Did you see Carmen's publicity stunt?"

"It was hard to miss," Lucas said, uncertain of how critical he should be.

"That Adam kid was ugly as hell," Jason said. "I'm amazed she could stomach it."

"Which is why it went viral," Jays said, his eyes fixed on the whiskey he was swirling. "She knew exactly what she was doing."

Lucas tried to decipher the current running through Jays' voice. Was it resignation? Disgust? Admiration? A little bit of everything?

"Honestly, man, you should have kicked her curbside when you had the chance," Jason said. Then he turned to Lucas. "But your boss is a sucker for beautiful women. And Carmen is at least that."

Jason was playing all of this as a big joke, but Lucas saw Jays' eyes darken. Then the anger was gone. "Carmen's helping us sell more magazines. Can't fault her for that."

"No, sir," Jason said, and looked at Lucas for further confirmation—as though his inclusion here were completely normal.

Lucas's drink arrived along with half a dozen small plates. "I'd like to make a toast," Jays announced. "To our newest venture. The College. May it prosper and thrive."

"The College?" Lucas asked.

"Jason, would you like to explain?"

Jason was busily chewing a bacon-wrapped date. "You were born between the years of 1982 and 2004, am I right?" he asked, still chewing, his mouth open too wide. Lucas nodded. "Good." Jason swallowed and Lucas watched a grotesque lump drop down his gullet. "Now let's say you aren't just a millennial but a very wealthy millennial, with a net worth upwards of ten million."

"Yes, please keep saying that," Lucas said, thrilled to see Jays laugh.

"Now our research shows a couple of things. One: You are

educated, but you do not have a full-time profession. Two: You do not *want* a full-time profession, because it would interfere with your frequent travel, luxury consumption, and need for constant excitement—that is, ways to spend your money. Three: You are self-conscious about your wealth and the lux lifestyle you lead. The Great Recession, turmoil abroad, the widening inequality gap, the rise of social media: All of these things have made you acutely aware of your good fortune in contrast to everybody else. You're guilty because you're not a contributing member of society, even though, let's face it, you don't actually want to be one. So what's the solution?" Jason gave Lucas a moment to consider.

"Well, you mentioned college, so . . . give up some portion of your wealth to help defray the cost of student loans?" Lucas offered.

Jason and Jays looked at each other and smiled, as though to say, *Adorable!*

"The College," said Jason, "is a membership-based lifestyle brand with physical locations in six cities, on three continents, for young people of means who want to save the world. Each will include a luxury apartment complex—called the dorms— complete with a hip restaurant, a high-end bar, state-of-the-art gym and spa, and an exclusive club. As a member, you'll be able to move seamlessly between Paris and Tokyo and London and LA, meeting with like-minded individuals with equal passions for making a difference, without feeling like you're some wealthy asshole hopping between continents. Instead, you'll simply be 'going home' to the 'dorms.'"

"And we'll offer classes," Jays said. "We're still designing the curriculum, but they'll be subjects that help our members achieve their vision, such as 'How to Cultivate Your Humanitarian Brand' and 'Locavore Mixology.'"

Lucas was afraid to react. He wasn't sure if it was a joke to laugh at or a serious idea to nod at. "Each course is designed to let the student feel that he or she is doing something good for the world," Jason explained. "It's about emphasizing the larger contribution."

"So . . ." Lucas frowned. "Forgive me, but how are these members going to save the world?"

Jays smiled. "They can use their newfound passion for lo-cavore cocktails to support small-batch distillers or their humanitarian brand to raise money for a good cause. If they ever get around to it anyway."

"Oh." Now Lucas was even more confused.

"Remember, Lucas, these kids are not like you and me," Jays said. "We've struggled against significant odds to claim our place at the table. We can call our achievements our own. These kids . . ." Jays shook his head, but he was watching Lucas intently. "They don't know how to strive. They want a safe space that indulges their best impulses, but without actually demanding action from them. We can provide that. But if you don't agree, you can be honest with me, Lucas. I will respect your opinion."

Lucas tried to process all this. So was Jays . . . taking these kids seriously? Or exploiting the rich by indulging their self-obsessions? Jays certainly seemed sincere about one thing: the insurmountable divide between himself and his potential College patrons. It was extraordinary to think about the audacity required for a poor Kansas boy to believe that he could make it to the pinnacle of the empire. *These kids aren't like you and me.* And the same applied to Lucas. "You're targeting your desired audience with a message that appeals to them," Lucas finally said. "Nobody says you have to like the people you're selling to. As long as you offer what you advertise."

Jays nodded. "Very practical," he said. "I knew you'd under-stand. And here's something else that I think you'll appreciate. I'll be using funds from this venture to bolster and expand the magazine. This new source of revenue will make us less dependent on ad sales. It will allow us to build out a television studio, maybe even finance movies based on our most popular stories. There are numerous possibilities."

"It's just a question of locking down the right investors," Jason said. At this remark, Jays shot his friend a look. Jason cleared his throat. "Well," he said, "looks like you're moving into the shop talk part of the evening, so I think that's my cue to scram." He slapped Jays on the back. "Talk to you," he said. "And nice meeting you, Luke. You've got a big fan with this guy."

"Thanks," Lucas said, leaning back into his chair. He was starting to like it here at the Wild Boar.

When Jason had left, Jays folded his hands over on the table and leaned over his whiskey. He hadn't touched the appetizers, which made Lucas reluctant to continue eating, now that Jason had gone. "I asked you to join me for dinner, Luke, because I think your talents are being underutilized. I've enjoyed the short pieces you've done and your fact-checking has been excellent, but I told you a while back that I saw in you the potential for greater things. Especially with the right mentor guiding you." Jays nodded to indicate himself as precisely this man. "I've got a project for you. A magazine profile. Would you be interested in that?"

"Absolutely," Lucas said, trying to contain his excitement. "That would be amazing."

"Excellent." Jays opened one of his Milanese notebooks and tapped the page with his Lamy 2000. "The subject is an individual named Nicholas Spragg."

"Oh!" Lucas burst out. "I know him."

Jays didn't seem all that surprised. "What do you think of him?"

"He's nice but hard to get a handle on. He likes to embellish." Of course, Lucas had far more to say on the matter: That Nicholas was eccentric, uncomfortable, and at times plain weird, that he was both highly insecure and also guilelessly generous. But he didn't say any of this, because oddly, it seemed unfair to Nicholas. "We've had some interesting talks," Lucas added.

Jays made a note, and Lucas imagined him writing "interesting talks" in his tight, quick script. If Jays' notebooks contained enough references to Lucas, then decades hence might not a biographer list Lucas among the Editor's inner circle?

"I'm glad to hear that you and Nicholas have a good rapport," Jays said. "As I'm sure you know, he is poised to take over the family company. And yet, on the eve of his ascension, he flees for New York. I'd love to know why."

"You think he's running away from something?" Lucas felt his pulse quicken. Perhaps this article would establish Lucas both as a profile writer and as an investigative reporter.

"Not necessarily anything so dramatic," Jays said. "Still, I'm thinking of something like, 'The Heir to the West comes East.' Readers respond to those kinds of romantic notions."

Lucas was already responding to romantic notions of another sort. He could see the photo art, featuring Nicholas standing against a big sky backdrop with a tiny replica of the Manhattan skyline sitting in his open palm. Inside a snow globe, maybe. And of course, he could see the byline: his own. Lucas wondered if he'd get paid anything extra—he could really use the money—or if the story would be a cover.

As though reading his mind, Jays said, "If done right, this piece could really launch you, Luke. If it's got the wit and panache that I'm anticipating, you might just find yourself moving up the masthead. The staff writing pool could use some fresh blood."

"I won't let you down," Lucas said, making this promise with the conviction of his entire being. In so many ways, this article was going to be a game changer. Finally, he'd publish an article under his own name. He wouldn't just be Nice Guy; he'd be Lucas the Writer. He couldn't wait to send the issue to his family as proof of his success. Hell, once he got a raise, he'd sign his parents up for a subscription.

CHAPTER 20

Carmen was feeling good. She was renewed, re-energized, reinvigorated. Not since her early days sneaking around with Jays had she felt so empowered. Kyle Carter had been a game changer. By the next morning, the YouTube clip had racked up 1,200,000 views; within the week, she had signed with a major talent agency, which now had three separate people—one for literary, one for film, and one for media appearances—working on her behalf. There was talk of a TV show.

So now, just days after her star had shot into the stratosphere, Carmen luxuriated on a hotel bed in the Times Square Marriott and waited for Lucas. She was dressed in black lace lingerie, complete with garter belt, sheer stockings, and high heels. She was not taking the high road. She was angry, despite all her great success—not just because Lucas had hurt her, but because she had *let* him. She hated him and she hated herself a little bit and she was going to play with his head: She would make him want her so badly that he melted into a puddle of desire, confusion, and failure.

Only when Lucas arrived, he looked different, older some-how, as though he'd been airbrushed, not with makeup but with a patina of maturity. He looked, she admitted to herself, *hot*. Not that she would let this influence her in the slightest. And yet, as he stood in the doorway, he seemed less wowed by her semi-naked, tarted-up body than expected.

"You're not drunk," she said.

"Are you shooting a Victoria's Secret commercial?" he asked, ignoring her opening line. He walked toward the bed.

"I was thinking about what you said last time, about chang-ing our approach," Carmen said, trying again. "I agree."

"Really? And what changed your mind? I'd think that sud-den celebrity could go to a person's head."

Carmen tried not to roll her eyes. Men were so transparent. Even back in elementary school, she understood that the boys who teased her actually liked her.

Carmen sat up on her knees, her legs hip-distance apart, and leaned toward him. "Let's just see what happens," she said. "No stopping. No note-taking."

"I thought you'd made an executive decision that we weren't going to—"

Only he wasn't able to finish the sentence, because her mouth was now pressed against his. When she finally pulled away, he was out of breath. *Got him*, she thought. This was going to be a cinch. But before she had a chance to make her next move, he'd pulled her toward him, returning the kiss with an angry, almost smothering passion. She had not expected such an immediate or forceful response. Lucas was still kiss-ing her, moving down her neck, his left hand cupping her right breast so hard that it was starting to hurt. This was becoming a sport. Suddenly, he slipped his hand up under the bra and tweaked her nipple. She yelped. So this was how he was going to play? She grabbed his shirt and pulled him down to the bed and, before he could outmaneuver her, pinned him beneath her. She ground her lower body against his erection and suctioned her lips to his neck, but he was surprisingly stronger than his lanky frame suggested, and he quickly flipped her down onto the comforter and pinned her arms above her head. She opened her eyes and realized that Lucas's eyes were open as well. For a moment, they just stared at each other, radiating hunger and fury.

The next twenty minutes involved some of the most rapacious sex that Carmen had ever had. She couldn't even remember the exact moment in which foreplay morphed into full-on intercourse. It seemed to her, while they were fucking, that they'd always been fucking—had never *not* been fucking. This was hate sex in its purest form. Desire fueled by an impulse to destroy.

Afterward, they didn't talk or touch. It was as though they'd been to battle. And unlike last time, Lucas didn't get up and leave. He was staying, a conquistador. He still had things to prove.

Rolling to separate sides of the bed, they fell quickly into sleep.

PART TWO

CHAPTER 21

Lucas entered room 116 at the Ace Hotel. "Screw the Critics" had been running for seven weeks now, and it was paying off in ways nobody at the magazine had anticipated: Advertising pages were up 25 percent, and website traffic was up 50 percent on the strength of the columns alone. This thing wasn't just a hit; it was practically a business model. Carmen was doing regular TV appearances. And finally Jays was paying for decent digs.

As usual, Lucas and Carmen didn't greet each other in any real way. No hug hello, like friends. No kiss hello, like lovers. They were neither of those things. They were like work nemeses.

Their past few columns had been consistently hateful, though the sex, Lucas had to admit, was pretty fantastic. *Cathartic.* But the good feeling evaporated post-coitus as he considered the inevitable war of words. Carmen was a superb insult generator.

In recent weeks, she'd called him a "sweaty-palmed man-child" and said that he grunted "like a college student lugging a couch up the stairs." In turn, Lucas went for the emotional blows. "All you are is beautiful," he wrote in his last column, pleased with the poetry of meanness.

"Jays has a demand," Carmen said now. "A weekly theme."

As though on cue, there was a knock at the door. "Room service," said a voice from the hall. Carmen secreted herself in the bathroom as an Ace employee wheeled in a cart of desserts. There was a banana split. A brownie sundae. A fruit plate. Cookies. Chocolates. And, straight from the hotel kitchen's pantry, an industrial-sized bottle of chocolate sauce.

"I guess we have to eat this shit off of each other," Carmen said when they were alone.

She and Lucas looked at each other in silence and, for a moment, Lucas felt something new toward Carmen, something like camaraderie. But it didn't last. "Well, for fuck's sake," she said. "Take your shirt off."

No sooner did Lucas comply than Carmen hurled a handful of whipped cream at him. It hit his chest and splattered. It was his turn.

"Lick it off me," he said.

"No."

"I'm not going to lick it off myself."

Carmen shrugged.

"Fine." Lucas grabbed the chocolate sauce and squeezed a goopy mess of it onto his palm. "OK, then take *your* shirt off," he said, "or this shit is going all over it."

Carmen did. And with a heavy hand, just shy of smacking, Lucas smeared the chocolate across her breasts, then went to lick it off—to show her how it's done. Almost immediately, he started to gag. It was just *so much chocolate*. He swallowed, trying not to cough as the disgusting mess slid down his throat.

He looked at what was left on her body: at least three or four mouthfuls more. *No fucking way.* He stood up.

"You look ridiculous," she said, as if scolding a child.

"Well, you look like you've been in a mud-wrestling match."

This, he thought, was actually pretty fun. He pushed her onto the bed and, feeling a rush of heat in his groin, dove down like her chest was a Slip 'N Slide. Aside from the additional stickiness of their skin and the occasional mouthful of sweat, the sex that followed was the same as always: angry and impassioned.

Carmen would later write that Lucas totally botched the experiment: "Food is the trickiest test of a man's maturity," she said. "With skilled hands it's a kind of physical art. With Nice Guy's grimy paws it was like a toddler playing with finger paint."

But Lucas saw this coming and had countered: "There should have been something carnal about it, like fucking a woman who has just devoured prey. But Carmen treated our encounter like she was dining at Jean-Georges and insisting on the precise usage of fifteen different forks. Where's the fun?"

Empire was billed $4,926 for cleaning services.

CHAPTER 22

In the weeks that followed, Jays messengered an assortment of items to their hotel rooms: handcuffs and a cock ring, erotic graphic novels and a copy of the *Kama Sutra*. He had them screw in the shower, screw while watching porn, screw while using sex talk from a best-selling romance novel.

At work, a ritual had sprung up. Whenever a new column appeared, Lucas's colleagues read Carmen's best lines and zingers to one another, sometimes shouting them across the office. Lucas asked why nobody seemed interested in Nice Guy's quips and Franklin replied, "Because he's sincere, which is, like, boring."

The glee everybody took in Carmen's arrows was pure schadenfreude—exactly what she'd said about people craving judgment. But Lucas wondered if the column's popularity was really an acknowledgment that deep down everyone felt embarrassed and inadequate about sex. Maybe they were so eager to skewer the underdog because they empathized with Nice Guy.

Or maybe that was overly generous. Maybe people just sucked.

Lucas hadn't felt this bullied since middle school. Back then, his nemesis was a kid named Max Ostera. Lucas never understood why Ostera picked on him. Lucas wasn't a nerd and he wasn't competition. He was, simply, normal. But the taunting was relentless and, one day, Lucas had had enough. He couldn't remember precisely how the fight began, but soon he and Max were shoving each other on the baseball field, in front of ten other kids. Whenever Max pushed, Lucas staggered back two full steps just to keep his balance. When Lucas pushed, Max barely budged. It was an impossible matchup. Like juiced-up Barry Bonds against an eighty-year-old George Steinbrenner.

Then Max reached back for a punch. Lucas saw it coming. He could have ducked, thrown up his hands to block. Instead, he had a thought—or maybe it was more intuition, some evolutionary mode that asserted itself: *Win by losing. Take it. Take it publicly.*

The punch landed squarely on Lucas's nose. Blood erupted. Lucas fell to the ground. And then everyone rushed over to Lucas, to make sure he was OK. Max—the obnoxious thug— was suddenly isolated. He walked away, feigning victory but left all alone. And once Lucas got over the pain, he stood back up, face bloodied, and asked to be next at bat. Because he was still on the field and Max wasn't.

Now, thanks to eighth-grade Max Ostera, Lucas the adult had an idea for how to deal with Carmen.

Nice Guy,

I've had sex in many bar bathrooms. I've done it in the Uniqlo changing room. I gave a guy a blow job in the back of a taxi, and was so stealthy that the driver thought he had only one (very relaxed) passenger. A public quickie is never really about the quality of the sex. I'm damn well guaranteed not to get off. But we ladies do it because giving in to passion is terrific fun. Because the moment you think "I want to fuck that person" happens to also be the best moment to fuck that person. And because the risk of getting caught makes everything more exciting. It more than makes up for the absence of a decent O.

But here's the rub: I'm not some restaurant critic. Half the city knows what I look like, so now, when I'm out, I can feel myself being watched. My anonymity is blown. You're lucky you still have yours, Nice Guy. And so, the irony: Our challenge this week was to have a public quickie, something that's impossible, given my current notoriety. Don't get me wrong. I appreciate risk, and as my previous gentleman callers know full well, I have very little fear. But I'm also practical, and I wasn't about to parade myself out before the ogling masses.

I'm sure it was to your relief that we did it on the balcony of our hotel room. Safe. Boring. Good view, though.

How real men begin a quickie: They know that time is tight, so they double down on everything. This isn't half of a sexual liaison; it's a full one, compressed. Every kiss is harder; every grip is stronger. They push me up against a wall. They slide their hand up my chest and to my neck, the way men do when they're feeling carnal. They act as though they control my body. They don't, of course. It's all make-believe. I play the submissive, because sometimes that's hot, because the brief charade lets me get what I want out of the encounter. Unfortunately with you, I found it impossible to suspend my disbelief.

Here's what you did. Standing in the center of the balcony, you put your hands on my hips like we were at some middle-school dance. Then you kissed me. Your eyes opened occasionally to scan our surroundings—oh yes, I was checking. And then, silly boy, you asked if we should get down on the floor. And if I wanted to lie on a towel.

Now let's explore how real men get going: Clothing comes off quickly, and purposely. We just need access here. Clear a path! And then I'm being fucked. Sometimes they spin me around and we do it doggie-style, but the strongest of them just grab my legs, wrap them around their waists, and lift me up. I am pinned to a wall or a bathroom stall or a door. It is vigorous. It is not considerate. And this is how we want it—because if we felt like making love, we'd have wanted some wine and rose petals and a towel shaped like a swan. But no. We felt like fucking, and fucking cannot wait. For fuck's sake, Nice Guy! Fucking is fucking.

But you—you stripped fully naked, your dick in the wind. Optics matter, Nice Guy. The other men could fuck me in the dingiest of places—New York dive bar bathrooms are not sexy, even after three drinks—but they moved so quickly, and with such force, that I didn't care. With you, I saw it all: our sad little staging ground, you thrusting on top of me, the people in the buildings across the street going obliviously about their lives. The weather was nice, at least. And you came relatively quickly, which was also a plus. And then, mercifully, we went back inside.

Carmen,

There's a moment that haunts me. It was about two years ago, when I was dating my ex. We'd been invited to some fancy corporate party at her father's law firm—everyone in dresses and tuxes. And after both of us were a little buzzed, my girlfriend whispered in my ear, her breath hot and sweet from the alcohol: "Let's have sex in the bathroom." I was afraid, honestly. I could only imagine the shame of a security guard finding us, screaming at us, and kicking us out in front of everyone. My girlfriend felt rejected, though, and the rest of the night was awkward. I stewed on this; I was annoyed at her for forcing me into the role of the prude. Why was I the one who had to do what's right and responsible, and protect us from social disaster? But now I look back on that moment and think: What an idiot I was. You accomplish nothing by playing it safe.

I'm sure you've had quickies in many public places and will tell all our readers about how I don't measure up. But let's be clear about this one thing, at least: We were challenged this week to have a public quickie, and I suggested we sneak out some-where in the world to do it. You insisted we stay in our hotel room and just go out on the balcony. I was ready to take the risk; you backed down.

Under normal circumstances, you'd get no protest from me. In a lot of ways this column is basically every guy's fantasy: to have a beautiful woman show up, as reliably as if she'd been ordered through Amazon Prime. Let's go out on the balcony this time and have sex? Yes, let's! Yes is what I always want to say, since that time I said no. Yes to new things. Yes to chocolate sauce and handcuffs and cock rings. Yes requires more courage, but it leaves you with fewer regrets. To have gotten myself into this situation with you—to be repeatedly and viscerally insulted, and then face you anew anyway—requires a lot of yeses.

This week I'm not going to insult you, Carmen. I know the encounter was awkward. I know you wanted me to be more aggressive. The problem is, those feelings can't be faked. You'd know it in a second. Instead, I began kissing you, because that's at least something real. And doing it out on the balcony, overlooking the impossibly dense, beautiful city with the fresh air and the distant possibility that someone could see us—well, all of that reminded me just how secretive our very public relationship is. For me, that was turn-on enough.

Admittedly, the aesthetics of our aerie didn't exactly suit a softer approach to sex. The balcony had two uncomfortable-looking chairs and a dirty table. I felt bad guiding you to either. So I asked if you wanted a towel, so we could lie on the floor. You said yes. I got one. Seemed like the right call. When I have sex on the floor, I'm reminded of just how firm our bodies really are. A bed has give: When I thrust into a woman there, the downward motion is accommodated, the springs and cushions an extension of our own movements. There's none of that on the floor; it's just body on body, more raw and physical. Carmen, your body on a bed is soft. On the floor, it is firm. It feels smaller, somehow. More fragile, but also more physical. It's a turn-on. In the moment, at least, before we return to our laptops, you feel good.

When I go home after our visits, I think about you. I do. I know you think about me, too—you have to write your half of this column, which means, at least, that you have to think about why you hate me this week. But I think about your body. I think about the corners of your mouth; your lips form this perfect little wave, equally sexy and adorable, and it turns me on to think about how, in short order, those lips will be on mine again, and on my body. I think about your neck. I think about your tits. I think a lot about your tits. I've jerked off while replaying our last night in my mind. Is that embarrassing? I don't know. It's true.

What will next week bring? Who knows? You can keep lodging protests. We may both have agreed to this, although obviously that doesn't mean we have to like each other. But I'll keep saying yes. I'll keep trying to please you, because that's the goal of this game, but it's also just what I want to do. I don't like selfish sex—I'm excited more when I'm exciting the person I'm with. Exploit that how you will, I suppose. But if I said no, if I walked away from all this, I wouldn't have just had sex with a beautiful woman, overlooking the city I love. Even if I'm insulted for it, I'll still have the experience. Yes at least gives me that. Yes, I want it.

Lucas was pleased with himself. *Yes requires more courage, but it leaves you with fewer regrets.* It was good, honest stuff. And on the day it was published, he felt the need to read it again and appreciate it fresh. But now, as he pulled the column up online at his desk at work, he encountered a poll on the *Empire* website.

"Whose Side Are You On?" it read.

And then, underneath: "Perhaps you read 'Screw the Critics' some weeks and think, 'Are these people even reporting from the same bedroom?' Now it's time to keep these two honest. Each week, we're inviting you to vote for Carmen or Nice Guy. Who made the most convincing case? Who deserved the better sex? It doesn't matter what qualifications you use; it only matters that you pick a side."

Lucas laughed. The Editor must have read Nice Guy's column and felt inspired—a further sign that he and Jays understood each other. If only Jays knew. Lucas imagined revealing himself as Nice Guy one day, over glasses of bourbon. At first Jays wouldn't believe it, of course. But then he'd realize, yes, of course: *Lucas.*

There was a little poll on the screen: "Carmen or Nice Guy." Each had a clickable box next to their names. "Whose side are you on?" Lucas clicked "Nice Guy." And then the poll disappeared and was replaced with the vote tally so far. Out of 39,528 votes, 97 percent were for Nice Guy.

Lucas laughed harder.

"What's so funny?" Franklin demanded.

"Oh," Lucas said, trying to contain himself. "Nothing."

CHAPTER 23

Lucas hurried into the elevator at The Standard, avoiding the urge to look over his shoulder. Rogue Empire had posted a worrisome comment on Tyler's "Screw Off!" column: "Snuck a peek at some *Empire* expense reports and either Jay Jacobson is charging his one-night stands to the company credit card or we know where CK and NG have been hanging out. I say we post volunteer investigators at the Ace and Financial District's W hotel. Fake mustaches on me."

Lucas knew that reading "Screw Off!" only fed his anxiety, but he couldn't help himself. On the upside, reader comments had decidedly tilted in his favor this week. "Nice Guy just laid out the realest shit I've ever heard from a man, and now I'm like, where's my Prince Charming who'll say he jerks off to me?" one woman wrote. In addition, he'd won *Empire*'s readers' poll by a ridiculous margin, which was a resounding personal triumph and a public validation. But Carmen would be furious.

Be cool, he told himself. *If you can handle failure, then surely you can handle success.* He took a deep breath and went in.

"Look at this fucking thing," Carmen said before he'd even crossed fully into the room. She was sitting on a chair in the corner, holding a small object. He'd expected that upon his entrance, she would start clapping, issuing her sarcastic congratulations about the readers' poll. But clearly something else was on her mind.

"What is it?" Lucas said.

Carmen tossed it underhand at Lucas. It was an egg-shaped thing with a bunch of buttons on it and one of those U-shaped vibrators that Lucas never quite understood. Where did it go, exactly? Inside and out, like a genital clasp? Lucas looked up at Carmen. "It's a . . ."

He stopped. He had no idea what it was.

"It's a remote-control vibrator," she said. "Our new challenge."

"Oh," Lucas said.

"Jays, that sadistic fuck. He had it mailed to me from Adam & Eve. You see what he's doing here, right?"

"I . . . might . . . ?" Lucas took note: Carmen's bitterness toward Jays trumped whatever antagonistic feelings she had toward him.

"He's putting you in control. It's a *remote-control vibrator.* I wear it; you control it. God, he couldn't be more obvious."

"At least he didn't send a paddle for me to spank you with," Lucas said.

Carmen stared blankly at him.

Lucas put the vibrator on the bed. "Well, listen," he said, "this one's all you. If you don't want to do it, we can figure something else out. We can go hide the vibrator in the hotel lobby and turn it on to startle people. And then we'll just file the columns as if—"

"Yes," Carmen said.

"Yes?" Lucas said.

"Your column. Yes. It's a good theme. You got me, OK? You win. If I say no to this, then you'll have an easy line of attack and—"

"That's not what I'm going for right now, Carmen."

"Fine. Right. Whatever. Yes. Yes, I'll do it. Give me the vibrator." Carmen held out her hand. Lucas stood frozen, unsure what was expected of him. Carmen wiggled her fingers. "Seriously. Give me the vibrator."

Lucas handed it to her and she slid it inside her pants. She closed her eyes as she maneuvered it and then reopened them as she slid her now-empty hand back out.

"Turn it on," she said.

"I'm serious, Carmen. I wouldn't call you out if—"

"Turn it on."

Lucas took the remote out. What did these buttons do? There was no instruction manual. So he just hit the button on the top, which he figured was a good place to start. A small hum began in the corner of the room. He looked over at Carmen.

"A little stronger," she said.

He hit the top button twice.

"How's it feel?" he asked.

"Like a vibrator."

For lack of anything else to do, Lucas sat down in a chair clear across the room from her.

"Let's see what else it does," Lucas said, and hit one of the other buttons. The steady hum was interrupted by a pulsating rhythm—*zzt, zzt, zzt, zzt*. After a few seconds, he hit another— *zzt, zzt, zzzzzzzzzz, zzt, zzt, zzzzzzzzzzt*. He looked down at the remote, selecting the next button to push, then aimed his finger and—

"Don't change it," Carmen said. "This is good."

"Oh?"

Carmen took a deep breath. "This thing is pretty good."

"Oh."

They looked at each other. They'd had sex. They'd had lots of sex. He'd looked into her eyes during some of it, when she was willing to hold his gaze, but it always felt distant somehow. And yet this ridiculous scene right now—she, there in the corner with a vibrator in her pants, and he, clear across the room, with a confusing tablet of buttons—was the most intimately they'd ever looked at each other. He felt it. He was pretty sure she did, too.

Carmen took another deep breath. Her cheeks were getting flushed. But she was doing her best to keep a straight face.

"Do you want it more intense?" Lucas said.

"No," she said. "This is good for now. This is good. I like how this thing, um, this is good. Listen, hey." She sucked in air. "That column you wrote. That was nice."

"Oh," Lucas said, a third time now. Did he have any other words? But she kept surprising him. "Thank you. I mean, I meant it. It wasn't just some—"

"Jerk off," she said.

"Yeah." Lucas laughed. "That part is kind of embarrassing to think about now, but it's, you know, true that—"

"No," she said. "Jerk off now."

Don't say "oh" again, Lucas thought. He searched for something else. Nothing came.

"You said you do it," she said. "I want to see it."

"But I mean, that's at home."

"Are you fucking kidding?" Carmen was suddenly no longer breathing deeply; the rose on her cheeks was fading. "I'm over here with your remote-control vibrator and you can't even—"

"Y-you're right, y-you're right, y-you're right," Lucas stammered. She was right. He'd never touched himself in front of anyone else before, and he was embarrassed to do it now. But he'd opened himself up to this. *Yes, remember? "Yes" is the word.* He stood up and took his pants off. Then his underwear. He'd been fully erect since their eye contact a moment ago.

"Um, should I sit or stand?" he said.

"Whatever you fucking want," she said. The deep breathing had returned.

He stood, his penis in his right hand and remote control in the left. They watched each other. *Touching yourself in ways nobody else has seen you do—now that is intimacy.* He loved the idea that the thing he does in his bed by himself—the loneliest of acts—is actually sexy, is something a woman like Carmen desires to see. *God, this feels good.* He squeezed both his hands harder. He was breathing heavily now, breathing out of his mouth; for whatever the hell reason, as he reached orgasm he always switched from nose to mouth. Easier to heave, perhaps.

His eyes widened.

What was Carmen doing? She looked—

His eyes shut. He couldn't focus.

Release.

"Unnggh," Lucas said involuntarily.

He opened his eyes. Carmen was still sitting in her chair, but she was now holding the vibrator, which sounded like it was about to blast off to outer space. He looked at his left hand; it was gripped tightly on the remote, practically crushing it. "What the fuck!" Carmen said.

"What! What happened?"

"You cranked this thing so high that it hurt," she said. "And you didn't hear me when I told you to turn it down. And then you blew a load on the carpet."

He looked down. It was all true. Again, *Empire* would have a cleaning bill.

————

The next day, Lucas sat at his computer, trying to anticipate what Carmen would write. Was it possible that she'd be kind? Maybe, had he not gotten so carried away. His last column had actually worked—she read it, she thought about it, and she'd softened to him. But he blew it (literally), so she was guaranteed to come out swinging. And what would the readers think, with this new voting system? He won last week; he wanted to win again. But if he wrote another column admiring her and she revealed his carpet-staining bumbling, readers would turn on him. It was a prisoner's dilemma.

"You can't let go," he finally wrote into his column, resigned to the continued war. "You can't even sit back and let yourself feel good—because, I think, it would be an admission of failure. If this feels good, what else feels good? What else did you wrongly reject? Your whole persona, everything you've built your career on, is based on the piddling lie that you know what's best. But maybe that's just a lie you tell yourself."

A few days later, the columns went live online and Lucas pulled Carmen's up to see what the damage was. It started nice—talking about his last column, how perhaps she, too, should say yes more often, how it inspired her to go along with this week's column. She described them sitting across the room, staring at each other: "I felt you, Nice Guy, in a way I've never felt your body. I felt you, and it felt good." Lucas smiled slightly; so she *was* thinking the same thing he was. But he didn't want to indulge in the moment; he was sure the sharp insults were just a paragraph away. The searing exposure. His flaws reflected back at him once more, this time as he held his dick in his hand.

"Until the end—when that vibrator almost buzzed my clitoris off—you'd given me the sex of my life," she wrote, in the column's last paragraph. "It was out-of-body—I was torn between sitting in that chair, letting you control me from afar, and wanting to summon you to me so I could feel the real you as I reached my peak. But I was selfish; I wanted to ride this feeling to its conclusion, and keep watching you as I did it. And so at no fault of your own, you pushed me to the painful edge as you achieved your own climax. All in all, this was good for us, Nice Guy: We needed time apart, and we got it, and you made the most of it. We'll see what brings us together next week."

And that was it.

It was the sort of column Lucas always wanted to read from her—honest and truthful but also, most important, kind. And yet he'd miscalculated. Missed the signs. But how could he have known? What reason did he have to trust her?

His phone pinged. A text from Carmen: "So that's what I get for being nice? Noted," she wrote.

More than ten thousand readers had already voted on whose side they were on. Lucas had 87 percent of them. He wished they hated him as much as, at this moment, he hated himself.

CHAPTER 24

Sofia stood in the lobby of The Ritz-Carlton wearing a drop-waist beaded dress with a sloping back. She kissed Lucas on the cheek.

"You look handsome," she said, assessing his rented tux. The outfit, ordered from a new formalwear start-up, had set him back eighty bucks and the start-up clearly hadn't worked out the kinks. The jacket shoulders were boxy and the collar too wide. Lucas knew Sofia would notice these things, but she said nothing. Which is to say, Sofia was being generous.

"You look stunning," he said. It was a phrase he'd often heard in the movies but had never actually spoken. Certainly not to Mel. With her, he always felt restricted by his own history. Since he'd never used those words with her, he couldn't abruptly start. It would sound forced, and she'd get mad. But with Sofia, he could start over. He was now a man who gave elegant compliments. And the words were true. He could have admired her for hours—and he must have been doing so now because Sofia laughed nervously and asked if he was all right. "Never better," he said, and meant it.

This party was a badly needed hiatus from work. Lucas had never been so busy. In addition to "Screw the Critics," his dates with Sofia, and his daily fact-checking duties, he'd been submerged in the Nicholas Spragg profile that Jays assigned him. He'd managed to sit Nicholas down for a couple of formal interviews, but more often than not, he was forced to collect information by chasing his subject around the city, often with Saint Regis the dog in tow. On the nights when Lucas stayed home, he scoured the database LexisNexis (using a friend's password) for information on Nicholas's family, Kingswood Hotels, and Apex, Idaho.

Tonight he was technically on the job, but he didn't want to think of it that way. Tonight was about letting loose at the Roaring Twenties–themed fete that Nicholas was throwing for his twenty-fifth birthday. *Tonight*, thought Lucas, *we should party like people who never saw the Great Depression coming.*

The elevator doors parted and he and Sofia stepped into a sequined sea of inebriation. Flappers darted among a reef of cocktail tables, their feathered headpieces floating like fins, while schools of tuxedoed gents circled the ballroom's three oval bars. The whole room was a quick-flowing current, moving in time to a sixteen-piece jazz band. The scene looked plucked directly from the pages of Fitzgerald.

But when the host appeared, he looked dejected, sadder than Gatsby after Daisy returns to Tom. Nicholas Spragg had a trust fund that rivaled the economy of a small country, and lived in an opulent hotel. But he looked very much alone. Nobody else seemed to notice. The small group nearest was having a merry old time, toasting one another.

"He *is* ugly," Sofia whispered as she and Lucas headed over.

Lucas had given her a full accounting of Nicholas's awkward features and social ineptitude.

Nicholas saw Sofia approaching first, and his face brightened as though hit by a spotlight. Then he noticed Lucas beside her, and his excitement dimmed. Lucas let his annoyance go. Nicholas had never met Sofia, and he must have thought this stunning woman had taken a fancy to him. Spragg immediately masked his disappointment, however, and opened his arms in welcome.

"My dear friend Lucas Callahan," he announced, clearly for the group's benefit. "Superstar of *Empire Magazine.*" Lucas made to shake hands, but Nicholas pulled Lucas toward him and kissed him on each cheek. Sofia had barely managed to introduce herself before he'd done the same to her. "It's the Mediterranean style," he explained unnecessarily, not seeming to notice that the new arrivals were wiping their cheeks.

"You didn't tell me that Nicholas had Mediterranean roots," Sofia said. "My grandparents are Italian. Where's your family from?"

Nicholas looked a little confused. "No, no," he corrected. "I'm from Idaho. Or should I say that I'm a *New Yorker* by way of Idaho." He leaned toward her with grave concern. "Do you think that sounds silly? I mean do you think people"—he glanced over at the small group of well-heeled individuals nearby—"would laugh at that description?"

"Lucas is from North Carolina," Sofia said. "And I'm here by way of Connecticut. We're all immigrants to this city."

Nicholas nodded as though Sofia had just legitimized his very existence. Then he turned to the others and made a swift round of introductions. It was a strange mishmash: a hot young architect, whose name Lucas recognized from the magazine; his painter girlfriend, whose work was being shown at galleries that sounded impressive (but what the hell did Lucas know); a couple of preppy Wall Street types; a thirtysomething literary agent; and the twenty-eight-year-old CEO of a Silicon Valley start-up that had a $1.6 billion valuation, despite having yet to turn a profit. The only thing these people seemed to have in common, Lucas decided, was a mutual derision of Nicholas.

"Lucas is profiling me for *Empire*," Nicholas said. "It's going to be a cover story."

"A whole feature about Nicholas," said the literary agent. "Dax, didn't you only get like five hundred words?"

The architect glowered. "And a photo shoot."

"And Stephanie," Dax continued, "I'm really sorry about *Empire*'s review of your writer—what's his name, Anderson somebody?"

"Anderson Stedman. But nobody's reading *Empire* for book reviews." The agent flashed Lucas an obsequious smile. "No offense."

"None taken," Lucas said.

"Nicholas's story is really fascinating," Sofia said, and turned his way. "I've heard some of your history and it's so fantastic— oh, I hope I'm not embarrassing you!"

Color shot to Nicholas's ears. Lucas himself beamed with gratitude. A woman this beautiful could have been selfish and aloof. Instead, she was empathetic. She saw that Nicholas needed help, and knew just how to remold the conversation.

"Are you referring to my great-great-grandfather on my mother's side?" Nicholas asked. "He was the archetypal self-made man."

Lucas wondered if Nicolas was about to give his Bavarian/ Hungarian count/duke spiel—all of which Lucas's research had definitively debunked.

"He came from nothing," Nicolas continued. "Left his family in Missouri at the age of fifteen without a penny and trekked alone across the country. At nineteen, he founded the town that

I grew up in. He called it Apex, the pinnacle of his dreams. He built a log cabin. And today, in that exact spot, is a Kingswood hotel—the very first. There's wood in that hotel that's nearly a hundred and fifty years old. He helped erect it with his own hands—in fact, he lost his life because of it, in a terrible, tragic accident."

"What happened?" asked one of the bankers.

Lucas wondered what Nicholas was going to say. To his surprise, everything recounted thus far was supported by the historical record. During their first taped interview, Nicholas said that a grizzly bear had come out of the woods and mauled his great-great-grandfather to death. Another time, Great-great-grandfather Spragg was high atop the building in a thunderstorm and struck by lightning. When Lucas had raised this discrepancy, Nicholas shook his head with force. "It was absolutely, one hundred percent lightning," he'd said. "I can show you the death certificate." When Lucas followed up, Nicholas said the document was in Apex but could be accessed "shortly." It had not materialized.

To Lucas's amazement, if not quite his surprise, Nicholas was now giving everyone a wholly different tale.

"It was vital to my great-great-grandfather that he and his sons worked with the laborers on every part of the hotel's construction. But there was a problem with the rigging on the crane. It snapped and a giant log crashed down. My great-great grandfather was crushed. Afterward, he was buried outside the hotel. A plaque lets all guests know that they are walking on hallowed ground. My great-grandfather was only ten at the time of his father's death, but from that moment he, too, insisted on helping to build the rest of the hotel with his own bare hands."

"He wasn't crushed by any falling beams?" the architect asked, barely masking his sarcasm.

"Oh no." Nicholas shook his head with complete sincerity.

"He was killed in a duel over his mistress. It's actually something of a family scandal."

It was true, Lucas had read, that the great-great-grandfather was interred in the front walkway, but he'd died of a heart attack at the age of eighty-three. As for the great-grandfather, his death was attributed to lung cancer at the age of fifty-five. There was no public record of a mistress.

"So no other deaths by duel then?" the painter said, glancing sidelong at the architect, who, in turn, rolled his eyes.

"This is all pretty fascinating," said the agent. She, unlike the rest, seemed genuinely intrigued. That or she was paying the toll of attending his party. Lucas couldn't tell.

"Now, if you'll all excuse me, I've got to get my friends Lucas and Sofia a drink." At that, he turned on his spit-shined heels and pulled them away.

The band had gone on break and the guests encircled the three bars, pressing forward, four and five people deep. The bartenders looked a little fearful, like they were under assault. For his part, Nicholas looked downcast.

"What's the matter?" Lucas asked. "Everyone seems to be having fun."

"Perhaps so," Nicholas said again. "It's just that—I'm not sure any of these people like me very much."

Lucas and Sofia looked at each other. He wasn't so oblivious after all. Lucas felt a twinge of sympathy for Nicholas Spragg. Ignorance, for all its downsides, surely beat whatever state he truly lived in.

"Why would you say that?" Sofia asked.

"They don't seem to like my stories. I've worked hard on them, you know."

"So some of that stuff is . . . made up?" Sofia asked gently. Lucas knew she was the only person in the room who could have gotten away with such a question.

"Well, yes," Nicholas said.

Lucas was stunned. Did Nicholas not realize that this admission could be printed in the magazine? Was he too drunk to care? He didn't seem intoxicated. In fact, he seemed quite sober. He must have seen the perplexed look on Lucas's face.

"I know it's a, well, shall we say *unconventional* approach to one's biography. But I'm reinventing myself, you understand. I certainly couldn't have done that in Idaho, where everyone has known me since birth. Here you can be anything."

Nicholas's face expressed a mix of hopefulness and disappointment, and Lucas realized how cruel it would be to expose his subject's naïve and fragile dream. Especially since Lucas was doing something similar. He just wasn't so explicit about it.

"Why not reinvent yourself a little less dramatically?" Sofia asked. "See how that goes over?"

"Or just be who you are," Lucas offered.

Nicholas observed the rollicking, flapper-outfitted crowd. "The city—it's like this party, you know. You come here with an idea of who you want to be, you throw yourself into that idea, and eventually, it's who you become. I guess I haven't hit on the right idea yet—the one people will really like. I didn't think it would be so difficult." Nicholas drained the rest of his champagne. "Well, I'm going to be a good host," he said. "Sofia, it was lovely to meet you—and please stay, because there's much more to come this evening." He kissed her on the cheek and, as he shook Lucas's hand, Sofia wiped her cheek for a second time. Then Nicholas allowed himself to be swallowed into the crowd.

Lucas turned to Sofia. "Thank you for being so kind to him. You're really amazing."

"It's nothing," she said, but glanced away, as though evading his adoring gaze.

"Listen, Sofia . . . ," Lucas said, taking her hands. "I wanted to talk to you about something." He hadn't planned on broaching the subject of their relationship—certainly not right here. But something about the party, and Sofia's kindness and even Nicholas's own dissatisfaction, had stirred him to action. Lucas wanted to be real. He wanted to be up-front: They never talked about Carmen anymore or the columns. Not since the night of the casket factory. And surely that meant something. "I really like you," he said. "I was thinking that we should make this—"

He was going to say *official*. But the band cut in, kicking off its second set with an abrupt cymbal crash. The horn section jumped headlong into a raucous, freewheeling Charleston.

"We should make what what?" Sofia bellowed.

"Official!" Lucas yelled, not quite hearing her.

"What do you mean?"

"You and me!" He smiled.

"What?" she shouted, possibly pretending not to have heard him.

But before he could answer, a waiter appeared, as though from thin air, proffering Lucas an envelope with his white gloves. "For you and the lady," the waiter said into Lucas's ear. Lucas opened the envelope and removed a piece of thick card stock. Inside, printed in gold, was a suite number and a time—"12:07 A.M."

"Mysterious," Sofia said. "And oddly specific." She checked her watch; they had eight minutes. "We better get going," she said, and turned toward the ballroom doors. Lucas had the uncomfortable feeling that she was anxious to get away.

The suite was lavish. Everything was braided and brocaded. There were two bars, one of them exclusively for shellfish. The other was devoted to whiskeys, along with a full array of muddled fruits. Women in fishnets and bustiers strutted through the room, offering cigars and chocolates. A magician in a top hat pulled coins from people's ears.

Some of the women had discarded their heels. Gratefully, Sofia slipped off her shoes and slid her stocking feet along the velveteen carpet. Spragg, upon seeing them, bounded over. "Welcome!" He'd undergone a rapid transformation. The earlier gloom had lifted and now everything was wonderful. "Welcome to the Extraordinary Society!" he exclaimed, and began to point out the luminaries: the CEO of a cosmetics company, an award-winning physicist, a poet who had recently been published in the *New Yorker*. In the far corner the drummer for a quickly rising indie band chatted with the winner of a popular reality show and the producer of a late-night comedy program. There was even a woman Nicholas described as a "former princess," which filled Lucas with questions. "Former" sounded far more interesting than "princess." But he dared not ask. He sensed that the glittering monument Nicholas had constructed inside this hotel suite could not withstand even the mildest of wind gusts.

"I'm flattered that you think I'm extraordinary," Lucas said.

Nicholas squeezed Lucas's arm, but he was looking at Sofia. "Now I have to prepare for the big event. Please, drink something!"

As they headed toward the bar, Lucas spotted Katie, the socialite from the love hotel. She was sitting on a window seat across the room, leaning seductively toward a man in a velvet tuxedo. He'd never gotten a full answer to what had really happened that night. "You seemed to be having a delightful time," was all Nicholas would offer when Lucas had asked a few weeks later. And now Lucas felt slightly excited, but mostly terrified, to be in the same room with a beautiful woman he had (probably?) recently slept with and the beautiful woman with whom he was (definitely) currently sleeping. Would he have to introduce Katie and Sofia to each other? What would happen if he did? But these questions resolved themselves; the second he caught Katie's eye, she looked away as though she didn't know him.

Sofia tapped Lucas on the shoulder. "Isn't that Jay Jacobson?" she asked.

Sure enough, Jays strode through the door, surveying the party as though he were its host. Whatever doubts Lucas held about the authenticity of Nicholas's "Extraordinary Society" now dissolved. If Jays had come, it meant that people must be starting to recognize Nicholas as a maker of taste, or at least a respectable and credible social linchpin. Maybe the circle of naysayers from earlier were simply bitter for not being invited in.

Sofia was staring at the Editor. Ogling, really. It annoyed Lucas, but he couldn't blame her. Jays was a strapping specimen. And he walked right over to them as though no one else at the party existed.

"Of course you'd be here," Jays said, shaking Lucas's hand. "On the job at all hours. And who have we here?"

"This is Sofia, my girlfriend." This wasn't the first time that Lucas had introduced Sofia as his girlfriend—it was part of his cover after all. And yet this time, the words caught in his throat.

"Hello," she said happily. She was so easy. So much easier than Lucas could ever be. "It's lovely to meet you." She reached out her hand.

Jays glanced at Lucas, clearly impressed.

"Young love," Jays said, observing Lucas's nervous smile.

"You're not making fun of us, I hope?" Sofia said, raising a fulsome eyebrow.

"Certainly not!" Jays put his hand over his heart. "In fact, I think we should make a toast. To you," Jays said, glancing at

Lucas, "and you," lingering longer on Sofia, "and maybe to me as well, but not the rest of these self-important assholes in here."

Sofia laughed, basking in Jays' smile. "To us," she said, and tapped her glass against Jays'. Lucas brought his own glass up quickly, feeling like the moment had somehow, nearly, passed him by.

But a new moment was tumbling forward. "Ladies and gentlemen!" Nicholas threw open the French doors between the living room and bedroom and stepped through them like the master of ceremonies at a three-ring circus. He had exchanged his black tux for a white one with tails. "I have invited you to celebrate with me, because you are all extraordinary people. Each and every one of you is outstanding in your intelligence, your creativity, your style, your wit. It is my great honor to share this extraordinary evening with you. Please, raise a glass of Moët and Chandon Bi Centenary Cuvée Dry Imperial—1943!"

"This champagne is seventy years old?" Sofia whispered, lifting two glasses from a passing server and handing one to Lucas. "Are you sure it's safe?" Her eyes seemed to laugh and Lucas felt a powerful urge to kiss her, right there, in front of everyone, including Jays. *Especially* Jays. He even leaned his head forward, but Sofia raised her glass, almost preemptively, and took a long sip. Lucas felt a hard knot clench in his stomach, but he didn't have time to poke at it because now three cigarette girls were wheeling in a gigantic cake. It was the size of a small table, three tiered and frosted with ribbons and flowers, sparklers blazing all around. "Do you think there's a stripper in there?" Sofia asked. "I don't know whether I'd be horrified or delighted."

Lucas felt the same way. It was over-the-top but thrilling in its ostentatiousness. He felt, as he watched the cigarette girls roll the cumbersome, glorious cake to the center of the room, that he was seeing the opening of his story unfold before his very eyes.

"In celebration of my twenty-fifth birthday, I wanted to give something back to all of you," Nicholas said. "To show my immense gratitude. To make this evening truly Capital."

A man with a snare drum appeared and produced a drum roll. Lucas wondered whether he should prepare to shield Sofia from an explosion. The sparklers were burning down.

And then—

BOOM!

The air was a blizzard of confetti. But something else—something heavier and wider—had been launched into the atmosphere. The room filled with a familiar inky smell. Sofia reached out and plucked an object from the air: A one-hundred-dollar bill. All around them, money. Cash. Twenties, fifties, and hundreds, crisp and pristine. Lucas and the other guests stood transfixed amidst a blizzard of green and white. Then the reality of the thing registered. A mountain of money had just erupted in the room. Money for all. Money for nothing. Money for the taking.

And then, chaos.

Lucas was pushed and jostled by the stampeding partygoers behind him. These people had money. These people did not *need* money. And yet. He and Sofia finally edged their way to safety behind the raw bar—the bartender having abandoned his post to join the mêlée. From here they could observe the incredible scene—these tastemakers and executives and even a possible (former?) princess stuffing cash into their pockets and purses. Sofia began to take pictures. Lucas caught the eye of a cigarette girl, surreptitiously stuffing money into her bustier. All the while, Nicholas cheered them on. He seemed almost manic, watching his well-heeled guests crawling on the floor, reaching under chairs and rooting between cushions.

Lucas saw that not everyone had been consumed by the insanity. Jays stood against the wall, his arms folded across his chest. He caught Lucas's eye and shook his head. Lucas felt the flush of recognition, of camaraderie, though in truth Lucas had been hoping to find a couple of bills that had just happened to land in his vicinity. Bills he could swiftly tuck away. Unlike most of these people, he actually needed an infusion. He was barely making his loan payments. (Tyler, having caught wind of the situation, was now overstocking their fridge.) But in the company of Jays, Lucas was forced to stand idly by.

After every bill had been collected and the cake was rolled away, the party resumed. But everything felt different. There was a palpable awkwardness, like waking up after a one-night stand and thinking: *Now I have to live with this thing.* People seemed eager to flee, to forget how they'd come by the cash in their pockets, to mix it with less shameful dollars. But they knew it was rude to go this soon. And so the party dragged on, crankily, until finally guests began sneaking out. Sofia said she was tired. "Of course," Lucas said. "Let me just say good-bye to Nicholas." But she assured him that he should stay. "I don't want to be a drag," she said. "It's still early."

"Oh, but I don't mind," he said softly, and interlaced his fingers through her own. "I've been wanting to take you home from the moment I saw you. No lesson," he said. "Just fun."

Sofia frowned. "But I really am tired," she said.

"Oh. OK. But things really are winding down. Let me just say good night to Nicholas and we'll head out."

Sofia seemed like she was about to object, but Lucas turned from her before she had the chance. He felt an uncomfortable vibrating sensation along the top of his scalp, a kind of buzzing. Maybe it was nothing. Maybe she really was tired.

Someone had seen Nicholas go into the bedroom, so Lucas went in. It was empty, so he followed a short hallway toward a dressing room. As he neared the door, he heard talking. The voices were slightly agitated. Rounding the corner, he nearly crashed into Jays, who was hurrying toward him.

"Lucas," the Editor said, stopping short. "You're looking for Nicholas?"

"Yes, is he . . . ?"

Jays nodded. "In the back." He leaned forward a little too close. His face was flushed, his breath sharp with scotch. "You're making progress with the profile, Luke?"

"Terrific progress."

"Good, good. Just keep observing, taking notes, digging in. That's what makes a story come alive." His eyes shone. "Spare no detail, my friend."

"Not a thing. I promise," said Lucas. Then he opened the dressing room door.

"I told you I didn't want—" Nicholas said sharply as he sat up and wiped his nose.

"I didn't mean to interrupt."

"Nonsense. Luke, come in! I thought you were someone else. Would you like some?" He indicated the paraphernalia and white powder on the counter.

Lucas shook his head.

"I suppose I should ask you not to put this in the story. And while we're on the subject—the love hotel? It goes without saying that's off-the-record, too." He flashed an ingratiating smile.

"Oh yeah, sure," Lucas said.

"It's not really a habit or anything," Spragg continued.

"Of course not," Lucas replied, but now that Spragg had brought up the love hotel, Lucas was needled by how Katie had ignored him earlier. He shouldn't say anything, but the question was like an itch, and he had to scratch it. "So . . . I saw Katie earlier."

"Who?" Spragg squinted as though Lucas was out of focus.

"Katie, the socialite from the love hotel. She kind of blatantly ignored me."

"Well, she's probably with a client," Nicholas said. "Professional courtesy."

"What do you mean?" Lucas said. But he knew, in that moment, exactly what it meant. He felt dumbstruck, unable to speak. He watched Nicholas do another line. He no longer felt like saying good night or thanking Nicholas for his hospitality. But he forced himself to do it.

"Impossible," said Nicholas. "The night is young."

"Sofia's tired."

"I hoped she'd stay." Nicholas sounded like he was blaming Lucas for her departure. "She's an extraordinary woman. Beautiful. Intelligent. Kind. Are you smitten?"

Lucas wouldn't have thought to use such a flowery word, but it was dead accurate. His heart swelled.

"You are!" Nicholas exclaimed. "You're positively full of her."

"Well, I—" Lucas was growing embarrassed.

"No, you are. It's apparent. Though honestly, I don't know how you managed to persuade her."

"I'm sorry?"

"Well, the other men here tonight, men like Jay Jacobson, they have that innate confidence and charm. Men like us . . ."

"Men like us?" All this time, Nicholas hadn't been looking up to Lucas; he'd seen something of himself reflected *in* Lucas.

"You're not offended, are you?" Spragg said. He looked genuinely concerned, as though the possibility of offense had only just occurred to him. As though he hadn't just admitted to lying about Katie and Corinne. Though had he lied about them?

Or was Lucas just exceptionally stupid? It should have been obvious all along. "We're friends, aren't we?" Nicholas asked.

No. But that was the wrong answer. That answer meant his magazine profile would be finished. "Yes," Lucas said.

"I hoped so!"

Lucas was almost frantic to be gone from this place, from Nicholas. He yearned for his small, shabby apartment. For the real world. "I'll see you Monday for our interview," he said.

"Of course," Nicholas replied. "I wouldn't miss it." He turned back to the vanity and began preparing another line.

When Lucas returned to the party he couldn't find Sofia anywhere. By now, the room held only a smattering of people, drunkenly sprawled on the couches and propped up against walls. The oyster bar was being packed up. The whiskeys and champagne looked pillaged, like the bar at a college frat. Lucas's phone buzzed in his pocket. "Looked for you and couldn't find you," she texted. "In a cab home, headache. Thanks for a fun night."

"I hope you feel better!" he typed, hoping to seem upbeat and nonchalant. "Will call you tomorrow."

He waited a moment for her response. None came.

A caterer wheeled away the oyster bar, and Lucas spotted a twenty-dollar bill that must have fluttered underneath. He hurried over and grabbed it.

CHAPTER 25

The next morning Lucas woke up alone. He wasn't hungover, but the evening had left him feeling heavy and dull. It wasn't just because of the revelation that he'd slept with a prostitute. Or Nicholas's insults. Or even the grossness of the money cake. It was Sofia: They'd been so happy, drinking and dancing. And then it had all turned sour, because he couldn't leave a good thing alone. He needed to hear from her, to know that they were all right, that something vital had not been ruined. But when he looked at his inbox, a whole other mess was there waiting for him.

It was from that architect who not-so-subtly mocked Nicholas Spragg last night. Subject line: "Between us."

"I don't know what kind of story you're doing about Nicholas," the guy wrote, "but if you're interested in more than pandering fluff, I'd suggest looking into Spragg's college career. My best friend's sister says he sexually assaulted a girl and then paid her to keep quiet."

Lucas sat with that for a second. *Shit.*

After the way last night ended, he wasn't sure what to think of Nicholas. The guy was much seedier than he'd thought. And weirder. And creepier! But a rapist? That seemed hard to—

Lucas stopped himself. *This is how rapists get away with it,* he thought. *Nobody's willing to believe that the guy they know is a rapist.* And yet why would Nicholas rape someone when he clearly had no hang-ups about just paying someone for sex? Wouldn't that just be—

Lucas stopped himself. He was doing it again. He couldn't just excuse this information away. Even if it came from the sister of a friend of a guy whom Lucas had met for thirty seconds at a party—which seemed like a pretty weak link, to be honest, especially considering that said guy had shown up to eat Spragg's food and drink his booze but hadn't exactly shouted "rapist!" while doing it. In which case, maybe this architect dude was just sour that he didn't get invited into the after party and—

He had to stop making excuses. He sat up in bed and looked out the window at the windy street below. He was the one person who'd given Nicholas the benefit of the doubt, despite all the kid's posturing and fabrications. No more. He had to take this seriously—as a man, certainly, but also as a journalist. He was going to follow up on the accusation. Jays himself had ordered Lucas to spare no detail. And if the rumor was true and Lucas missed it and he ended up writing a puff piece about a man who turned out to be a rapist, his career would be over before it even began.

Jays asked no questions when Lucas approached him on Monday and asked to take a last-minute trip to Wisconsin. "Whatever you need," the Editor said. "I'm sure what you're chasing is important."

The next day, Lucas landed in Milwaukee. The minute the plane touched down, Lucas checked his phone. Nothing from Sofia. He'd sent a casual text the day before asking if she wanted to have dinner, and she hadn't responded until well past dinnertime, thanking him for the invitation. He'd heard nothing from her since. There was that vibrating sensation in the top of his head again. He wondered if he had a brain tumor, if something was seriously wrong with him. But the feeling was not omnipresent. In fact, it seemed to strike mainly when he checked his phone and found his inbox empty.

Lucas picked up his rental car and began the hour-long drive to Nicholas's college. Icy snowdrifts pocked the median, and the cars around him were so dirty, they seemed to have all driven through mud pits. He'd promised himself not to check his phone until he reached his destination, but over bad pizza at a highway rest stop he couldn't help himself. As he already knew, she hadn't written. Maybe Sofia was just busy. Or grappling with her own intense feelings for him. Or maybe it was nothing at all. He pulled back onto the highway.

The architect's best friend's sister told Lucas that Nicholas Spragg had allegedly assaulted a girl named Sara Porter three years ago on the eve of his graduation. Porter was now a senior, but her online footprint contained just a single photograph on her sorority website. She was cute: petite, brown haired, button nose, nice smile. Over the phone, the sorority president said Sara Porter had quit two years earlier. Lucas asked if he could meet with any of her old friends. The president hesitated, then said one of the sorority's university-mandated career talks had just fallen through. If he'd fill the slot, she'd try to help him.

At Kappa Alpha Theta a young woman in flannel pajamas, a sorority sweatshirt, and clotted mascara opened the door.

Lucas stepped inside, plunging into a sea of femininity. Upwards of fifty young women sprawled about in the house's spacious living room. They sat on couches, on overstuffed chairs, on the floor, most of them dressed in KAT paraphernalia. Standing there, Lucas recalled those many nights he'd visited Mel at her sorority house, grabbing her hand as she hurried him up to her tiny third-floor bedroom. Once safely tucked away, they would hook up to the same Sarah McLachlan playlist.

The KAT president was a senior named Jamie, a woman whose smile had the force of a battering ram. She introduced Lucas to the room and said he'd come all the way from New York City to answer their questions about magazines.

"Do you know Anna Wintour?" one of the girls asked.

"Um, no, sorry," Lucas said.

He watched the collective sisters go from disinterested to actively annoyed. He tried to impress them with tales of booze events—all the free alcohol and no commitment to coverage! But this didn't register; the girls in this room were living a nonstop booze event already. Finally, somebody asked Lucas what he made. His answer more or less shut down the conversation.

Afterward, Jamie led Lucas into a library at the back of the house where another sorority sister was waiting. "This is Amber. She used to be friends with Sara."

"Was?" Lucas asked.

Amber glanced at Jamie, clearly uncomfortable. Jamie nodded. *Let's just get this over with.*

"I've got a class with her this year," Amber said. "But we don't really talk anymore. It's awkward. Because I was with her the night the whole thing happened with Nicholas."

Lucas took out his recorder and asked Amber to start from the beginning.

"The first thing you should know," she said, "is that Sara

was always really nice to Nicholas. Significantly nicer than the rest of the house."

"The whole house knew him?"

Amber and Jamie exchanged looks. Jamie stood up. "I'd rather pretend this conversation wasn't happening," she said, and left the room.

"When Sara and I were freshmen," Amber resumed, "Nicholas started hanging around. He dated like a quarter of the house. Or tried to."

"Tried?"

"Oh, you know, wooing them. He'd take girls out to fancy dinners, buy them things, send them flowers. He became a total joke, but nobody wanted it to stop exactly. He once hired a fancy spa in town to come out and give free manicures and blowouts. It was insane."

"But why?"

"He wanted a girlfriend. But he was, like, trying to buy one. It didn't seem to matter much who the girl was. People said he was a virgin—at twenty-two! I mean Jesus, just hire a Pretty Woman. It's not like he didn't have the money."

"Do you know if he tried paying anyone for sex?"

"That's not what Nicholas was about. He'd often tell Sara that he was a total romantic. He wanted to sweep women off their feet. Be their Prince Charming. It felt desperate, not sleazy."

"And nobody obliged?"

"Lord no."

"But you all encouraged him."

"Sara in particular thought we were stringing him along. I still don't understand why she sympathized. These girls aren't poor and it's not like a boy had never sent them flowers or fancy jewelry before. But Sara was one of the few who came from, I guess, more modest circumstances. She had loans. That set her apart. And I remember one of the girls, a senior at the time, saying that if Sara really felt bad for Nicholas, then she should go out with him. Stop complaining about how everybody else was taking advantage of the guy and actually help him."

"So Sara went?" Lucas asked.

"Well, she agreed to a date on the condition that Nicholas not give her anything. They went out a few times. Ultimately, Sara decided what the rest of us had known all along: Half of what Nicholas said was blown out of his ass and the other half was pompous as hell. And on top of that, he lacked basic inter-personal skills."

"I'm assuming she broke it off?"

Amber nodded. "It was spring fling weekend and we were having a big party. Nicholas was totally coked up. He's disgust-ingly nice until he gets high. Then all that ingratiating bullshit flies out the window. Anyway, they went to her room to talk. She wanted to dump him in a dignified fashion. But her rejec-tion really hurt him, I think because she'd actually gotten to know him."

"So he . . . ?" Lucas couldn't bring himself to finish the thought aloud.

"All I know is, the next morning Sara banged on my door. She said Nicholas had assaulted her the night before and we needed to go to the police. I took her to the station and she filed a report. But then she called the cops later and said she didn't want to press charges. I tried to find out more, but she just clammed up. Everything was different after that. She quit the house, stopped talking to us. It was like she blamed us for what had hap-pened. I kept trying to check up on her, but she ghosted me."

The next morning Lucas went to the local precinct and re-quested a copy of Sara's report. He didn't have high hopes for it turning up, but to his surprise, it was still there. Getting rid of such a document apparently required more effort than simply forgetting about it. And there, in plain English, was a detailed description of what had purportedly happened between Sara Porter and Nicholas Spragg. He'd shoved her on a bed, grabbed her breasts, and tried taking her pants off. She kicked him away and bolted to the door.

Lucas took a deep breath. That report was pretty clear.

After the police department, Lucas went to the seminar room where Amber said Sara Porter had class. Amber came out first. She and Lucas exchanged glances and then she quickly disappeared into the crowd of exiting students. Sara emerged and Lucas followed her into the quad. She was smaller than he'd expected and dressed in sneakers and a parka. It was obvious that she'd left the sorority fold.

Lucas had never done any reporting like this. Hell, he'd barely ever approached someone and introduced himself as a reporter, let alone a possible sexual assault victim. He was nervous; his hands shook. Was this even ethical? He wasn't sure. But other magazine stories revealed sexual assaults, so what did those reporters do? "Hello, I'm a reporter," he said to himself. "I'm a reporter I'm a reporter I'm a reporter."

He walked a little faster and caught up with Sara. "Hello, I'm a reporter," he said, and immediately realized this could not be what real reporters said. It just sounded so stupid.

Sara stopped walking. "Um, OK," she said.

Lucas plowed ahead, explaining that he worked for *Empire* and was writing a story about Nicholas Spragg. She stiffened visibly at the name.

"What do you want?" she said, now clearly more nervous than him.

He told her about the profile, about the police report. He wanted to verify the facts, get more of her story.

"You're going to mention me?" She looked frightened.

Lucas felt bad, but it was too late to turn back. He wondered if he could appeal to her on the basis of kinship. They'd both belonged to Greek houses where they didn't quite fit. Surely, like him, Sara was financially strapped. And why should the rich and powerful get to dictate everything? He felt himself channeling Jays' indignation—which was quickly becoming his own. It wasn't fair.

"Why'd you let some rich kid get away with it?" he asked. "Why not press charges?"

Sara looked through the trees on the quad. A light rain was starting to fall. "Don't write that I talked to you," she said. "You will fuck me up so hard if you do."

She waited for Lucas to nod. Reluctantly, he did.

"The irony," she continued, "is that if he'd actually managed to rape me—if I hadn't gotten away—I could have been tested. Instead, it was his word against mine. And he has money and lawyers."

"But people need to know, Sara. What if he tries this again? Maybe he already has."

She shook her head. "I can't."

"Is there . . . some other reason you didn't press charges?" Lucas asked as gently as he could, remembering the architect's email. "Is it because he paid you?"

Her face went white. "Who told you that?"

"It's what I heard. Look, I get it. I have a lot of loans. I know how it is."

"A check arrived, OK? But there was no threatening letter, no bribe. The money basically dropped from the sky."

Lucas thought of the cake exploding hundred-dollar bills.

"And if you really 'get it,'" she scoffed, "then you get what it means to be debt-free. Now leave me the fuck alone."

CHAPTER 26

That night, Sofia finally called. "Sorry I've been MIA," she said.

"Oh, it's OK. Work. I totally understand." He tried to sound nonchalant. If he pretended that everything was fine, then maybe it would be. "Sof, you won't believe what I've found out about Nicholas," he pressed on. "I'm in Wisconsin right now, flying home tomorrow. I can't believe how gullible I've been, thinking that he was just misunderstood, thinking that he—"

"Luke, we need to talk."

"OK."

"This is getting to be too much."

"What do you mean?" The prickling sensation was coming on full force, the top of his scalp hijacked by bees.

"I told you at the outset that I wasn't looking for a relationship. But I think your feelings have changed."

"OK?"

"Mine haven't."

"OK."

"Say something more than 'OK.'"

But Lucas couldn't speak.

"It's been amazing spending all of this time with you. But we're not on the same page. . . ."

"If being together is amazing, why stop?"

"Because it's not real."

Lucas felt everything spin. Not real? He had a vision of Sofia in the abandoned casket factory, shivering and smiling as she posed for him. *You're my muse, Lucas.* "How can you possibly say that, after everything we've shared?"

"Lucas—"

Yes, they'd been playacting at first. But over time, that had changed. If only he'd kept his mouth shut at Nicholas's party, they could have gone on as before. And then one day, Sofia would realize that there was no distinguishing the fantasy from the reality. Instead, in the spirit of open communication, he'd been honest with her. And that honesty had forced Sofia to make a real-world—as opposed to a pretend-world—decision.

"You're deluding yourself," he said now. "You're scared to admit the truth."

"That's extremely patronizing," she replied. "Telling me I don't know myself. However this feels to you, Lucas, it's not like that for me. I'm sorry. I thought you understood. I thought you could handle this kind of relationship. But you haven't been single for very long. It makes sense that you'd grow attached."

"And you call me patronizing?"

There was a pause. "I'm sorry," she said. "That wasn't nice."

Lucas snorted. *Nice.* Like they were kids on the playground.

"Look," she said. "You don't need me anymore. Your columns have been great. You've got Carmen on the defensive."

"I don't care about the fucking columns!"

"I'm sorry," she repeated, but meekly as though shrinking from his outburst.

Something occurred to him. "How long have you known I had feelings for you?"

She said nothing. His head was buzzing so badly, he wanted to scratch his scalp off.

"How long, Sofia!"

Silence.

So it had been weeks, if not months. "You knew how I felt and you strung me along, letting me hope? Why would you do that? You want to talk about nice? *That* wasn't nice."

"We were having fun," she said. She sounded defensive. "*You* were having fun."

"I was falling in love with you and you let it happen!" Lucas heard her start to protest, but he quickly ended the call and threw his phone on the bed. All along he thought he'd been competing with Carmen. But she was not his adversary. She wasn't some formidable foe he needed to vanquish. Sofia was right. He was handicapped by his own vulnerability. He'd learned how to have great sex—so what? What was the point, if that's all it was? That knowledge didn't seem so important up against his emotional shortcomings, especially the lack of armor around his heart.

CHAPTER 27

A week later, Lucas was back on an airplane and flying to North Carolina for Christmas. He'd made the decision to return weeks ago, when life was splendid and he was eager to showcase his success. Now he was too depressed to gloat. In the past week, he'd lost his not-quite-girlfriend, Carmen had called him "a frozen toaster strudel with a penis" in the magazine, and his big story seemed to be falling apart. The moment Lucas broached the subject of Nicholas's college career, Spragg had suddenly, suspiciously disappeared. It was only now that Lucas realized how much he'd wanted to believe *in* Nicholas (if not exactly believe him). He'd admired the guy's determination, his romantic Gatsby-esque notions as contrasted with his cynical, churlish peers. But Lucas had it backward. Nicholas wasn't Gatsby. He was Daisy and Tom. Careless and selfish, shielded by his money.

Lucas's older brother picked him up from the airport. Sam

was a louder, larger, blonder version of Lucas and invariably southern. During the week, he ran marketing for their father's car dealership. On the weekends, he participated in "man club," in which he and his friends drank cheap beer and messed around with power tools. Lucas had always considered his brother remarkable. He was so content with his abilities, his prospects. It wasn't a good life that led to Sam's happiness but the other way around. Around Sam, Lucas couldn't help but wonder if his ambition was a sickness. If only he'd inoculated himself—married Mel and become a tax lawyer—maybe he'd be content, too.

"You should know," Sam said as they drove home, "that Mom is freaking out about you. Those sex columns where the people review each other have her up in arms."

"I'm aware of them, obviously."

"Right. Well, she's worried that your association with that magazine might affect your future job prospects. Even your next law-school application."

"The depths of her delusion are astounding."

"So you won't give up the magazine and come home?" he asked.

"You're not serious?"

"Don't shoot the messenger, Bro. I promised her I'd ask."

Theirs was a tony suburb, though the Callahans had barely managed to squeeze themselves into the zip code. A portion of their backyard actually fell over the town line. This didn't affect their school district or their bragging rights. And yet Lucas had long wondered whether this part of the yard— overgrown with ivy, the fence starting to rot—was left untended due to negligence or protest. Either way, he saw that corner as a symbol: Despite his parents' ceaseless efforts to cultivate

a perfect picture of Charlotte society, no amount of horticul-
tural finesse could pull up those thick middle-class roots. His
parents—his mother especially—were constantly on edge
about their finances, the mortgage, the property taxes. In short,
their place in the world.

Entering the house, Lucas was struck by the polished floors,
grime-free windows, and dustless corners. His parents might
be on financially precarious footing, but their kitchen had cab-
inets for miles, filled with all manner of foodstuffs purchased
at a membership grocery store and carried home in the trunk
of an SUV. Lucas thought of Carmen carrying her grandmother's shopping bags. How far he was from New York.

And yet here his mother's drapery sconces and headache-
inducing paisley wallpapers passed for style. Here charm was
an overabundance of Christmas decorations and the cloying
scent of synthetic cinnamon. Lucas had always enjoyed Christmas, never caring that people decorated their lawns with fake
snow. Now this seemed a poor imitation of what Christmas
should be. In Manhattan, everything looked exactly like the
movies: the pine-scented stands of fir trees, the outdoor gift
markets, the opulent window displays. Over the past week, as
he wallowed in his disappointment, Lucas had walked for hours
after work each night, imagining himself in the center of a
romantic comedy. He kept to the wide boulevards where everything looked so bright and beautiful.

Patricia Callahan was pulling a tray of homemade pigs in blan-
kets out of the oven when Lucas and Sam walked in. She wore
the typical uniform of pleated slacks, a fitted Talbots button-
down and oxfords. Her hair was flipped under and sprayed into
her signature brown helmet. Like the house, she was orna-
mented in red, gold, and green. "Lucas!" she exclaimed, and,

still in oven mitts, rushed toward him. She drew him into a hug, rocking him back and forth. "You look good!"

Lucas bristled at the surprise in her voice but then caught Sam's eye. *Not worth it.* Lucas took a deep breath. "I'm happy to be home."

"Do you really mean that?" She looked elated. "I told your father it was high time we put the whole thing behind us."

"Where's Dad?"

Patricia's face tightened. "At the dealership. It's been a slow month. But I'm sure there are still some Christmas shoppers out there."

Feeling surly, Lucas said, "I never understood how anyone could buy a car as a Christmas gift. What if you take it home and your husband or wife doesn't like it?"

Sam shot Lucas a look: *Shut up, idiot.*

Patricia put her oven mitts on the island and began to arrange the appetizers on the plate. "So you know who I ran into at Starbucks yesterday?"

"Mom, don't you want to give Luke a minute to settle in first?" Sam said, his tone putting Lucas on alert.

"I'd just ordered a Pumpkin Spice Latte," Patricia continued, "when I heard the woman behind me place the same order! It was Lucille Woodward. I mean what are the chances of Lucille and me ordering the same drink?"

Exceedingly high, Lucas thought.

"Lucille was tickled by the coincidence, and of course we got to talking. And you won't believe it, but Mel's engaged!"

Lucas nearly choked on his mini hot dog.

"To a young man from Pinecrest named Cal Braden. He does real estate law for Palmer and Coletta, which is apparently one of the top firms. Lucille said he is definitely going to make partner, that he's a real go-getter."

As if Lucas wasn't. As if Lucas was a bum.

"Mel is very happy, so the good news is that last summer is water under the bridge. It's such a relief!" Patricia had not looked this elated since Lucas had announced his own engagement.

"This is crazy. Mel's only been dating this guy for like five months!"

"When you know, you know." Patricia shrugged. "Look, honey, don't be upset. You'll find the right person."

But what if he already had and she wasn't interested?

"Once you get your life on track," his mother added. "Women respond to men who have a plan."

Lucas opened his mouth, but Sam shook his head.

"But for now," Patricia said, "be happy that Mel doesn't hold anything against you."

Lucas couldn't contain himself any longer. "Mom! Mel broke up with *me*!"

Patricia frowned. "You did back her into a corner—running out on your own engagement party?" She cleared her throat. "And everything else."

"What's that supposed to mean?"

"I know we haven't discussed the specifics—"

"That's damn right."

"But Lucille says you didn't give your all to the relationship."

As if he and Mel were a baseball team. This was absurd. "Are you really going to believe Lucille over your own son?"

"Luke," Sam interjected. "Lucille's right about—"

"Shut up, Sam."

"I'm just saying, honey, that the Woodwards don't hold a grudge against us."

"Of course!" Lucas slapped his palm on the island. "It's not me you care about. It's Mel's parents. My marriage was your ticket into their social circle, to all of Lucille's committees. That's why you care about Mel 'forgiving' me." Lucas pumped air quotes so hard, his fingers cramped. "You just want a bet-ter table at the country club."

"That is not true." Patricia shook her head, her eyes brim-ming. "Not true at all." She rushed from the kitchen.

Sam shook his head. "You've been home for what—five min-utes?"

"She started it!" Lucas protested.

"You're a moron," Sam said, and hurried after their mother.

Sam's rebuke made Lucas's cheeks burn, so he popped a pig in the blanket into his mouth and focused on the rush of fat and salt. He was smart to have left this place. Smart and brave to have cut the cord. He didn't need anyone's forgiveness—least of all Mel's. He popped a second hot dog into his mouth and chewed vigorously. He could eat these things all day and won-dered if his mother had made enough for him to take extras back to New York.

That night, Sam tried to talk some sense into Lucas. "Cut Mom a break," he argued. "Think how she feels, trying to fit in here."

"She and Dad put themselves in this situation," Lucas said. "If she didn't base her self-worth on these unattainable goals, she'd be a lot happier."

"Aren't you doing the same thing?"

"That's different, Sam. I'm trying to build a career. Mom and Dad are social climbers."

"And why is their ambition any less noble than yours?"

Because theirs is petty and insignificant. But Lucas knew how offensive that sounded, so he kept his mouth shut. Instead, he announced his need for a stiff drink.

"Well, fortunately," said Sam, "we're going to a bar."

Each year their high-school friends gathered at the Pig and Whistle Pub the night before Christmas Eve. Lucas had been nervous about entering the fray; he hadn't seen any of these people since the broken engagement. He spent the first hour regaling his friends with tales of New York. He had plenty— enough, in fact, to mute his own depression. But halfway through a rollicking tale of the love hotel (in this version, Katie and Corinne were indeed socialites), the currents in the bar begin to shift. People who'd been eddying around him were flowing away, pooling elsewhere. And Lucas saw why. Not more than twenty feet from him, stood Melanie Woodward, his ex. Mel held a Michelob ULTRA in her right hand. A cluster of young women gathered around her left, as though waiting to kiss the ring of Don Corleone.

Everyone in the bar was now highly aware of the situation. Lucas was aware that everyone was aware. And Lucas did not want everyone to see him crumble.

"Shots!" Lucas exclaimed to the remaining friends who were sticking to their territory. "Why haven't we done shots?" And so the group of them marched toward the bar and promptly threw back a round of tequila shots. After the second round, Sam sauntered over and asked Lucas if he wanted to take a break. Lucas did not. "How 'bout another round?" he asked.

"How 'bout some water?"

But only one thing would come between Lucas and a disastrous next drink, and that was—

"Hi, Sam!" Mel said, appearing suddenly beside them. She leaned in for a hug.

—yes, well, Lucas thought, perhaps another drink would be preferable to this.

Sam put on a big smile. "Lucas," he said unnecessarily, as if talking to a senile relative. "Mel's here!"

"Melanie," Lucas said. He never called her that, and he

hoped she noticed. But Mel only smiled and went in for a hug. She smelled different, which for some reason felt like a rebuke.

"You're looking really good, Luke."

How long was this conversation going to last? Why was it even happening? He looked around for his brother, but Sam had sidled away. Lucas turned back to Mel, his head swinging around too quickly. Mel wavered in his line of vision, so he blinked hard, trying to stabilize. He leaned backward, and the bar steadied him. There, that was better. Mel had stopped moving. She was wearing a dress he'd never seen before and knee-high boots. Her brown hair was smoothed and straightened with the usual meticulous attention. And, per usual, pinned above her forehead was a little hump of hair.

You look good, too, but why do you smell different? Why all of a sudden do you smell like somebody else? Lucas opened his mouth, but what came out was, "Your dress is new."

Mel gave a little twirl. "Cal bought it for me when we went to the Rebecca Minkoff sample sale in SoHo."

"When did you guys visit the city?" Lucas asked, trying to sound nonchalant. For some reason, knowing they'd been in the city, while he was living there unawares, made his heart pound.

"Cal lives in New York. I was visiting him."

"*New York* City?"

Mel nodded. "Crazy, right? After the big fuss I made about not wanting to move there. And now here I am just a few months away from joining him!"

"Hold on. You're *moving* to Manhattan?"

"Well, we are engaged, Lucas. I've applied to a couple of grad programs. Though if I don't get into school right away, it won't be the worst thing, since Cal owns a one bedroom in Chelsea. It's right around the corner from this amazing southern restaurant called Tipsy Parson. The food is like my mom's cooking but on crack. And they have the most incredible cocktails. Have you been? Anyway, the point is that I don't have to freak out about rent—you know how crazy rents are in the city."

Hell no. She was *not* trying to commiserate with him about the Manhattan real estate.

"Anyway, I'll let you get back to it." She nodded at the shot glass on the bar. "But I wanted to clear the air between us. We've both moved on. I'm happy for you. I hope you can be happy for me."

Last summer, all Lucas wanted was for Mel to have shown even a little enthusiasm about New York. Now her impending arrival felt like a declaration of war. She had no right to invade *his* city, just glide in on somebody else's mortgage—and not because she really wanted to be there or could appreciate being there, but because her fiancé just happened to be a rich real estate lawyer with a one bedroom in fucking Chelsea. "And where is Cal?" Lucas felt anger rumble in his stomach.

"He's flying down tomorrow. Closing a deal. But maybe once I've come to the city, we can all get together. I'm sure you can introduce us to some really cool spots."

"You keep calling it 'the city,' like it's your home or something."

"Well, it will be," Mel said plainly.

Lucas scowled under his breath. "I can't believe this."

"Believe what?" Her face was so open, so innocently inquisitive, that he almost didn't answer. But then he did.

"You think that I want to spend time with you and your new fiancé? After I begged you to move with me? After you made it absolutely clear that you would never live in New York and that I was ridiculous for even considering it myself? After you broke off our engagement and then jumped into bed with some other guy, like what, a month later? And then posted a million pictures of the two of you online so you could prove to everyone how much better than me he is? And now you want to hang out? You want me to show you the 'cool' spots as you call them."

Mel stared at him, shocked. But Lucas wasn't finished.

"The thing is, Mel, cool isn't about where you go. It's a way of looking at the world. It's about what you want out of life and the risks you'll take to get it. It's about opening yourself to new opportunities, taking risks, being open—" Wait, had he already said that? Maybe, but he needed to make sure she understood his point. "Whether you live in Podunk, North Carolina, or Chelsea or on the moon, Mel, you'll never be open-minded enough or ambitious enough to be cool or understand cool or even experience cool."

"Lucas," Mel breathed. "What in the hell are you talking about?" Her eyes were starting to tear, and she wiped at them fiercely. "Honestly, I don't know why I'm crying. You're drunk and you're being an asshole." She looked around, as though in search of a witness. Fortunately, Sam was already making his way back.

"What's going on?" Sam asked.

"What's going on," Lucas spit, "is that the *city*, as she insists on calling it, doesn't want her, doesn't need her, has no use for her. Mel-an-ie." He lifted the shot glass from the bar and raised it high into the air. He was the fucking Statue of Liberty, holding aloft the light of freedom, and if Mel didn't get that, then she could suck it!

Sam reached up and removed the shot glass from Lucas's hand. "OK," he said. "We're calling it a night. I'm sorry about all this, Mel."

She nodded, dazed, though by now she was safely ensconced by her squad.

"Tell your mom thanks for not holding a grudge!" Lucas shouted as Sam pushed him toward the door. "Tell her we don't give a shit about your country club!"

"What the hell is wrong with you?" Sam demanded, once they were outside.

"I can think of a couple things," Lucas muttered. Then he leaned over and vomited in the parking lot.

CHAPTER 28

Carmen walked home from Mira's, despondent. She couldn't remember any Christmas having gone so completely and terribly awry. She had spent a lovely day with a small, eclectic group of Mira's friends. And that night, per the usual tradition, settled down to play Gin. But as Carmen searched the kitchen for playing cards, she discovered a stack of mail beneath a pile of catalogs. They were notices from Mira's landlord—or, to be precise, his lawyers—stating that she'd broken the law by living on the rent-controlled lease of her deceased partner. Since the couple wasn't married, the letters explained, Mira must pay market rate if she was to stay. Further, the landlord was ordering her to make up the difference in rent for the time she'd been "scamming" him. The sum was $48,750, which Carmen knew her grandmother didn't have. The letters went back months.

Carmen's heart seized up. She carried the envelopes into the living room. "Were you ever going to tell me about this?" she asked.

"He's just a bully trying to make me flinch," Mira said, fiddling with her iPad. "But I won't."

"Mira, they're threatening legal action. Eviction."

This word captured Mira's attention. "I am eighty-six," she said pointedly to Carmen, "and I have lived here for decades. I'm not going anywhere."

Carmen walked over to her grandmother. Did she really not understand what these letters meant? Or that by ignoring them for so long she'd made herself even more vulnerable? And yet Mira's refusal to take any of this seriously meant that Carmen was going to have to step in and find a solution—and that was going to take a lot of money.

"Nobody's going to throw a little old lady out of an apartment the size of a manhole," Mira said, having noticed Carmen's silence.

"If that manhole is on Barrow Street, they will," Carmen said. "We need a lawyer."

"Forget it. Neither of us can afford that."

"I have savings."

Mira shook her head. "This will work itself out. You'll see."

"Mira, these kinds of problems don't just vanish. You can't ignore them."

Mira gave a dismissive "hmm."

Carmen couldn't take it. "Don't shrug this off like it's nothing. Don't you understand?" She was standing directly over Mira now and she was still looking at her iPad. "Mira, you are going to get kicked out of here if you don't do something. It may already be too late. How could you have just ignored this? Pretended it wasn't happening? It's like you live in a fantasy world." Carmen shook her head and started pacing back and forth.

"That is an unkind thing to say to me, Carmen."

"I'm sorry, but it's true. Why do you think you and Mom don't talk anymore? Why do you think you spent your life bouncing from job to job, never being able to stick anything out for more than five minutes? It's because your version of reality doesn't match up with anyone else's. And it impacts the people around you. It impacts me. Now I have to fix this for you. Because you insist on being completely irresponsible. Like a child." Carmen was aware, as she said these terrible things, of how truly awful they were. But she couldn't stop herself. She was terrified for her grandmother—for what would happen should Mira be forcibly removed from her home. And so this assault, these accusations, seemed the only way to reach her. But Mira was looking at her granddaughter with hard, unloving eyes, her lips drawn tightly together.

"I have lived my life as I wanted to live my life. And I have never asked you for a thing, so don't talk to me as though I am such a burden to you. Don't talk to me like you know so much better, because you don't, Carmen. You don't know."

"But I do!" she nearly screamed. "Evicted, Mira! Evicted! That means you have no home. That means you have nothing. And it's happening. It's going to happen."

Suddenly, to Carmen's horror, Mira began to weep. Carmen ran to the couch and knelt down. "I'm sorry. Mira, I'm so sorry." She reached for her grandmother's hands and Mira allowed Carmen to take them, but they remained flaccid and unresponsive. "Mira, please!" Carmen pleaded. "I didn't mean it. I'm just worried. We have to do something."

Mira pulled her hands away and dried her eyes with the corner of her robe. "I'm very tired," she said. "I'm going to bed now," she said almost mechanically. "Please lock up on your way out."

Carmen turned out the lights and left the apartment. Walking home, she realized her mistake. Mira, who had lost her partner of decades only one year ago, had been ignoring the letters out of a deep-seated fear. In letting her own anxieties escalate, Carmen had inflamed that fear. She'd not only taken a verbal battering ram to the woman she loved more than anything—she'd also blown a hole through her grandmother's tenuous optimism.

And Mira was still being threatened with eviction.

Carmen arrived home, put on her pajamas, and sat down to wait for Lucas's call. It may have been Christmas, but the magazine's publishing schedule wasn't taking a break. A column needed to be published. And Jays had issued a decree: The next "Screw the Critics" theme would be video sex, via Skype. Carmen and Nice Guy were to lead each other through a verbal maze of kinky entertainments to see who could make the other come first. "And no cheating," the Editor instructed via email. "Record the conversation so that I can adjudicate if necessary."

I bet he'd like to adjudicate, Carmen thought. *Adjudicate into a wad of Kleenex.*

Carmen wasn't sure what turned Jays on more: the sexual exploits of his ex-girlfriend—he was always a little masochistic like that—or the rapidly climbing newsstand sales and Web subscriptions that "Screw the Critics" continued to produce. But neither Carmen nor Lucas had any interest in creating a visual record of their interaction, so the two joined forces and pushed back: They'd do phone sex, but no Skype. And there would be no recording. It was the first thing they'd agreed upon in ages.

Now, phone in hand, Carmen felt overwhelmed by the amount of meanness in her small world. The cruelty of others— and her own.

When Lucas finally called, she answered with exhaustion. "What?" she groaned.

"Did we not have an appointment? I need my weekly dose of humiliation."

How much of Lucas's sarcasm masked genuine hurt? "I—" she started in, but couldn't get any further. All at once, she was sobbing, struggling to muster the control to apologize and hang up. The phone shook in her hand.

"Carmen, what's wrong? Are you all right?"

She swallowed her tears, but more came.

"Carmen, seriously, what's happening?" Lucas was starting to sound panicked.

"Why do you care?" she sobbed.

"Please." He sounded genuinely concerned. "Tell me what's wrong."

So she did. Because suddenly she couldn't bear the thought of being alone with her own self-loathing. Because for the first time in these many months, Lucas was being kind. And hell, despite their emotional distance, they knew each other in ways nobody else did. He listened patiently, asked her some questions. Slowly, she began to calm down. When her eyes were finally dry, she asked him to hold on a moment and went into the bathroom to splash water on her face. Worried that Lucas might hang up, however, she hurried back.

"I'm here," she said. "Sorry."

"It's all right. I'm just sitting in my childhood bedroom staring at my Green Day posters, regretting being here."

"You should never, ever leave New York," she said, managing to laugh a little. "Unless you're going somewhere exotic and far away."

"Yeah," he said. "I know that now."

"You had a bad Christmas, too?"

So he spilled. About seeing Mel again and the disaster at the bar. Before he knew it, he was telling her all about his profile of Spragg and, finally, about Sofia—who, now that it's over, he might as well admit: She'd been his sex coach.

"You little cheat!"

"Yeah, well, add it to my indignities."

Carmen seemed not to have heard, she was laughing too hard. "Honestly, I was wondering how you'd suddenly started performing so well."

"Wait, you admit that I've been performing well?"

"Sure."

"But you've been writing all this—"

"Lucas, it's the game. You're telling me that you've been honest this whole time?"

"Yes."

"Wow," she breathed. "I guess I respect your integrity."

"But wait, so are you going to let everyone know about my sex coach?"

"Nah."

"I've just given you deadly ammunition, and all you have to say is 'nah'?"

It was strange, Carmen thought, how she and Lucas had been physically intimate for all these months but had never had an actual conversation. Now, all of a sudden, with thousands of miles between them, she felt able to talk to him. "Sounds like you *want* me to let the cat out of the bag."

"No!"

"Then I won't. Anyway, the playing field has been leveled."

"Ladies and gentlemen, Carmen Kelly speaking on the record!"

Carmen groaned. "But Sofia's gone. You're on your own now."

Lucas was silent.

"Were you in love with her?"

There was a beat. Then, "I was—am—in love with her."

"It sucks," she said. "But it'll get better." And she meant it. Though it was difficult to admit, she'd been in love with Jays. It must have been in love, because what other emotion could have cut her open so violently? Yet now, when she searched for that familiar searing pain, there was nothing. No wound even. All of the powerful emotion she'd felt for Jays—both the love and the anger—seemed to have never existed.

"Better?" Lucas said. "Right."

"I've been there. You've got this darkness pressing in from all sides. You can't see your hand in front of your face. But every day the darkness will recede a little, and then suddenly you'll be able to see for miles."

"One day."

"Take heart. Everything worth seeing is out there right now, waiting for you to get your vision back. And all those people—new loves, friends, frenemies even—make Sofia seem as boring as a stock photograph."

"Frenemies? You wouldn't, by any chance, be talking about a certain sex columnist?"

Carmen chuckled. She liked this version of Lucas. Not the ambitious, indignant Lucas she sparred with on paper or the overeager, self-conscious Lucas she fucked, but the Lucas who was doing his damnedest to keep his head up.

"Perhaps 'frenemies with benefits' is more accurate."

"Do you think—I mean, how would you feel if . . ." He paused, and Carmen, sitting on her couch, raised her eyebrows in anticipation of whatever was coming next. ". . . we were just friends with benefits?"

"Oh, man, Nice Guy. That's a loaded question." What was she doing, flirting with him?

"Carmen Kelly seems to like things loaded," he said, which sounded vaguely like a playful innuendo. Though if Carmen asked him what he meant, she suspected he wouldn't really know. Still, was he flirting back? This was starting to feel weird.

"Yes, Lucas," she said. "We can be friends."

"Détente!" he said. "The best news I've heard all week. Now, what's next?"

"Phone sex?"

"Ugh."

"Why don't we just make something up?" Carmen suggested. "Like we should have been doing all along."

"Isn't that, I don't know, kind of dishonest?"

"We're not exactly reporting on matters of national security."

"I know, but—"

"Stuff in the magazine gets invented all the time. Like that stupid column 'Ask a New York Barkeep.' Where do the 'reader' questions come from?"

Lucas sighed. "The editors make them up."

"That's right. And the answers from the barkeep?"

"The editors write those, too. I know, but—wait, hold on a second. Who's that bartender in the photo they run?"

"He's an actor."

"What? But that guy looks so . . . convincing! Like he's straight out of Central—"

"Casting. Yup. He probably was. Did you know Central Casting is an actual company? And here's another one for you: Jays' editor letter? Housman writes it."

"Shit," Lucas says. "That one's just depressing. I'm a fact-checker at a magazine full of un-checkable facts! But still, it feels like someone's got to stand up for honesty around here, and if it isn't me . . ."

"I'm not trying to pressure you. If you feel really strongly, we'll keep going like before. I'm just saying that it seems we could both use a break."

"You think readers would buy it? You think Jays would?"

"I do. I'll write my column and send it to you. You can base your response on that."

"You're going to show me what you say about me? How is this not a trick?"

Because, she thought, for the first time since all of this started, the game failed to excite or even interest her. "Do you remember when you said you wanted the columns to help people? I know I shot you down. But I think you're right. And I think if we really want to help people with their relationships and their sex lives, we should be working together."

"You really mean that?"

He wanted to believe her; she could hear it in his voice. "I'm tired of fighting with you, Lucas." She stood up and paced the apartment, waiting for his answer. For reasons she couldn't quite explain, she felt a lot was riding on it.

"All right," he said finally. "I'm in. But let's write the columns together, as a team. We can make them so hot that we'll have half of New York coming in their cubicles."

Carmen laughed. "That's the spirit! It'll be a frenzy of sexual release. Then the city will pass out and finally get some sleep."

CHAPTER 29

Nice Guy,

Like many New Yorkers—that is, the people that moved here but are not of here, who call themselves New Yorkers as a badge of honor because they can afford to pay the rent—you are out of town visiting family for the holidays. I'm still here in the city, because I never leave. So this week, our assignment was to do what many New York couples do during the holidays: have phone sex. Which for you apparently means saying the words "suck my cock" over and over again, until you ejaculate into your pants. It was a pleasure, to be honest: For the first time since we began this sordid affair, there was no cock that I had to actually suck.

People will be reading this while still on their holiday vacations, so I feel obliged to tell them what to do and what not to do, and we can use you as a cautionary tale. So let's start here: Do not ask, "What are you wearing?" I know, I know: It seems standard. But it is a joke, Nice Guy. It's a cultural joke, as cliché as it gets; whenever you get married, you're also not supposed to walk up to strangers and say, "Take my wife, please!" (Though perhaps she'd be relieved.) Instead, you ease into it. You say something honest and a little jarring, something that makes a woman's heart flutter. You say that you like imagining me sitting there, that you wish you were there with me now. You take control. You tell me to start running my hand up my shirt. You tell me to breathe deeply; you like to hear my breath. You tell me it makes you hard.

You do not tell me to take my clothes off. Come on, Nice Guy. I'm sitting here in a room all by my fucking self—what, I need to be naked on my couch, too? You're supposed to be creating a moment, a fantasy we can both live inside while also, truth be told, just being turned on by thinking that the other one is far away, somewhere, their hand in their pants, thinking only of each other. There's something powerful in that, isn't there? To know: This person, in this room, is all alone right now, sliding their hand up and down their cock, thinking of me. Indulge in that, Nice Guy. Say you love picturing me there. Say what you're doing, how it feels, how it really feels.

"Suck my cock," you said again. No. What was I going to do—say, "I'm sucking your cock"? I was clearly not sucking your cock, because I was speaking those words to you on the phone. And I was sure as hell not going to make some cock-sucking noise to you.

"Do it, do it," you said. I mean, Jesus, enough with the imperative! For a writer, you're not very good at telling a story. Phone sex is literature, not a shouting match.

Ultimately, I had to take control. And I know what men want: They want to be acknowledged. They want their sexual power to be noticed. "I want you to keep stroking yourself," I told you, "as you listen to my voice. Go slow. Slow. That's right. Touch yourself like that."

And so on. I think the slowness thing got you. It gets me, too, to be honest. People always picture passionate sex happening fast—bang, wham!—but slowness is underrated. You can feel small movements when you go slow. You can feel more intimate. You came on the slow stroke. I knew you would.

But I will say this, my unfortunate, contractually obligated friend: For all its awkwardness, it was surprisingly nice to hear your voice. It made me realize how little we talk during sex. That's surely my fault, at least in part. But voices are nice; in the heat of the moment, you can say things that sound silly in any other context, but that feel sexy just because you happen to be saying them while fucking. It's a form of letting loose. Of giving in. We got a little of

that on the phone, and I'd say we're better off for it. I
hope other New Yorkers do, too.

Carmen

Lucas finished reading the column and, for the first time
since this project began, he felt genuine joy. He wasn't reading this in the magazine or online, as he usually was. He was
reading it in his inbox, because Carmen, true to her word, had
sent it to him to review, along with a little note: "If we're violating
the rules of fact-checking, we can't suddenly act nice to each
other. People would notice. But I slipped in the word 'friend'
there. Ignore the few words that come before it."

Now Lucas felt inspired. Some people read these columns
for the judgments, sure.

But some read them because they were undersexed schmucks
like he used to be, and they genuinely wanted pointers. And
Lucas was going to help them. Even though, well, he'd never
actually had phone sex—with Carmen or, frankly, anyone else.

Carmen,

Let's work our way backward. I think the last thing
you told me before hanging up was, "I really need to
wash my hand now."

When Carmen read this, she laughed out loud. Lucas was
clearly ribbing her here, for all the times she made sex as un-
sexy as possible. And then she laughed again because he was
right: It was the kind of thing she'd have said. He knew her.

And before that, I came. And before that, you were
giving me instructions on jerking off—go slow, speed

up a little, slower now. It was a turn-on, to be honest, although it also felt a lot like a live-action version of those "jerk-off instructions" videos you find on Pornhub. I'll admit, I watch them sometimes. Some woman is sitting in a room, looking into a camera, making a jerk-off motion in the air as she sweet-talks a viewer into orgasm. Those videos are weird if I think too hard about them, but in the moment, with enough hormones flooding my brain, they're just intimate enough to bring me over the top. I wouldn't have thought you'd ever watch them, but I suspect now that you have. Carmen, you try so hard to seem organic, but I'm on to you. You've taken inspiration from the Internet, just like the rest of us. There's nothing wrong with doing what works. If I like the porn, I'll like it coming from you, too.

Before the instruction manual, I think you came, but I just have no idea.

I haven't told you this before, but here it goes: I am genuinely, crazily turned on by a woman's breath in my ear. That deep, sexual sigh, that small moan, that quickened pace. I once told a girlfriend about this, and she began putting her mouth up to my ear every time we had sex, which was great except for how quickly it made me come the first few times. I wasn't prepared for such an overdose. Usually, those breaths only happen in passing.

But the phone is a different beast. Your voice was right there in my ear the whole time. It felt more intimate, in a way, than your actual body. I wish you

had indulged that intimacy. Carmen, you were so
busy speaking, so careful with your words, that you
forgot how impactful your wordless breath could be.

In Lucas's first draft of the column, which he emailed her,
that last line wasn't in there. Carmen wrote it herself and
sent it to him. "It's an artful insult," she wrote. It felt strange,
giving Lucas a weapon like that. But also, she was surprised to
discover, it felt less strange than she'd expected. The columns
had always been performative—both in the real sex and in
the word fights that followed. If it was all an act at this point,
why not perform both sides?

And before that, I tried to walk us through a little
fantasy. I pictured us together, here, in my
childhood bedroom, trying to be quiet and not alert
my family. I whispered instructions to you—to take
your shirt off, to unbutton my jeans, to blow me.
You didn't seem that into it. I think the dialogue
went like this:

Me: "Suck my cock."

You: [silence]

Me: "Yeah. Like that."

You: [silence]

Hey, listen. I tried. I'm not really sure how I could
have been more elegant without sounding like a bad
erotic novel.

Before that, we awkwardly talked about how we were going to start this thing. The transition from normal talk to sex talk is . . . not easy.

And before that, I dialed your number and you said hello. It was the first time I'd heard your voice in days and it reminded me that I felt more lonely outside of New York than I'd been in a long while.

Nice Guy

Carmen had to hand it to Lucas: Since they started this thing, he'd become better at sex, better at writing, and now, it seemed, better at being an actual nice guy.

CHAPTER 30

It was New Year's Eve, and Lucas was back in town—back in a city with no girlfriend and a still-evasive Nicholas Spragg. Tyler tried his best to cheer Lucas up, inviting him out for the evening, promising a "gentlemen's night."

"Did Sofia tell you what happened?" Lucas asked. He was anxious that Sofia had been too forthcoming. But mostly, he was looking for any clue that her conviction might be flagging.

"She thinks you're great. I don't think you should beat yourself up over this."

Lucas longed to ask Tyler whether Sofia had genuinely felt something for him. Just a week ago, he would have sworn his life on it. But now, without her around, he was starting to doubt himself.

"I think maybe you got too close too fast," Tyler added.

"It wasn't some casual fling!" Lucas protested.

"I know I'm not your shrink, but would you permit me a moment of analysis?"

Lucas shrugged.

"You were with one girl for ages. You were engaged! Then you're suddenly single. But all you know is Relationships with a capital *R*. So when you fall for someone, in your head, you're right back in relationship mode—the place that's familiar. You don't know how to moderate your feelings, to check your emotional pace with hers. Maybe you took off at a sprint, left her in the dust."

"You're saying I rushed things."

"Well, yeah, that's a simpler way of putting it."

"We dated for three months! We saw each other all the time! We were close, Tyler. In lots of ways. We opened up to each other."

"I'm sure you opened up to her—and I'm sure she listened. She's a good listener. But what do you really know about her? I mean beyond the outlines?"

"I know her," Lucas said miserably. "I'm sure I do."

"Look, man, I'm sorry if I upset you."

"It's not your fault," Lucas said. "It's all kind of raw."

"I bet. So look, if you want to come out, text me. We could go hunting for Nice Guy, and reveal his identity. I'd let you share the byline. That'd cheer you up."

When Tyler had gone out, Lucas shut himself in his room. He felt like crying, so he channeled his sadness into anger. It was time to wrap up the Spragg profile. Lucas was done chasing. He wasn't going to let Nicholas tank this story. That's not how journalism worked—the person being written about doesn't dictate what's written. Lucas opened an email draft:

Dear Nicholas, I've been trying to reach you for some time now to discuss an incident that occurred

between yourself and a young woman you knew
during your senior year of college. I'm on deadline. If
you'd like to talk about it, please call me tonight.
Otherwise, I'm filing the story without your comment.
Sincerely, Lucas.

He hit "send." He'd done his due diligence and now it was time to get to work. He began typing, barely looking up from his screen for hours. Midnight arrived with bursts of cheering and drunken revelry on the street, but the noise was drowned out by the clicking of keys and the voice in his head—as though some independent, maybe even celestial, entity were dictating the story to him. Not since that initial rebuttal to Carmen's column had Lucas written with such conviction, purpose, and speed.

He finished writing and reread his work. It was 3,476 words long, and it was honest and biting and real. Nicholas would be furious—would possibly even feel betrayed—but Lucas didn't care. Jays would be impressed, which was all that mattered. "Spare no detail," the Editor had said. Lucas had not. It was 5:00 A.M. and Nicholas hadn't called. Lucas filed the story. It would now begin its long descent into Empire's bureaucratic editing process—with one editor reading it and making notes, then sending it to another, who would read, edit, and send to yet another, and on and on until it eventually reached Jays. That could take weeks. Lucas would have to wait for his rewards.

In the meantime, his romantic depression deepened. As winter dragged on, only his writing sessions with Carmen could truly lift his spirits. They sat across from each other or side by side in the hotel room of her choosing, room service platters between them—all on Jays' tab—constructing the perfect epistolary repartee. They divvied up the attacks and rebuttals, the concessions and jabs. They were no longer relying on snark but striving for wit—which was only possible because they were communicating. The experience was new for Lucas. He'd never worked so closely with another person before, certainly never written with someone else. They'd become a real team, he and Carmen. Not a romantic team; the downside was that friendship had replaced sex. The most physical contact they now had was a hug or a high five. But aside from losing the pleasure of her body, Lucas had to admit that their relationship had become otherwise more gratifying.

They also started getting creative with the circumstances surrounding their fictional couplings. Freed from the constraints of reality, they sent Carmen and Nice Guy into the city. They climaxed together at the new interactive natural disaster exhibit at the Museum of Natural History as volcanoes erupted in 360 degrees. They had sex in a box at the Metropolitan Opera during a performance of *The Merry Widow*. And they crashed a cotillion ball at The Plaza, in which Lucas went down on Carmen in the corner of a crowded room, by hiding beneath the ample layers of her gown. All of this created a new frenzy over their identities. Now Carmen and Nice Guy were *out on the town* somewhere. They could be spotted. Newsstand sales and online subscriptions spiked anew.

"They're getting careless," Tyler wrote in *Noser*. "And sooner or later, they're going to get caught, in mid-coitus, by me. I promise to *expose* Nice Guy for the cowardly sex-crazed maniac he really is. Nobody can stay anonymous for this long, especially when boning and insulting a very public woman. It has to end."

CHAPTER 31

By February, having heard nothing about his article, Lucas checked in with Jays. The reply by email was enthusiastic: "Haven't had time to read it, looking forward, if it's as good as I suspect could see a staff writer promotion." Lucas wanted to print out this missive and frame it. He wanted to send it to his family, to Sofia, to everyone who had ever doubted or rejected him. More than this, he saw the forthcoming promotion as a kind of formal induction. He would be able to confidently call himself a New Yorker. A man who didn't just live here but who was *of* here. Gone would be his days of gullible innocence, ahead the wisdom of experience. He fixated on this victory to keep his mind off of Sofia.

And then, more than a month after Lucas had turned in his Nicholas Spragg profile, he was summoned to Jays' office. Lucas had not been inside *Empire's* seat of power since August, and the place had not changed. Not a scrap of paper was out of place.

There was not a speck of dust. It reminded Lucas of an article he'd fact-checked, about the Russian and Chinese multimillion-aires who were buying up penthouses across the city. Dwellings not for people but for their money. Whole blocks of ghost towers, empty year round.

"Lucas, thanks for coming by," Jays said. He was sitting on the corner of his desk, his hands folded in his lap. There was something unusually stiff about his demeanor. "Why don't you take a seat?"

Lucas sat. He pulled out a notebook and a pen, ready to take edits.

"That won't be necessary," Jays said.

Was his story so good that it required no revisions? That seemed impossible. But who knew? Maybe he'd knocked it out of the park.

Jays hung his head; when he looked up again, he was frowning. Something was wrong. "Lucas, I assigned you this profile about Nicholas Spragg because I saw great promise in you. I thought, 'Here's a young man who is ambitious and eager, who after only a short time at our magazine understands its vision. My vision.'"

"I do—" Lucas began, but Jays put his hand up.

"And then you turn in your assignment. Three thousand words spent disparaging a young man who is only trying to make his way in this great and complicated city of ours. Much like yourself, I might add. I assigned you a simple profile and yet you bring me a screed, impugning Nicholas's character, bringing allegations against him that, frankly, seem absurd given his character and standing, and which, if printed, could ruin his career, not to mention his reputation. It's as though you've taken great pleasure in bringing him down. You may as well be working for some tabloid. Is that what you think *Empire* is? Because if so, this is not the magazine for you."

Lucas could feel the dampness spreading across his back and under his arms. He felt dizzy. The top of his head stung horribly. This must be a joke. Maybe an initiation? What in the hell was happening? Lucas's article was well reported. It was harsh but fair.

"I am disappointed in you, Lucas," Jays continued. "But mainly, I'm disappointed in myself. For giving you this remarkable opportunity and believing that you were mature enough and professional enough to handle it gracefully. I misjudged. To think of the public backlash we'd get, not to mention the libel charges."

"But it's all true. There's a police report. I did exactly what you wanted," Lucas protested. "I don't understand."

"Imagine if I had actually promoted you to staff writer!" Jays continued, shaking his head. "In any case, I'm sorry to say it— or maybe I'm not sorry—but your employment at this magazine is terminated."

And then, as though on cue, somebody snorted. Lucas whipped his head right, then left. He and Jays were the only two people in the room.

"What was that?"

Jays was fumbling with something in his hand. His cell phone.

Lucas stood. "Is someone listening to this?"

"Absolutely not."

But he'd heard a snort! "But I—" Lucas said, and stopped. If he could only compose himself, identify what had gone wrong, figure out what the hell he was missing. But he needed to figure it out fast. If he left this room, he'd never be allowed back in.

"You've got ten minutes to pack your things and get out of the building, Lucas. Otherwise, I'm calling security."

No, no no! Everything was moving too fast. If he could only find the right words. The right explanation. There had to be one. There had to—

And then Lucas burst out laughing. He laughed like a maniac. He literally pounded the armchair of the seat he was in, because it was all just too much. Because he'd never expected that this was how his Ace in the pocket would be played.

"You can't fire me, Jay," he announced, gleefully, like a man transformed. The blood that seemed to have drained from his body gushed back in. He sat up straighter, confident, invincible. He flashed back to Sophia's advice, after Carmen went on that late-night show. *That's the very definition of the upper hand, Lucas. When you know what the other person expects, you can throw them off guard.* Lucas stood up. He took a deep breath. He looked Jays right in the eyes.

"I write the best column in your magazine," he said.

Jays froze, but his eyes darted back and forth. "What the hell are you talking about?"

"I'm Mr. Nice Guy. Pleased to meet you."

Now the Editor looked truly stunned. Lucas smelled blood. He kept going. "You don't believe me? Call your ex-girlfriend. Ask her who she's been fucking."

A shadow crossed Jays' face.

"I could quit right now," Lucas continued. He was on a roll. Nothing could touch him. "I'll take my show on the road. Maybe take it to *Noser.* Then what'll you do?"

Jays closed his eyes. When he opened them, his face was as calm and clear as the reflecting pools, many stories below.

"Yeah," Lucas continued. "Maybe I will quit. See how you'd like that."

"You're right," Jays said, his voice even. "If you're Nice Guy, then I'd prefer for you to stay." Lucas felt himself deflate a little. Where was Jays' anger? Why did he look so preternaturally calm?

"Oh, so now you want me to stay?" Lucas said, trying to keep up the momentum. "Well, if you want me to stay, then you're going to have to publish my story about Spragg."

Jays shook his head. "The magazine's owner won't allow it. We can't afford that kind of lawsuit. Even if there is proof, as you claim."

Lucas felt the fight drain out of him. How was he supposed to argue against the *owner*?

"What else?" Jays asked, the epitome of patience.

"I . . . uh . . ." Lucas felt himself flailing. "I want a promotion to Staff Writer. I want a raise. At least twenty-five K more." This was his moment; he needed to milk it. "I want to be more involved."

"Involved in what?" Jays asked, and Lucas wondered if the Editor wasn't smiling, just a little, out of the corner of his mouth.

"In editorial decisions," Lucas pronounced. He didn't really even know what that meant, but he saw the top editors of *Empire* in a room together on a regular basis, making the real decisions. He wanted desperately to be in that room. "I'm a lot more talented than you're giving me credit for."

Jays nodded. "All right," he said.

"Good," Lucas said. But now what? The Editor seemed to be waiting for Lucas to say something else. "Good," Lucas repeated.

"Anything else?" Jays asked. There it was again, that infuriating glimpse of a smile.

"No." Lucas turned and walked quickly out of the room. But as soon as he'd stepped through the door he turned around and went back in. "Yes!" he said, fumbling furiously with his Ferragamo tie. He balled it up and then threw it on the rug. "I'm done with these stupid ties. From now on, I wear whatever the hell I want."

CHAPTER 32

Lucas burst out of the doors of One World Trade. If he could, he'd have kicked those doors down like a fucking boss. Lo, what powers he had felled! That's how he felt. He walked with swagger. His chest felt larger. *When you come at the king,* he thought to himself, *you best not miss.* Jays had missed. Lucas was king.

"Fuck yes!" he yelled, startling a woman in a marshmallow coat. He walked a few blocks. He had no destination. He just felt the need for movement. For the blast of air. He felt like a minor-league baseball player must after getting promoted to the majors—all pride and energy but nowhere to channel it. You don't get tapped and then magically appear in a major-league stadium, with thousands calling your name. You're shown your locker. You're given a new uniform. You do the mundane things, as the energy inside you builds, until you're thinking *just give it to me just give it to me just give it to me.* And then, finally, you step out onto that big stage, where the greatest are tested against the greatest, and you become the man you always knew you were.

That time was coming for Lucas. The city wanted to know who Nice Guy was. And he was going to show them that it was Lucas Callahan, motherfuckers. He smiled, thinking about how the news would shock—would physically knock people to the floor!—some of the people who doubted him. His parents. Mel. Everyone.

His parents. Mel. Everyone. *Oh, man,* Lucas thought. The whole city and half the country were going to know about his sexual exploits. His identity would be revealed, and then his private life would be revealed, too. He took a deep breath. This was not a moment to wilt. This was the opportunity he'd been waiting for, through all those months of loneliness and heart-break. "Fuck yes!" he yelled again. A few feet away, an old lady pushing her dog in a baby carriage sped up, eager to avoid him.

Fifteen minutes later, Lucas was standing outside Carmen's building, incessantly pressing the buzzer. Finally, the front door's lock clicked open and he flew up to her apartment, panting, and opened the door to find her curled on the couch with a book. The sight of her bare neck and oversized Columbia sweatshirt, drooping off one shoulder, delighted him. Here she was, just living life like it was any other day, unaware that the universe itself had changed.

"You won't believe what just happened!" he said, and in a rush told her everything.

When he was finished, Carmen furrowed her brow. Why wasn't she jumping up to hug him, to pour them drinks? Why wasn't she ecstatic? "You're not going to congratulate me?" he said, feeling hurt.

"So you're saying that Jays tried to fire you because he was unhappy with a story you wrote? And that someone was listening in? Lucas, that all sounds really off to me."

Lucas shook his head. "I'm sorry—did I bury the lede? When Jays woke up this morning, he did not expect to be outsmarted by his fact-checker. And now I have a seat at the table. Now I finally have some power. That's going to be amazing for the column, for *both* of us!"

Lucas walked to her bar cart and began fixing them both drinks.

"Well, as long as we're sharing, I have some news as well," she said.

"Yeah?" he said, searching for the ice tongs.

"I'm leaving."

Lucas spun around. "What?"

She nodded slowly.

"Leaving *Empire*? Not now. Why?"

"Will you sit down please?"

Lucas shook his head. He'd finally gotten everything he wanted; why did she have to blow it?

"All right. Well, I've been offered my own Netflix show. It's a documentary series where I'll be coaching the sexually and romantically inept. Not literally—not like Sofia. But they want me to star and co-produce."

"I'm happy for you," Lucas said, returning to the drinks.

"Come on, Lucas. This isn't—"

"No, really, I am. You've been working so hard to break out of the sex-writer ghetto. At long last, you get to do the exact same thing, basically, but on TV. For a lot more money."

"That's not fair. I have the chance to shape a new cultural product without Jays looking over my shoulder. And yes, I'll have some money. Enough to afford a good lawyer, so that my grandmother won't be out on the street."

Lucas still wouldn't meet Carmen's eyes, only now he felt ashamed. "I'm sorry," he said. "It's just that without you, I'm screwed. Nice Guy goes public and then Carmen Kelly quits? The public will eviscerate me and Jays'll play it up for the publicity."

"The column is too valuable. You'll get a new partner. Someone you actually like."

"Don't joke about that. We're a team. I can't do this without you."

"That's sweet of you," she said. "But I have to get out of *Empire*, Lucas. I *need* to get out. You have no idea how much."

"Can't you do both?"

She shook her head. "They want me in LA. This is my chance to be truly free."

Lucas leaned forward, drew his palms together. "Carmen, please. I need you."

Carmen bit her lip, observed him coolly. "Get on your knees," she said.

Lucas didn't hesitate; he dropped to the floor.

"Jesus! I was kidding!" Lucas didn't move. "OK." She groaned. "Let me talk to my agent. If it's OK with Netflix, I'll give you six more weeks. Because you're right about the public. And definitely right about Jays. But that's it. Six weeks, and I'm done."

Lucas felt the clouds of disaster lift. "Thank you, Carmen," he said, suppressing the urge to hug her. "I owe you big-time."

He was just handing her a drink when her phone rang. "Oh, hi," she said, and Lucas immediately knew that it was Jays. "Yes," she said. "Yes . . . well, you lost that privilege when you—" Carmen stopped abruptly and frowned.

Lucas didn't know much about her relationship with Jays or its dissolution, but watching her now, he understood how complicated and painful it must be for her to work under him. *This is my chance to be truly free.* She didn't just mean creative freedom or professional freedom, but something much deeper. Which gave him pause. Was he asking too much of her? Yet without her, he'd be lost. And it was only six weeks. Such a short amount of time.

"Yes, I will be there," Carmen said. "And yes, I'll tell him." She hung up. "Well, it's official. I don't know what Jays is planning, but he wants us in the office first thing tomorrow morning. Also, he says to wear a tie."

"Asshole!" Lucas muttered.

Carmen looked at him quizzically, then said, "Right now, I suggest you take a walk." She pointed to the door.

"Are you kicking me out?"

She shook her head. "No, my friend. I'm literally suggesting that you go on a walk. As of tomorrow morning, you won't have an ounce of privacy in this city."

CHAPTER 33

The next morning Lucas and Carmen met in the lobby of One World Trade and rode the elevator together to the twenty-ninth floor. The news of Lucas's identity had already leaked; the person calling themselves Rogue Empire had published it in "Screw Off!" "Yesterday," the mole reported, "an *Empire* fact-checker named Lucas Callahan entered Jays' office looking nervous and emerged looking triumphant. Jays soon followed, looking like he'd eaten salmonella-tainted kale. This morning, *Empire* will reveal that Lucas is Nice Guy. Whatever Jays says, those are the facts. Take them as you will."

Lucas hadn't actually seen the post, but he was alerted to it by a text message from Tyler. "You son of a bitch," it said. This warmed Lucas's heart. Never before had he been the man of intrigue, the one who left people guessing. He imagined what his friends and colleagues were thinking of him now. *If Lucas is capable of this,* they might wonder, *he must be capable of so much more.*

"Are you ready?" Carmen asked now, in the elevator.

"I feel like it's my birthday," Lucas said.

"More like your media cotillion," she said with a smirk.

The elevator came to a rest. Silence. Then the doors opened. "They're here!" somebody shouted, and the pair walked out of the elevator and into a waiting crowd. The entire *Empire* staff, along with dozens of editors from other magazines in the building, broke into whooping applause. "Well, man, you surprised us all," said a guy Lucas had never met. Lucas scanned the crowd for familiar faces. Alexis looked a little stunned, if nervously supportive; she now knew *way* too much about his sex life. Franklin lackadaisically moved his hands together and apart while rolling his eyes. It seemed a mark of honor: Lucas was now important enough that Franklin pretended not to give a damn about him. But as Lucas scanned the room, he began to feel self-conscious. What did these people expect of him now? To look different. To *be* different. He was suddenly overwhelmed. A glance at Carmen edified him. Thank god she was here.

Jays appeared from the throng. He kissed Carmen on the cheek and shook Lucas's hand. Then he quieted the room. "As you all know by now, our Lucas—dogged fact-checker, tie aficionado, and all-around *Nice Guy*—has been moonlighting as Carmen Kelly's partner in our wildly successful column 'Screw the Critics.' I know this comes as a shock to many of you. Probably to all of you. I mean, *this* guy? With Carmen?"

"He's hotter than Adam the PA!" somebody shouted.

Jays chuckled. "Yes, well, as soon as I hired Lucas to be an *Empire* fact-checker, I knew he'd be the perfect man to co-launch our most ambitious column—all the more so because no one would ever suspect him."

Lucas looked at Carmen again and raised his eyebrows as if to say, *Is this guy for real?* She responded in kind.

"But there's more," Jays continued. "In the coming year, *Empire* will be expanding its national and global reach, transforming from a magazine and website into a broad-scale media force. And Lucas and Carmen, as our most popular—if notorious—writers, will be at the forefront of this effort. So I am proud to announce their promotion to Brand Ambassadors for *Empire Magazine*."

The room cheered. Lucas imagined what Carmen was thinking. If she was going to leave "Screw the Critics," it would be all the more satisfying to do it while Jays was heaping on the praise—not to mention placing so much of the brand on her shoulders. Here Lucas was, standing in between the strangest of cold wars. Jays, deftly rewriting history to place himself at the center of it. And Carmen, letting Jays believe that he was in control—of the situation, and of her.

"With their help," the Editor continued, "we'll be launching an event series, a podcast network, exploring entertainment opportunities. I think it's safe to say that Luke here is going to need a few more ties for all the TV he'll be doing!" Jays winked at Lucas. "This is an exciting time for *Empire*," he concluded. "And I'm thrilled to have all of you here with me to make the most of it."

Out beyond the Editor, dozens of phones homed in on Lucas's face. Within minutes, these videos would be unleashed upon the world. These were the images all of New York would be looking at. Lucas's life really was about to change. His chest tightened. But then he felt a warm pressure in his palm. Carmen had taken his hand.

After champagne and chitchat and selfies, Jays convened the newly knighted Ambassadors in his office. He cataloged their upcoming itinerary of photo shoots and interviews, the meetings they were going to have with producers, the event series they were going to host, the partnerships with up-and-coming artists, designers, and DJs. "I hope you two appreciated screwing undercover," Jays concluded. "Because from now on, it's all hanging out for the world to see."

Ribbing aside, Lucas was taken by the Editor's professionalism. It was as though the botched firing had never happened. People accused Jays of having a big ego. They said he held a grudge. But Jays wasn't going out of his way to punish Lucas. Just the opposite; he was turning a potentially awkward situation into an advantageous one for the magazine. Lucas respected that. And Carmen, meanwhile, just let it happen, nodding along with a smile. Not a mention of Netflix. Maybe she was rethinking the deal after all? This *Empire* gig suddenly seemed pretty good.

At the end of the meeting, Jays took Lucas's arm and said, "There's so much in store for you, Lucas, and you deserve all of it." With a swelling heart, Lucas answered, "Thank you, sir."

From the office, Carmen and Lucas were whisked to the SoHo headquarters of a no-nonsense style guru, who hosted a TV show called *Take That Off!*, where he ripped people apart for their terrible fashion choices. As Lucas was being manhandled like a mannequin, his phone started blowing up. Interview requests flooded in from reporters across the city along with emails, texts, and voicemails from friends and family. His mother left repeated messages, her voice increasingly frantic and higher pitched.

Sam texted: "don't know what 2 thnk Happy 4 u? call me."

Tyler texted: "Fuck you, you brilliant man!"

A text arrived from a number he didn't recognize; he opened it to find a photo of a very nice pair of breasts, along with the message: "Call me any time, Nice Guy." His number had gotten out creepily fast, but he wouldn't be entirely upset about more messages like that one.

Finally, Carmen and Lucas headed into the city for their photo shoot. In less than twenty-four hours, Jays had developed an ad campaign to announce *Empire's* new Brand Ambassadors and managed to secure Lucian Moreau, one of the city's hottest photographers, to direct them. The theme, Moreau explained, as they rode uptown together, was Meet Un-Cute. "Jez Jacobzon hez a *brrrilliant* vision!" Moreau leaned animatedly over his pointy-toed shoes. His accent and attitude seemed pompous, even for a French photographer. "Bet of cuz, zat is why Jez calls me," he continued. "I only do *brrrilliant* campaigns."

Carmen looked askance at Lucas, who just shrugged.

"We shoot ze anti-romantik gestures in the citi's most romantic locashionz. You see et ees about con-*trast.*"

And so it was. At Jean-Georges, they sat across from each other with an untouched dessert between them, fabricating the steely aftermath of a fight. At Tiffany's, Carmen was directed to look longingly at the engagement rings, while Lucas checked his watch. "Isn't this kind of sexist?" Carmen asked. "And not very interesting?" Lucas added. Moreau looked horrified and said, "It is ze ord*er* of Jez Jacobzon!" as though the Editor were Caesar himself.

After this, they were driven to The Standard Grill, where Jays waited for them at the very same table where he'd bullied Carmen into joining "Screw the Critics" all those months ago. He'd chosen the spot purposefully, Carmen was certain. But was it a boast? Or a more menacing message: that all roads truly did lead to Rome, back into the emperor's hands? But Carmen was no longer a tangle of conflicted feelings. No more longing, hatred, regret, or the remnants of love. Her only feeling for the Editor at this juncture was distrust.

As the trio awaited their drinks, Carmen explained her frustration with the photo shoot. The setups, she said, mischaracterized the columns, the nature of her and Lucas's relationship, not to mention their new role. "Ambassadors are supposed to work together," she said. "But if you insist on presenting us as adversaries, at least make it sexy."

"Moreau makes everything sexy," Jays said.

"Moreau is a clown," Carmen said.

"What if we're photographed in a boxing ring, in our underwear?" Lucas suggested.

Jays slapped the table. "Yes! Excellent. And *that's* why I hired you, Luke." He looked at Carmen as he spoke, as though she'd pushed back. Which she hadn't. Lucas, meanwhile, was blushing. Carmen hoped he wasn't getting caught up in Jays' flattery.

Jays pushed back his chair. "Well, I'll give you both some time to eat before the press arrives. I believe you've got interviews with *Cosmo, Vanity Fair,* and BuzzFeed."

"You're not staying?" Lucas seemed disappointed. "What about your drink?"

"Don't want to step on your toes." Jays gave Carmen a maddening wink.

"So you'll set it up with Moreau?" Carmen pressed. "Lucas's boxing idea?"

"Oh, sure," Jays said, distracted by someone he saw across the room.

They had not been in the restaurant for long before the other patrons began to realize that the lanky sandy-haired kid sitting beside Carmen Kelly was Nice Guy. Since the announcement that morning, the blogosphere had swelled with the revelation and word was spreading. Half a dozen people interrupted the interviews to ask for selfies. A full dozen leaned over Lucas and

Carmen like they were statues, snapped a selfie, and walked away without even saying thank you.

That afternoon, the photo shoot continued. In a taxi outside the Washington Square Park arch, Carmen was asked to recoil from Lucas as he leaned in for a kiss. At the Majestic Theatre in Times Square, they were painted as mimes and posed before a panel of stern-faced judges. Finally, after the working day had ended—late even for Manhattan's corporate lawyers and bankers—Carmen and Lucas were taken to a hotel and posed in a picture of post-coital disappointment: side by side beneath the sheets, staring at the ceiling.

"Nize Guy!" Moreau snapped his fingers. "He-lo! Nize Guy!" Lucas's eyes snapped open. The king-sized bed was soft and cool, and he'd briefly dozed off.

Carmen glanced at the clock. "I think we've had enough for today." She looked at Moreau's four photo assistants, who hovered around the bed like timid medical residents. "I hope you're all being paid overtime."

"Can I just sleep here?" Lucas mumbled, and closed his eyes again.

"Good idea," Carmen said. "Everybody out. Now!"

The assistants began packing up their equipment as Moreau stood frowning in the corner. "Maybe I take images of thees?" he said. "Nize Guy and Ms. Kellee—"

"Out!" ordered Carmen.

"Thank you, Carmen," Lucas said, his eyes fluttering. "You're my—"

But Carmen never learned what she was, because suddenly he was snoring. She was exhausted as well, though in the sudden quiet she couldn't sleep. She watched the rise and fall of Lucas's bare chest. It was a nice chest, not as broad as some, but sturdy enough. And practically smooth. Before Lucas, she'd preferred a healthy layer of chest hair—at least enough for the man in her bed to seem sufficiently like a man. But she'd grown to like the proximity of her nipples to Lucas's skin. It was a different kind of closeness than she was used to. It was, for lack of a less saccharine word, tender. She wanted to lay her chest against him now, but their relationship had changed. They didn't do things like that anymore. Which made her feel . . . well, she wasn't sure. Part of her missed the sex. But she was no longer the same woman who'd fucked Lucas every other week. She'd needed to be that person—judgmental, fierce, and proud—to have become this new women. Wise. The columns, unexpectedly, had been an education for her. They'd transformed her into a person with much more complicated feelings about whom she slept with, when, and why.

Gently, Carmen ran her finger across one of Lucas's cheekbones, the feature that had first caught her attention. He stirred but remained asleep.

She should be packing her bags for LA, drawing out the physical and psychic distance between herself and Jays. But she couldn't just leave Lucas here. He was too enthralled with his sudden success, too vulnerable. Too eager to say yes. He'd made a stirring case for yes during their dark ages, but it was a naïve one. Yes could be dangerous. Especially when you didn't really understand what you were agreeing to. Carmen had learned this the hard way. Nobody had guided her or helped her, and as much as she'd achieved, she had also suffered at the hands of a master manipulator. It had taken her a long time to understand that Jays was always making a play. He cared only about himself, and screw everyone else. Carmen had internalized more than a little of this outlook. But then Lucas had appeared and shown her just the opposite—how to be part of a team. She was grateful for that, more than he would ever know. For that, she could give him six more weeks.

CHAPTER 34

The next morning, the weather chilly and windy, Lucas and Carmen were styled and driven to their final location: Bow Bridge in Central Park. The bridge was iconic, a cast-iron architectural beauty meant to resemble the bow of a violin, and voted many times over as the most romantic spot in Manhattan. Lucas realized he must have seen it in a dozen romantic comedies, though he couldn't recall a single one.

"Well, at least the sun's out," he said to Carmen as they walked up the bridge's gentle slope, both of them shivering. Lucas was sick of posing, of pretending to be lonely, angry, and awkward. There was enough of that in real life; why did anyone need to spend a second make-believing? Moreau posed Lucas on one knee, holding a bouquet of roses up to Carmen, and had her looking down at him with a notebook and pen, critiquing the gesture.

"Give me annoy-*ance*!" Moreau shouted at Carmen. "Yes,

perrrfect. *Brrrilliant!* Now irritashion! Perrrfect. Now exasper-ashion! Beautiful. *Brilliant.*"

Lucas watched Carmen cycle through the slide show of emo-tions. She was frowning (at Moreau's direction) and bearing it. But she was also cold. As she gripped the notebook and pen, her fingers had turned white.

"Thank you for doing this," Lucas said through clenched teeth as the camera snapped away.

"All I can say is, I better get to keep these clothes," she said testily.

"I didn't know we'd have to do any of this, I swear. Just six weeks and—"

"Nize Guy!" Moreau snapped. "Show me dezperashion. You are pathe*tic*. Yes?"

"Hearing him call you names in that ridiculous accent kind of makes this nonsense worth it," Carmen said.

"Nize Guy! What ess thees? You are, what do they say—a hopelees romantik, but more hopelees than romantik, yes?"

"Is he referring to my romantic gesture or this photo shoot?" Lucas murmured as Carmen shook with laughter. She tilted her head back and opened her mouth. A glorious, throaty laugh spilled out. And then, all at once, people were shouting their names. Someone must have tweeted their location, because now scores of gawkers were pushing farther and farther toward the center of the bridge. "Stop! Stop eet!" Moreau shouted, but to no avail.

Only then they did stop, because a black object swooped out across the water and sped like a missile toward the bridge. The black object was now hovering just before Lucas and Carmen, a camera lens pointed at their faces.

Lucas jumped to his feet. "Is that a drone?"

"Oh for Christ's sake!" Carmen moaned. But she looked de-lighted. "I've never gotten this kind of attention before. Lucas, you've single-handedly quadrupled my star status. I'm going to have to hire a publicist and a stylist and an assistant. I'm going to have to start blowing out my hair every fucking morning."

Meanwhile, Lucian Moreau was losing his shit. "Zees ess *my* shoot, you stupeed metal object!" He waved his hands at the drone, and when that didn't work he grabbed the bouquet of roses from Lucas and, to his and Carmen's astonishment, hurled it off the bridge. The drone drifted lazily out of the bouquet's path, and the flowers fell into the water with a plop.

Lucas and Carmen went to the edge of the bridge, where the roses were slowly sinking. "So who sent that thing?" Carmen asked calmly. "*New York Post, Us Weekly,* or *Star?*"

"I have my money on somebody else," Lucas said, and held up his phone. On the screen was a text from Tyler: "Smile, kids!" Lucas scanned the crowd for his roommate. The number of onlookers had ballooned. Who were all these people? Didn't they have jobs?

"We're not famous enough for this!" Carmen shouted at the drone. "We're writers—and he's not even really a writer. He's a fact-checker!"

For the first time, Lucas's former position filled him with pride. He'd barely stood on the lowest rung and yet had flown skyward nearly as fast as the elevators in One World Trade. For a moment, he was lost in reverie, imagining all of the 30 Under 30 lists on which he was about to land. Then an incoming text from Tyler called him back. It was a link to a Facebook Live stream called CriticsCam. "Carmen!" Lucas pulled her over. "Look!" There they were, on the screen, looking back at themselves.

"I think we're having a moment, Lucas," Carmen said. "We should make the most of it."

Lucas looked directly at the camera as it hovered in front of his face. "For days," he announced to it, "we've been taking depressing, pseudo-antagonistic pictures for an ad campaign.

We've been pretending to hate each other. But we're *Empire's* new Brand Ambassadors and we don't think that's the spirit of our magazine." Lucas was on a roll, now that hundreds, maybe even thousands, of people were watching him. "*Empire* is about excitement," he continued. "It's about taking chances. It's about saying yes!"

"And yes to what exactly?" Carmen asked, pretending not to know.

Lucas did not hesitate. He pulled her close, and in the next moment they were kissing. The crowd went wild. Lucas's phone was having a seizure in his pocket. Lucian Moreau was practically having a seizure on the bridge. Lucas was vaguely aware of all of this. But mostly, he was aware of Carmen: Her warm, soft mouth. The smell of her shampoo. The impossibly soft threads of her sweater. Their hearts pounded so fast, fueled by the adrenaline of the moment, that each could have sworn they were flying. Carmen and Lucas were rushing toward each other at the speed of light.

CHAPTER 35

I f you continue to go rogue, I don't know what I'm going to do with you." This was Jays on speakerphone, sounding and feeling very far away. Carmen and Lucas half-listened. They'd set the phone on the ledge of a Jacuzzi tub, in an insanely large bathroom, in a suite at the Mandarin Oriental. Carmen was wearing one of the complimentary snowy bathrobes over her clothes and had stretched out in the dry tub. Lucas leaned against the vanity, wearing Mandarin slippers on his feet. He and Carmen had been installed here for the night to work on their next column—the first of Lucas's public career—and Jays had finally, truly, ponied up.

When Jays called, they'd been struggling to write. Balled-up pages of false starts were scattered around the bathroom.

"That photo shoot was totally stupid," Carmen said, sipping the Moët that Jays had sent them.

"People want drama, tension, and angst," the Editor said. "They don't want *feelings*."

"I'd say some things were felt on that bridge," Lucas said, suddenly a wise guy. He refreshed the page at Empire.com where the video had been posted. It had been viewed 247,327 times. He refreshed again: 247,328. How could Jays be anything other than thrilled?

"And they also want sex, because we're not a sanitized network TV show," the Editor continued, ignoring Lucas. "*Empire* isn't middlebrow; it's boundary pushing. So that's why I'm telling you two: You have to embrace the conflict. Don't get soft on me."

"Fine, fine. Bye," Carmen said, and hung up the phone. Then she downed the rest of her champagne like it was a shot. "Maybe we should write these columns tomorrow. When we're fresher."

"Or maybe . . . ," Lucas started, then paused.

"Maybe what?" Carmen yawned. Her eyes were closed and she was absently running her index finger along the edge of the tub. Lucas watched it: the finger, the perfectly shaped nail moving along the smooth porcelain. "Maybe . . ." He swallowed. What was wrong with him? He'd been so decisive on the bridge, but now, alone with her, he'd lost his nerve.

Carmen opened her eyes. She followed Lucas's gaze through the bathroom door and toward the bed. "Oh," she said.

"Well, why not? This afternoon was amazing."

"It was." She sat up in the tub. "But we have a good thing going—writing together."

"We can still write together. We can be writers with benefits! I'm just saying that maybe we need some new material, to help us get over our, um, writer's block."

"A lot of men have tried to talk me into having sex with them," Carmen said. "But writer's block is a first."

"The thing is, I haven't had sex in forever. Not since Sofia and I . . . ," he trailed off.

At times, he and Carmen had each privately wondered about their new platonic condition. Each had occasionally felt hungry for the other, turned on by what they were writing. But neither wanted to disturb the equilibrium they'd established.

That afternoon had changed things.

"You're saying sex will jump-start the creative process?" she asked now. The kiss on the bridge had been pretty amazing. It had put her in the mood for a good fuck. She stood up in the tub and pulled off the bathrobe. "OK."

"Really?" He scrambled up. "Great!" He kicked off his slippers and led her into the bedroom. Standing in the middle of the room, they began kissing. Lucas pushed himself against Carmen and she stumbled backward. She countered with her own weight and Lucas tripped back. They staggered to the left, then right. They were like a human Ouija pointer, jerking this way and that. They looked at each other and laughed as though to say, *Ha-ha, we're really making a mess of this.* Then they dove back in.

"I want you against the wall," Lucas said, and walked Carmen backward. He unbuttoned her jeans easily enough but, after some tugging, realized he couldn't get them down. "Can . . . you . . . ?" he panted, looking hopefully up at her. Carmen braced herself against the wall and began pulling at her own pants. Lucas, not wanting to lose momentum, bent over her feet to help and crashed his nose into her rising knee. He flopped onto the carpet as Carmen landed on top of him.

"Oh my god!" she shouted.

Lucas cupped his hand to his face. When he pulled it away, his fingers were red.

She rushed into the bathroom and returned with a hand towel. "Tip your head back." She helped him into an armchair and guided his head against the seat. "These jeans should come with a warning." She laughed nervously.

"You kicked me in the face," Lucas groaned. "I knew we had our differences, but . . ."

"More like you kicked yourself in the face with my leg. You basically tried to pull my femur from the socket."

"So we're both casualties," he said. "I hate to say it, but . . ."

She nodded and finished the sentence: "This isn't working."

Lucas laughed. "It felt off somehow. Like, forced. Which I don't understand because I really, really wanted this."

"Me too," she said.

"Really?"

"Oh, don't look so shocked." Carmen waved at him dismissively. "But look, just because two people *want* there to be chemistry doesn't mean there's going to *be* chemistry."

"But this afternoon on the bridge was full of chemistry. What, did we just lose it?"

"I don't know. It's not like we haven't been off—way off—before."

Lucas drew the towel away from his face and gently touched his nose. The bleeding had stopped. "But things between us are different now. Right?"

She smiled. "Things are different now."

Lucas felt a sudden flood of joy. What an odd reaction to a humiliating sexual failure. He leaned back and closed his eyes.

"Are you sure you're OK? Should I call a doctor?"

"I've never been better."

"Well, then, let's call this a fluke." She was decidedly businesslike. "And I think we should get out of here. That's what made the bridge so great—don't you think? The audience."

Lucas nodded slowly. The irony began to dawn on him: They used to have sex in private for the purpose of public performance. Now that *they* were public, they had no private spark.

"I guess we only have chemistry when there's an audience," he said, realizing that this sealed their platonic status.

"We only have chemistry when there's an audience," she replied.

Lucas considered the meaning of this. Out of her mouth, those words didn't sound so fatal. They sounded like a revelation. Like a discovery. Like a . . . plan?

"We," he said, repeating the words back to her slowly, "only have chemistry when there's an audience."

And soon they were out the door.

They did not return to the Mandarin that night. The bars closed at 4:00 A.M, and deposited them out onto Bleecker Street in the frigid pre-dawn, their bodies pressed together as much for stability as for warmth, the last strong drinks still circulating through their veins. They were laughing, had been laughing for what seemed like hours now: about the comical number of people who'd offered them a threesome; about the selfies people took without asking, just shoving their faces up next to Carmen and Lucas and blinding them with a camera flash; about the CEO of some sex toy start-up who'd handed them "his-and-hers" vibrators; about the woman who showed them a tweet that had just gone out: "I'm at the same bar as Carmen Kelly right now and she looks a lot older in person." When Carmen saw that, she grabbed the phone, hopped up on the barstool, held it aloft, and yelled, "To whoever just tweeted that I'm old, I want you to know I'm going to take young Lucas home tonight and screw his brains out!" The bar erupted in cheers.

And that's where the two of them finally went. "We're home," Carmen announced, taking Lucas by the hand and leading him into her building. They tripped up the stairs, giggling like little kids. After some effort, she managed to unlock her door.

And then they were inside, kissing, shedding shoes and clothes, high on the night, the booze, the attention, the excitement of it all. They were still laughing. Whenever they came up for air, they laughed. Which, for all the sex they'd had, was something they'd never done before. And so, laughing, they fell into the bed—the glorious cloud bed. They made good use of it until dawn, at which point, exhausted, happy, and finally sated, they passed out.

CHAPTER 36

The first time Lucas visited the New York Public Library, he'd just gone to find a book. Still, as he climbed the stairs past those stately lions he imagined himself entering one of the world's great cathedrals. Now, nearly a year later, he discovered that the private after-dark library was far more magical than the public daytime one. A veteran gossip columnist in the city, Stu North, was having his annual Stu's Survivors benefit gala. And for the occasion, the library had been transformed into a glamorous Wonderland. Guests in black tie sipped jewel-hued martinis. Waiters passed cocktails, both alcoholic and crustacean. And in the atrium, petit fours dangled like delicate flowers from trellis set pieces. Now and then, Lucas saw a movie star float by, on a current of small talk and champagne.

Unlike Spragg's birthday fete, the evening had a leisurely, almost somniferous quality. Everything was charming, and in the dim light everyone was attractive, no matter how overzealous their makeup job. Lucas wasn't entirely clear who Stu's Survivors were or how the gala benefited them, but the issue seemed unlikely to be raised. Jays had brought Lucas along to "show support," which meant they would appear and shake some hands. Lucas liked this; his mere presence was *supportive*.

It was the first time since their public debut that Lucas and Carmen weren't doing a big event together. Which did seem odd. But Carmen appeared unconcerned. "It'll be more Greenwich, Connecticut, than Greenwich Village," she'd told Lucas. "I'm too uncouth for the stuffy old suits there. You go play the southern gentleman."

And so Lucas did just that, following Jays around and meeting the attendant philanthropists and executives. Carmen was right about the retro scene. When couples walked together, the men led, subtly, by touching the low-mid backs of their dates. When women went off to the bathrooms in small groups, their husbands clustered ever closer. It occurred to Lucas that most men were drinking brown cocktails, while most women were drinking clear or brightly colored ones. Most attendees he met didn't register even a flicker of recognition—no knowledge of Nice Guy, or "Screw the Critics," or, it seemed, anything about *Empire* aside from its powerful place in New York media and the importance of Jay Jacobson. And so, by way of introduction, Jays often went full Nicholas Spragg on Lucas's family history—transforming Lucas into a deeply connected son of the southern elite.

"If you buy a luxury car in North or South Carolina," Jays told one mustachioed man, "you can be sure that Lucas's father was somehow involved."

Lucas just smiled and shook the man's hand. The lies made him uncomfortable, but he had to admire the narrow line they walked: The amped-up details sounded impressive but begged no questions that Lucas couldn't answer. None of the men in this library had ever, or would ever, buy a car in the Carolinas.

"This crowd seems outside *Empire's* demo," he said to the Editor as they waited at the bar. "Are they really useful to us?"

"The College needs some fresh capital," Jays said. "And the kids of these people are half our audience." Then he leaned in and whispered, "I'll be providing them a valuable service: baby-sitting the scandal-prone set."

Later, Lucas stood at the second-floor balcony, watching Jays maneuver through the crowd, shaking hands and smiling with the fluidity of a politician seeking campaign donations. The Editor kept his disdain for these people well masked.

"Incredibly stuffy down there, right? Full-on nasal congestion."

Lucas turned to see none other than his roommate, Tyler, gnawing on a lamb chop. "I haven't seen you in a week!" Ever since Lucas had been named Brand Ambassador, he'd spent almost every night at a fancy hotel or at Carmen's apartment.

"And whose fault is that, *Nice Guy*?"

"I'm really sorry, Tyler. I wanted to tell you the truth. I really did."

"No need to apologize. *Noser's* the enemy. And anyway, I figured it out a while ago."

"What? How? Did Sofia tell you? She promised—"

Tyler shook his head. "Sofia may be fickle, but she's true to her word. It was simpler than that. About two months ago, you left your laptop open in the living room when you went to the bathroom and I saw a very mean description of oral sex written out in a Word document on your screen. A few days later, I saw it in the magazine. Case closed."

"I'm a moron," Lucas said. "Why didn't you out me?"

"I'm your friend, dude. I'm also not especially interested in drawing attention to the fact that we're roomies. It wouldn't look good for either of us, especially since, these days, I'm on the Jay Jacobson financial ruin beat."

"Hyperbole much?" Lucas felt a little defensive on behalf of his boss. After all, he was here to show support.

"This is obviously off-the-record and I'm still putting the pieces together, but if those blue bloods down there knew how overextended Jays was, his rock-hard ass would be hitting Fifth Avenue. Follow the money, right?" Tyler sucked the fat off his lamb chop. "This is delicious," he said, and looked around for a waiter. "Oh, and I have it on good authority that the Wild Boar is closing."

"But that's horrible. The Wild Boar is like his child. It's an institution."

"An institution *you* can't even set foot in without an invitation." Tyler flagged down a waiter carrying a tray of cocktails. "Although for all I know, with your new fancy status you can go whenever you damn well please." Tyler deposited the lamb bone and lifted two martinis. He handed one to Lucas.

"You *are* pissed at me."

Tyler shook his head. "Not at all. Jays is doing all right by you. Though I have to ask—roommate-to-roommate—why come out as Nice Guy now? And don't try to tell me that it was Jays' decision. He didn't have a clue who you were, am I right?"

Lucas wasn't eager to talk about his near firing. The Spragg profile was like a shirt tag scratching at his neck. If he could ignore it long enough, he could probably get used to it. But Tyler would most certainly want to cut it off and examine the rough edges.

"Fess up," Tyler said. "Don't I deserve something for my decency?"

Lucas groaned and, after extracting a vow of silence from

Tyler, explained what had happened in Jays' office. When he'd finished, Tyler merely observed the scene down below, contemplatively chewing an olive.

"You have nothing to say?" Lucas asked.

"Sorry, what?" Tyler looked up at Lucas.

"To my story. You have no response?"

"Well, yes, but . . ." Tyler glanced back at the party. Jays had ceased chasing WASPs and was now casting about the room. "Is he looking for you?" Tyler asked. Sure enough, Jays caught Lucas's eye and pointed toward the doors. A sufficient amount of support had been shown for one night.

"I guess we're heading—" Lucas began before he realized that Tyler was no longer standing beside him. Lucas looked up and down the gallery, but his roommate had vanished.

"Let's take a drive, Lucas. Do you feel like a drive?"

They'd reconvened in Jays' car, the heat blowing full blast. Before Lucas could answer, the driver was already heading toward the FDR. It felt odd, going for a late-night drive with his boss. But also a good sign. Jays was taking Lucas seriously in his new position. He wasn't just trotting him out to events. He wanted to develop a relationship, maybe even a friendship.

"Fucking freezing out there," Jays said. "February in this city is a special kind of hell."

"At least you don't have to take the subway," Lucas offered.

"Can you imagine?" Jays said as though Lucas, too, had the luxury of being driven around in a private car.

Not that Lucas was going to point this out. He was in Jays' world now—literally inside the Editor's car—and so the moment required a Jays'-centric point of view.

"Can't you just jet off to your house in Anguilla when the weather turns nasty?"

Jays looked amused. "This car is one thing, but a house in Anguilla! Who told you that?"

Lucas's colleagues spoke about this with such certainty that he'd never thought to question it. "Well," he said. "I guess everybody."

"Huh." The Editor looked amused. "Tell me, what else do people say?"

Lucas hesitated.

"I don't want any names. But indulge me. What's something especially outrageous? It's been a long, draining night."

Lucas pondered. "People say you commissioned a sculpture of yourself modeled after Michelangelo's *David*."

"Life-size?"

"They didn't get that specific."

Jays nodded. "Fair. Because most of them have never been to my home, so how would they know?"

"So you won't be hosting the next *Empire* book club meeting?"

Jays laughed brightly. "This game is fun. What else?"

"Let me think. Well, people say that you primarily subsist on gel capsules—like futuristic food substitutes? And that you wax your arms. Oh, and that you wear foundation."

"Honestly," Jays said. "Why is it only acceptable for a woman to artificially correct her skin tone?"

"They say you get manicures."

"That, in fact, is true. Go on."

"They say you're into kinky sex stuff."

"Who isn't?"

"Oh, and people say you tell gossip columnists fake things about your love life." Immediately after blurting this out, Lucas knew he'd gone a step too far.

"Oh?" Jays said with exaggerated incredulity. "And like what?"

Lucas swallowed. They were galloping full speed toward a precipice. "It's just talk. I'm not even sure—"

"Like what?" Jays said sharply.

"Like you say you're dating women you aren't dating."

"Such as?"

Cursing himself, Lucas said, "That indie singer Felicity Koh."

"Who else?"

"Well, I might have heard something similar about Karen Scarpelli, the MMA fighter."

"Who else?"

"That's all."

As the driver pulled onto the FDR from 96th Street, Lucas racked his brain for a credible way to change the subject.

"That can't be all," Jays said. "I'm something of a man-about-town, you know. Surely I've fabricated more than two relationships."

"I really don't—"

Jays shook his head. "Don't be a buzzkill, Luke. We're having fun!" He gave Lucas a playful, if forceful, nudge.

"I think there was one other? Jasmine Washington, the actress."

At once, Jays' smile vanished. "That's not office gossip."

Shit. Now Lucas remembered that Washington had not been lumped in with the other women. Carmen had told him about Jasmine Washington. How after just a few dates Jays was convinced the actress was in love with him. He'd boasted about it everywhere, made it seem like Washington couldn't keep her hands off of him. It wasn't true. And even if it had been, no woman deserved to be humiliated like that. When Washington discovered what Jays had been saying, she threatened to make a public statement that would not only damage the Editor's reputation but also put off other actresses from wanting to be in the magazine. To keep Washington quiet, Jays had run a feature-length advertorial about her new business—a line of cocktail-scented incense.

"I could have sworn that somebody from the office said—"

"Don't bullshit me, Lucas. Carmen's the only one who knows."

"I'm not going to tell anyone," Lucas said. "I promise."

"That—"

Lucas was sure Jays was about to say *bitch*. Instead, the Editor turned to the window. "She's the last person who has any right to talk about inventing things. Especially relationships." His face striated with shadow, Jays turned back to Lucas. "Did she mention any of *that* to you? I'm sure she didn't. It's not really in her interest to do so."

"Any of what?"

"Only that a lot of the men she's written about are totally made up."

"What do you mean?"

"It's simple, Lucas. Carmen invented a large number of the men she claims to have slept with, dated, what have you. Probably in the columns she wrote about you—all that talk of banker boys, and whatever bullshit she wrote. Those aren't real men. Those are her imagination. Go on and ask her about it. I'd love to know what she says."

Lucas was stunned. What was Jays trying to pull? "That can't be true," he said. And yet. She'd been the one to suggest that they start inventing sexual escapades for "Screw the Critics."

"Truth be told, when she wrote the first Nice Guy column, I thought it was just another fake. When the rebuttal came in, my first thought was that she'd written it herself."

"But why would she have done that?"

"Oh, why does she do anything? She has all sorts of excuses. Here's my take: It's much easier to sit at home with your laptop and a glass of wine than to actually go out and report. I have to give it to her; she's pretty good at making stuff up. You'd never know which columns are about actual human males. Even you—the actual human male who's been screwing her—didn't know that she was approximately sixty percent less experienced than she claimed to be."

"Or maybe I was so inexperienced, I couldn't tell the difference," Lucas said, feeling suddenly morose.

Jays appeared not to pick up on this and burst out laughing, a deep guffaw. "I like you, Luke. I really do. I'm happy we're in this together. At any rate, thanks for indulging me. This was fun."

The car was now wending its way through the East Village. It stopped outside Lucas's apartment. Fun, Lucas thought as he got out, was not how he'd characterize that conversation.

CHAPTER 37

For the next two weeks, Lucas and Carmen took meetings during the day and reveled through the city at night. They began developing an event series and podcast called 21st Century Sex. They were treated to dinners at Mission Chinese, Momofuku Ko, and The Spotted Pig—the kinds of restaurants most New Yorkers had to wait hours or days to get into but where Lucas and Carmen could now enjoy seats whenever they pleased. At the trendy bar Death & Co, they celebrated the launch of a new cocktail called The Screwed Critic (it contained two beaten eggs, which symbolized . . . balls? Breasts? Lucas was unclear). They faked merengue moves at Bembe, hooked up in the bathrooms at Le Bain, shared a blunt with hipsters at Output, and whispered snarky comments about the glam crowd at Provoc as sparkler-capped champagne bottles bobbed by. They also had a lot of sex. The public's enthusiasm energized them, fed their hunger for each other. The chemistry was back in a big way.

Carmen was impressed by how well Lucas did in the spotlight. He was confident but never cocky, always willing to pose for selfies, always upbeat. She was also happy to see that he'd taken the initiative on innovating the column. It had been his idea to have readers suggest their weekly assignments—finally, no more ideas from Jays!—as a way to expand the audience. So far, there'd been dozens of requests for anal (Carmen: no thank you), role play (Lucas: yes to *Hamilton*; Carmen: no to *Frozen*), and the switching of traditional gender roles (Carmen drew on a mustache and Lucas donned a skirt). Suggestions came from every state, from the most ordinary people: from civil engineers to insurance agents. Often, there'd be a letter attached. Readers, it seemed, were curious but embarrassed and shy. They wanted to try new things but were afraid to ask for them—and so they lived through Lucas and Carmen, as if these two could test-drive their desires and give them a sense of the potential pitfalls.

One afternoon, they lay naked in her bed, their bodies slick. "I'm going to miss this," Lucas said. "When you leave."

Carmen smiled. "So will I. Can you believe we're *here*? Considering how we started."

"Well, you're different," Lucas said.

"How so?"

You're unguarded. You're real. You're lovely. He wanted to say these things, but he was suddenly embarrassed. Instead, he traced his index finger down her sternum, slowly circling each of her breasts. He saw goose bumps rise on her arms. "The way that people look at you, when we're out together—they admire you. I admire you."

He'd thought a lot about Jays' revelations the other night and decided not to dwell on them. The woman Carmen had been back then—who thrived on judgment and created suitors from whole cloth—she was not *this* woman.

"They don't admire me, Lucas," she said. "They admire us and what we're doing."

Us.

They began to kiss, but there, very quietly in Lucas's ear, was a voice. *Careful*, it said. *Remember what happened the last time.* So Lucas told the voice: *This is nothing like last time.*

"Lucas," Carmen murmured, sliding her hands down his thighs. At which point, the voice shut up.

CHAPTER 38

Halfway through Carmen's remaining tenure, Jays summoned his critics to discuss a new assignment. Lucas had not stepped foot inside One World Trade since he'd been appointed Brand Ambassador, and he imagined that his colleagues had been speculating avidly about his new, if modest, celebrity. He couldn't wait to regale them with tales from the sexual trenches. But riding to the twenty-ninth floor, Lucas began to worry. He thought about Franklin, his head buried in copy, his days spent checking the details of other people's lives. He thought about Alexis, deferring solely to Jays on all matters large and small. His own schedule was exhausting, but it was also downright bacchanalian, tumescent with pleasure: eating, drinking, screwing. It was pretty ridiculous when you stopped to think about it. More than this, he now knew what it felt like to be wanted. Producers wanted his ideas. Journalists wanted interviews. The public wanted his advice, wanted selfies, wanted even just a glimpse of him. Carmen clearly wanted him. Jays wanted him to keep a successful thing going.

He was a little worried about how his colleagues would react to his swift success. But Lucas had worked for his new role. Like Jays had said, he deserved it. The important thing, he decided as the elevator doors opened, was to show gratitude and humility. In short, not be a dick.

The office was typically quiet for a midweek afternoon. He stopped by Alexis's desk, but she wasn't there. Should he wait? The Sphinxes were watching him; at least some things never changed. He continued on. A few of his colleagues looked up. They seemed a little perplexed to see him there, like he might be a mirage. Lucas smiled, waved. Word of his presence began to spread. Chairs swiveled. But nobody got up. Lucas slowed his walk. Still, nobody got up. He hadn't thought this through. What had he expected people to do—form a conga line behind him? At last, he reached the exurbs. He'd intended to stealthily slip into his old desk chair, but his chair was occupied. The new fact-checker, short and trim with thick dark hair and rimless glasses, looked a few years younger than Lucas. His face screamed high-school chess champion. He was in the middle of relaying a story to Franklin and Alexis—something about a magazine feature and his dad and an elephant. He was cracking them up. Lucas felt like he was intruding. But that was ridiculous. "Hi, guys," he said.

The new kid craned his neck around. "Oh my god!" he exclaimed. "You're Lucas Callahan."

"Lucas!" Alexis gave him a big hug. Finally.

"The king returns to his kingdom." Franklin lifted his hand lethargically. "But what are you doing here?"

"I still work for this magazine," Lucas said.

"Well, yeah," Franklin said, although he sounded dubious.

"Hey, I'm Pete." The new kid stuck out his hand. "It's great to finally meet you. I've heard so much—and *read* so much, of course."

"Pete's your replacement," Alexis said.

That word—"replacement"—made him feel weird. But why? He'd never wanted to be a fact-checker and now he wasn't.

"Pete's dad is Richie Sullivan," Alexis added. And all at once, the spotlight above Lucas's head flickered crankily. He was standing before the son of a literary superstar—famed *New Yorker* writer, National Book Award winner, *New York Times* best-selling author. If your dad was Richie Sullivan, you could walk into any magazine you wanted. Pete smiled huge at Lucas, and Lucas tried to hide his annoyance.

"So anyway, to finish the story," Pete continued, not even bothering—Lucas noted—to fill him in, "apparently the editor had told the art director that my dad's story was really about 'the elephant in the room.' And 'we really need to focus on the elephant in the room' and 'just don't forget the elephant in the room.' So when the photos came in, they featured a picture of an elephant—a literal elephant—standing in a room. They spent like fifty grand on it."

"Oh, come on!" Franklin said, wide-eyed in a way that Lucas had never seen.

"Well, this was back when magazines had fifty K to throw around." Pete said this like he'd been there.

"What was the story about?" Lucas asked.

"Oh, I don't know. Something about the economy."

Could Pete have been any more dismissive?

"I can't believe the magazine OK'd the bill!" Alexis said.

"I can't believe the art director was that big an idiot," Franklin said.

"Well, I've got a meeting with Jays," Lucas said.

The three of them turned to him. "Oh, OK," Alexis said. She seemed a little disappointed, which Lucas appreciated. But he wasn't feeling especially social anymore.

"It was great to meet you, Lucas," Pete said. "I know I've got big shoes to fill."

Here was the praise that Lucas had been expecting—except he was being congratulated for the wrong thing. "I just did my job," Lucas said. "No shoes to fill really."

"But fact-checking is integral to making this magazine. My dad says that anything you can do to actually *make the magazine* is admirable and honorable. That's why I'm here."

Was this guy for real? How was Franklin's bullshit meter not about to explode?

"Hey, these guys were telling me about a story you'd been reporting," Pete continued. "Sounds like you're really following the scent of something. It would be so cool if I got to fact-check it. When do you think it'll be ready?"

Alexis and Franklin knew he'd been writing a profile of Nicholas Spragg and that he'd followed a lead to Wisconsin just before Christmas. But that was all.

"You know how long these stories take," Lucas said now, shifting his weight, eager to get away. "All the drafts . . ."

"Sure, sure," Pete said, nodding. "Well, I'll keep my eye out."

"Great," Lucas said. With that, he hurried away. He couldn't understand it. His friends didn't care one whit about his new position and his replacement had basically accused him of selling out by becoming Brand Ambassador. Which obviously wasn't true. He was writing. His byline was there, right beside Carmen's. In every issue. He'd tried to write a feature, and it wasn't his fault that Jays killed it.

The Editor showed Lucas and Carmen into his office, where Lucas was surprised to see a tumbler of scotch on the coffee table. Jays never drank at work. Something was off. Carmen must have noticed it, too, because she asked if everything was all right.

"Of course!" he snapped, shutting down further inquiry. "Look, I know you two are very busy, so let's get to it. We've been inundated with requests from around the country. America wants you to date."

For a moment, neither Lucas nor Carmen said anything. "I don't understand," Carmen said finally. "Dates are all we've been doing. Drinks, dinner, dancing, parties, more drinks."

"And sex," Lucas said, as though they needed a reminder.

"Frankly, I'm exhausted. I can't keep up with this. Lucas, aren't you?"

"I'm having fun," he said meekly.

"People want you *to date*," Jays said, clearly annoyed. "They want romance. So: Monday, it'll be fancy reservations, flowers, a good night kiss. Tuesday, an afternoon in the city, doing something date-y—a museum or ice skating."

"Hold on a second," Carmen interrupted. "You said no *feelings*."

"I know. But we did some polling and romance is what people want—or what they think they want." Jays continued the schedule. Tuesday afternoon they'd get to Second Base. Wednesday there'd be another romantic dinner, after which Carmen would take Lucas upstairs. "And then on Thursday you'll stay home and fuck each other's brains out."

"And what happens on Friday?" Carmen asked. "Do we have boring relationship sex and then bicker about taking out the trash? And then break up on Saturday?"

"Not break up," Jays said, refusing to acknowledge her sarcasm. "Just decide that you're better as lovers than lovebirds. But after each date, you'll write something for our website. You'll take pictures, shoot some video, let people experience the romantic tension."

"I don't like this experiment," Carmen said. "Lucas and I have known each other for months. We've been having sex for months. We can't just push some imaginary 'reset' button, playact a relationship."

"But you're terrific at playacting," Jays said.

Carmen's face went white. But Jays simply continued, "What I mean is, this entire column has been largely performative, has it not?"

"And in fact," Lucas interjected, "a PhD student at Brown just tweeted at us. Her dissertation title is 'From Carrie Bradshaw to "Screw the Critics": The Politics of Sexual Structuralism, Media, and the Male Gaze.' She wants an interview."

"How the hell did she fit all of that into a tweet?" Carmen demanded.

"Come on, Carmen," Lucas urged. "It's just a game. We'll have fun."

"Are we finished?" Jays sounded uncharacteristically impatient.

"Fine," Carmen groaned. "But I'm not participating in anybody's dissertation."

CHAPTER 39

The following Monday night, Lucas arrived at Carmen's apartment holding a bouquet of roses in one hand and his phone, already recording video, in the other. "Seriously?" she said opening the door. "We're really doing this?"

Lucas did not respond right away. He was still taking her in: her sleeveless knit dress, slinky and gray with a slight metallic sheen; her dark waves swept back; her neck bare save a penny-sized gold circle, attached to a delicate chain. "You look incredible," he said.

Carmen glanced down at herself. "Yeah, pretty good, right?" Then, as though suddenly embarrassed, she hurried off in search of her shoes. "The vase is above the sink!" she called back. "And turn the camera off. You got your footage."

Lucas complied and was filling the vase at the tap when she came up behind him and slid her arms around his stomach. "Wouldn't you rather just stay here?" She squeezed.

He turned her around. "We're on assignment," he said. "It is ze order of Jez Jacobzon!"

She seemed to laugh in spite of herself. "Come on!" he said, and led her out of the apartment and into a taxi, opening every door. They rode around the block a couple of times.

"Why are we going in circles?" Carmen asked.

The taxi pulled over just a few blocks away in front of Mira's building. "What are we doing here?" she asked, but Lucas was already scrambling out of the car and around to her door. He helped her out and they walked up the front steps. She was surprised to see him produce a key both to the front door and to the apartment. "After you," he said, and followed her inside. When he flipped on the light, Carmen gasped. The tiny space had been transformed. Ropes of twinkling bulbs hung above them, turning the ceiling into an arbor of pale white light. The end tables bloomed with vases of Winter Jasmine, Sweet Alyssum, and Calendula. In the center of the small room, Mira's card table was set with her best tablecloth and china.

"What is this? Where's Mira?"

"We've been getting the royal treatment these last few weeks, and I worried that Mira was feeling left out. So I asked whether she'd like a night out." Lucas glanced at his watch. "Right about now, she and a gentleman caller are sitting down to dinner at Eleven Madison Park."

"You're paying for that? Lucas, that's like two hundred and fifty dollars. Per person."

"Not me," he said, flashing a satisfied smile. "*Empire*. Mira and her friend are using our reservation. Don't worry, I spoke to the maître d'. He knows what's up."

"Th-that's . . . th-this is . . . ," Carmen stammered. She walked farther into the apartment, looked up at the lights. "It's gorgeous."

"Well, I figured there needed to be *some* element of romance for our non-date date."

"And you're not even following me around with a camera!"

"Oh," Lucas said, clearly pleased with himself, "I took photos beforehand. Didn't want to ruin the atmosphere once you arrived. And hey, at least I didn't fill the place with rose petals and candles. I didn't want you walking out on me." Carmen turned to him. He'd never seen quite that look on her face before. For a moment, he wondered if she was going to cry. Then the buzzer sounded.

"And here's the best part!" Lucas exclaimed. "Dinner!" A moment later, a deliveryman appeared holding a large pizza box. Lucas carried it over to a side table. "Sausage and mushroom good?"

Carmen nodded, still dumbstruck.

Lucas busied himself opening the wine and serving them. When they were finally settled, Lucas offered a toast. "Here's to a quiet night in," he said.

They clinked glasses. For a moment they ate in silence, enjoying the lights twinkling overhead and the hot, gooey cheese.

"So," she said when the silence began to stretch on a bit too long.

"So," he said.

"First dates sure are awkward."

Lucas chewed. She was looking at him, waiting for him to say something. And so he might as well admit it, because at this point, why not? "This is my first-ever first date."

"No kidding."

She looked fascinated, so he began to tell her about Mel. They'd gone to the same high school but hadn't really known each other until college, when they realized they lived a floor apart at UNC. Eventually, he rigged up a small basket on a piece of twine and would lower snacks and stupid notes down to her room from the window. Just before he left on winter break, he lowered down an envelope with a handful of rose petals and a card that said: "From L."

"That's so adorable . . . and sappy." Carmen was trying not to laugh.

"Hey, cut me some slack," he protested. "I was nineteen. I'd never been in a serious relationship before. I was a virgin." Lucas paused to see how she would take this. But Carmen merely nodded for him to continue. "I knew Mel liked me and that we were both just really shy and one of us was going to have to make a move. But all around us, people were hooking up and having flings and it was impossible to know whether anything *meant* anything. I didn't want her to spend all of winter break guessing and worrying."

"Your attempt at clarity was a note that said 'From'?" Carmen was full-on laughing now. "And what did Mel do—no, wait, I know. She spent the entirety of break guessing and worrying?"

"Pretty much. She was in Georgia at her grandparents' house, so we didn't see each other at all. But we came back to school early, just before rush started. And, well, it happened."

"You slept together?"

Lucas shook his head. "We didn't actually sleep together for another five months."

"Jesus Christ! You innocents."

"But we were together from then on. Until she dumped me last May."

"You were engaged, right?"

Lucas nodded.

"Did she get cold feet?"

Lucas shook his head.

"She fell in love with someone else?"

"Nope."

"You cheated?"

"No!"

"Then what? She didn't suddenly decide that she no longer believed in the institution of marriage?"

Aside from Sam, Lucas had told no one about what precipitated the breakup. He'd been too embarrassed. But now he felt ready—a new-enough man to observe his old self with some distance. So he told Carmen: "I was a coward."

"Not what I was expecting to hear," she said.

"Second semester of our senior year, Mel decided that we should break up. She said we obviously weren't getting married anytime soon, but we'd survived, as most relationships around us hadn't. Which, by default, put us on the marriage track. So, before we started developing our real, post-college lives, she thought we should take the opportunity to explore new things. And, like, other people. She said if we still loved each other a year out of college, we'd pick things up again."

"I am *super*impressed with Mel right now," Carmen said. "I mean, sorry, you know I'm on Team Lucas all the way, but it takes a strong and smart woman to propose something like that. What did you do?"

"I said OK. And honestly, it wasn't an especially difficult decision. *That* should have been the red flag."

Carmen nodded thoughtfully.

"But then our parents stepped in. It didn't make sense to them—deciding to temporarily dissolve a relationship like that. They thought we were perfect together. Our mothers, in particular, were practically planning our wedding. They had our lives mapped out. Law school for me. Then I'd go to work for Mel's dad. And Mel studied art history, so she'd open a gallery in Charlotte and host society parties. And both of our parents just kept working at us—'you're making a mistake; you're so happy together.' And we freaked out a little. Because what if we *were* making a huge mistake? What if our relationship was the best relationship either of us would ever have? What if there was nothing better out there?"

"That's exactly how people feel when they're stuck."

Lucas nodded. "We were both cowards, I guess. It was just easier. It was comfortable. So we didn't break up, which of course thrilled our families. We moved in together. And then, honestly, it was like sleepwalking toward the inevitable. We would get engaged. Only it took me a long time to do it. I kept putting it off and we'd get into these horrible fights and she'd be crying and eventually I told myself that enough was enough."

"You broke things off?"

"No, I bought a ring and proposed."

Carmen just shook her head. "Were you even a little bit happy?"

"I mean, yes? But I wasn't giddy. I was like, *I've done the right thing.*"

"Shit, Lucas, those are like the worst five words in the world. Nobody ever wants to be proposed to because it's 'the right thing.'"

"God, I know. But I told myself that I was going to have a good life. And how could anyone not want that—a good life? My brother, he has a good life."

"But good isn't necessarily right—like, *actually* right."

"I figured that out." Lucas said that before long he grew annoyed with dumb things, like how Mel teased her bangs and shredded her napkin and insisted that they always go to bed at the same time even though nothing much ever happened in the dark. New things bothered him, too. Like how Mel told nearly every person she encountered that she'd been forced to explain precisely what kind of engagement ring she wanted, down to the cut, clarity, and color, to prevent Lucas from fucking it up. She threw herself into the wedding planning with a fervor that drove him nuts. It was just a dress, just dinner, just a band!

Why did she care so much? Looking back, Lucas understood that his attitude was born out of resentment—the (mistaken) belief that Mel had forced him into all this. And so, Lucas checked out. He made plans with his friends and didn't tell Mel. He was late returning her texts. He made halfhearted apologies, blamed his crappy phone battery. He forgot to do the small errands and favors that he'd always been meticulous about in the past. He'd come too far to walk away from the relationship, but it seemed he was begging to be pushed out of it.

It all erupted the night of their engagement party on Memorial Day weekend. Mel's aunt and uncle hosted what seemed like half of Charlotte on the deck of a new upscale BBQ restaurant. All night, Lucas had been aloof and laconic. He'd tried to be amenable, but he couldn't muster the energy. He felt claustrophobic.

Toward the end of the night, when a few of his buddies said they were heading to a bar, Lucas decided to go with them, even though the party wasn't exactly over—just dwindling. He'd announced his decision to Mel, kissed her on the cheek, and left before she could yell at him. Later that night, he arrived home to find her waiting up, red-eyed and furious. She ended things promptly, employing a level of fortitude and decisiveness that both surprised and terrified him. The next day, Lucas moved out of their apartment and back into his childhood bedroom. He refused to talk about what had happened, and Mel, driven by familial propriety, was similarly tight-lipped. Nevertheless, it was assumed that Lucas was to blame. His mother was beside herself, his grandmother mortified, his father furious. Their friends flocked to Mel's side. Everyone hated Lucas, and yet he'd never felt so relieved.

"I let it get further than it ever should have," he told Carmen now. "I was a coward for not standing up for myself and a real asshole for putting Mel through the humiliation of that engagement. Sure, she wanted us to test the waters before settling down. But she was in love with me and I knew it—and I let her believe that I was in love with her. It was the worst thing I could have done."

"It was a betrayal," Carmen said.

"Yes," he said. "It was. Did the same thing happen with Jays?"

Carmen sighed. "I think at one point, for the briefest moment, he was in love with me. But it frightened him. And instead of letting me go, he kept up the charade of love. And I was so in love with him, and so certain that I was different—more special than all of the other people whom Jays mistreated and manipulated—that I didn't notice. And Jays knew that. He kept me around, by giving me *just enough* of himself to satisfy me."

"But why would he go through the trouble? Why not just break things off?" As soon as Lucas asked, he realized Mel's friends had probably asked her the same questions.

"I think that kind of manipulation is second nature to him. He probably didn't think much about it. But I did start to see past the fog. I started to realize that he was stringing me along. And that's when Jays broke it off. I'm sure he was afraid I'd leave him, so he did it first. He's *never* rejected if he can help it."

"Do you think you would have left him?"

Carmen considered the question for a long, silent moment. "Having someone want you is intoxicating," she said, "and Jays is an addict for validation. I think that's why he pretended for so long. But that's also why I stayed. I wanted so badly to be wanted, Lucas. And when that security started to slip, I just held on. Tighter and tighter."

She was gripping the table, staring past him. There were tears in her eyes. "I know that I should let go," she continued. "But I can't. The more I struggle, the tighter the grip. Lucas, I—"

She stopped and looked down at her hands. She began to rub the feeling back into her fingers. Lucas suddenly understood that she'd never shared any of this before. Not even with Mira.

"Hey," he said. "It's all right." He rose from his seat and knelt beside her chair. "If you want to tell me, I'm listening." He took her hand.

Carmen blinked a couple of times. She kept her gaze fixed on their hands, his on top of hers. "I felt out of control," she said. "Like I'd allowed Jays to gut a basic part of me. All that was left was this terrible wanting. I swore I'd never let that happen again."

And there it was. All of Carmen's judging and criticizing and dissecting was a buffer against her own wanting. It *was* really about control, but it was so much more complicated than Lucas could have imagined.

"But you have to let yourself want things at some point, Carmen. You'll miss so much. If I've learned anything through Mel, it's that. Chase the things you really do want."

He was desperate to kiss her then, to show her how much she was wanted. He was still holding her hand. But at that moment, the sound of a key turning in the lock startled them both. The front door swung open and there was Mira, bedecked with beads and holding a small bag of complimentary chocolates. Lucas sprang backward and Carmen sat up, stiff and straight in her chair.

"Well, isn't this a chaste sight," Mira said, and gave her granddaughter a not-so-subtle wink. Lucas was surprised by how deeply Carmen blushed.

After Mira described her fabulous dinner and wished them good night, Lucas walked Carmen home, their arms linked, their bodies pressed close for warmth. They were alone on the street, the city quiet in a way unique to winter nights. He pressed closer to Carmen and she pressed back. He felt, simply, happy.

At the steps of her building they stopped. "I guess this is where I'm supposed to kiss you," he said.

"It seems a little silly, doesn't it?"

"I guess." Lucas shrugged, glanced at his feet.

"You want a real good-night kiss!" she exclaimed. "You're taking this seriously!"

"Oh please."

"No, no. I admire your conscientiousness with this assignment."

He was about to ask whether she was serious or joking when she kissed him. The sudden warmth of her mouth sent a rush of heat through his body, straight down into his toes. He could feel the cold, like fingers, trying to pry them apart. But the chill couldn't get a grip. He leaned into her. She leaned into him, and she sighed.

Lucas had heard Carmen make many sounds. He'd known her to moan, yelp, pant, murmur, and laugh. And yet he'd never heard her make a sound like this: at once breathless and substantial, the audible turned physical. It sounded like she had finally yielded some deeper part of herself.

Neither of them noticed the photographer in the shadows, snapping away.

CHAPTER 40

The next afternoon, they went skating at Rockefeller Center. Afterward, as Lucas bought them hot chocolates, two young women approached Carmen. They wore pom-pommed knit hats and overlarge puffy coats and a surfeit of foundation. "That looked so hot last night," one of them said to her.

Carmen looked up from tying her boots. "Excuse me?" she said.

"The kiss at the end of the night," the other one explained. "Tell us everything."

"I really don't know what you're talking about."

The women's faces started to sour. "What, you think you're too good to talk to us?" the first one said.

"Nooo," Carmen began, slowly, unsure of where this was going but instantly familiar with the women's expectations. Hers was a terrible kind of fame. She wasn't Peter Dinklage out walking his dog, or Maggie Gyllenhaal buying her adorable children ice cream, or any other at-a-distance New York celebrity people recognized but didn't feel they truly *knew*. Internet-famous people like Carmen gained fame by exploiting their personal lives, which led the public to feel a sense of ownership over them. "If you'll excuse me—"

"God, you really are rude," the second woman said. "It's all over TMZ and you play dumb?"

And with that, the two women left, no doubt off to tweet or Snapchat the encounter. Carmen immediately pulled up TMZ to find pictures of her and Lucas kissing. His hand was on her ass. The headline: "Nice Guy's Naughty Good Night." She ran over to Lucas at the snack bar and handed him the phone.

"Whoa!" he said. "Paparazzi!"

"Don't sound so excited. You realize that Jays sent someone to stalk us."

Lucas led her away from the rink. "So what if he did? It's not like the public hasn't seen us kiss before. A million times now."

"That was *in* public. That was *intentional*."

"I'm not sure I see the difference," Lucas said. "This was intentional, too."

"The bridge was a show. We were performing."

"OK—and this time we were 'performing' the assignment. Like Jays said."

"It's not the same thing."

"Why not?" But Lucas was already answering his own question. *It's not the same, because this time you felt something. Something new.*

"It's an invasion of privacy," Carmen answered.

"You have to admit that it's pretty smart of Jays," he said. "Drumming up this buzz."

"What's up with you defending Jays all of a sudden?"

"What do you mean?"

"Well, you have no problem with him sending paparazzi after us. You've been totally into this whole dating thing."

"I just think they're good ideas. What's the problem?"

Carmen stopped walking and folded her arms like a school-teacher about to scold a child. "Lucas, listen," she said. "You, me—we're a team. Jays is not on the team. You may think he's doing something smart today, but tomorrow he'll do something smart at your expense, and you won't like it as much. And I'm not going to be here for much longer—"

"You think I can't take care of myself?" Lucas said.

"That has nothing to do with it," Carmen said. "All I'm saying is, he tried to screw you once already."

"What, by killing my Spragg story?" Lucas said. "I outma-neuvered him. Here we are."

"You *think* you outmaneuvered him."

Lucas looked hurt, and Carmen realized she'd made her point as best she could. "Of course you can take care of your-self," she said. "Just don't forget who you're dealing with."

The realization, when it came, was part of a simple mental exer-cise. It was the middle of the night on Wednesday, only midway through what was supposed to be a relatively chaste week of theatrical romance. The prior day's ice-skating date had led to museum tours and dinner at a lovely restaurant along the East River. Wednesday featured an afternoon helicopter ride, a move so knowingly ripped from The Bachelor that Lucas and Carmen felt genuinely embarrassed by it, though the views of the city from above were worth the fuss. Then they'd eaten dinner at a hidden gem in Queens. Finally, they dispensed with Jays' silly rules and returned to Carmen's place. "We only have two weeks left together," Carmen had said, "so let's make the most of it."

And they did. Carmen had fallen into a deep slumber moments after her last orgasm, leaving Lucas awake beside her, listening to the rain as it clattered against car hoods and air-conditioning units. He was counting the kinds of sex they'd had over the last six months. It was a veritable rainbow: vigorous, sensual, angry, and awkward sex; passionate, gentle, humorous, and competitive sex; abortive, drunken, embarrassing sex; hurried, laconic, turbulent sex. The list left him no closer to sleep. Presently, he was stalled on the kind of sex they'd had that very evening. He turned over and looked at Carmen, half-buried in the pillows, her dark hair fanned nest-like around her head. Something about tonight was different: newly intimate, especially intense. But to use either of these words—"intimate," "intense"—felt romance-novel generic. They were generalizations. And when you really knew someone, your physical connection was specific and precise. It was, Lucas realized, the difference between having sex and making love. Sex, on the one hand, was something you did. You could do it poorly or well. You could practice and improve. But it was, essentially, an activity, like yoga or checkers. Love, on the other hand, was something you made. Something you fashioned with great care from the raw materials: your body and someone else's, your heart and theirs. Tonight, corny as it sounded, he'd made love to her.

And he'd made love to her, because he loved her.

I love her.

Lucas froze as though the slightest movement would cause those three words to skitter off. Where had they come from? Were they real or a flourish of the game he was playing?

I love her.

No, the words—the feeling behind the words—had been gathering for weeks now. Maybe all the way back to Christmas, when they first realized that they actually liked each other. And

this *like,* as he knew sometimes happened in arranged marriages, had turned to love. His body vibrated; his heart thumped;
his lungs constricted; his eyes burned. *This is real,* he concluded.

This is a mistake, the little voice said.

Shut up, Lucas said back. He was so excited, he couldn't
think straight. This would upend everything—the column, his
career at the magazine, his life in New York. But he didn't care.

Sofia, the voice insisted. *Don't forget Sofia.*

This thought did, in fact, bring him down to earth. His
mistake last time was to declare his feelings based on a hunch.
He had to treat his relationship with Carmen like a magazine
story, and you didn't publish a magazine story based on your
gut. You reported it out, checked the facts. He needed something to confirm his gut now. In most relationships, that was
impossible. If love was blind, so was the route to admitting it.
But not this relationship. Now, finally, Lucas knew the advantage of sleeping with someone who was contractually obligated
to record her feedback in a notebook.

Slowly, so as not to rouse Carmen, Lucas climbed out of bed.
The pounding rain absorbed the sound of his footsteps across
the floor and the creak of her desk drawer. He lifted her notebook out and carried it to a window. Here was Carmen's catalog of their sexual history. The scribblings from their many
encounters, notes for the column. It felt like an invasion of her
privacy, and he hesitated—but rationalized that, hey, this was
all written for public consumption anyway. He wasn't prying
into her thoughts so much as getting an advance peek at what
everyone would soon know. He flipped to the end. The last entry was marked two days prior, the same night he'd kissed her
on the steps.

*Well fuck. I did not expect to fall for L. I did not want to fall
for L. I fell for L. I wish*

Fall for L. Fell *for L.* Lucas returned the notebook to her desk. He was smiling so hard, his face hurt. Proof! Her feelings as naked on the page as her sleeping body on the bed. And yet that tantalizing fragment! *I wish*—what?

I wish I knew what Lucas wanted and whether he wanted me?

I wish I wasn't so afraid of my own wanting?

I wish I could say yes to wanting him?

Lucas could plainly see the upward sweep of a letter, half-formed, beside the word "wish." She'd been interrupted midsentence. But any of these wishes would suffice. The question now was how to respond. Of course, he would pen a response. His column would convey without a shadow of a doubt that she was wanted. That *he* wanted her. He would do for Carmen what Jays had not: tell the world how much she was desired. But Lucas couldn't imagine her reading his declaration on a computer screen. What he needed was a grand gesture. A statement bold enough to demonstrate the force of his feeling.

CHAPTER 41

Carmen woke up late the next morning to find a cappuccino and croissants on the table. Beside them was a note: "Meet me outside MOMA at 3 p.s. How's this for boyfriend material?" The overture was lovely, and yet . . . She was leaving in two weeks, and all of a sudden this relationship had become incredibly complicated. As she showered and dressed, she tried to sort things out. First: She had powerful feelings for Lucas. Second: Those feelings were obviously mutual. Third: The timing was fundamentally, almost existentially wrong.

One more date before they wrote their "better off as fuck buddies" columns. That would be a good opening for a heart-to-heart with Lucas, a way to settle things gracefully before she left.

She'd just gotten dressed when the door buzzed. She peered out the window, checking for paparazzi. The street was empty.

"Lucas?" she asked into the intercom, assuming he'd forgotten something.

"Not quite," said the voice.

"Jay?"

"Can I come up?"

She buzzed him in.

He appeared at the door, and immediately Carmen noticed the uncanny smoothness of his skin. It was makeup, which he resorted to on the rare occasions he'd slept poorly. Something was very wrong; Carmen had never known anyone to sleep more soundly than Jays.

"The Boar is closing," he said, entering and sinking into her couch.

"Oh, Jay," she said. "I'm sorry." And she was. She'd been there from the restaurant's beginnings, had traveled the city with him scouting locations. He'd wanted that spot in the Village so badly, and his joy at securing it had been so pure. It reminded Carmen that Jays had been a boy once. He rarely spoke of his childhood—he was embarrassed by it—but she liked to imagine him running beneath the endless Kansas sky, massive wind turbines churning the air. They were the closest thing to skyscrapers in his world. Jays' young Kansan life was a constant search for the real towers, a yellow brick road to take him to New York, his Emerald City. "What happened?" she asked now. She sat down on the opposite end of the couch.

"The restaurant industry is a bitch," he said. "I thought The College would have been taking applicants by now, and that tuition could have helped prop up the Boar. But instead, investors have dragged their heels and The College is behind schedule."

Carmen nodded sympathetically but said nothing. She'd never thought The College was a good idea, at least not as Jays envisioned it. In his eagerness to bilk superwealthy millennials of their inheritances, he'd taken on too much debt and made unwise investments. It was all very un-Jays, actually: His ambitions usually led him to make crystal-clear decisions, but somehow in coming so close to building his dream he'd let ambition get the better of him. And the first casualty was the restaurant, one of the few things he truly cared about.

"I'm sorry," she repeated. She didn't know what else to say and wondered what he was doing here.

"How's the little dating experiment shaping up?" Jays glanced around the apartment, as though searching for some sign of Lucas. "Are you sick of him yet?"

The Editor sounded uncharacteristically defensive. Was he jealous? It seemed impossible. "Why are you here, Jay?"

"I wanted to see you, Carmen. We need to have a heart-to-heart." He shifted closer to her on the couch. "You know I'm not good with apologies. But I admit it. I fucked up. I took advantage of you, of your feelings." Jays was moving closer. She could now see how wan he looked. Tired and sad. "I'm not used to opening up. So I pushed you away. It was the biggest mistake of my life, Carmen."

Carmen felt off-balance; like a reflex, she wanted to comfort him. But then she remembered that she'd steeled herself for a moment like this. Many months after their breakup, she'd paused to consider what might happen if Jays came back to her. *If he does,* she told herself, *it's not because he wants you. It wasn't about you before, and it won't be about you in the future.* And now here Jays was, proving her right. He'd lost many things and wanted to even out his property. Lose the Boar, regain Carmen. One for one.

"Jay," she said, "I'm sorry you're losing the restaurant. I am. But this apology is too late." *And completely insincere.*

Jays leaned toward her. He took her hand. "I am a flawed man. I can't continue like this, alone, with everything falling apart. Please, Carmen."

She expected him to try to kiss her, pull her hungrily onto the cushions. But Jays did not move. He held her gaze, his eyes supplicating. She'd never seen him look this way before. *Could this be real?* Jays extended his arm and brushed his finger slowly along the ridge of her shoulder. Carmen shivered. Then she caught herself again and stood up.

"You've been manipulating me for years," she said, as if it were a cold fact delivered by a law professor. "You did it emotionally, and you did it professionally. You promised to get me out of the sex-writer ghetto that *you* put me in, but instead you pushed me into 'Screw the Critics,' knowing I didn't have anywhere else to go." Jays opened his mouth to protest but Carmen just shook her head. "You think that because I said the idea for the column first, that absolves you? It doesn't, Jay. You came into that lunch knowing *exactly* what was going to happen. Knowing that I'd let you degrade me just a little more. But I'm done with all that. You see things slipping away, and you're grasping for me. But the truth is, Jay, you're losing me, too."

"What are you talking about?"

"I'm leaving," Carmen said. "I'm moving to Los Angeles to work on a show. I'm done with this magazine and with you. I quit."

"When were you going to tell me?"

"Right now," Carmen said. "Two weeks' notice is right now."

Seconds passed, and Carmen watched the Editor's face for some sign of emotion. There was none. Finally, Jays stood up and walked toward the door.

"Go find someone else to prostitute out for your magazine," she said, just to get a rise out of him. His quietness was disquieting. But he gave her nothing; as he left the apartment, he didn't even look back.

———

That afternoon, at the appointed time, Carmen arrived at MOMA. It was a blustery day and the museum was crowded with tourists in flight from the cold. The lobby was aswirl with movement: museumgoers laden with winter coats and scarves, sucking down the dregs of their Starbucks, plotting the most expedient routes to Dalí, de Kooning, and Kahlo. Lucas was already there, clutching a bouquet of yellow tulips. Carmen maneuvered her way to him. He kissed her on the cheek and handed her the flowers.

"You're really doing your due diligence," she said. Yellow tulips were her favorite. He must have asked Mira.

"Shall we?" He presented his arm and they walked in silence toward the elevators. Lucas smelled very good and looked freshly groomed.

"Sorry I'm not looking fancy," Carmen said, glancing down at her jeans and PUMAs. It was just a trip to the museum after all.

"You're beautiful," Lucas said. And then the elevator doors were opening on the fifth floor—van Gogh's floor. Lucas stepped out.

Carmen hesitated and looked at him across the threshold. Another detail obviously offered up by her grandmother. It was no big deal. So why the sudden nerves?

"It's sweet of you to bring me here," she said as they walked through the gallery. "I'm guessing Mira told you the story— about how I went to Amsterdam to see a painting that was back in Manhattan. I know it makes me look a little foolish."

They were approaching *Starry Night,* though Carmen could barely see it through the crowd, pressed shoulder to shoulder. But then the crowd gave way, almost like it had been waiting. Soon she and Lucas stood before a velvet rope. And there was Charles, the security guard, unhooking the clasp and letting them through. A small space had been cordoned off directly in front of the painting.

"What—?" Carmen turned to Lucas. But she stopped abruptly, because there, just to the side, was Mira, dressed in her flowing finery, her gray hair coiffed and studded with tortoise-shell combs. Beside her stood a stocky, muscled young man. Carmen knew him from somewhere. He nodded at Lucas. It was Tyler, Carmen realized all of a sudden. He'd been an intern at *Empire* maybe five years ago, back when Carmen still came to the office on a regular basis. Tyler was a trip. She frequently ran into him at parties, where he worked the room, wooing women twice his age and height. Then, at summer's end, Tyler's internship was over and Carmen forgot all about him. It had never occurred to her that Tyler the intern and Lucas's roommate—a *Noser* reporter named Tyler—would be one and the same.

Lucas cleared his throat. Carmen saw Tyler turn his phone toward them.

"Lucas," Carmen whispered. "What's going on? What is this?" Her heart was starting to pound. There were so many sets of eyes on them now, so many lenses pointed in their direction. She was suddenly hyperconscious of the bouquet, dangling upside down from her hand, stems in the air.

"'Dear Carmen,'" Lucas said, reading from his phone. He took her free hand.

She looked at him with terror. Surely he wasn't about to propose? But why bring her here? Why invite Mira?

"'Months ago, you and I became involved in an experiment. It was an exploration of physical intimacy that had never before been attempted—at least not on such a public stage. We had nothing in common. We had very little chemistry. Actually, we kind of hated each other.'" Lucas grinned sheepishly. Carmen returned a weak smile. "'But over time, things changed. As we explored each other's desires and expectations, we built a different kind of connection. We became friends, then partners, then confidants. We became truly vulnerable to each other in ways I've never been with any other person. I did not expect to fall for you, Carmen. I did not want to fall for you. But I fell for you.'"

Carmen's heart beat hard against her sternum. She recognized her own words, of course. And though she had not intended him to find them—had not *wanted* him to find them—she could not blame him. Because they were heartfelt and true. They just weren't the only truth, the only thing in her heart.

Lucas continued. "'I fell for you,'" he repeated. "'It's not just about falling in love, though. It's about how much I want you. I want you more than I've ever wanted anything in my life. As long as we are together, you will know how much you are loved, appreciated, and desired. As long as we're together, you will never feel unwanted. Sincerely, Nice Guy.'" Lucas looked up at her. "I will be filing this for my next column, but I wanted to read it to you first."

Carmen closed her eyes as the tears rose behind them. She knew exactly what Lucas was doing. He'd designed this moment to be a foil to Jays and everything the Editor stood for—or, more precisely, didn't. No one had ever thought so carefully about what would touch her as this expression of love. And yet, as much as she loved Lucas and did not want to hurt him, she could see the future as he could not: everything falling apart and both of their careers ruined in the process. In the present, though, she needed to get him out of the spotlight and away from these cell phones. "Let's go somewhere and talk," she whispered. "I want to be alone with you."

"Don't be shy," he whispered back, but she saw that she'd planted the seeds of doubt. Because she hadn't pulled him into a passionate embrace. Because she hadn't yet said, *I want you, too.*

"You're amazing," she whispered. "This is all incredible. But not here. Please."

Lucas pulled back. "Why not here?" he asked in his normal voice.

Carmen took a deep breath. "Please, Lucas." She tugged gently at his hand, encouraging him to walk. He didn't move. Now what? She couldn't very well just leave him standing here. And she couldn't fake the response he wanted.

"I read what you wrote," Lucas said, a slight amount of pleading in his voice. "Your next column was going to be about your love for me. About falling for me. It's mutual, Carmen. Don't you see? It's not just some game we're playing for a bunch of magazine readers. It's us."

Carmen shook her head. "I do love you, Lucas. I feel more strongly for you than I have for anyone. But I—please, can we talk about this somewhere else?"

"No. Here." His bottom lip was quivering. It made her want to cry.

"I am leaving in two weeks to start a new life, and I need to be free. Completely."

"So what, you're just going to pretend that I don't exist?"

"Of course not. But we're going to be three thousand miles apart. A relationship doesn't make sense."

"We can make it work. I'll move out to California. This is once in a lifetime, Carmen. This is right."

"I'm going to hate leaving you, OK? It's going to be hard. Very hard. But it's not—" She'd gone too far.

"It's not what?"

She pleaded with him, silently, but he only shook his head. "It's not once in a lifetime. You're twenty-five. You've been in one long-term relationship. Who knows what else is out there for you? Settling down with you right now would be a terrible decision for both of us."

"All of a sudden I'm too young for you? You've been fucking me for months, confiding in me for months, and suddenly I'm a child?"

"That's not what I'm saying. But this is about me, too, Lucas. Being with you—it's taught me a lot about myself. What I want, and what I need, and who I am. I owe you so much."

"I'm so happy to have been the vehicle of your self-discovery," Lucas said, his face contorted with scorn. Carmen hated this. She hated to be the person who'd done this to him. All she wanted was to wrap her arms around him, to shield him from this hurt. But that would be like trying to protect him from fire by dousing him in gasoline.

"Well, it's the truth. You've made me a better person. A stronger person. And I know it's not fair. I know it sucks, being where you are right now. And this is not how I wanted it to happen. But I've been tethered for too long. Lucas, you *know* what I'm talking about."

Lucas's bottom lip had stopped shaking. "The truth," he said, parroting her. "What *is* the truth? Was it not what we've experienced over these past few months? Was it not what you wrote about me? What's the goddamned truth, Carmen?"

"That was all true. But it's also true that—"

"Of course," Lucas said. "So many truths. So many truths! I should have known better than to trust your version. Maybe people would like to know that we've been making our columns up for months and it was your idea."

"Lucas, be careful," she said. Carmen wasn't going to retaliate; she'd stand here and take insults from him. She was leaving in two weeks, no matter what. Had there been any doubt in her mind—and, at their most intimate moments, there had been some doubt—it was gone now. But Lucas was on the verge of harming himself. He could still have a gig at *Empire* after she left, if he was smart about it.

"Oh, I don't need to be careful. You do," he said. "I'm not the one who's been making up columns for years."

Her stomach dropped, just plummeted into her feet. She was suddenly hyperaware of the cameras: dozens of phones trained on them. *The Lucas and Carmen meltdown was filmed before a live studio audience.* How did he even know this? Jays. It must have been Jays. "Lucas . . ." She touched his arm, but he shook her off.

"When we first met, you raked me over the coals for months because of my lack of experience. But the whole time—long before I arrived—you'd been lying to everyone. You pretended to go out and meet men, date men, take men home. For column after column after column. But you weren't doing very much of it. How many of those bankers and lawyers and artists were based on real people? Thirty percent? Forty? Sure, writing a sex and relationships column isn't exactly serious journalism, but readers expected honesty, Carmen. They expected the truth. I expected the truth. That's all we've all expected from you, but you just keep on lying."

Shivers of heat ran up Carmen's arms. Sweat prickled the back of her neck and her upper lip. This had not happened. Lucas had not exposed her to the world. He had not retaliated against her with flippant, destructive cruelty. Not her lover and best friend.

Briefly, she considered arguing with him. She could make a case for herself, expose the inherent sexism in her professional situation, the power imbalance that had compelled her to act as she had, wrongly or not. Or she could throw this all back in his face, condemning him for being complicit in so much of it. But as stunned as she was that Lucas had sunk so very low, she couldn't summon the energy or the will. She meant what she'd told him at Christmas: She was done fighting.

And so there was only one thing to do. Carmen pushed into the crowd. They stared at her like she was naked, like she was dirty. Couldn't they just get out of her way? Everywhere she looked, there were phones trained on her, bodies hemming her in. She felt like she might throw up.

"Put your phones away!" The emphatic voice rang through the gallery, as though from a Broadway stage. Behind the voice came a frail, eccentrically dressed woman, elbowing gawkers left and right.

"Is that Miranda Kelly?" someone whispered loudly.

"You should be ashamed of yourselves," Mira pronounced, finally reaching her granddaughter. She looked back at Lucas with fiery eyes before collecting her granddaughter and leading her away.

In the elevator, Carmen felt she could breathe again. "It's true," she whispered. "What Lucas said."

Mira slipped her gnarled, ring-studded fingers into Carmen's. "Honey," she said. "I don't care."

PART THREE

CHAPTER 42

New Yorkers know exactly what to expect of their seasons. Fall is crisp and blissfully prolonged. Winter is interminable. Summer is glorious when you're sitting in an air-conditioned room. And then there is spring, the season of budding trees and brownstone flower boxes, of oxford shoes and ballet flats, of Meg Ryan and Tom Hanks finding true love. The city savors spring like a wartime ration. Come spring, even the most cynical New Yorker believes in serendipity.

But not Lucas. MOMA had left him heartbroken and humiliated, feeling that he'd misunderstood or mistaken everything he knew about Carmen. How had this become his pattern? Carmen, Sofia, Mel—all horrible, unnecessarily cruel miscalculations. He felt stuck in a kind of at-bat purgatory: there at the plate, forever on his second strike, destined to bean balls into foul territory for eternity. And yes, he felt guilty for exposing

Carmen. But given what she'd done to *him*, wasn't it justifiable—
at the very least, understandable?

Still, whenever Lucas closed his eyes he saw only Mira's pro-
found disappointment as she led her granddaughter away.

It was all too much. Lucas called in all of his vacation days
and spent two straight weeks floating facedown on the living
room couch, takeout containers lapping at his feet. The only
screen he'd look at was the television, a device mercifully void
of social media.

Finally, Tyler staged an intervention. On an afternoon in
mid-March, he thrust open the windows and a blustery wind
hit Lucas like the shock of cold water.

"Hey!" Lucas moaned. In response, Tyler handed over his
phone.

"Look at the 'Screw Off!' comments," he commanded.

"Are you serious? Can't everyone move on?"

"Just do it."

Lucas sighed, took the phone, and winced. "This one says:
'If Nice Guy was any nicer, he'd be Hitler.'"

Tyler snatched the phone back and groaned. He scrolled
around for a few seconds, then handed it back to Lucas. "Here,
now read."

Lucas did. There was a stream of comments going back
weeks, not all of them nice but many of them sympathetic. Men
of all ages, and even some women, seemed to understand his
heartbreak—to celebrate it, even. "'Every man has been in Nice
Guy's shoes. The rest of us are just lucky no cameras were
around,'" Lucas read aloud. Then he looked at Tyler. "And the
point of this is?"

"The point is that you're not a villain. You had haters before,
and you have defenders now. It's OK. People are complicated.
And look at this!" Tyler pulled Lucas's phone from beneath a

pile of lo mein cartons. "You've got a dozen missed calls and texts from your family. Fuck it, I'm reading them.

"'Mom and Dad are really worried. Call them!'

"'Honey, we love you. Please call us!'

"'Luke, your mother is beside herself with concern.'

"'L, Mom is freaking! Dad says he's sorry for being so judgmental.'"

Lucas took the phone from Tyler. "OK, not what I expected."

"And check out your inbox. Look at all those interview requests."

"You looked through my email?"

"Dude, I was worried."

Lucas scrolled through the list, stunned. Instead of ridiculing him, as he'd assumed, the masses wanted his side of the story. Instead of a laughingstock, the Internet had turned him into a lovestruck, lovelorn everyman. Maybe his career wasn't over. He got up off the couch. "I'm done with this shit," he said, surveying the mess he'd made. "And you know what?" It might have been the cold air or the MSG coursing through his bloodstream, but suddenly Lucas felt high. "Screw her!" Lucas announced. "Screw. Her!"

"Yes, exactly," Tyler said. "Now for the love of god, go take a shower."

The other thing Lucas had missed during his hibernation was Jays' public apology in the magazine:

To our valued readers,

As you are likely aware, our Brand Ambassador Lucas Callahan brought forward disturbing accusations against his "Screw the Critics" partner, longtime *Empire* sex columnist Carmen Kelly. He claimed that Kelly had fabricated portions of her columns for years, deceiving readers by manufacturing men she supposedly slept with and describing sexual escapades that did not actually happen. We take accusations like these seriously; *Empire* is nothing without the trust of its readers, and we would never knowingly violate that bond. An internal team investigated these accusations, and I regret to confirm that they are true. It hurts me more than I can say to have let down our loyal readership. You expected the highest standards of journalistic truth and were sorely disappointed. As of this morning, Carmen Kelly is no longer a writer or Brand Ambassador for *Empire.*

And yet there is reason for optimism. As of print time, over 14 million of you have watched Lucas face his toughest critic. You have seen his generosity and his courage. But more than this, you have seen his genuineness. In a culture where so much is faked, fabricated—and, in the parlance of reality TV, "produced"—Lucas has always been honest. Even when that honesty opens him up to scrutiny and criticism, he is a model of integrity. You, dear readers, understand this. In the last two weeks, we have received hundreds of emails, tweets, and Facebook posts from you. And all of you want the same thing: to see our Lucas pick himself up again. Which is exactly what he's going to do.

This is not the end of Lucas, or of the column "Screw the Critics." And I hope that you will once again put your trust and faith in *Empire,* so that it will not be the end of our relationship either. There is so much of this story left to tell.

Lucas didn't actually see the letter until he walked back into *Empire*'s office, a day after he finally took a shower. As the elevator opened up, he remembered the last time he walked in after an extended absence—only a few weeks ago, after his star had risen, and he was disappointed that the office largely ignored him. Now he wished for exactly that—knowing he wouldn't get it. Alexis was the first to spot him and rushed over for a hug. "Lucas, you poor thing," she said. Everyone gathered around, wanting to know how he was holding up. Franklin strung together multiple sarcasm-free sentences of support. Even that braggart Pete Sullivan, the kid who took Lucas's job, seemed genuinely supportive. "My dad was just saying how romantic disasters make for the best memoirs," he said.

Jays noticed the commotion and emerged from his office. The staff hushed as the Editor walked toward Lucas with arms open wide. (The hug would quickly be reported on "Screw Off!," thanks to Rogue Empire: "Jay Jacobson just bear-hugged Nice Guy, the first confirmed hug Jay Jacobson has ever given another human being. It's getting real here.") Soon Lucas was installed on Jays' distressed-leather couch. "I'm happy you've come back," the Editor said. "Now it's time to find you a new partner."

Jays, as Lucas might have guessed, had plans. "Screw the Critics" would be reborn as "Love the Critics." No longer simply a critique of sex, it would become a raw and detailed exploration of an entire relationship—from friendship, to intimacy, to love. The new column wasn't, Jays assured him, about the mushiness of romance but rather the complicated process of melding two lives. "Carmen wasn't capable of it," Jays said. "But I know you are. And we'll find you a partner who will be, too. So let's get you out on the town—keep your profile high—and we'll find a new lady."

Within days, Jays had whipped together a nonstop social calendar, and Lucas threw himself into his post-Carmen life, grateful for the distraction. Now there were nightly parties full of It-Girl artists and fashionistas, twentysomething magazine editors, novelists and Instagram influencers. A lot of these women were eager to jump into bed. Two women in particular— impossibly skinny and always greeting him like the third in a trio of besties—seemed to show up at every party. Were these his first stalkers? His groupies? He enjoyed the attention, and yet it all felt wrong. Like these women simply wanted to take him for a test drive, to find out whether Nice Guy performed as advertised. If only he could have sex with abandon. If only he could do it with the anonymity that Carmen once told him to savor. But he couldn't. All he wanted was to find his new partner, a woman he could fall in love with, someone untainted by all this nonsense.

The parties did serve at least one valuable purpose: They were a distraction. Alone, away from his beautiful crowd, he thought only of Carmen. He recycled their last few weeks together, searching for answers. He loved her and hated her, and he didn't know how to reconcile the two. He was desperate to know what she was thinking, but he had no way to find out. Contacting her directly was out of the question, and she'd deleted all of her social media accounts. He was sure she'd done it on purpose, specifically to hurt him. Instead of taunting him with the chronicle of her fabulous new LA life, she'd cut him out. She didn't care enough about him to make him jealous.

At the end of April, *Empire* began accepting applications for "Love the Critics." Women submitted a thirty-second video introduction, a résumé, and a writing sample. Any New York–based female between the ages of twenty-one and thirty could apply. The response was overwhelming, so Alexis was brought in to filter out what many in the office began calling the slut slush. Lucas sat beside her in the conference room with his laptop and headphones as the eligible women of New York flashed like subliminal messages before his eyes.

"That one's cute," he'd say, and Alexis would move her into the follow-up folder. "Oh no," Lucas would then say a moment later, "this next one is way cuter." And then the previous one would go into the slush. It didn't make him feel good, sorting women this way, although doing it with Alexis felt mildly better. At least another woman was involved in the ugly task. "It's really no different than swiping left or right," she said. And in truth, there was something cathartic about moving so many applications around however he wanted to. Pathetic as this might have been, it was the only thing that made him feel even moderately in control.

CHAPTER 43

On a gray Monday afternoon in April, Carmen trudged up from the Christopher Street subway. Another day wasted. She'd spent the morning applying for jobs she wouldn't get: copywriting, native ad writing, grant writing—basically, résumés and cover letters hurled into the darkness, on the off chance one landed with a manager who didn't immediately recognize her name. If only she had another marketable skill. But writing was all she could do. At the Legal Aid office, where she'd just had a fruitless meeting about Mira's eviction case, she'd started thinking about the benefits of practicing law. Not thankless public interest law of course, but high-powered, big-firm law. She'd hired one such lawyer after signing her Netflix contract. He was smarmy, racking up the billable hours, but he was also flush.

Which Carmen decidedly was not. After Jays published his apology—"An internal team investigated these accusations, and I regret to confirm that they are true"—Netflix's legal team had canceled her contract. Carmen was then forced to ditch her high-powered lawyer for Legal Aid, but the nonprofit's office was overextended and Mira's eviction date was swiftly approaching. It went without saying that Mira would move into Carmen's apartment. But Mira could barely manage a single flight of stairs, let alone four. And then what? "I'm an aging sex columnist who lied," she told her grandmother. "I'm unemployable." Mira assured her that things would change. "People have short memories," she said. "Take heart." But according to public opinion, Carmen didn't have one.

If she couldn't drum up work, she and Mira would have to move, even leave the city. Carmen had begun to fantasize about the open plains of Nebraska and the thick forests of New Hampshire, places where nobody had heard of "Screw the Critics" or *Empire*. Online, she'd been reduced from a person to a persona, a target that people were eager to hit with misogyny and schadenfreude. Terrible hashtags—it was her misfortune to have a name beginning with the letter *C*—proliferated like weeds. Carmen deleted her social media accounts, but it didn't stop the assault.

And how could she leave the city? Being from here—*of* here—had given her the confidence to scrimmage with Jays, back when they were merely flirting. It was the source of her nerve, what allowed her to bite back, to test his limits and her own. It had made her fearless in the face of an absurd power imbalance. So what if he drew a little blood? She'd been a survivor in this town; she could handle it. When she first started at *Empire*, she was so smug around the other new hires—her peers from Michigan, California, and even New Jersey—because she drank crappy bodega coffee and knew the subway map by heart. But she'd taken the city for granted, underestimated it.

——·——

Carmen had barely exited the subway station when a cold spring rain began to fall. Cursing, she ducked into the closest doorway. It was Kettle of Fish, one of the many local haunts she'd been avoiding—and not just because it was where she'd first met Lucas. The close quarters of the Internet were no match for those of the West Village. For nearly a decade, Carmen had walked these streets, frequented these stores, encountered many of these people. She knew her neighbors and they knew her, and her business. Since MOMA, they'd been watching her, judging her, pitying her. People call New York vast and impersonal, but those people are strangers to the town. On an island merely 13.4 miles long and just 2.3 miles wide, neighborhoods are like small towns. When people ignore one another, they're simply providing the illusion of privacy. Most days, it's a gift: emotional space, where physical space doesn't exist. But in reality, everyone is seen. Everyone is watched. Which meant that when Kettle of Fish's longtime bartender caught Carmen's eye through the window, she had to go in—or suffer a new groundswell of hyper-local gossip.

The bar was mostly empty, save a couple of NYU students procrastinating over pints in the back room. The bartender Aiden, who'd she met shortly after arriving in the neighborhood, was already pulling out a glass and a bottle of Pinot Noir. He looked straight from Central Casting: hairy arms, cleft chin, belly, and a bar towel slung over his shoulder. He was even Irish. But Aiden only turned on the gruff bartender act when he wanted to have a little fun with a tourist or gullible student.

"Ms. Kelly! It's been ages. I hope you're well—and that lovely grandmother of yours."

It was sweet of him to pretend he didn't know, but she didn't need his pity.

She sighed, turned the stem of the wineglass. "Come on, Aiden," she said. "We've known each other too long for that."

Aiden frowned. "What do you mean? Is there news? I've been in Ireland these past few months. My sister's been ill."

"Oh. I'm so sorry," Carmen said, and they spent the next few minutes talking about Aiden's family obligations. If his sister passed away, he'd likely return home for good. He had three nephews and his parents were aging. They'd need him. Hearing all of this made Carmen feel ashamed of her wallowing. She and Mira had their health. They had each other. "I'd be sad to lose you," she said. "I doubt many bartenders would have been as lenient with a regular as stingy as myself."

Carmen hadn't thought about it in ages, but she and Aiden had become friendly in the early days, when she was new to the Village. This was before she'd gotten a regular job, let alone her own column, and she was still scraping by. Nearly every day, she'd come in, set her laptop on the bar, and write magazine pitches—ideas she'd email to editors, who were almost guaranteed to ignore them—all the while subsisting on free bar nuts. A couple times a week, when she got a promising email back or, miracle of miracles, had a story accepted, she'd reward herself with a glass of wine.

"What you call stingy I call industrious," Aiden said. "Most of the kids who come here to 'write'"—he flashed air quotes—"are just flattering themselves. You know it by the size of their tab. They have trust funds and aren't getting shite done."

When she'd first met Lucas here, they were each at work: he scribbling in a notebook, she on a napkin. He'd offered her paper. And though she derided him—called him a grad student—there was an earnest way about him. Something reminiscent of her younger self. It was, she realized now, the reason she took him home: nostalgia for the Nice Girl she'd been. For the ambitious young woman who believed that in putting pen to paper she could make her voice heard.

And all at once, she made a decision.

"I'm running home to grab my computer, Aiden. Get out the bar nuts."

CHAPTER 44

One month later, Lucas sat in a TV studio as a *TODAY* show makeup artist applied flesh-colored war paint to his forehead. She was efficient, her fingers less than forgiving as they blotted and smeared. In an hour, Jays would announce Nice Guy's new partner on national television. And he'd also announce the column's new spin: Henceforth, it would be called "Love the Critics."

And who was the lucky lady? Lucas had narrowed it down to two women. They were both attractive, of course. But they were also superb writers and witty, thoughtful human beings. Each was deeply invested in her own career—and neither worked in magazines. Lucas had insisted on that point. He didn't want someone motivated by the spotlight, and he wanted a partner, not a competitor. "Love the Critics" would not be a cage match of judgment. Jays whole-heartedly agreed. In fact, the Editor had been terrific since the MOMA debacle: amenable and fair, available and consistent. So much for Carmen's warnings about Jays' duplicity.

Since Lucas had approved both finalists, Jays said he'd like to pick the winner and, in a genius stroke of marketing, reveal her identity on live television. Lucas would learn who she was when the rest of America did.

Now Jays sauntered in. He'd already had his makeup done. "How're you feeling, Luke? Excited?" But before Lucas could respond, the Editor held up his phone. "Just a sec."

Lucas turned to the windows, observing the pool of eager tourists who'd been waiting for hours. They flooded to the city, as they did each summer, with their subway maps and fanny packs. Soon the weather would grow sweltering and sticky, but for now it was welcoming. A glorious day to wait outside of 30 Rock, holding signs that read: "Happy Birthday, Grandma!," "Breast Cancer Survivor," and "I ♥ Nice Guy!" It thrilled Lucas to be part of the occasion for these salt-of-the-earth types, these first-time New York City explorers. He felt an outpouring of love for them. *I was once like you, my face pressed to the glass,* he thought. To think that he was on the inside now, part of the show. And yet he couldn't quite muster the excitement that he knew the moment deserved.

"Yes, at the studio!" The rise in Jays' voice drew Lucas's attention. The Editor rolled his eyes at the caller and made a yapping motion with his hand. "Yes, of course," he said. "It's all set. The story will go live after the segment."

Lucas marveled at how well Jays masked annoyance with false enthusiasm.

"I don't know where I'd be without you," Jays said. He went quiet for another moment. "Well, yes, I guess that's where I'd be. Good-bye, Nick."

Nicholas Spragg? But no. *Empire* had two Nicks on staff.

"It's almost time," Jays said brightly. "You look terrific, Luke. Are you ready?"

Lucas stood up and smoothed out his shirt. *Get psyched!* he told himself. *The rest of your life is about to begin.*

As the production assistant led Lucas and Jays onto the set, the Callahan family waved excitedly from their VIP seats. Gone was their snobbish disapproval of big-city life. They'd flown in from Charlotte to see their son live on national television, and the night before, over an *Empire*-expensed steak dinner, Lucas's father even apologized. "I'm proud of you, Son," the elder Callahan said in a tone snatched right from TV Land.

Kathie Lee Gifford and Hoda Kotb arrived with an entourage of producers and cameramen and settled into their chairs. It was almost go time when the lead producer hurried over, talking feverishly into her headset: "The network wants to keep references to *screwing* to a minimum. We're live in ten."

She counted down from commercial, and the hosts snapped to life.

"This morning, America's most-dissected bachelor is about to become one half of America's most-watched couple," Gifford said. "You all know Lucas Callahan, part of the wildly popular *Empire Magazine* column—yes, *that* column."

Lucas felt his undershirt dampen beneath the lights. Beside him, Jays looked like he was lounging on his own living room sofa. Lucas tried to affect a similar posture of repose and nearly tipped over.

"So, Lucas," Kotb was saying, "have you always been such a nice guy?"

Lucas blushed. "I don't know if I can say that."

"Look at that!" Gifford exclaimed. "Adorable. But sexy, too."

Lucas blushed deeper.

"Ladies, this is the one you want to bring home. But before we reveal who will have that honor, let's take a look back."

The lights dimmed and there on a screen beside them was a short NBC clip about "Screw the Critics," followed by a voice-over recapping Lucas and Carmen's tempestuous relationship, followed by footage from *Noser's* Facebook Live stream of them on Bow Bridge. "But it all came to an abrupt end," the voice-over said, "when Nice Guy laid his feelings on the line." Lucas struggled not to cringe—or tear up—when he saw himself standing before Carmen at MOMA. He hadn't seen the footage; he'd hoped he never would. But he couldn't look away now. All at once, the lights came up.

"It's been quite a road, Lucas," Kotb said, nodding sympathetically. "We wanted to know, if you don't mind us getting a little bit personal—"

"Hoda, have you read his column?" Gifford asked. "I don't think he minds."

Everyone laughed.

"So, Lucas. We know you're excited about starting 'Love the Critics' with your new partner. But I have to ask: It's only been a few months since you declared your love for Carmen. Have your feelings for her faded?"

The screen was now showing images of the two of them ice-skating at the Rockefeller rink, just feet from where Lucas currently sat. In what now seemed a lifetime ago, they'd held hands on unsteady legs, laughing about their own clumsiness. This was the cruelty of New York City. It moved on without you; when you left a space, it simply became populated by someone else.

"It's always difficult getting over an ex," he said, swallowing hard. "But I'm excited to move forward."

"I think Lucas is being overly kind," Jays interjected. "Which is precisely why he's such a Nice Guy."

The anchors chuckled.

"But seriously," the Editor continued, "Nice Guy has become a cultural touch point. He's the genuine, chivalrous suitor. The man women want to love, and who men want to be. Since this column began, the phrase 'nice guy' has gone from an insult to a compliment. And that's why we're eager to tell the next chapter of this nice guy's story."

"That's right," Kotb said. "We asked viewers to send in examples from their Instagram feeds. This one is from Alexander in Traverse City, Michigan." A picture appeared on the screen of a boyfriend surprising his girlfriend with flowers. The comments were littered with #NiceGuy.

"But #Carmen is also trending," Gifford said.

Jays nodded. "It is. A 'Carmen' is a—well, I can't say it on national television. Suffice it to say, America has decided who they support."

"That must make you feel good," Kotb said. "Especially considering how tough Carmen was on you in those early columns."

"It does," Lucas said, though he preferred to leave it at that.

A brief, awkward silence followed. "I'd say Carmen's been punished enough," Jays piped in. "She was hired to write and co-produce a TV show based on her experiences at *Empire*. But once her dishonesty came to light, that opportunity evaporated. I'm sure by now she's learned from her mistakes. At least I hope she has."

Wait, what? Lucas stiffened on the couch and struggled to maintain his composure, aware that cameras were trained on his every move. Inside, he roiled with questions: How had he not known about this? Was it reported, and he missed it? Had he really been *that* self-absorbed these past months?

He suddenly saw the dominos fall: Carmen, publicly shamed into hiding, trolled endlessly online. Netflix, canceling her show. Mira, dependent upon Carmen's money to afford her apartment, now evicted with nowhere to go.

Lucas felt weak. Sweat prickled down his back. He couldn't get enough air. He took a large sip of water from his *TODAY* show mug. He needed to get off this set, away from these lights. But he was stuck, pinned beneath the indomitable gaze of America's eyeball.

"So tell us about 'Love the Critics,'" Kotb said.

Lucas took a deep breath. He'd memorized this part. He could make it through. "Physical attraction is easy," he said. "But now we're looking for emotional and intellectual attraction as well."

"Sounds a little bit like *The Bachelor*," Gifford said. "But without the cocktails and trips to Tahiti?"

Jays shook his head. "You'll read no platitudes in our pages, Kathie. No 'journeys,' no clichés about true love. Lucas and his new partner will be giving us the nitty-gritty of what a developing relationship looks like. It will be honest and raw and, above all, real. Nothing of this kind currently exists in modern media."

"Well, then," Kotb said. "I think it's time for Lucas to meet his new mate. Am I right that you don't know the young woman's identity?"

"That's right," Lucas said. "I narrowed it down, but Jay made the final choice."

Gifford feigned shock. "That's a lot of trust to put in your boss! Picking out your potential wife. And of course, next week that relationship gets even more intimate, because your first kiss will be at your boss's house!"

Lucas looked at Jays; this was more news to him. "That's right," Jays said, "and Kathie and Hoda, your invites are already in the mail. We're going to pack my apartment with the most exciting people in New York, and watch Lucas and his new partner have their first kiss. And everyone at home can watch, too. We'll be live-streaming it on *Empire*'s website, so be sure to watch."

"Well, we can't wait. OK, Lucas, are you ready to meet your

new 'Love the Critics' partner?" Kotb asked. Lucas's brain felt like an overworked computer. Before he could process one surprise, he'd been hit with another and then another. But now came the most important moment—the surprise he'd been waiting for. He was finally meeting a woman whom he was allowed—in fact, encouraged—to fall for, head over heels. He took a deep breath.

The audience cheered as Kotb announced, "Let's bring out Lucas's new partner between the pages."

She walked out, tall and lithe in a white tunic and strappy high-heeled sandals. Her long brown hair shone like brushed silk and her face seemed, literally, to glow. She carried with her the scent of freshly cut grass. Lucas stood on shaky legs. He wasn't sure how he was going to support himself. It was only with the help of her hands, taking his own as she leaned in to kiss him on each cheek, that he managed not to buckle.

"Surprise," Sofia whispered into his ear.

CHAPTER 45

After the segment, there was a flurry of activity as Lucas's parents shook hands with Jays and exchanged hugs with Sofia. Then a woman who introduced herself as Sofia's agent arrived and they all—Lucas, Sofia, Jays, the agent, and the three other Callahans—went to brunch at the Wild Boar.

"We have much to celebrate," Jays said when they had all ordered their drinks. "In addition to our new hire, the lovely Sofia here, we are also congratulating Lucas on his first cover story in the magazine."

"My what?" Lucas asked, astonished. He'd been given no time to process Sofia's appearance, Jays' trickery, the reversal of Carmen's fortunes, or Mira's looming homelessness. For the last hour and a half, he'd been mannequin-like, letting people move him around, a fake smile gelled on.

"Lucas!" Mrs. Callahan exclaimed. "Why didn't you tell us?

That's incredible. Jim, isn't that incredible?" She nodded with the enthusiasm of a dozen mothers.

"Er, yes. Absolutely," Mr. Callahan said.

"I'm sorry I don't have the print edition to show you yet," Jays apologized to Lucas's parents. "But the story has just gone live."

Lucas fumbled with his phone. And there it was. Headline: "Heir Apparent." And underneath that: "The Prince of Apex, Idaho, Claims His Throne in New Amsterdam. By Lucas Callahan." Only it wasn't his story. It was a grotesque Frankensteinian assemblage of sentences that he wrote, shoddily nailed and glued onto those he did not. As everyone at the table watched him, he furiously scrolled through the piece. Huge swaths of his reporting were absent. There was no mention of the rape allegations or Spragg's contradictory origin stories. The money cake, too, had become a casualty of Jays' red pen. Only small scraps of truth hung from the story's bones, mostly related to Spragg's strong desire to leave Apex and strike out on his own. There were oblique references to an ambitious, innovative hospitality company that Spragg would be helming, though his ridiculous Wharton-esque references to "taking rooms" and "spending the season" had been excised from the discussion. Here Nicholas Spragg appeared the picture of intelligence, sophistication, and dignity.

Jays led the table in a round of cheers. Lucas drank with the others, but his beer tasted like soap. The joy on his mother's face made him want to cry.

The appetizers came and the group tucked in. Everyone seemed to be having a terrific time. Sam chatted with Sofia. Jays casually gossiped with her agent. But Lucas was immobilized. He'd walked off the *TODAY* show set into an alternate reality. He'd been given everything—Sofia, an *Empire* cover story, a heartfelt apology from his parents—but it was horribly twisted, all terribly wrong.

When Sofia excused herself to the restroom, Lucas waited a beat and then followed. He found her standing before the mirror, reapplying her lipstick. "Hello," she said, as though the two of them hanging out in the Wild Boar bathroom was nothing unusual.

"What are you doing?" Lucas spit.

"Touching up," Sofia said. "What are you doing?" She blotted her lips with a tissue, then pulled a small bottle of lotion from her purse. She massaged the cream into her palms, rubbing deep and slow, as though giving herself a hand massage.

"No, what are you doing involved in all this? With me? You broke things off. We're supposed to be done." *I'm not supposed to have to talk to you again, let alone fuck you, let alone try and date you! You hurt me. Just like Carmen hurt me. And now I'm—* But he banished this train of thought. He would not get sucked into a sinkhole of self-pity.

"But you're over me, right? It's like starting fresh."

He was, but that was beside the point. "Love the Critics" was about giving readers an honest look into a fledgling relationship. It was about dissecting intimacy as it grew and blossomed into something stronger and, perhaps, permanent. He doubted Sofia wanted any such thing.

"You're saying that this time around you *could* fall in love with me?"

"I *could* do many things," she said, inspecting her face in the mirror. "I don't know what will happen. It's an adventure. Come on, Lucas. What's the matter?" She looked at him. "It'll be fun."

"Because!" he retorted. "This isn't just some urban exploration. Some exciting new door you can throw open. This is my life, Sofia. You being here means I'm trapped in another relationship with no future, no potential." Sofia's eyes narrowed slightly. "With you, the conclusion has been written, and we'll just be pretending—no different from before. And I don't want another fake relationship. It's why I couldn't marry Mel. Why I despise Nicholas Spragg. It's why I can't stand you!"

Sofia raised an eyebrow. "Are you finished?"

Lucas continued to stare at her. Something was just sinking in. *Why I despise Nicholas Spragg.* "You didn't apply to be my partner," he said. "How did you even . . ."

She shook her head. "Jays came to me and asked if I'd like the position. Of course, I said yes. How could I not?"

Lucas felt the air rush out of him. All of this was connected. The timing wasn't coincidental. Somehow, Jays, Sofia, and Spragg were all pieces of a larger puzzle. But . . . why? How? What the hell was the point? Lucas tried to mentally snap the pieces together, but it was like a baby banging a cube into a round hole. Who was secretly on the phone that day Jays tried to fire him—Spragg or Sofia? Whose idea was it for Sofia to join "Love the Critics," and why was she picked over the actual candidates Lucas wanted?

Lucas knew who could figure it out—who might have even seen this coming. Carmen. She kept telling Lucas that Jays was motivated solely by self-interest, that he played a long game. And Lucas, in the end, had acted the same way. He was equally selfish, equally careless. He'd screwed Carmen, destroying the reputation and career of the one person who'd been there for him, who'd cared for him, who'd believed in him. The one person who'd been generous with him.

My god, he thought now, *how generous.* She had tried to protect him. And when his own myopia threatened to rain humiliation down on them both, she had pleaded with him to step out of the spotlight, away from the crowds and their cameras. She'd fought for her and Lucas's privacy in the one moment when it really mattered. But he'd forged ahead, heedless of the consequences. How ignorant he'd been. How callous. And then to sit back and do nothing as everyone piled on? To revel, even privately, in her evisceration, and not just by strangers but by the magazine she'd devoted herself to. So she'd lied in those early columns. So what? She'd been trying to forge a career, doing whatever she could to stay relevant—not to mention employed—without completely sacrificing her dignity. Lucas, careless person that he was, had sacrificed it for her.

Now his reward was to become a pawn in a game he couldn't understand.

He ran out of the bathroom without saying another word to Sofia and left the restaurant. As he hurried toward Sixth Avenue, he shot off a text to Tyler. "Meet me at Union Square," he wrote. "VERY IMPORTANT." He didn't know what he was going to do, but he needed to do *something*. Anything to make things right with Carmen.

Tyler found Lucas at the northern outskirts of the farmers market, pacing frantically between the baked goods and heirloom vegetables. "Jesus Christ," he said, and put his sturdy hands on Lucas's shoulders. "You need a drink." He steered Lucas toward Pete's Tavern, installed him in a booth, and brought over two shots of bourbon.

"Now," Tyler said. "The *TODAY* show! Sofia? Tell me everything." He looked legitimately concerned but clearly relished his proximity to the drama.

"Spragg," Lucas sputtered.

"Spragg!" Tyler exclaimed. "I knew he'd show up again."

Lucas nodded miserably. He told Tyler everything—how the day unfolded, what he learned about Carmen, and what just transpired in the bathroom with Sofia. "If I can just figure out who was on the phone in Jays' office, and why," Lucas said. "Everything else seems connected to that."

Tyler looked Lucas directly in the eyes, held up his hand like he was being sworn in for jury duty, and said, "Lucas, I have a confession—and please don't bite my head off."

"Are you serious?" Lucas yelled. "It was you?"

"No! No. Fuck no," Tyler said. "But listen, here's the thing. Remember months ago when we ran into each other at the Wilde's party and you asked how I knew the Sphinxes?"

That's right—Tyler had referred to Jays' secretaries by their code name. It struck Lucas as odd, but he'd promptly forgotten about it. What with meeting Sofia for the first time.

"Well," Tyler continued, "I used to intern at *Empire*. For a summer in college."

"Hold up," Lucas said. "That's something you might have mentioned, like, the first time we met."

"I know. I'm sorry. But I was covering Jays for *Noser,* and you worked for him, and I didn't want to create a conflict of interest. But look, something weird happened to me at *Empire* that could explain what's going on. You and I actually had really similar paths at the magazine. I came in superambitious, just like you, and Jays took an outsized interest in me. I was thrilled, of course, and chalked it up to my extraordinary talents."

"Just like I did," Lucas said quietly.

"To make it here, man, you've got to be at least a little full of yourself, a little bit deluded."

Lucas shook his head. Was that really true?

"Anyway, Jays put me on the event beat—sending me out to parties with instructions to peek into the personal lives of various prominent individuals. I was good at it. I'd come back with all kinds of dirt and write these short columns exposing everyone's little secrets, which Jays said would run as gossipy stories in the magazine. But they never appeared. Eventually, I went back to school, assuming I'd failed to impress Jays. But here's the strange thing. After a while, *Empire* started running stories about the people I'd reported on—and without fail, instead of all the dirt I found, the articles would be superpositive. Basically giant blow jobs. So I started keeping track. And three things were always the same. You ready?"

"I'm not sure."

"Well, buckle down, because a lot of shit is going to come together at once. Here we go. Number one, these people were all superrich. Number two, they were all the worst of the worst—like they'd committed serious ethical lapses, or had done something straight-up illegal. And three, within a few months of *Empire* running a positive story about them, they'd all start palling around with Jays. Sometimes, a news report would even say they'd gone into business with him."

Lucas sat with this information for a moment. Spragg fit this pattern perfectly. Lucas finds dirt on Spragg. The dirt never runs. A positive profile appears instead. Spragg and Jays seem to have some social connection.

"And," Tyler said, "you know Jays is having serious financial trouble, right? The Wild Boar is closing next month and Jays' new project—"

"The College?"

Tyler nodded. "It's rumored to be in trouble, too. Jays is close to defaulting on his loans. But I'll bet you anything that he's about to receive a huge influx of capital, if he hasn't already."

"You think he's blackmailing Spragg? Isn't that illegal?"

"I think it's more like whitemail. Jays is basically telling people: 'I won't just protect your secrets from public scrutiny—I'll let everyone know how fabulous you are. And in exchange for my generosity, maybe you could help me out.'"

Now it began to make sense. Lucas could imagine the scene. Jays calls Spragg and makes him an offer: He'll kill Lucas's story and make sure no word of Spragg's rape accusation ever becomes public, in exchange for a major investment in the restaurant and The College. Spragg accepts but wants vengeance as well: He wants Lucas to be fired, and he wants to hear it happen live. So then Lucas gets called into the office and—

Or maybe it went down differently. Maybe Jays called Spragg and said, "You're a very impressive man and I hate how this kid Lucas treated you, so I'm firing him right now and I want you to hear it." It would have been Jays' way of building Spragg's trust, before asking for the money. So Lucas gets called into the Editor's office for a lashing and—

Or maybe Spragg called Jays and demanded that Jays kill the story. Jays said he would, for a price. And for a mere $250,000 more, Spragg can listen as Jays fires Lucas. So Lucas gets called into the office and—

Whichever way, Jays clearly didn't expect Lucas to reveal himself as Nice Guy. But that didn't deter the Editor. It just changed his game.

"And instead of Jays being the bad guy, extorting Spragg, I become the enemy," Lucas said.

"It's kind of brilliant, right?" Tyler said. "I mean, that's the problem with blackmail—the person you're extorting hates you, which makes you vulnerable. But if you can establish yourself as the advocate and protector, then you get what you want *and* a thank-you. The manipulative faculties required to pull it off are really quite impressive."

Lucas put his head on the table.

"Cheer up, man; it's not so bad."

"So how did Sofia get into this mess?" Lucas asked.

Tyler shrugged. "You know what she's like. She craves new opportunities, but she's also kind of an opportunist. I bet Spragg's just using her to fuck with you. That dude hates you now."

Lucas lifted his head, dejected. "Carmen tried to warn me about something exactly like this, but I wouldn't listen. And then I let Jays spoon-feed me that crap about Carmen's made-up columns. I need to fix this, Tyler. I need to blow this whole thing open."

"You want to apologize to Carmen by committing professional seppuku? Lucas, ruining your own career isn't going to save hers."

"But it's the right thing to do." Lucas looked imploringly at Tyler.

"Well, with any luck, we'll see a financial transaction between Nicholas and Jays soon. In the meantime, we need more proof to make our case. I've got an idea, but it's a long shot."

"What is it? I'll do anything." Lucas leaned eagerly over the table.

"Those are words people usually regret."

Lucas sighed and sat back.

"During my internship, Jays occasionally had me bring dry cleaning and other packages to his house. Once, he even called me on a Saturday afternoon to bring him coffee."

"What a dick."

"Yeah, well, I was happy to oblige. That house is legendary. Very few people in the office have been there. And suddenly I—*an intern*—am at Jays' kitchen table eating a sandwich! Or in Jays' sitting room having a nightcap! I mean, my god. I thought I was the luckiest person alive. Of course, he was only kneading me into a pliable piece of dough. But one night, when we're drinking in Jays' sitting room, he goes into his closet. It's this massive walk-in, basically the size of our apartment, and covered in mirrors. It's *the* most narcissistic room. And he's taking off his shoes and his tie. And I'm thinking, is this about to become some weird sex thing?"

"Please tell me it was a weird sex thing." Lucas was again leaning over the table.

"He stops at the tie. But because of all the mirrors, I see him climb a ladder. All along the top shelf are notebooks. Just like the ones he's always carrying around. He pulls one down. And then he asks me questions about one of the people I've been investigating for him. Just casually, like it's no big deal. But I can see him making notes. Then he pulls out another and asks me more questions."

"And this didn't make you totally suspicious?"

"Was it weird that Jay Jacobson kept slam books in his closet? Sure. But did I think he was going to use it for a series of elaborate manipulations to help prop up his personal investments? I know you find it difficult to believe, Lucas, but I haven't always been a hard-boiled reporter. I was nineteen!"

"Right, but this was what—seven years ago? Aren't those notebooks gone?"

"Those notebooks cost a thousand dollars each! And yes, I think he's arrogant enough to keep them. The worst people in history are always great at paperwork." Lucas quickly flashed back to college classes about Nazis and communists. It was true: both meticulous notetakers. "They're like his arsenal. But imagine if we could cross-reference his notes with the positive press and then trace each person's financial contributions back to Jays? It's a pretty damning picture."

Lucas regarded his roommate: the muscled arms folded over his chest, the dark expectant eyes, the mischievous grin. "Wait," Lucas said. "Is all of this the reason you're writing for *Noser* under a pseudonym? Jays doesn't realize you're snooping around."

"J. P. Maddox at your service."

"You're like the caped crusader of New York media!"

Tyler laughed heartily. "If I am, then you're Clark Kent and together we're unstoppable. But seriously, can you get me one of those books?"

"How am I going to—" Lucas said, but then stopped. He

knew exactly how he'd get into Jays' apartment, because Jays had already invited him there. The very next week, the Editor was opening his home to New York society in celebration of Lucas and Sofia's first kiss—or "first" as far as the public knew.

Despite his height, Lucas had often felt small in the shadow of Tyler's bombastic personality. But at this moment, he felt robust, like he could stand in the middle of Broadway and stop Ubers with his bare hands. Like he could morph from credulous, selfish peon into a skeptical, altruistic warrior faster than Superman changed clothes in a phone booth. "I'm in," he told Tyler. "I am so in."

CHAPTER 46

Carmen was writing. And writing. And writing. For nearly two months, she'd visited Kettle of Fish daily, sitting at the bar with her laptop or, when the place was crowded, holed up at a corner table. She felt a little guilty: She should be out looking for a job. But Mira quickly squashed that suggestion. "This work you're doing is too important," she contended. "You're on a roll. You can't stop now."

But rolling toward what? For the first few weeks, Carmen didn't consider the document to *be* anything. She was flushing a lot of pain from her system, just words purged onto Microsoft Word. She was—god forbid—indulging herself. It was a point of pride that she had never done so in the past. She was a reporter and a critic. Her columns weren't *about* her personal life so much as they *covered* her personal life. Every detail, every admission, served to buttress an argument or strip down a source—and, really, until Lucas came along, that's how she thought about these men: as sources. The writer Janet Malcolm famously called journalism the art of seduction and betrayal. Well, then, the sex and relationships beat was journalism distilled to its purest form.

Only now, for the first time, Carmen wasn't trying to seduce or betray anyone. Instead, she stripped herself down, layer by protective layer. The voice in these pages wasn't the character she'd created to protect her heart or her ego from the world's judgment. Nor was it speaking at someone else's command. It was her voice, talking her truth: about how vulnerable she'd been, how mean, how proud, how gutsy, how jaded, how repressed, how judgmental. And she did so here at a bar, where everyone could see her. It was a kind of personal affirmation: *Fuck you, haters. I'm done hiding.*

Slowly a story emerged. If was, of course, her own: a tale of scrappy ambition, of romantic-professional entanglement, of manipulation, self-delusion, and the forfeiture of her dignity for the sake of love and career, all set against the backdrop of New York media. And that was just the part about her and Jays. She hadn't even gotten to Lucas yet.

Mira, bless her heart, was already kicking around titles and sketching out cover designs, while Carmen could barely bring herself to say the word "book." It seemed grandiose, if not downright impossible. But this being the West Village, it was perhaps inevitable that one evening, the *New Yorker* writer, National Book Award winner, and *New York Times* best-selling author Richie Sullivan would saunter in with Lydia Rothsfeld, his estimable powerhouse literary agent. And it was, perhaps, further pre-ordained that Sullivan, who'd gotten Jays to hire his son Pete in exchange for a 650-word column on silk socks, looked over, saw Carmen typing away, and whispered, "Lydia, it's that disgraced *Empire* sex columnist."

The agent nodded and sighed. "She got a raw deal. Her work was smart, even if some of it was fiction."

As it happened, Rothsfeld was just complaining about her upcoming seventy-fifth birthday party at the National Arts Club, planned by the new forty-year-old head of her agency. The city's literary elite had been invited and they were *all* coming, which meant just one thing: "It's not a celebration," Rothsfeld said. "It's a send-off. I'm being pushed into the abyss on a burning barge. I won't have it." She latched her wrinkled, manicured fingers onto Sullivan's arm with startling force. "Be a dear, Sully, and buy me two Manhattans."

"Two?" Sullivan asked.

"One for me." Rothsfeld nodded at Carmen. "And one for her."

CHAPTER 47

Jay Jacobson lived in a Greenwich Village brownstone, but he was increasingly fed up with the neighborhood. It wasn't because of gentrification; by the time he arrived, the beatniks and artists were long gone and the gays and first-generation yuppies priced out. (Just because you could afford a five-ingredient latte seven days a week, that didn't mean you could pay five thousand dollars a month for a studio.) But lately, not even high-end boutiques could afford the rent. Jay didn't know what was worse—five Marc Jacobs properties on a single block, or none at all. And then the community board had the gall to reject his remodeling application—his ideal building façade, the ultra-modern love child of Shigeru Ban and Snøhetta—on the grounds that it would "disturb the character of the neighborhood."

Such were the thoughts that needled Jay as he arrived home on a Thursday afternoon in mid-May. Most days, he could banish them once the front door closed and he was safe from the community board's clutches. His four stories hummed with efficiency and convenience. If only his employees and business associates took direction as obediently as his speakers and thermostat. Because today, the house was abuzz with activity. His event planner orchestrated her team like a conductor, slashing her arms through the air. Caterers rushed around the chef's kitchen, covering the Italian-sourced marble counters with canapé trays. Furniture was rearranged and the origami-like decorations, built from living flora, were arrayed on mantles and shelves. Candles were placed among the succulents' dark green and deep purple leaves. Jay hated bright colors and had refused the event planner's desire for even "pops" of orange or red.

It was loathsome to see his private domicile of minimalist sophistication invaded by these armies: the battalion of workers, followed by the onslaught of guests, and finally the reinforcement of cleaners. But he understood that infrequent and highly curated access to his sanctum created a useful sense of exclusivity. The occasional soirée, followed by well-placed photographs and brief write-ups, gave the uninvited masses a tantalizingly brief glimpse of what they'd missed. And in just a few hours, Nicholas Spragg would no longer be a member of that unlucky group: He'd finally be in.

Of course, inviting Nicholas into Jay's home was like opening a town car window as it drove by a skunk. But there was no way around it. Not long ago, Jay routinely complimented himself on how well he'd aligned Spragg and the other chess pieces. He'd met Spragg and Lucas within months of each other and immediately identified them as twins and foils. Both were outsiders, equally naïve and ambitious, and yet Lucas appeared to have everything Spragg wanted: influence with a powerful media mogul, a beautiful girlfriend, and, eventually, an adoring audience. These were only the broad strokes, of course. Up close, both Lucas and Spragg were equally powerless and mal-leable. But neither could see the fine details. They'd play off each other perfectly.

But the game had not gone according to plan. Many months ago, Jay invited Spragg to coffee and presented him a draft of Lucas's profile. Jay had a finely choreographed performance for moments like this. Step one: Indignant apologies. He'd instructed his reporter to write a glorious puff piece and was shocked—and genuinely embarrassed!—to see his employee taken in by these jealous, lying backbiters. Step two: Jay would theatrically stop, as if a terrible thought had just occurred to him, and he'd stammer it out: "Th-that is, well, I don't even want to think this, and I'm sorry to even ask, but, for my own reputational sake, I must: Those stories aren't *true*, right?"

At which point, his subject would either come clean or lie . . . and then eventually come clean. And so on to step three: The Editor would suggest a way to protect his subject's reputation. By helping Jay bolster this investment or skirt that regulation, they'd both win. Never threaten: That was Jay's cardinal rule. Instead, flatter, massage, cajole.

But unlike the others, Spragg didn't bite. Were the rape accusations true? He just shrugged, as if to say, *Who cares?* He seemed unconcerned about exposure, as though his money were an impenetrable force field. No, what infuriated Spragg was Lucas. "I'm very upset," Spragg had said, pushing his coffee away with disgust, "about Lucas's betrayal."

"Betrayal of what?" Jay had asked.

"Of my friendship," Nicholas said like it was obvious. "Of all I've done for him."

Jay barely managed to contain his laughter. Spragg had done exactly zero for Lucas except buy him a couple of meals and some (unrequested) sex. And yet Spragg believed that Lucas was in his debt, simply for being around. There was also more than a little jealousy there—Spragg seemed personally offended by the fact that Sofia wasn't *his* girlfriend. So Jay altered the deal. If Spragg would invest in The College, Jay would fire Lucas.

"I want to be in the room when it happens," Spragg said. "I want to see his face crumble."

This sounded like the making of a dozen different lawsuits, so Jay countered: "What if you just listened by phone instead?"

Then, lo and behold, Lucas turned out to be Nice Guy. It was so wholly unexpected that Jay wasn't even upset. He was actually kind of impressed. But it made everything more complicated. Spragg became pouty and petulant. He wanted Lucas fired—and if Jay *really cared* about getting the investment, he'd do it. But Jay had to balance his interests, and casting off his most popular columnist was a nonstarter. At this point, he considered blackmailing Spragg outright, but the kid was so indiscreet that he might just go blabbing it to the nearest hooker, who'd then sell the secret to TMZ. And so, Spragg packed up his moneybags and scampered after somebody new to stroke his ego.

Jay continued searching for money to no avail. He'd kept it together during those dark weeks, with the help of energy supplements and an ample amount of La Mer under-eye concealer. He'd had one slip. On the February morning he'd learned the Boar would have to close, he'd walked the city for hours and, eventually, ended up outside Carmen's apartment. He cringed at how weepy and pathetic he'd become. And then to have Carmen throw it all back in his face! He still felt disgusted—with himself, with her. He couldn't stand thinking about it.

But then divine intervention rescued him. A few days after Lucas and Carmen imploded, Spragg returned of his own volition. The MOMA spectacle had been a call to action for the

young man. He would invest in The College on three condi-
tions: First, Jay must make him an official partner; second, Jay
must publish the aforementioned glowing article under Lucas's
own byline; and third, if Lucas couldn't be fired, he'd at least be
tortured. Sofia would be his new partner in "Love the Critics."

Some legal finessing would be required to ensure that
Spragg didn't actually own much of The College. Jay wasn't
surrendering anything to that Wharton-loving nitwit. But he
could stomach the rest. Sofia was actually a brilliant candidate
to be Lucas's partner. Sure, Spragg chose her as retribution:
The woman who broke Lucas's heart would now be his new romantic partner. But she was beautiful and TV ready. She'd
keep the columns interesting.

As for the cover story under Lucas's byline—well, Jay felt
the smallest twinge of guilt about that. Jay liked Lucas. The
kid had gumption. He applied himself. He was decent. But he
was also broke, which meant he wasn't useful where it mattered most. Such was the sad truth of life: The good-hearted
rarely had power or money, and the powerful and moneyed
were rarely good.

Almost immediately, Jay regretted getting into business
with Spragg. The bastard would not stop calling, full of terrible
ideas for The College. He was the neediest Richie Rich Jay had
ever met. And so Jay found himself in the unenviable position
of constantly kissing his benefactor's twenty-five-hundred-dollar
camel calf Stefano Bemer–clad feet. Every time Spragg called,
Jay wanted to shout at him: *I came here from a place equally
remote as Apex, Idaho, and with nothing. I worked and struggled
for my position. And you—pathetic, ineffectual, ugly, weak—think
that you can have whatever you want without taking any risks?
Without producing a drop of sweat? You make me sick!*

Instead, Jay was throwing a party where he would introduce Spragg to New York society as his official partner in The

College. At long last, Jay would give Nicholas the legitimacy he craved, the one thing Daddy Spragg could not buy.

It was now 5:00 P.M., and Jay walked the ground floor of his town house for a final inspection. In the dining room, a cleaning woman stood on a step stool, dusting the massive chandelier that an interior decorator named Chandra had convinced Jay to buy. It didn't match anything in the house, but Chandra had been so persuasive. So *very* persuasive with her impossibly tall stilettos, endless legs, and the skintight dress that zipped all the way down the front. At least the money hadn't come from Jay's own pocket. That's what his *Empire* expense account was for.

"Careful with that!" he snapped at the cleaner, and headed upstairs to his bedroom for a few hours of restful grooming before the city's fashionable, powerful elite stampeded in. These the people he loved and loathed with equal conviction.

CHAPTER 48

Lucas stood outside Jays' house in his new Armani suit. It had come straight from *Empire's* fashion closet and was tailored on the magazine's dime. The open windows were ablaze with light and lively chatter, a deceptive cocoon of warmth and welcome. Lucas took a deep breath, walked up the steps, and entered the dragon's den.

Around him, fashionables stood proudly in their brushed silk and polished leather. There was an assurance in how they tipped champagne flutes to their lips, a silent, mutual agreement of their belonging, though many of them had nervously awaited their invitations. A year ago, Lucas would have come here wide-eyed and breathless from the orgasm of wish fulfillment. But life, he now knew, was not like the lottery: You didn't get what you wanted in one exciting jolt. Instead, you got it by way of scrapping and sacrificing and stepping on toes. And when the prize finally arrived, you might not even want it anymore. Which was a good thing, because if the night went according to plan his access to all of this was over.

Now the Editor approached Lucas, his eyes shining, his demeanor perfectly lubricated. "I was wondering when you'd turn up," he said. "You have many people to meet. I've slipped MDMA into all the drinks, which means everyone is going to be especially receptive to Nice Guy's charms."

Lucas looked uneasily at his glass.

Jays continued, "At nine thirty P.M., Sofia will make a dramatic entrance. Are you excited for your big kiss? Not that it's your first . . ." Jays gave Lucas a nudge. Lucas wondered if the Editor really was on drugs. He seemed uncharacteristically garrulous. He leaned toward Lucas with an air of conspiracy and said, "What's that infuriating phrase Nicholas Spragg always uses—'capital evening'? Well, it'll be very capital."

"So there's a money cake involved?" Lucas didn't see Spragg and was dreading the encounter.

Jays didn't pick up on the joke. "Tonight, Lucas, anything is possible. Now come with me, and grab a canapé if one passes by. They're delicious."

And then Lucas was slapped hard on the back. A booming voice behind him yelled, "Nice Guy! Right here in the flesh!"

Lucas turned around. It was Jai Rogers, one of Silicon Valley's youngest and most prominent VCs, grinning like they were best friends. "Big balls on you, kid." Rogers shook his head in admiration. "That Carmen Kelly, she really deserved what she got, humiliating you like that."

Lucas barely had time to cringe before Jai Rogers was gone. And in his place was a Pulitzer-winning journalist, a state senator, a Broadway star, a guitarist for Lady Gaga, a celebrity chef, the Yankees' new draft pick, and on and on, passing Lucas around the room like a joint. The conversation was always the same: excitement, empty compliment, trashing of Carmen, farewell. Lucas kept introducing himself by name; the party-goers kept calling him Nice Guy anyway. Walt Frazier, the legendary New York Knick, called him Louis. At least he tried.

Meanwhile, Lucas kept glancing at his watch. He needed to find Jays' notebook collection and be back downstairs in time for the kiss. And if there was no notebook to be found? Lucas put that possibility out of his mind. He dashed off a text to Tyler: "Operation Cockblock commences 9:30. What's your status?" While Lucas played burglar, Tyler wasn't sitting idly by. He had his own part in the plan.

Five minutes passed, then ten, then fifteen. Lucas's stomach lurched as he waited for Tyler to respond. Maybe silence was a positive sign. Maybe he was too occupied with his own task to respond. Lucas checked his watch again. He couldn't wait any longer. It was nearly nine o'clock. Go time.

Lucas ducked through the crowd and scurried up the stairs, hoping that nobody was paying attention. Soon he stood alone on the silent second floor. He followed Tyler's instructions to Jays' bedroom. The door opened with a small whoosh, revealing a sparsely styled space in hues of gray with a few glints of silver and navy. The walls displayed black-and-white female nudes. Plush cream carpet underfoot. Lucas peeked into the spacious marble bathroom. The tub was like a small swimming pool. The shower had more heads than a car wash. Lucas looked at the bed and thought of all the nights Carmen had fallen into those sheets. She believed that she'd seen inside Jays there. But all she'd seen was a persona, which Jays eventually sloughed off like dead skin.

How many layers could be peeled off of Jays? Did a core even exist?

Lucas walked across the bedroom and entered a sitting room. He'd been hoping that the door between the two would lock, but it didn't; he'd have to do this exposed. There, across from the leather chaise, was the closet. Just as Tyler had said. Lucas pulled the handles and entered a dressing room half the size of his apartment. In the center was a wooden island, lined with drawers. *An island in a closet?* Lucas had never heard of such a thing. Jays' suits were organized in showroom fashion. There was an entire wall of designer shoes, including, oddly enough, more Manolo Blahnik pumps than Carrie Bradshaw owned. Lucas snapped a couple of pictures. Was Jays a secret cross-dresser? Did he collect the shoes of his conquests like trophies? But Lucas was getting sidetracked. He looked up and, sure enough, a long row of notebooks lined one of the top shelves.

Lucas pulled over a sliding ladder and climbed it. Tyler had given him the names of half a dozen sources Jays had likely whitemailed. But there were twice as many notebooks, and time was running out. There was only one thing to do. He reached up and, one by one, began flinging the notebooks off the shelf. One after another, they flew out behind him and tumbled to the floor. There was something wonderfully cathartic, almost joyous, about it, and Lucas was sad when there were no more books to throw. He hopped down and got to work. He'd worried that it might be difficult to find all the names he was searching for, but Jays made it easy: The notebooks were labeled alphabetically. Lucas started taking photographs of the relevant entries. He was about to leave when something occurred to him. He pulled out the notebook labeled "C–D" and flipped until he arrived at "Callahan, Lucas." There he was, summed up in a single word that Jays had written in neat, small letters: "Jackpot." Lucas felt the sting of recognition. From day one, he'd been the mark Jays was searching for. Well, no longer.

Lucas dashed off a text to Tyler: "JACKPOT!!!" Then he grabbed the notebook labeled "S–T" and hurried from the room, leaving the mess of books behind him.

CHAPTER 49

A few days before Jays' epic party, Carmen received an email from *Noser*'s media critic, J. P. Maddox. Reflexively, she went for the "delete" key. Then she paused. All spring, publications had taken turns swinging at her like she was a piñata. But *Noser*—which should have been handiest with the bat—had been conspicuously silent. Now, out of nowhere, Maddox was politely requesting a drink.

Carmen also considered turning him down, because she was busy. Her new agent, Lydia Rothsfeld, had given her a tight deadline. Back in April at Kettle of Fish, after Lydia and Carmen had finished two rounds of Manhattans, Richie Sullivan took Carmen aside with a word of warning: "Before you sign with Lydia, know that she will be the single toughest critic you've ever had. She will make you question your talent, your skill, and definitely your self-worth. But if you can stick it out, you'll produce the best work of your life."

Carmen had faced plenty of critics in her day, but none whose goal was to make her work better. Jays certainly never did. Now she was excited and nervous to have someone finally treat her writing—treat *her*—with respect. So did she really have time for drinks with a *Noser* reporter? But curiosity got the better of her.

On the second Thursday in May, she agreed to meet J. P. Maddox for a beer. Only into the bar walked none other than Tyler, erstwhile *Empire* intern. He stretched out his hand. "J. P. Maddox," he said. "I believe we've met?"

Carmen stood up to leave. "You have half a second to explain."

Immediately, Tyler dropped the act. "I've been writing under a pen name at *Noser* to shield my identity from Jays. I'm also—"

"Lucas's roommate. I know."

"So then you understand why I didn't say who I really was. I worried you wouldn't come. Any other questions?"

"Keep talking," she said, and sat back down. "I'll stay as long as I have a reason to."

And so she listened to Tyler explain the assignments Jays had given him, the resulting positive press, and the Editor's secret notebook collection. He told her about Jays' partnership with Nicholas Spragg and how he'd used Lucas and Spragg against each other. None of this surprised Carmen, but the details made her queasy. She'd seen those notebooks but never been brave enough to sneak a peek. Even so, she'd tried to warn Lucas that something like this would happen. He simply hadn't listened. And even now that he saw the truth—or supposedly saw it, according to Tyler—what had changed? She'd watched the *TODAY* show segment; Lucas knew about the Netflix deal. And he was well aware of the financial consequences it would have on her. And yet Lucas never called—if not to apologize for ruining her career, then at least to see if she and Mira were OK. There had been nothing. No communication of any kind.

Instead, Carmen caught glimpses of Lucas online and in the society pages, flashing here and there, from this party to that premiere, a fading trail of light in his wake. She couldn't imagine that he was enjoying himself, especially after Jays had published that horrible article under his byline and thrown him back into bed with Sofia. More likely, Lucas had simply given in, submitted to the powerful forces that now dictated his universe. Carmen had seen it before. It depressed her.

"Look," Tyler was saying as he glanced at his watch, "there's something we want you to see." He put his phone on the bar and slid it toward her.

"We?"

"Lucas is about to do something, which is either incredibly brave or incredibly stupid. Or both. But the point is, he's doing it for you."

Carmen shook her head. "No," she said. "Not interested." She stood up.

"Carmen, please. This is important."

She backed away. "I don't want to know what Lucas is doing. I don't *care* what he's doing. I'm not the only one Lucas screwed over, Tyler. Doesn't he get that?"

"Carmen," Tyler said slowly, deliberately. "Just watch. Two minutes. That's all."

She could see herself reflected in his expression; she was a small animal he was desperate to capture. But she would not let herself be netted. "I'm sorry," she said, and hurried away.

CHAPTER 50

Lucas returned to the party with the notebook tucked awkwardly into the back of his pants, hidden beneath his suit jacket. No one seemed to have missed him.

"There you are!" Jays materialized. "Let's get you ready for your big moment." Lucas held his breath as the Editor looked him up and down. "Armani's a good look for you," he said. "Now follow me."

They made their way into the tented backyard and up onto a stage where the band was playing. At Jays' signal, the music stopped.

"It's a thrill to bring you all together," the Editor said, his voice as smooth and rich as the passed foie gras. The guests listened, rapt. The only sound was the wind chime of clinking ice. "You know how much I love opening my home for these gatherings. And tonight is particularly special. I know you're eager to witness the big kiss—"

At this, the party erupted into cheers. But Jays held up his hands.

"But first, I wanted to formally introduce you to a special person, the subject of this week's cover story. Mr. Nicholas Spragg!"

The tent flaps parted, and there stood Nicholas, half-blinded by the glare of an actual spotlight. The theatricality of the moment was crude, hardly of a piece with the party. And yet the moment felt very Spragg-like. Lucas was certain Jays had engineered this subtle humiliation on purpose.

"As you already know, the superb profile of Nicholas was penned by our own Lucas Callahan, aka Nice Guy." Jays clapped Lucas on the back. Lucas, in turn, felt the notebook shift precariously in his pants. "Mr. Spragg is a courageous and ambitious young man, newly arrived in the city from Idaho. For those of you who don't know, that's one of our fifty states, located roughly in the vicinity of Washington and Montana. I'm told it has a lot of potatoes?"

There was laughter. Nicholas smiled, clearly unsure of whether he was being praised or mocked.

"Though seeing as I'm from Kansas," Jays added, "I can't really judge. You've heard of Kansas? Also a state?"

More laughter. Lucas looked around the room and spotted Jai Rogers in the corner, sidling up to a runway model. A recent profile of Rogers in *Businessweek* said the guy was from small-town Illinois.

"You're going to be seeing a lot from Mr. Spragg in the coming months," Jays continued. "He has plans to build great things in this city. I hope you'll welcome him into the fold and make him feel at home here—as much as you did for me nearly two decades ago, when I stepped off the bus at Port Authority."

The guests chuckled. Some shook their heads, as though

public transportation were the quaint remnant of a bygone era. Lucas caught sight of the Pulitzer-winning journalist at the bar. He'd heard him speak on a panel once and was pretty sure the guy mentioned growing up in Toledo. And there, discreetly tapping his cigarette ashes into Jays' landscaping, was the Lady Gaga guitarist. He had a southern accent.

"Back then, I didn't know Tribeca from Southampton from my ass," Jays said, and the room laughed again. Lucas laughed, too, weakly, because it seemed inappropriate not to. But now it was dawning on him: Most of the guests weren't originally from New York. A lot of them had likely arrived long after Jays received his Port Authority "welcome." So what was so funny to everyone? But Lucas didn't have any time to think about it, because Jays had moved on to the main attraction.

". . . and so it is due to the insight of Nicholas that we are lucky enough to have a beautiful and talented writer for our new column, 'Love the Critics.'"

Sofia appeared beside Spragg, glorious in a rose-colored jumpsuit with a plunging back and cream heels. As he took her in, her gorgeousness, Lucas's heart ached. But the feeling was fleeting, like a shiver on a hot day.

Nicholas took Sofia's arm and, as though leading her down the aisle, walked her to the stage. Now the four of them stood in a row: Lucas, Sofia, Nicholas, and Jays. In between the party's two most handsome guests, Nicholas should have looked even uglier. Instead, he seemed to be siphoning light from them, filling himself with confidence and bravura. This was his moment, and not even biology was going to get in his way. Except then Jays nudged him aside.

"Well," said the Editor, turning to Lucas and Sofia. "Are you two going to kiss or what?"

There were more cheers and more laughter, and Jays reveled

in their adoration. Never for a moment did he question the outcome of these events. Nicholas turned a gloating, almost maniacal smile on Lucas. He looked ready to piss himself.

"What do you say, Lucas?" Sofia smiled like the fresh-faced ingenue she most certainly was not.

Lucas looked steadily back at her. He'd made big, important decisions before, but never had he watched the future split, right before his eyes, into alternate paths. It was time to choose: kiss the princess and live unhappily ever after or pronounce himself the frog. He stepped forward.

CHAPTER 51

Carmen ran home so fast that she was gasping for air by the time she made it up the four flights of stairs to her apartment. Immediately, she pulled up the live feed of Jays' party. Like hell she wasn't going to watch. (At the very least, she was now obligated to do so in the name of book research.) But she certainly wasn't going to give Tyler the pleasure of witnessing it. And she didn't want Lucas to know. Or think that she cared.

And yet. The two of them were tied together, not just because of what they'd been to each other but also because of who they were to Jays. Not so long ago, Carmen had stood in Lucas's shoes. She could empathize with his entrapment. For that reason alone, she felt compelled to watch. Like it or not, she was part of this reality show.

Carmen had come to the proceedings a few minutes late, and it took her a moment to orient herself. Jays, Lucas, Sofia, and Nicholas Spragg stood on a stage, beneath a tent, in Jays' backyard. It looked like one of those childhood jokes where a priest, a rabbi, and an atheist walked into a bar: What were they all doing together up there?

"Before I smooch the leading lady," Lucas was explaining, "I'd like to say a few words."

Carmen felt sick. She wasn't sure if she could stomach this apparent display of Stockholm syndrome. But then she noticed a look of doubt cross Jays' face. This, she realized, was not part of the program.

"This is why Lucas is such a nice guy," the Editor said, quickly recovering. "He wants to have a conversation before jumping into bed!"

Carmen heard the guests laugh. She didn't need to be among them to know that they were completely within Jays' thrall. But she was more interested in Lucas, who kept glancing from his phone to the camera and back again. She realized that he was waiting for word from Tyler. Confirmation that she was watching. Well, too late for that.

Finally, Lucas put his phone away. "For the longest time," he began, "I dreamed of coming to New York and working in magazines. I thought that my determination to make it here made me special. I thought that I was better than everyone back home. But it turns out I'm not so special, and I'm not any better."

He sounded sincere, but she wasn't going to soften. Whatever this was, it was too little, too late.

"I have made terrible mistakes," he continued. "I hurt the person I loved the most."

"That's right," Carmen said aloud. "You did. And this isn't going to make up for it."

"But, Carmen," Lucas said straight to the camera, as though responding directly to her. "You are my best friend."

Carmen swallowed. It was unnerving, the way he seemed to be there with her, talking just to her.

"You are the most generous, most genuine—the most honest—person I know. I mean"—and here he turned to the assembled crowd—"I get why you all jumped on her so quickly. If 'Screw the Critics' taught me anything, it's that judgment is human nature." He started to pace back and forth across the small stage, not unlike a professor giving an impassioned lecture or, Carmen thought, a lawyer trying to persuade a jury. "Against our best intentions, we seek out other people's failures. Anything to make us feel a little bigger, a little stronger. But Carmen is decent. She is *real*. She doesn't deserve your judgment. But I do."

Lucas stopped. The room was silent. Jays was frozen, his expression inscrutable. "Jay calls me a nice guy," Lucas finally said. "Well, I'm not." He turned and looked meaningfully at Nicholas and the camera zoomed in on them both. Carmen had never seen Nicholas Spragg in person. She'd only seen the photos of him that *Empire* ran with Lucas's cover story. There the photo team had proved its merit; they'd nearly made Nicholas handsome. Here, on the screen, he looked every bit as awkward as Lucas described. The constipated smirk on his face didn't help either.

"My cover story about Nicholas Spragg is a lie," Lucas said. "More than that, it's an intentional cover-up."

Nicholas's head popped up. Jays turned sharply. Carmen shot forward and punched at the "volume" key. Did Lucas realize what he was doing? Of course, he must. But she could hardly believe it.

"Nicholas assaulted a young woman and paid her to keep quiet. I've known about it for months."

"This is absurd," Nicholas said. "Jay, make him stop!"

"Lucas," Jays said calmly, "what you're saying makes no

sense. I never would have allowed such a thing. Frankly, I'm worried about your mental and emotional health."

"Oh please!" Carmen exclaimed at the exact moment that Lucas said, "Oh, fuck you."

The camera was still trained on the stage, but Carmen heard a collective gasp from the guests.

"For years," Lucas went on, "you've dug up dirt about wealthy, famous people and then printed glowing pieces about them. And they, in turn, have been doing you a lot of favors and paying you a lot of money."

Carmen jumped up from her chair. She had no words for this. "Oh!" was all she could manage. Then, "Holy fuck!" She felt ridiculous—she was shouting to an empty room—and also conflicted. Lucas was doing the right thing, the brave thing, and, admittedly, the dumb thing. Which were all reasons to root for him. But he'd nearly destroyed her life. And Mira's.

Jays shook his head with parental disappointment. "This slander is an offense to every upstanding person in this room, starting with Nicholas here."

Carmen wished she could see the partygoers. She imagined them nodding along. Because of course Jays' guests would be so credulous. She'd been to plenty of his parties. She knew that the Editor hadn't just welcomed them with his bounty but had made them feel deserving of it. He'd united them in an exclusive, self-congratulatory embrace. And it was obvious to her that no one felt better about himself at this particular moment than Nicholas Spragg.

"You're a lying piece of shit," Spragg spit. "And you're a nobody. You're a nobody who thinks he's a somebody. It's pathetic."

"Come on, Lucas," Carmen said aloud, still on her feet. "Let's see what you've got."

"That may be true, Nicholas, but you'd better take a hard look at your relationship with Jays. You think he's your ally? He just needs your money. He doesn't give a shit about you—or about me for that matter. You should see what he's written about you here."

And with that, Carmen watched Lucas pull an object from his jacket. She leaned toward the screen. It was a notebook. One of the grotesquely expensive ones that Jays billed to the magazine and secreted away in his closet.

"What's that?" Nicolas was still boasting a haughty expression.

"Lucas," Jays said quietly, "give me that."

Lucas took a step away. "This is where Jay keeps tabs on his marks, Nicholas. It's where he lists their character flaws, records their petty crimes, their *serious* crimes."

"Give me that," Jays repeated, his face hardening.

"Jay and I have a shared vision," Nicholas said, though his voice faltered. "He understands that I—"

But before Nicholas could finish the thought, Jays lunged for the notebook. Carmen watched it happen, her mouth wide open. The events on the screen seemed to unfold in slow motion: the Editor hurling himself at Lucas like a lion pouncing on a wildebeest; Lucas canvassing the party for a way out and then yelling, "Walt, help!" as he tossed the book offscreen.

Whoever was holding the camera quickly panned left. The book was caught by an outstretched arm, far above the sea of bobbing heads. Carmen recognized the catcher instantly: It was Walt Frazier, the basketball player. Mira often said that Frazier, in his 1970s-era short-shorts, had the sexiest thighs in sports.

Then there was a crash. The sound of a microphone thumping to the ground, followed by screeching feedback. The camera jerked back to the stage, where it landed on Jays, grasping idiotically at the air. Below him, Lucas lay on the stone patio, clutching his leg. The Editor had knocked Lucas off the stage! It was so surreal that Carmen began laughing. Here were the men who'd done her the most harm, and they were now enacting some moronic WrestleMania scene, all for her benefit. Two enemies, canceling each other out. But she had to root for Lucas, if only because there was work left to do.

Lucas pulled himself up to standing and yelled, "Walt! Flip to Spragg and start reading!"

The camera panned back to Frazier; whoever was operating this thing deserved an Emmy. "'Nicholas *Spragg*,'" Frazier read in his butter-smooth baritone. "'Entitled. Sycophantic. Dull. Needy. Naïve. Gullible. . . .'" There was a pause. Was that it? Then Frazier licked his finger like a librarian and turned the page. "'Paid off sorority sister to keep quiet about attempted r—'"

"It's all lies! Lies!" Nicholas yelled over the reading. "Jay, tell them!"

"I wrote nothing of the kind," Jay said.

"He's got a dozen of those notebooks upstairs in his closet," Lucas announced. "You can see for yourselves."

Carmen smiled. She knew exactly how the rest of this would play out. And indeed, there it was: Jays threw Lucas a look of pure fury, jumped off the stage, and pushed his way through the crowd, presumably to go and hide the evidence. Nicholas Spragg was fast on his heels. The camera followed them, but a bunch of partygoers had a head start. They might be grateful to Jays for their invite, but that didn't make them loyal. Whoever got to the notebooks first, Carmen knew, was going to have a fabulous few seconds of fame. And who wouldn't want that?

CHAPTER 52

Lucas looked around the party for Sofia, who hadn't said a word during all this. In fact, it turned out, she'd excused herself from the fracas entirely. As he hobbled off into the house, and out the front door, the guests just looked at him, a little bit awed, a little fearful, as though he really was mentally and emotionally off-balance. Finally alone in the quiet night, he hailed a cab. He was only going a couple of blocks, but the fall had done something awful to his knee.

En route, his phone buzzed. "You were amazing!" Tyler sounded out of breath. "I mean, holy shit!"

"Carmen!" Lucas demanded. "Did Carmen watch?"

Tyler paused a beat too long, and Lucas's stomach sank. "But you talked to her, right? How . . . did she seem? Did she say anything about me?"

"I mean, you know," Tyler said. "She said some things."

The taxi stopped outside Carmen's building.

"Tell me, Tyler!"

"Are you getting out or what?" the driver said.

"Yes, sorry." Lucas pulled out a twenty, the only money he had, and pushed it through the window. Then he slid out of the car, accidentally stepping out on his bad leg. He groaned. "What did she say?" he huffed.

"That her life wasn't the only one you ruined. What did she mean?"

Lucas lowered the phone from his ear. Carmen was sitting on the front steps smoking a cigarette. Lucas had never seen her smoke before, and yet she seemed practiced. She hadn't spotted him arriving, and so, for a moment, he was able to just watch her. He hadn't seen her in months. The physical urge he felt seeing Sofia earlier that evening was nothing compared to the longing and pain that gripped him now. How he wanted to pull Carmen close, breathe in her hair, kiss her lips, the bump on her nose, her sternum. He missed her voice, her sarcasm, her confidence. He just missed her.

"Carmen," he said. It came out like a plea.

She raised her head. When she saw him, she exhaled and then stubbed the cigarette out on the steps. Lucas opened his mouth, but before he could speak even a single word she smirked, stood up, and went inside.

Had she watched? Lucas entertained the thought, but he couldn't decide what outcome he preferred more. If she had watched, her reaction now would be all the more devastating. It meant he'd sacrificed everything and still lost her.

He knew it was useless to stay, but he did. He watched her windows until the lights went out. Even then, he didn't leave. He imagined that her head appeared from behind the curtain and she called down to him. At one point, his phone rang, and his heart leapt. But it was only a reporter calling for comment about Jays' party. Lucas hung up on him. Eventually, the pain in his knee grew intolerable and he had no choice but to go home.

CHAPTER 53

Alexis was always the first to arrive at *Empire*'s offices, at 7:30 A.M. sharp. No other editor would stroll in until at least ten, and the graphic designers wouldn't deign to show their faces until at least eleven. But as Jays' third assistant—the young, disposable one—Alexis couldn't afford to enjoy the largess of media hours. It was one of the many reasons she never felt like she truly worked for the magazine. She really worked for Jays. Which meant she had to get in early in case he needed anything.

The Sphinxes, it went without saying, arrived at ten. Media hours.

Typically, Alexis would have an hour or so to sip coffee and search the Internet before Jays sauntered by. But today, the morning after his disastrous party, he was already standing by her desk, arms folded, when she arrived. She was startled to see him, and also anxious: Was she supposed to say something about last night? Of course, she hadn't been invited to the party, but she'd watched the live stream.

"Alexis," Jays said, the moment he saw her. "Call I.T. My email isn't working." Then he went into his office and closed the door.

Alexis knew something Jays didn't: *Empire*'s I.T. guys also ran on media hours. She quickly checked her work email; it was functioning fine. This wasn't a system-wide problem. This was just Jays' email. Which meant that I.T. had come in early. Which meant that someone higher up had called them.

Which meant this was going to be an interesting morning.

Alexis sat down at her desk and opened *Noser*'s "Screw Off!" column, which she'd been constantly refreshing since last night. The conversation was heated—a mix of love and hatred for Lucas, Jays, Carmen in absentia, and even Nicholas Spragg, who had somehow won himself some admirers last night. Alexis moved her mouse cursor over to the "Log In" button and paused to consider.

Like so many of her peers, she'd come to New York and to *Empire* to thrive inside a glamorous bubble. Was this her dream job, doing tasks for Jays? No. But she knew that nobody succeeds sitting on the sidelines waiting for the perfect opportunity. Instead, you play every hand you have and follow the one that works out. Lucas had done this, though admittedly not well. She'd been doing it, too, moving carefully, working cautiously, making sure she played the odds. And now, it seemed, one hand she'd been playing was about to cash in.

She clicked, then signed in.

"Username: Rogue Empire

"Password: Rightnext2uJays!"

Then she posted her first message: "Has anyone tried to email Jay Jacobson this morning? You may not get through. A sign of things to come? Stay tuned."

As soon as she submitted her comment, the Sphinxes walked past her desk, looking even grimmer than usual—as if two dead bodies could somehow be *deader*. Alexis saw the dominoes setting themselves up. If Jays lost his job, they lost theirs. And so did she.

"Jay Jacobson has retreated to his office," she now wrote on *Noser*. At this point, she was giving her identity away: There was nobody else in the building. But who cared? It was game over. "I think he's cowering under the desk. His formidable secretaries, the Sphinxes, are guarding the door. Shit is about to get real."

Next, two men in security uniforms exited the elevator and walked up to Jays' office. Alexis began typing.

Rogue Empire: "Security is facing off against the Sphinxes. 'Mr. Jacobson isn't available right now,' the two of them just said in unison, like they're the *Shining* twins. We have a standoff. What's Jays doing inside—burning thousand-dollar notebooks in the trash can?"

Rogue Empire: "More security here. Two men the size of refrigerators just literally picked the Sphinxes up like statues and moved them out of the way. The door is locked. Battering ram? Are we about to see a battering ram? Please tell me we're about to see a battering ram."

Rogue Empire: "This is amazing. Security just tried to unlock Jays' door, because apparently Security has keys to everything around here, but Jays had *changed the locks*. Maybe we really will see a battering ram!"

Rogue Empire: "Security guy is now picking the lock. Bummer. No battering ram."

Rogue Empire: "They're in. There's rustling . . . now arguing."

Rogue Empire: "Jay Jacobson and the Sphinxes are being escorted to the elevator. Nobody is saying a word. Jays is wearing a coat and scarf, and holding one notebook. If I had to guess, that notebook is what the scuffle was about."

Rogue Empire: "Elevator door closed. It's over. Now what?"

But Alexis knew what to do now. She'd wait a few minutes for Jays, the Sphinxes, and Security to go wherever they were going, and then she'd head straight to *Noser*, reveal herself as Rogue Empire, and be rewarded with a staff position.

She was confident they would not turn her down.

CHAPTER 54

Lucas sat on the train as it swayed and rumbled toward Grand Central Terminal. It was his first major excursion since his knee surgery six weeks before, and he'd already been impressed with the simple charity of strangers. As soon as he began limping toward a door, someone would rush to open it. When he'd step on a subway train, people would leap out of their seats to let him sit. The rest of the country thought New Yorkers were cold and uncaring, but that simply wasn't true. A certain amount of introversion—call it psychic breathing room—was necessary to maintain peace of mind in such a crowded city. But when a person needed help, New Yorkers noticed, and they sprang into action.

The day after Jays' party, a doctor informed Lucas that he'd torn his ACL. "How did this happen?" he'd asked, gently palpating Lucas's knee. Most people probably said they were skiing. Lucas wasn't sure how to reply. What would he say—*I was attacked by my boss after exposing his dirty secrets to New York society, and you probably read about it in today's* New York Post? Instead, he simplified it: "I fell off the stage at a party."

"Must have been a good party," the doctor said. Lucas left it at that.

After the surgery, Tyler had taken exceptional care of him. Franklin and Alexis visited frequently, bearing food, alcohol for themselves, and constant friendly bickering, now that they worked for competing publications. In his Percocet-induced delirium, Lucas half-expected Carmen to appear as well, sidling up to his bedside with sympathy and chicken soup. Of course, she didn't. Lucas spent a long time wondering if she'd seen his very public apology. Tyler assured him that, at this point, it was impossible to miss; the video from Jays' party had redefined the meaning of "virality." But Lucas knew that if she'd made up her mind to excise him from her life there was nothing he could do about it. Which sucked. Now that he was laid out at home, he had ample time to drill down into his heart and excavate his true feelings. And also to consider Carmen's.

As the painkillers wore off and the fog lifted from his brain, he realized that his performance at Jays', bold as it had been, was also selfish. He'd apologized to Carmen, but he didn't *do* anything for her. He wasn't *there* for her. The actions of that night were, frankly, all for himself and his own conscience.

He thought back to what Carmen told Tyler: *I'm not the only one Lucas screwed over.* At this point, Carmen was gone. He would never win her back. Still, he owed her. She deserved as much generosity *from* him as she'd given *to* him. It wasn't a debt she expected him to repay or, frankly, would want him to repay. But he wanted to. He'd dug too many holes since moving to New York. This was one he needed to fill.

Lucas racked his brain. How could he right his wrong? And then, one day while he was on Facebook, a photo from his mother's feed popped up in his timeline. There she stood in a row of society ladies, their gauze-brimmed hats set just so atop their heads, gin fizzes in their hands. It was, Lucas gleaned quickly, taken at Mel and Cal's engagement party. Lucas clicked through to see Mel looking not only happy but also relaxed. And why wouldn't she be? This time around, her groom wasn't sidling off early. This groom had the self-awareness to know exactly what he wanted. This groom was sticking around.

Jesus, Lucas thought, *what a dick I've been.* He opened an email and began typing out an apology but stopped halfway through. All at once, a solution presented itself: a way to make things right, not just with Mel but with Carmen.

He called Mel from Tyler's phone, guessing that she'd screen his name. He then pleaded for her not to hang up and, once that was accomplished, begged to see her and Cal. Begrudgingly, she told Lucas to meet her that Saturday morning at Grand Central, under the information booth clock. "You can say whatever it is you need to say before we catch our train. Be there at nine forty-five." Then she hung up.

Lucas arrived early, giving himself and his busted knee ample time to reach the appointed spot. The Main Concourse was like a sanctuary, an echoing temple of stone and light. Lucas stood among the weekend travelers, tilting back his head as they did, taking in the seventy-five-foot ceilings. As the blood rushed to his brain, the sea-green sky and gilded constellations seemed to swim overhead. It was jarring to find majesty here, amidst such a crass, cosmopolitan city, as opposed to, say, anywhere in Europe. It reminded him of Carmen's experience finding *Starry Night* not in Amsterdam, but at MOMA in New York. Which, of course, reminded him of the terrible thing he'd done to her there. Lucas felt tears rise, so he stood up straight and collected himself. He was on a mission. He must remain focused.

At exactly 9:45, the couple strode in, Mel wearing a pastel sundress and Cal in khakis and oxfords. Seeing them together made it clear to Lucas that he and Mel had never been right for each other. Or maybe they had been for a brief moment, years ago in college, before Lucas figured out who he was and how much he didn't know. Mel spotted him and nudged Cal: *Over there.* Cal smirked. As he approached, Lucas felt himself being inspected. Did the crutches make him look sympathetic or weak? But Cal's appraisal was clear: Lucas was a piece of worthless junk.

"I'm Lucas," Lucas said unnecessarily, and struggled to offer his hand while balancing on one crutch.

"This better not be some kind of stunt," Cal said after he dropped Lucas's hand. "Like the one you pulled at that editor's party. If we're being filmed, I will take legal action."

"Whoa, Cal. Hold on. Nobody's being filmed. I'm here to make peace, and if you don't like what I have to say, I'll leave, and you'll never have to hear from me again. OK?" Lucas knew how anxious he sounded, but this was his last shot.

Cal scowled, and Mel took his hand. "We have a ten-fifteen train. You have until they post the track."

Lucas glanced at the schedule board behind Mel. He didn't know how early tracks were posted, but he guessed he had about ten minutes. This was going to be tight. "Look, guys, I have something to offer both of you. Mel, yours is first, and it's an explanation. We're long past apologies. I know that. Though for what it's worth, I am deeply sorry for how I treated you at the bar in December, where I was a real jerk, and—"

"Yes, you were," Mel said.

"Yes, I was," Lucas agreed. "I was feeling lonely and stupid, and I lashed out, and you didn't deserve it. But more important, I'm sorry for everything."

"I thought you said we were past apologies," Mel said stonily.

"You're right. Sorry." He grimaced. "I mean, I'm not sorry for . . . wait, that came out wrong." Lucas stopped himself. This had all sounded a lot more eloquent when he ran through it in his head. Now Cal and Mel were looking at him with a mix of contempt and pity, like how you look at a salesman who's struggling to sell you snake oil. Lucas composed himself. "Mel, you've moved on and found a great man, and I don't flatter myself to think that you're up at night wondering how our relationship fell apart. But I know that my actions didn't make a lot of sense back then, and if it helps you at all to know the answer, it's this: We had a good relationship, but I had nothing to compare it to. I didn't know if giving it up would be the worst mistake of my life, or if we would actually both be happier with other people. And I didn't know *how to know*. I mean, we just didn't have the experience. So I became paralyzed."

Cal stretched out his arm—made a big show of it—and looked at his watch. Lucas glanced at the schedule board. Still no track. "You're a wonderful person, Mel, and I put you in a terrible position, and you were mature enough to once suggest that we break up, and I was never mature enough to return the favor. I felt stuck, and I took advantage of you, and I'm not going to ask that you forgive me, but—"

Movement on the board caught his eye. Lucas's stomach sank. But no, the track posting was for a different train.

"Lucas," Mel said, stepping into the momentary silence, "you made me feel like I only cared about getting married—about some stupid wedding. You made me feel like I was shallow and boring and somehow deficient for not being this adventurous person who would drop everything and move here with you. But I'm not those things."

"I know," he said. "I think, deep down, I wanted our relationship to fail, but I didn't have the guts to actually call it quits. So I just tried to poison it."

"That's fucked up," Mel said.

Lucas nodded. "It was awful."

Silence again. Both Cal and Lucas watched Mel as she took this in. Finally, she sighed. "And what do you want to offer Cal?"

At that moment, their track appeared. "Well," Cal said, "I guess that's that. Have a nice life, Lucas."

Lucas looked at Mel, silently pleading with every ounce of his being, *I don't deserve your help. I'm a dick for even asking. But I can't tell you how important this is. Please.* Mel's face was blank and Lucas understood that his time was up. He would not be able to help Carmen after all. But at least he'd made a good-faith effort with Mel.

Mel groaned. "Cal, just hear him out. Lucas, you'd better talk fast."

Lucas swelled with gratitude and relief. "Well, I'm currently unemployed. I'm not exactly the first guy magazines are looking to hire."

"I'd say not," Cal said, but he was listening.

"But I do have two years of law school under my belt, and since I now have a lot of free time on my hands I would like to offer you many, *many* hours of totally free work."

Cal's eyebrows rose. Of all the things he'd anticipated Lucas saying, this clearly wasn't one. "But why?"

"Like I said before, we're past apologies. But I want to do something for you—and for Mel. I know what kind of hours you must be working, and if I can help take some of the load off, and get you home to Mel earlier at the end of the day, well, that would make me happy."

Cal looked at Mel as though to say, *Is this guy for real?*

"And also," Lucas said, "to be perfectly frank, I've recently developed a newfound interest in real estate law."

EPILOGUE

Lucas hurried through Union Square Park, a book-filled messenger bag over his shoulder. He was supposed to have finished reading *In Cold Blood* before tomorrow's class, but he was behind—and in trying to catch up on the subway going downtown he'd missed his stop and had to double back. Just over a month in, journalism school continued to humble him. There was so much he didn't know. He'd never covered a school-board meeting or had to turn a breaking news story around within an hour. And with every new person he met, he had to explain that, yes, he really was Nice Guy from "Screw the Critics," and no, the experience hadn't created the opportunities he really wanted.

After Jays was fired, Lucas found himself in occupational limbo. The Editor clearly would have shitcanned him if given the chance. Instead, Lucas had to wait a couple of weeks to receive his personal death knell. Soon enough, though, *Empire* hired a new editor-in-chief, some bozo who'd run a food website and whose entire vision for the magazine seemed to be "let's make digital videos," and that guy's first true act was to send Lucas packing. Almost immediately, *Playboy* and *Cosmo* both offered him columns writing about his sex life, a porn studio promised a five-video series, and the website *Bustle* offered him the title of Guys Editor, whatever that meant. But he didn't want to feel boxed in the way Carmen had. So he turned it all down, applied to journalism school, and hoped to hit the "reset" button on his career. Now, carrying his Capote through the mid-September dusk, he knew he'd made the right decision. He felt purposeful, happy to be a student again.

He approached the Barnes & Noble, and there was her face, printed on a poster. Lucas's heart skipped a beat; he hadn't seen Carmen in nearly two years. He'd expected a severe and brooding author photo, a warning to readers: *Don't mess with this bitch*. Instead, Carmen Kelly, author of the new memoir *Screw the Critics,* wore a wide and gracious smile.

Lucas entered and walked past the "New Nonfiction" table with its phalanx of hardcovers, and felt a little queasy. Months ago, the publisher had mailed him an advance copy of Carmen's book. He still hadn't cracked it—not because he feared her criticism, but because he'd worked so hard to get over her. He worried that reading even a page of her book would be like an alcoholic having just one sip: an inevitable relapse. But then she'd invited him to the launch—the first real contact they'd had. He wanted to support her. He felt ready. So here he was.

Lucas was very late and the reading—standing room only— was well under way. He couldn't see Carmen through the crowd, but he could hear her well enough.

"'After all,'" she read aloud, her voice assured, "'he hadn't even taken his pants off yet.'"

The audience laughed.

"'And I wasn't going to do it myself,'" Carmen finished, and everyone laughed again. Lucas figured there was a 90 percent chance the pants in question were his.

"Thanks again for coming out tonight," Carmen said. "I'll take a few questions, and then would be happy to sign books."

Someone wanted to know if she and Jays were still in touch. "Nope," was all Carmen said. Another person asked if she still regretted losing the Netflix show. "At some point," she answered, "you have to focus on the opportunities you have instead of the ones you don't, or you'll never move forward."

A college-aged woman with pink hair raised her hand. "You say that you're sick of writing about sex," the woman said. "So why write this book?"

Carmen smiled and shook her head. "This book is really about desire," she said, "and that's far more interesting. Sure, there's sexual desire in there, but it's also the desire to be wanted, to be successful, to be important, to be worthy. And it's about the trouble we have when our desires get entangled with other people's—which is exactly what happened to me and Lucas and Jay. And also, I think it's important to talk about how our strongest desires are rarely fulfilled. We will *always* want more. And like I said, that can make us forget about what we already have. The real struggle of living in this city isn't the constant striving to get what you want—it's being able to simply live. To be content."

Amen, thought Lucas.

"So are you done with sex?" shouted an overeager member of the audience.

"Writing about it, or having it?" Carmen said, and everyone laughed. "Of course I'm not done with having sex. But I'm most certainly done telling you all about it. I spent so long thinking that sex was the singular source of my power and my voice. But that's not true. So now I'm figuring out what else I have to say. Sorry, no more juice from me."

Carmen signed books for over an hour. When she finally emerged from the bookstore, her writing hand numb, she almost walked right past the bearded figure leaning against the window.

"Lucas?" she asked, breaking away from her agent and editor.

He looked startled, despite the fact that he'd clearly been waiting for her. "Oh, hi," he said. He shut the book he'd been reading. Truman Capote, she noticed.

"You grew a proper beard. I didn't know you could."

He reached up and touched his cheek as though this were news to him. "Yeah, me either. Finally hit puberty I guess."

She chuckled. "It suits you."

They looked at each other, unsure of what to say next. Carmen's companions tittered. All they wanted in the world (aside from a glowing review in the *New York Times* and booking *Fresh Air*) was to meet Nice Guy in the flesh.

"You were really great," he said.

"This is awkward," she said at the exact same moment.

They laughed. She thanked him for the compliment and asked if he was coming to the party. "We're taking a car." She nodded at the Uber pulling up.

"Actually," he said, "it's such a nice night. Want to walk?"

This—the two of them alone again—had been a long time coming. She took a breath. "Just a few blocks," she said. "Mira's already there. I don't want her waiting too long for me."

They set off toward Fifth Avenue. The air wasn't quite cool, and the leaves had barely turned. Had September always been like this—more summer than autumn? Carmen was excited for her book tour, but she would miss fall in Manhattan: the simple pleasure of sleeping with her windows open, apple cider donuts from the Union Square farmers market, the energy of everything revving up.

"How is Mira?" Lucas asked.

She felt him glance at her but didn't glance back. "She turns eighty-nine this year, if you can believe it. This isn't an easy place to be old, but she makes it work."

"I wouldn't expect anything else."

Carmen nodded and they walked on in silence. They'd left the hubbub of Union Square and were approaching the Washington Square Arch. She wondered what Lucas really thought about the book, about what had happened between them. Maybe it was the beard, but he seemed so strange to her now, an entirely different person. After nearly two years, he probably was. It made her a little sad to think about the space between them, because they had once been so familiar with each other, so intimate. But the space, the strangeness—these were good. Over time, it had allowed her to forgive him. She hoped it had allowed him to let her go.

"You know," she said, finally looking at him, "something crazy happened a while back."

"Really?" Now he was the one avoiding her eyes. "What?"

"I'm sure you remember that Mira was going to be evicted? It was a huge mess. And then out of the blue, this law firm calls, saying they'd like to take on her case, pro bono. I mean, how in the world did that happen? How did they even know?"

Lucas bit his lip. "Wow," he said. He'd spent a lot of time thinking about what he'd say if this ever came up. Shortly after meeting Mel and Cal at Grand Central, Lucas had joined Cal's firm with an unusual arrangement. The firm would take on Mira's case, and Lucas would do the bulk of the work himself for free. And whenever Cal had to jump in, Lucas would work twice as many hours, also gratis, on Cal's other cases. In total,

Lucas ended up spending five months on Mira's case and an additional eight months wading through documents for Cal and the other associates. At night he waited tables and relied on the generosity of Tyler and his parents to help make ends meet. It was exhausting but satisfying. By the time he made the decision to take on a whopping hunk of grad-school debt, his emotional debt had mostly dissolved.

At times, he fantasized about revealing all of this to Carmen; he imagined it was enough to win her back. But he didn't dwell too long on these scenarios, told himself it was foolishness. And also, not the point.

"I'm glad a law firm stepped in like that," he said. "I mean, nobody is more deserving than Mira. And you, frankly, for taking such good care of her."

"She's my grandmother. It's not like I'm a saint."

"Still, most people wouldn't stick by her like you do."

"I guess." Carmen was starting to feel uncomfortable. She worried Lucas was gathering up his courage for an apology. She wanted to stop him, make him see that it was unnecessary; he'd apologized already, at Jays' party. She looked at him, hoping to convey the message without having to speak: *I watched your dumb, heroic act on that stage. Of course I did. But that's behind us. The woman who could have forgiven you doesn't exist anymore. She only lives inside my book.*

"Carmen, I—"

"Was that *In Cold Blood* you were reading before?" she said quickly. "Very grad school of you."

"Oh, ah, yes." He was flustered, but he seemed to understand. "But you know, I *am* a grad student now! J school actually."

Carmen laughed loudly. "So I was right all along!" she said. "That first time we met, I could have sworn you were a grad student. Turns out, I was just seeing the future."

He smiled. "I guess I'm more predictable than I'd like to think."

They walked another few feet in silence.

"You know," Lucas said, "two years ago, we couldn't have walked this far without being mobbed by paparazzi. And now here we are, two anonymous people."

"It's the best and worst part of fame. The minute you stop giving people a reason to pay attention, they forget you. After everything blew up, I thought I was marked forever, but, you know, people just—Oh! Oh!" Carmen suddenly interrupted herself. "You won't believe! I was at this fancy event last week to promote the book, and Lucian Moreau was there shooting some model. Remember him, the photographer who shot us for all those advertisements?"

"How could I forget? 'Jez Jacobzon hez a brrrilliant vision!'" Lucas said.

"Exactly. So I go up to say hello to him, and he looks at me, and it's totally clear he has no idea who I am, and he says, 'If your book becomes very big, maybe I shoot you sometime.' And then he walked away."

"Amazing," Lucas said. "One day, Carmen, if all your dreams come true, Lucian Moreau might photograph you."

Carmen laughed. "And you?" she said. "Has everyone basically forgotten you, too?"

"Mostly. My classmates recognized me right away. They were like, 'Why did you come here if you already made it as a writer?' I told them to be careful what you wish for. Also, I dated this girl for a while who said she'd never heard of me and promised not to read any of our columns."

"She was obviously lying."

Lucas shrugged. "She said it would be like skipping to the end of a book. She said it was possible to know too much."

"She's right about that. So what happened?"

"She went off and read everything."

"As I said."

"And after that, things just got weird. It was like she suddenly expected me to be Nice Guy—to think like him, act like him. And when I didn't, she'd accuse me of being fake. Because she had all this evidence about who I 'really' was. It was crazy."

"That sucks. But I assure you, not every woman will be like that. Some women will understand that the person you were then—and the persona you put on—isn't who you are."

"The rare woman," Lucas said. He caught Carmen's eye, then looked away. She was quiet just a moment longer than expected—and what did *that* mean? "But how about you?" he asked, hoping he wasn't pushing too far. "Are you dating at all?"

"Like I said, it's possible to know too much."

Lucas went silent.

"I'm kidding." Carmen nudged him. "You haven't lost your sensitive side, I'm relieved to see."

Lucas smiled.

"Not exactly celibate," she continued, "but definitely not dating. A million lifetimes ago, when I told you I needed to move forward alone, I really meant it."

"And how has it been?"

"Vital. Eye-opening. And lonely, I won't lie. It may be time for something different. You know, it's crazy, but there's one kind of romantic experience that is totally new to me."

"What's that?" Lucas asked.

Carmen stopped a moment and looked at him, as though it should be obvious. "A serious, committed, monogamous relationship. I wonder sometimes: Can I even do that? *How* do I do that?"

All it takes is generosity, which you have in spades, Lucas wanted to say. But he wasn't sure how far down this path she, or he, wanted to go. "Or maybe," he said instead, to lighten the mood, "a groupie will fall for you on the road. He'll be loitering next to the cheap white wine, hoping you'll take him back to your Courtyard Marriott midlevel whatever hotel."

"The glamorous life of an author." Carmen sighed. "At least, for a moment, we had a tab at the Mandarin Oriental."

They were approaching the park.

"We should probably get a cab the rest of the way," she said. "I'm pretty late to my own party and these stilettos are killing me." It was an invitation but also an exit. Lucas wished they didn't have anywhere to go. He wished they could just keep walking. But already he'd gotten more than he expected from her. So now, go to the party with Carmen or go home? He imagined the night—being spied as Nice Guy by everyone in the room while just longing to talk more to Carmen, who wouldn't have the time. It wouldn't be good for either of them. He should take a lesson from Carmen herself and walk on alone. For now anyway.

"I've actually got an early class tomorrow," he said. "But when you're back in town, I'd love to hear about the tour and, you know, your life for the last two years. If you're up for it, I mean."

"I think we can make that happen," Carmen said, and as she stepped into the street Lucas swore she winked at him.

As Carmen often did when hailing a cab, she thought of Mira. She liked to boast about her youth: how she routinely walked thirty or forty blocks in pussy bows and pumps, navigating the grit of a far less welcoming city. "Young ladies today are so spoiled," she'd joke. And yet both women knew that Carmen had made her own long walk these last few years and navigated plenty of potholes. She'd tripped on some of them, but like her grandmother before her, she kept on going.

A taxi pulled up.

"It was really good to see you," Carmen said. "A welcome surprise."

They hugged and Carmen opened the door. Just before she climbed in, she turned back to Lucas. "I noticed that your messenger bag says 'Palmer and Coletta,'" she said.

Lucas looked down. He'd been using this messenger bag for years, and it had become so common to him that he'd forgotten the significance. "Oh," he said. "Yes, it does."

"What a funny coincidence. Because the law firm that took on Mira's case was also Palmer and Coletta."

"Wouldn't you know it," Lucas said.

"Wouldn't you know it," Carmen said, and climbed in.

Lucas crossed the street and looked up at the Washington Square Park arch. It seemed incredible that the majestic edifice was simply here, in what was otherwise a regular park, populated by students and, currently, a large group of Jedi cosplayers, balletically waving their light sabers. There was so much strangeness in this city, so many particular cultures. Each had its own social hierarchy, filled its adherents with unique ambitions and desires. But maybe the trick to wrestling these insatiable wants was to try to live across cultures. Instead of letting the city trap you—in the magazine world, the society world, the Jedi cosplay world, the grad-school world—you could use the city to be free. It wasn't Sofia's kind of freedom, that total abandon, but the freedom afforded to those with a strong sense of self and generous friends. With these things, you could walk through new doors and never get lost. With these, it was possible to do what Carmen said was so difficult: to simply live.

So many people came here to escape their simple lives. This, Lucas realized now, was why everyone at Jays' party laughed condescendingly when the Editor made fun of "irrelevant" places like Kansas and Idaho. It's because they'd all come from someplace equally irrelevant. They'd come to shine, to be bigger and brighter. Some, like Jays and Nicholas Spragg, had gone to extreme lengths to prove the totality of their transformation. But Lucas was equally a New Yorker, even if his life was smaller and dimmer. What mattered was that he was here to make it his own. And that he was happy.

Despite the vast amount of course reading he had to do, the night was too inviting. Lucas headed across the park, crossed West Houston, and wandered through SoHo. Soon he'd entered Tribeca, which meant he was closing in on One World Trade. His old stomping grounds. He decided to settle into a quiet bar and do his reading there, for old times' sake. He knew just the place, back from his days at *Empire*. He wandered along Hudson and turned onto Jay Street, a mere slip of sidewalk tucked between two larger avenues. But a block shy of his destination, he halted. Before him was an angled building of glass and chrome: a mini One World Trade, something Disney might have created for Epcot. The incongruity of the structure, among so much stone and brick, made for a disorienting sight. Then Lucas saw the flag, pointed stiffly over the sidewalk, like the sail of a warship. Smack in the center, embossed in gold, was an enormous *C*.

At that moment, the front doors swung open and a coterie of young, beautiful people spilled onto the sidewalk. The women wore lamé and silk, their dresses oozing over their almost nonexistent hips. The men were outfitted in velvet and plaid, their collars popped, their wing tips aggressively narrow. With their cigarette smoke and raucous laughter, the crowd was taking up too much space on the sidewalk. But did they care? *No,* Lucas thought. Caring was obviously something they didn't care much about.

And then, two more people appeared. Nicholas Spragg came first, dressed in simple slacks, a well-tailored button-down, and a preppy-ish haircut. He was unattractive as ever but cleverly remodeled by the man who followed. Jay Jacobson, erstwhile Editor of *Empire Magazine,* paused on the top step, assessing his protégé: his mentee, patron, lackey, and, Lucas was certain, constant irritant.

Of course! This was The College, the flagship location. Lucas pulled out his phone, snapped a picture, and sent it to Carmen. A moment later, she replied: "Like I said, nobody's marked forever."

She was absolutely right. But if it didn't bother her, Lucas decided it wouldn't bother him. From the shadow of a doorway, he watched Spragg smoke and smile, ingratiating himself with the group as they ingratiated themselves right back. Jays, meanwhile, had not moved from the steps. Lucas saw him grimace and his eyes squint with uncharacteristic exhaustion. He saw Jays draw in a breath, as though readying himself for an unpleasant task. And then, Lucas saw this process reverse itself: the blue eyes brighten, the handsome mouth smile. Jay Jacobson jaunted down the steps, his hand extended in greeting.

Observing all of this, Lucas felt a twinge of sympathy—or maybe just pity—for his old boss. Then it passed. There were too many other people and pursuits that now deserved Lucas's attention. Which meant that he was wasting his time here, hiding out in a doorway. He needed to be on his game in class tomorrow. So Lucas readjusted his tote bag and continued on his way, unconcerned about whether anybody noticed him.

ACKNOWLEDGMENTS

First, Jason and Jen would like to thank each other: Hey, we wrote a novel together, and it was about two people viciously criticizing each other's sexual performance, and our marriage is still intact! (High-fives!) You, our reader, are surely wondering how much of our own personal perspectives were conveyed in Lucas's and Carmen's columns. It's a good question! Moving on, now . . .

But seriously, if you would like to interview us and then tell a large audience about this book, we will gladly answer that (and any) question.

We'd also like to thank our families, and particularly our parents, for above all being supportive and caring. We are who we are because of them. They are so wonderful, in fact, that they enthusiastically read this book despite how awkward the reading experience must have been. Jason and Jen hope their toddler, Fenn, grows up to do whatever he sets his mind to, except, perhaps, to also read this book.

To the industry: Thanks to our agent, Libby McGuire, who provided us invaluable enthusiasm, confidence, and know-how—as well as the title of this novel! (We'd originally called it *Screw the Critics*.) Anna Worrell, we're lucky to have you spiriting this book across the finish line. Thanks to Adam Gidwitz, for connecting us with Libby. And thanks to our editor, Leslie Gelbman, for her thoughtful eye, and to the rest of the St. Martin's Press crew who has worked with us to launch this puppy: Brittani Hilles, Marissa Sangiacomo, and Tiffany Shelton.

Jen has written three previous books, which means she's written three acknowledgment sections, which means she's running out of people to thank. But for inspiring elements of this novel, she would like to give a nod to *The Custom of the Country* by Edith Wharton, *The Great Gatsby* by F. Scott Fitzgerald, and *The Devil Wears Prada* by Lauren Weisberger. Also, if fictional characters can have real-life stylists, then Nick Marino, that's you.

Now on to Jason. This is his first book, so please stand by as he transitions into the first person and attempts to pass an omnibus bill of gratitude.

Hi. Jason here. Because *Mr. Nice Guy* is set in the world of New York media, I've had the urge to thank literally everyone who's ever shared that world with me. I feel ever-fortunate to have such great, talented friends. Without them, the weirdest parts of this career wouldn't have been half as fun. They do amazing work. They are amazing people. They consume an amazing amount of free liquor, provided by publicists for reasons we'll never fully understand. But I've come to accept that I can't thank everyone by name. This book can only be so many pages. And also, I'd totally forget someone and regret it forever.

So to be woefully, inadequately brief about it, thank you to my friends from *Boston*, *Men's Health*, *Fast Company*, *Maxim*, and *Entrepreneur* magazines (and a special shout-out to those I worked with at previous jobs who have joined me in various capacities at *Entrepreneur*), and my Dudes Dinner dudes (née Dudes Night dudes, but now we're old), and the people who took a chance and hired me (some of whom overlap with the aforementioned), and the peers who have become friends after events and panels and after-work beers and freelancing and sometimes just a lot of tweets. Listen, you: If you think I'm talking about you in this paragraph, then I am. Thank you for inspiring me, and this book, and for not unfollowing me on social media as I transform into a self-promotional bot, because that's what friends are for.